BEING
IN A
BAND

Other books by Anthony Scott

On Ashover Hill

The Birthday Gift

BEING
IN A
BAND

Anthony Scott

Matador
9 Priory Business Park,
Wistow Road, Kibworth Beauchamp,
Leicestershire. LE8 0RX
Tel: 0116 279 2299
Email: books@troubador.co.uk
Web: www.troubador.co.uk/matador
Twitter: @matadorbooks

ISBN 978 1789018 929

British Library Cataloguing in Publication Data.
A catalogue record for this book is available from the British Library.

Printed and bound in the UK by TJ International, Padstow, Cornwall
Typeset in 11pt Aldine by Troubador Publishing Ltd, Leicester, UK

Matador is an imprint of Troubador Publishing Ltd

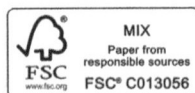

MIX
Paper from
responsible sources
FSC® C013056

Prologue

*"I got you to look after me, and you got
me to look after you, and that's why"*

John Steinbeck, Of Mice and Men

You can go through your whole life, making friends and
building relationships all the time – each day, each month, and
every year. It happens and you don't realise it is happening. It's
just the way of life. But I always thought that there is never
any substitute for the friendships you acquire in childhood
that then survive into your adult years. Those friendships
where you experience the joy, the knocks and the excitement
of growing up together. Those are the ones which bind us and
blind us and see us through our life – they are the constants,
the certainties and details which make up the people we are
and the people we are to become.

I first met Anthony Scott in 1979, when we were both 13 years old – we had a fist fight actually, and I remember his glasses falling to the floor. And I went away feeling guilty but also curious, as this person hadn't previously come across my radar, he had just been some nerdy, academic kid with specs. And then a few weeks later I am in town on a Saturday afternoon and I bump into him and he's carrying a copy of 'Rubber Soul' by the Beatles and I'm like, yes this guy is someone I need to get to know. And that was it. That's how it started.

And today it's a beautiful autumn morning and it's October 2018, and I'm driving down Huntingdon Street in Nottingham and I pass our old rehearsal rooms, called Rubber Biscuit, and I think about how many times we lugged our gear up those 5 flights of stairs twice a week. And even now 20 odd years later I can still smell that place – the damp, the constant smell of weed, the suffocating and putrid odour of what passed as carpets, like sulphuric brimstone and the long haired stoners who ran the place, working through a haze of smoke, with Led Zeppelin playing at full volume in the background. And I smile as I wonder how many chest infections and colds I got from practicing in that rancid and putrid building. And now I am thinking about all the songs we rehearsed up there. All the beads of sweat dripping across my forehead, the intro's, guitar solos, middle eight's, chord progressions, arguments, disagreements, disputes over set lists, broken guitar strings, snare drum skins, broken fingers and blisters, songs that weren't working, recording on cassette tapes, knackered old tape recorders. And I smile, because you know what – I wouldn't have changed it for anything. And I think about all those things happened in that shitty old building in the 1990's.

And as these thoughts are going through my brain, I happen to be listening to 'When You're Young' by The Jam and I start to think about when me and Anthony were drunk on youth, when it all seemed possible, when we would sit in his brother's bedroom listening to the White Album and talking about being in a band together, or trying to figure out the chords to Eight Days a Week, or Let It Be, when we would argue about what we thought was the best Beatles album or Bob Dylan album. And it occurs to me for the first time that the foundations for Wide Eyed Wonder were established back then, back in the late 1970's and early 80's when we were still just kids, when we were cutting our teeth on life, figuring out the best music to listen to and scoring girls in our school year out of 10.

And then it's spring 1981 and we are sat in my mum and dad's front room on Hereford Avenue, and it's lunchtime and by now we are prototype indie kids with skinny jeans, converse trainers and cropped hair and we should be back at school, but we've got a bottle of wine on the go and fish and chips and Lennon is blasting out Revolution at maximum volume and we're pretty fucked up – and I'm thinking this is about as good as it gets because I know with absolute conviction that in about 4 years' time this is what we are gonna be doing.

And then my mind is off thinking about the 1990's, and I remember Anthony ringing me at work and asking me whether I'd heard about this new band called Oasis and how I had to listen to their new album – but I'd heard of them and already had planned to get the record as soon as I was paid. And when I did listen to it, it changed everything, it changed the way me and Anthony wrote songs, it changed the way we dressed, it changed the way we spoke – it opened up a world of new and exciting possibilities for us – and Wide Eyed Wonder was the vehicle we used to explore this new found world.

The 1990's were a great time to be in a band – there seemed to be new bands and new music coming out all the time – Oasis and Blur are the obvious ones to think about, but there were others who were up there as good or better, like Embrace, The Bluetones, Shed Seven, Cast, The Charlatans, Suede, Manic Street Preachers, Supergrass, The Stone Roses, The Verve, Massive Attack, Portishead and Radiohead – all awesome and amazing bands and Wide Eyed Wonder were part of that whole scene and I was the lead guitarist in the band, and my best mate was the rhythm guitarist and singer. And we were simply awesome.

And I think about all the venues we played at like Rock City in Nottingham, The Princess Charlotte in Leicester, the Hope and Anchor in Islington or the Orange Club in Kensington – these were incredible experiences that you cannot replicate in a merry-go-normal life. It's like when we played Rock City for the first time and we are on stage, playing our own songs and me and Anthony for a moment midway through playing "Take You There" look at one another, and everything goes into slow motion for a split second, and we smile at one another and it's like yes, this is the best thing ever, better than a last minute goal, better than hearing 'Like a Rolling Stone' for the first time, better than fucking some fit bird, better than speeding, better than anything you want to think of pal. This is me and my best mate doing what we dreamt about when we were sat in that front room on Hereford Avenue, listening to Revolution. And I think back to that moment and I smile. Fucking mint.

And we loved going around the clubs and bars in Nottingham and people knew the band and knew who we were and it seemed like I was permanently pissed on adulation and the coolness of being in not just a band, but being in Wide Eyed Wonder. The other day I was listening to Glory Box by Portishead and it took me back to me and Anthony being in The Cookie Club probably around 1997 and being hammered and on the dance floor and we are just totally fucked up and the room is spinning and we are just having an amazing time. And people just coming up to us and wanting to talk about the band and telling us how awesome it is. I miss that. It was always me and Anthony v The World. And it still is.

Looking back on it all now in October 2018, the 1990's were the most brilliant time of our lives and being in Wide Eyed Wonder was central to all of that and it was a time when anything seemed possible. Thinking back when I was young – and I mean many years ago, probably when I was 13 or 14 – I wanted to experience the same emotions you read about in books or see in movies. I wanted them to overturn and disrupt everything I assumed about life. Being part of Wide Eyed Wonder with Anthony helped me to create and define new realities. I knew that I could do anything when Anthony was stood next to me (I still do) – I could stand up on stage and play guitar and sing – nothing daunted me. However, I think as you get older, you want your emotions to be more practical and mild – you want them to support your life as it has evolved and turned out. You want them to be safe. You don't want to be side tracked into blind alleys. You want them to assure you that things are ok. And I don't think there is anything wrong in that.

It was a brilliant time.

Steve North, Lead Guitarist,
Wide Eyed Wonder

"So it's time to leave you preview, so you too can review what we do, 20 years in this business, how do you sell soul, g-wiz, people bear witness, thank you for lettin' us be ourselves, so don't mind me if I repeat myself, these simple lines be good for your health, to keep them crime rhymes on the shelf, live love life like you just don't care, five thousand leaders never scared, bring the noise, it's a moment they feared, get up, still a beautiful idea…"

Chuck D – Harder Than You Think

1

Taking a journey on a bus is not necessarily the accepted way of receiving enlightenment that will change your life forever. It never happened to Michelangelo and despite the fact that some might argue that buses in their modern format did not exist then, I would argue 'who's fault was that?'

Anyway I was on the bus because my normal mode of transport had come down with an illness. My car, a name given to it because of its likeness to its distant cousin a real automobile, had not been quite itself for some time and had just been dropped off that morning. Jake, the family 'mechanic', wanted to take its parts and use them for car medical research but, as I said in no uncertain terms to him, my car had not signed any donor card. Until it did I was determined to see it continue to fulfil the work ethic to which I had been tricked into fulfilling along with so many other fools. I left the car, resplendent in all its mix of red paint, brown rust and various shades of grime, with Jake and a strict guideline that any repairs must not cost more than fifty pounds. He asked me if that included VAT and labour, and then walked away laughing.

Now to me when God was handing out natural comedian's job titles this obviously included mechanics. They look at your car and make deep noises that you suspect they also use for intimate foreplay. They umm and ah, and then you notice a smile begin to appear, working its way from the side of the mouth until it unfolds into a full blown smirk. At this point their plan has become crystal clear in their minds as the division between actual cost of work and cash in that back pocket has made its bountiful mathematical result into their brain. Now, with a RADA trained turn and look of absolute torture in their eyes such as the one Hamlet tossed over to the feet of his tragically beloved Ophelia, they dramatically turn back from the car and look you in the eye and utter the re-assuring words, 'leave it with me son.' Remarkably we invariably do just that; after all where else can we go with our car troubles? In fact perhaps our society is missing a trick. It seems to have every self-help group going for most things but I have not yet come across 'Done up like a Kipper Car Owners Anonymous!' We need one because later in the day, or week, month or year, dependant on how long the mechanic said he needed the car for, you return to find that the car has undergone a life changing and apparently much needed transformation, and that this transformation is to cost you your next month's wages. You could ask the mechanic how did this happen but you know that there would be an exhaustive list. This list will contain items that are even beyond the ancient Latin scholar. You therefore accept the bill, despite the fact that you only took the car in for the handbrake to be tightened.

And so there I was, on the bus. It was October and the weather had chosen today to turn a little chilly, inclement one might say. Being used to driving in my car like a true lord and consequently enjoying the benefits of a heater that remarkably still worked, I had not taken the precaution of wearing any type of coat. It was a huge and breath-taking mistake. I was now so cold that my nipples were sticking through my jacket and my willy had retreated into my inner stomach. I was reminded, as I always was during moments of being deeply frozen, of a house rugby game back in the late 70's when the scrum became a way of trying to get warm and as a result the ball did not see much of open play. I was a winger, which basically meant I never saw the scrum and therefore lost any chance of any bodily contact, and so my frozen lot was cast. How I never lost fingers and toes and other body bits to frostbite I will never know.

I sat towards the back of the packed single-decker bus, dating possibly to pre-war days and most certainly in need of retirement. A rather large old aged pensioner with a taupe furry hat that could have been a hamster had decided to sit next to me despite the fact that I had tried to look as menacing as possible. After trying to trick me into conversation with such questions as 'Are you going shopping? 'Are you local?' and 'Do you like my coat?' she had now decided to move up to me as close as possible without sitting on my knee. Still I was thankful for small mercies. She was after all giving off a certain glow of warmth, albeit with a tinged old lady smell that included some essence of onion, a hint of whisky, a far too sweet perfume, several cats, almost certainly a dog, rhubarb, a tinge of woodbine, and possibly a death or two. My stomach was not thankful for this mix of odours and was consequently spinning round like a washer full of shoes, and big enormous dirty shoes at that! Still, I was not going to chat. I was feeling sorry for myself and determined to revel in my discomfort. Eventually hamster head gave in and turned to a nervous looking young lady across the aisle and launched into a conversation about the price of eggs or milk or nuclear weapons or something. The 'conversation' was one-sided.

Feeling pretty miserable and still extremely cold despite old big leg's best efforts to warm me through, I decided to attempt to gaze through the classically condensation filled bus window at the world outside. Squinting through a hole I had created with a hanky my mother had kindly slipped into my jacket pocket, (I had a little sniffle and this had concerned her greatly as it should have done), it was then that I saw my future form in crystal clear clarity and my eureka moment was born! There, facing me with a force that wanted to hit me square between the eyes was a giant poster of the Band Oasis. These big attitude boys had been sticking up two fingers at just about everyone who cared to look for a little while now and their effect on the UK music world for the last 6 months had been mesmerising. I was attracted to their big in-your-face songs and classic bad boy rock and roll behaviour that screamed at you to stop and take notice. And I, along with many others, had taken notice. They were showing me right here and now a world I did not have, but that I could have if I could only get off my backside and find out how to get there!

Now to me the word Oasis had traditionally summed up a girlie shop to which my sisters shopped, or a welcome stop off point in an otherwise barren desert rather like a fish and chip shop on the long walk home after a down town drinking session. This had been the extent of my knowledge of the use of the word Oasis until this life-changing band had come along. Why they had chosen to name themselves after a girl's shop was somewhat lost on me, particularly given their hard boy image. Still mine was obviously not to reason why as the name did not seem to be holding them back. Thank god they had not gone for 'Dorothy Perkins...'

The poster happily declared 'Buy their debut album 'Definitely Maybe' now.' I had heard these boys singing on the radio and I had seen them performing on the TV. They were like nothing else around on the music scene. They were loud, abusive and wonderfully far too full of themselves. Even so, and probably especially because of the way they were, their music was cutting through the general music scene that had stuttered throughout the early 90's. The UK music market had become unsure of itself, no longer confident in its roots and looking across to America to see where it was going. In so doing much of our airwaves was lost in middle of the road mush and little that you could call cutting edge was getting the airplay it merited or needed. DJ's became characters of themselves and the days of the bright fires of Bob Harris and The Old Grey Whistle Test seemed far too distant.

Without really knowing it I had been, as so many other people had been, waiting for this Band to arrive, not necessarily because of their music, but as much about their desire to kick the door down and let some light in. I, and indeed the British people in some not so small way, had been desperate for something vibrant to come and grab us by the throat and consider that we too could master our masters and achieve whatever we wanted. In truth I had always been ambitious having written plays from the age of boyhood and performing them to whoever might give me the time of day, but the great drug of necessity to earn a living had come along and thrown the hum drum of existence over my now weary frame. And now this band, with their swagger and lyrics, were telling me, and the generation around me, that there was a big world outside my window waiting for me still. Seeing the smug expressions of the Oasis boys on that poster just took to reminding me that they were not under any of the work ties I was currently experiencing. Immediately I resolved to buy their album in my lunch break when I would be momentarily free from the capitalist clutches that held me strapped to the work ethic from hell. I was working in a bank! It wasn't slave labour but it sure felt like it.

So four hours later, my tortuous bus journey and a morning's work full of enough boredom to send a whole town to sleep for a fortnight over, I made my happy way to 'Andy's Records', presumably owned by Andy, although I have never met him. To be fair it could even be owned by a Mr Andrew Record who, seeing his name could make him a small fortune, opened the chain of record shops. This is one reason why I may change my name to Abel Dildo. It would after all make an excellent lead singer band name and have those lady folk queuing in their droves for me to sign their self-patented favourite toy. Of course I would probably need to take some time in choosing the right size of marker pen, and maybe get a few with different gauges, but nonetheless Abel could be my future...

I had in fact been very excited about buying the Oasis album for some time. The band had released some material, but the album would see what they were really made of. It would put the meat well and truly on the bones and hopefully prove that Oasis were a real band of substance. So often you would go out and buy an album purely because of the singles you had heard on the radio only to find why the other songs on the album were not the ones released. It was like going out with a girl because of her most amazing smile, only to find she kissed like a surly fish. Surely Oasis would be bigger than this and not make me regret parting with my hard fought for cash.

I walked up through the happy throng of shoppers on West Gate, a pedestrian area set aside for people to enjoy the delights of Mansfield's shopping paradise, and into the record shop which greeted me with warmth and music. I made my way past sixteen or seventeen amorous old women who had probably been let out of their OAP home for the day and were now for excitement thumbing through Des O'Connor's back catalogue. On my way through they tried to thumb through mine as well but I kept my eyes forward, thought of England, and made it to the counter intact.

The assistants were busy talking to each other about the previous nights TV, and it took several loud and lofty coughs to attract their attention.

'Are you wanting any help love?' Attention at last though the fierce gaze in the assistant's wonky left eye was somewhat discomforting.

'Yes, indeed.' I answered, grandly. 'Thank you, first of all, for deciding to serve me. It is good to see the wheels of industry still roll in this great country of ours is it not?'

'You what m'duck? Are you feeling alrate? You were coughing like a good 'un. Made me tabs laugh you did.'

The point was clearly lost on the assistant who, as I looked at her for longer, not only had the aforementioned off kilter eye but also had extremely small ears. Maybe the two were connected. I went on,

'Have you got the new album by a band called Oasis?'

'Oooh I'm not sure love. Oasis you say? Do you mean the shop?' she said loudly as though she had assumed my confusion was somehow linked to my ability to hear.

'No, the band,' I offered, aware that the old folk were coming closer behind me, leafing through the realms of higher alphabet letters to have a better view of the one male in the shop. I tried to keep focussed.

The assistant scratched her head vigorously suggesting a large colony of African fleas had taken residence in her haystack of hair. In fact some things did indeed start to fall out but I could not be sure if these were fleas, dandruff, or general bits collected over a period of days in a busy shop, or indeed a busy life.

'We have a got a song called 'Midnight at the Oasis.' Is that what you're after m'love?'

'No, no it isn't,' I countered, a level voice kept intact, 'the band are called Oasis and not just at midnight. They are a new band, a smashing new outfit from Manchester,' I added to amuse myself and sadly not the assistant.

'Oh, I see,' she replied nonplussed, clearly not seeing anything. This was possibly due to the fact that she was wearing more eye make up than I had ever seen on a woman before. This, I suspected, was the culmination of several weeks worth of make up applied in a classic house decorating manner that applied the logic always paint on top and never ever use sandpaper.

Our eyes met and she held my gaze with an almost mystic power. I realised the look was not one of the 'can I help you find your record' look, but rather one of the 'are you free tonight for a little nip and tickle' variety. It was certainly my day for pulling the ladies and I considered the thought of asking one of the pretty cashiers out for a drink when back in the safety of the banks vaults. The bank was boring as boring could be but my word it could pick out a bright young thing for my personal titillation to get me through the day.

I then noticed the assistant pointing to her name badge which was sporting the name Coco and was ideally located directly in the middle of her huge left breast. My eyes wandered down to where her finger was pointing, seriously I couldn't help it, and then I realised she was licking her lips. The shock of seeing this heady and brazen attempt at foreplay being played out in Andy's pad caused me to take emergency action. I pushed my tongue around my frothing lips and caused my eyes to grow very large and expectant. I then nodded my head violently in the direction of the stock room behind her whilst rubbing my hands up and down my body in an over exuberant manner. Admittedly I was running the risk of her actually wanting to take me in to the stock room but I knew my manic look would be enough to put off a wild boar. It was. She turned away in a disgusted fashion and grumpily muttered,

'Let me just ask Magenta.'

The assistant did not walk to the back of the shop to where her colleague had now gone. Rather she just shouted her name at a volume that should have brought every Magenta from around the town into the shop. Miraculously the name Magenta is not an overly used one and so the herds of Magenta's were not to come running. Magenta, an extremely thin and nervous looking girl, walked towards us. Her name, which matched her face colour, sang out to me from a similar badge to that of her colleague Coco, and which was also stuck on her much smaller left breast. My thoughts wandered to me asking Sandra back at the branch whether or not she had considered wearing her name badge on her breast and whether or not I could help put it there.

'Magenta, this young man is after a new CD by a band called Oasis.'

As Coco spoke she no longer looked at me. I was yesterday's news, no in fact last week's local news, but not local to this area but to an area she had no knowledge or interest in. To her I was now as interesting as the business section pages in the Adelaide Gazette, even though this week's addition ran an interesting article on the reducing profit margins of the hill wine and the recent failure of the latest vintage. It was riveting stuff.

'Is he indeed. Well you, m'duck, are in luck! We 'ave it rate 'ere! It's one of the ones we put in the headphones this mornin' along wi' new albums from 'Mike and the Mechanics' and 'Black Death.'

'Oh great! This is fantastic news! Can I listen to them?' I said with far too much enthusiasm.

Magenta looked at me. I was obviously very stupid.

'That is what the listening headphones are for youth!'

I looked over to the booth and its decaying headphones that had been slapped on to thousands of greasy Mansfield heads across many years, and thought about debating Magenta's use of the sole word 'listening' to describe the headphones. Perhaps we could have added the words breeding and infecting. Wisely I decided to leave the matter and keep my own counsel. I made my way over to the headphones and rubbed them vigorously on my arm sleeve. I then slowly, and deliberately, as though about to go through something of great significance, placed the headphones over my expectant ears. I turned towards the wall, closed my eyes and pressed play. After a few too many moments of perfect silence I opened my eyes and saw I had pressed pause. Moving my finger to the right I closed my eyes again as I pressed the magic play button.

Sometimes in life extraordinary things happen that cannot be explained by mere words. These moments are so precious and precise because they cannot be predicted. I had put on the headphones for the Oasis album and pressed play without any preconceptions. I had thought that the album might offer me something new, perhaps even something mildly exciting. I had no idea that it would change my life. Noel's guitar hit my brain and from that moment every note made my very insides tingle. I was listening to music that I had been waiting for all my life. From the opening 'Rock and Roll Star', through 'Live Forever' and 'Supersonic', and closing on 'Slide away' and 'Married with Children', the world became just a distant memory. In listening I felt myself become stronger, as though I could take on anyone and anything and for those brief fantastic moments I was King.

The album finished and I returned to Magenta a changed man. 'I'll buy that please.'

Magenta looked at me with a disdain that she probably normally reserved for shoplifters and perverts, and perhaps on a bad day perverted shoplifters.

'I should hope you bloody well will buy it. You've been clogging up our booths for ages you sicko.'

I handed over the cash and looked her straight in the eyes, making sure that she handed the CD over to me before my parting shot,

'Magenta,' I said, a smile filling up my face, 'I think you will find your booths have been clogged up for a very long time indeed.'

I turned and ran, spectacularly late for a job that I cared even less about than before. Oasis had made me free to go and be who I wanted to be.

As I ran down Westgate and back to my modern day workhouse, a new thought entered my head. Oasis had started in me a train of thought that was now screaming out 'this is your time, your life, your choice.' My lungs, now pumping air in and out so quickly that I sounded like an out of shape horse, carried me towards the bank as I crashed through the branch doors having decided there and then I would start my own band. Why not? What was good enough for the Gallagher boys was sound enough for me too. With that blessed relief throbbing through my veins I looked my first customer of the afternoon, who had already been waiting for 15 minutes, in the face and said, 'Today Mr Otto I will change your life!'

My head was buzzing and I longed to get home from work and ring my best mate, Steve. I would tell him all about Oasis and tell him that he too was about to become a rock god and lead guitarist in a kicking new rock band. He'd like that. He was born to do it. That and talking. He was brilliant at that too.

2

Steve is my best mate. We have known each other since we were very little and I can honestly say that I do not know anyone else like him. He is unique. Let me describe him.

Age: 24.

Looks: Tall, developing beer belly and yet still surprisingly sleek looking. Like a gazelle on an off day. He has spiky dyed black hair, a throw back to his 80's glam rocker days, with alert and yet cheeky eyes, and complimented by a fine hooked nose giving an air of confidence and sexual prowess that can hook in the ladies to his Stevie fly trap.

Pulling power: Exceptional. Can smell game from a distance not rivalled by any man I have ever known. In this respect alone he is very much like the western-clawed frog of the Western African rainforests.

Plays: At home and away and as often as possible.

Scruples: None.

Girlfriend: Chloe, his teenage sweetheart. He had been

something of a baby snatcher, she being four years his junior.

Musical talent: A guitarist of incredible talent. Has an original Gibson electric guitar that is so heavy I get a hernia just thinking about lifting it.

Musical roots: Beatles, Counting Crows, Dog's D'Amour, Stone Roses, Bob Dylan, Thin Lizzy, Pavement.

Character: Charming and coarse at the same time. Very funny. Regularly brings me close to wetting my pants. Occasionally causes me to actually let urine go when it should not have done. Can tell a story better than a storyteller from story telling land.

Sporting Ability: None whatsoever. Has always viewed any sporting gathering as a place for social interaction and as a result never made any school sports team other than badminton and that only because he latched on to the fact that it was a mixed sport and he could see up the girls short skirts whilst picking up his cock. Add to that the fact that the badminton and table tennis coach was incredibly camp, into his music and highly sociable. He would talk for hours and Steve saw past the man in a way that most of the lads at school could not. He was, of course and as a consequence, called gay himself, a fact in which he didn't give a monkey's.

Education: Not a chance. As with sport, education was something that stopped him talking. As a result he was inevitably constantly in trouble with the teaching staff for being disruptive. This was in every lesson other than maths, the subject in which he was taught by Mr Stevenson, the badminton coach.

Nick Name: The North, after his surname, North. Thought provoking and brilliant stuff that Ruskin would have been proud of.

If you'd known him at school, Steve was the one who stood out from the crowd. His hair was different, his clothes were different, and his attitude was different. As a result he was friends with everyone and yet no one at the same time. Everyone knew him or knew of him, but very few actually got into his inner sanctum of friendship. I was one of the lucky ones.

I don't know how we both got to be best friends. We knew some of the same people and messed around with the same crowd. We were younger then of course, unable to attract a fly never mind a girlfriend! At some point an opportunity arose for us to become the school gardeners and, along with another friend called John Wickson or Wicko for short, we took the chance. Being 14 and in charge of some school property to use as we wanted was reason enough for us to take the role over from sixth formers who had left. I only hope they never got to hear about the way we developed their work.

This fine green-fingered pursuit gave Steve the platform to build the largest selection of photographs of naked women that the school had ever seen. He set up the most fantastic display at the back of the school green house where we were growing offshoots of Begonias for sale at the annual school fete. Glamour shots have since never had the same feeling for me as it does for so many because I can't look at them without smelling that sweet whiff of Begonia's. Of course if I had found the smell sexual this could have caused all sorts of problems in the garden and of course those visits to the garden centre. Thankfully I do not.

I still do not know how Steve managed to amass so many rude photographs. In truth I have never known how Steve manages to do so many things. His ways remain so often a glorious mystery. The money he made from admission fees to his 'gallery' kept him in trendier clothes and with a much finer music collection than the rest of us. This scheming attitude would serve him well.

For the next 2 years the three of us had a ready-made love shack that would have been ideal had we had any girls interested in us. Steve was tall and bone like, 'Wicko' was short and round, and I, I was in National Health black-rimmed glasses. I never knew what I looked like without them because I couldn't see what I looked like. However the talks we had about what we would do with the many girls, or as we called them 'women,' who could benefit from calling in to our greenhouse, were tremendous. The plants we grew took on new meaning with cucumbers for example becoming a new and exciting addition to the school garden.

Word had got around the whole school, and I mean the whole school, of Steve's naked girl photographic selection. Steve was inundated with young spotty lads keen to spend a useful 5 minutes in the presence of beauties they could only fantasise about and, indeed, in the greenhouse this is exactly what they did!

As the 'business' developed, Wicko and I began to take a more active role in helping Steve primarily for the financial rewards, but also with the new 'cool' friends that we were beginning to make. Kids who were so hard that previously I had been unable to even dare look at them, suddenly began to ask me how I was. Top flight boys too who would normally talk in Latin rather than include me in their conversation began to speak to me in English and ask about how things were going. We were gaining respect with all of them, each wanting only one thing, and that was entry to the displays.

How our teachers did not find out about what we were doing I will never know, although we were very good at producing a wonderful smoke screen in that we were actually quite good at gardening and we produced some quality produce. In particular my summer plants were a delight and I was providing cuttings for nearly all the staff. Even the Head,

Mr 'Public Relations' Boulding, was furnished with hanging baskets to be proud of. If only he knew.

For three glorious summers it was my plants that adorned the school flowerpots and hanging baskets and that in turn made arriving at our school a more pleasurable experience than it might have otherwise have been had you driven in through Sunnydale and had your car decorated with eggs. The staff in turn used to delight in saying that it was their very own pupils who had grown the plants in the school's very own gardens and greenhouse. Our diligence was partly out of actual interest in gardening, which was very true in my case, but mostly out of keeping attention away from our other 'projects.'

I guess in all situations of pupils doing things they should not be doing you have to weigh up the good and the bad. For the three of us our ventures were, by and large, a good thing. We provided a good feeling to pupils of all social and intelligence standing. In turn we provided harmony and, I like to think, a little bit of sexual education that the school had no intention of providing. We also helped satisfy curiosity and, no doubt, let pupils let off a bit of sexual tension that meant they were freer, more rounded pupils in the days classrooms. In many ways we were the missing link, the glue that helped hold the school together, the bridge that allowed pupils to express themselves in and out of the normal school setting. An alternative view could be that we were missing a link but that would, I believe, be unfair.

Any teachers who did suspect, and I am sure there were a few, decided to leave us to our own devices. I can only suppose they took the view that if they were to blow the whistle then some blame may well be directed at them for having not done so sooner. It was the old 'guilty by association' tag, and certainly none of the staff would wish to be connected to what went on at the back of the school greenhouse. I personally never went into the back of the greenhouse save to store my potting plant pots and compost. Even then, when entering the North Hallowed Area, I would avert my eyes and whistle any tune that would arrive in my head. It was normally a hymn that suggested hell and damnation and made me rather sweaty and nervous.

It was Steve's idea to have the after school party that would bring to an end our garden work. Wicko and I were both unsure as to the wisdom of this venture because if we were found out we would lose everything. Why mess, we reasoned, with a banker of a business that had seemed untouchable. However Steve's idea was simple. He told us he had at least 50 pupils willing to pay £5 each and, with the thought of sudden large wealth exploding in our minds, our reservations were immediately set aside. The term half-wit would never be set aside for what followed.

We arranged the party for the last week of term on the Friday night. We figured that everyone would be so de-mob happy that any possible violence would be set aside for a feeling of friendship and conciliation. It was a similar kind of thought that meant after the famous football game in the Somme in 1914, the troops returned to their trenches to royally shoot the hell out of one another.

Steve had collected all the money, (it was pay in advance or no entry), and we had enlisted the help of ten exceptionally hard children, going on men/animals, to ensure:

a. The evening would pass by without problem and,

b. Entry would be on a ticket only basis to avoid unsavoury types.

Excitement built and we found ourselves taking bookings from 90 people including many girls, which added vastly to our excitement. What we failed miserably to realise was the ability of our greenhouse, albeit a very large green house, to hold this amount of people. The aged structure was quite long and wide. It was all glass and iron and brick and, in its day, was no doubt the pride of the local education authority as well as the school governors. It had been built with plants in mind; not rock and roll.

Still with 'ignorance is bliss' as our motto we were not about to stop and consider the downsides of why on earth a greenhouse could not double up as a venue. We were just 16 and beginning to think we were growing into real men with charisma to match any eau de toilette advert. Oh yes. We did not understand fire regulations and safety hazards and the dangers of loud music to plants. We just understood £5 per person entrance fee and that there would be lots of girls to look at. Simple.

Wicko was to be the music man and he set about kitting out a sound system that would fill the greenhouse with a 'kicking vibe.' The only problem we could have had would have been with the caretaker but, thankfully, he had been for a long time partaking in our 'display' facility. He even had his own key and we didn't ask too many questions. It was better that way. We gave him a brief outline of what we were doing i.e. having around 20 people over for an end of year party. He said he would keep well out of our way and to have a good time. Sorted.

We spent the week before meticulously preparing the greenhouse for a party to remember and, in turn, show the school's hip crowd that we were there to be counted. No more walking by us in the school breaks as though we didn't exist, but rather 'Ayup youth, what you doing later?' The school's beautiful people began to court all three of us and we, in a true show of dignity, lapped up every last minute of it.

Wicko set up his 'state of the art' stereo system towards the back of the greenhouse. It consisted of his home bedroom

Hi-Fi with his father's two 'Bush' speakers that supported
the Wickson family sound system in the lounge. He had told
his parents that he needed the extra power because he was
in charge of school sports day announcements. On top of
this he added on two 50-watt speakers 'borrowed' from the
music storeroom. We hid them all under the tomato plants.
We fastened black paper to the roof glass panes to ensure a
dark atmosphere for the night. An art teacher did enquire as to
what we were doing when he caught Steve and I taking a large
amount of card from the art stock room. Steve explained that I
would explain. I cast Steve a look of thanks and then prepared
for the best of lies which, as anyone knows, must be told fairly
and directly into the eyes of the beholder to pass the honesty
test. It was simple, I told him: we were on strict orders from
the Head to protect the plants as they were burning up in the
intense sun we were experiencing. The art teacher incredibly
bought it! This again summed up the tremendous respect we
had built for ourselves at the school, so much so that this guy
knew better than to argue with the School Gardeners who at
this stage were one of the school's treasures.

Friday arrived and school finished. We rushed home, got
changed into our trendiest clothes and returned. With so
many girls arriving and with us being the party organisers we
were all hopeful that perhaps this would be the night when
girls, ('women'), would begin to take us seriously. After all
we were the school entrepreneurs, the business leaders of our
generation, and our future signalled money, money, money
(read-doom, doom, doom).

Up to this point only Wicko had already experienced a
modicum of success with girls. Over the last two years he
had developed a physique, some hint of muscle, which was
something that for Steve and me remained sadly missing. Girls
actually began to 'fancy' him and he had been known to use

the greenhouse on more then five occasions that we knew of for extra curricular activities, two of which he had allowed us to hide in the corner and watch. Steve and I were quite simply jealous. Initial respect and fascination had turned in to a slight sour feeling at Wicko's inability to get his girlfriends to get girlfriends for us. In truth he probably never even tried but I suspect his girlfriends would not have been too helpful. Steve continued to be all out of shape in that he was rather gangly and awkward, and I remained spotty and hidden behind a pair of spectacles borrowed from NASA. Still as the new school party organisers we were hopeful of success on this night with or without Wicko's help.

Steve was wearing black, totally black, with black shades covering eyes sporting black eyeliner, and dyed jet-black hair. After I got over the initial scare and the laughter had come and gone, I told him that he looked very cool indeed. He gave me an appropriate look over the rim of his sunglasses, which he had apparently got with a recent purchase of a Smash Hits magazine. I smiled at him, nervously, and apologised for laughing.

Wicko was wearing Bermuda shorts and a bright red shirt opened down to his navel. He had developed a hairy chest at birth and was determined to show everyone, regardless of whether they wished to look.

I had not known what to wear. I had told my mother truthfully that I was going to a party, although not so truthfully that the party was at Steve's and that yes of course Steve's parents would be there. She had suggested that I wear one of my two ill fitting and dreadful Sunday suits. Mother has never been good at understanding modern fashions. As a child I was wearing velour-flared trousers made by my great aunty Norah for no reason that I could see other than to encourage the laughter of the whole school. This it duly did and still now I am stopped in the street by old school friends who will remind me of my earlier attire.

In the end I decided to dress down and let my gentle yet intelligent and quite frankly slightly sensual wit do the rest. Simple jeans and T-shirt were accompanied by a pair of cool prescription shaded glasses that I had bought at great expense with party receipt money. It bothered me immediately on seeing Steve that his free glasses looked far cooler than mine. Never mind.

The party was due to start at 9pm allowing for any extra keen teachers, and remarkably there were a few, and cleaning staff, of which there were far fewer, to be long gone. By 8.30pm we had our bouncers in place and music ringing out at a volume that would almost definitely be upsetting my precious plants. I covered as many of them up as I could with paper but stopped when I realised that the bouncers had cottoned on to what I was doing and were laughing accordingly. Any slight street cred I had now ruined, I made my way to the back of the greenhouse for a final party run down with the team.

By twenty to nine the queue was building and I began to get nervous. By ten to nine the queue was further than I could see. Steve mumbled something about having sold a few more tickets than he had told us about.

'How many more?' I worryingly asked.

'About a hundred.'

We were all silent. Disaster loomed in the air like the gathering storm clouds at the end of a far too hot and humid day. All we could do was enjoy the last few rays of sunshine.

Nine o'clock and 'Knuckles', the head bouncer and super keen Madness fan, opened the door. Tickets were handed over and people crowded in. As they did so I found myself being crushed against the greenhouse wall and immediately considered escaping home. If I wasn't there when the police inevitably came, how could I be blamed? Then I saw Wicko's current girlfriend, Michelle Bowler, walk through the door and my plan to escape disappeared. At the side of Michelle was her friend Alison Smithley, who was, in my humble opinion, a beauty. I had long since admired her from a distance but I could not have prepared myself for how she looked this evening. She was wearing her hair long, where at school it was always scraped back. Her dark locks fell on to her shoulders, which were wonderfully bare and tanned. Alison had chosen to wear a tight off the shoulder top that showed off her majestically formed breasts that I soon became lost in the thought of touching. As I did so I was aware of my tight jeans perhaps not being the best clothes choice as my manhood began to scream out for attention. I tried to take my mind off Alison's breasts only to see her tanned legs calling out to me as they flowed out of her tight black mini skirt. I was in heaven because there in front of me was a true Woodhouse angel. Tonight, I thought, perhaps my luck was in.

The girls fought their way straight to the back of the greenhouse and to Wicko who was mixing up a mixture of mid eighties music and alcoholic drinks, both of which would terrify us in years to come. I followed them, caught in the spell of short skirts and small tight tops. Delicious legs and cute pert breasts had swayed my shallow personality and my fears of impending disaster had been successfully averted. I suspect The Light Brigade were given such a show before promptly riding to their deaths in the Crimean War.

As I began to reach the crowd at the back of the greenhouse the darkness took over which meant with my prescription sunglasses I couldn't see a thing. I nonchalantly slipped them off and placed them in my back pocket, tripping over only twice before reaching Wicko. I had ordered contact lenses with loaned birthday money but unfortunately they had not arrived in time for the party. Tonight then I would have to let my senses take control. Having got no sense this would unquestionably add to my inevitable downfall.

By nine thirty around 150 people were crammed into the greenhouse which now seemed the size of a small wooden garden shed. There were many more people who had got no chance of getting in, shouting to hear the music outside. Wicko decided to oblige and he turned up the increasingly inaudible music for them to hear. The speakers turned into a sound of mush as they spluttered in their vain efforts to carry the pulse of the party music out into the night. It was like listening to a record with your head up to the fully turned up speaker, but with you wearing a crash helmet, which had several babies nappies fastened around it. Try it some time! Clearly the speakers were now working towards a blow out.

The bouncers had not really been enlisted but had more so volunteered. They had done so on the understanding that they could provide the drink on the side. We thought this was a truly great idea and they readily agreed. They were selling almost certainly nicked beer outside at £1 per can making a fantastic extortionate profit. For the punters though the accessibility of drink was a Mecca to behold. The drinks attraction also had an added bonus of keeping those outside fairly satisfied and providing a through flow of people getting out to buy alcohol allowing more to come in.

By ten o'clock the bouncers had left the door. It later transpired they had been charging a further £2 on the door. Steve was punched at least 4 times as a result from disgruntled punters.

I, on the other hand, had been in constant and deep conversation with Alison, my newfound friend. She was, as I told her, beautiful, although admittedly I couldn't really see her anymore. Still in the blurred way that I could see her, she looked very pretty indeed. As we talked she actually seemed interested in me and, remarkably, in my role in the greenhouse. It turned out that her father ran a garden shop and that she knew very much about gardening. In my head I fantasised of us planting begonias in her tubs in her back garden, naked.

By ten thirty the beer had run out and the ugly effects of drink had begun to take their toll. Several fights, thankfully most of them outside and away from the plants, had seen a few lost teeth and a pane of glass broken. I hoped it was not a sign of things to come and yet I guessed it probably would be.

In the greenhouse Wicko had been diverted to the back room after his girlfriend began to stroke his groin area. Imagine that, a girl stroking your groin without hesitation and with a gusto that would bring a shine to any cricket ball. He had left a friend in charge of the music who, had he been sober, would probably have been fine. It was not to be.

I was just outside the back room with Alison. We had found a little corner of our own just to the side of the display room and underneath a table which was hidden from public view by a black tablecloth. We had been in the same kissing position for about twenty minutes. To the naked eye we could have been a frozen ice sculpture.

Looking back I am not sure whether I heard the breaking glass first or smelt the smoke. It later transpired that 'Fuzzy', the young man Wicko had left in charge of the stereo, had taken to setting alight all the plants he could reach to add some fun and amusement to proceedings and create a cool atmosphere. One thing had led to another and without realising it the shelves holding some of my precious plants had begun to smoulder. The paper bags I had wrapped around many of the plants had clearly not helped the fire situation as they ignited easily and helped feed the fire at a pace all of its own. At the same time Fuzzy's fires had caught with the table that held Wicko's stereo. Before he knew it he was trapped behind a blazing inferno with nowhere to go. Luckily he was in a greenhouse and faced with any number of windows to break out through he made his successful escape.

By this stage the party had begun to spill outside with people rather wisely deciding to get out and enjoy the impromptu fire display from a distance of safety.

I had just managed to negotiate my right hand from a tenuous and somewhat tortuous journey from Alison's neck, down her back, up her arm and, crucially on to her left breast without her moving away or slapping me. It was a journey that I had dreamed about many times and was at last being allowed to carry out. The fact that cramp had settled into both my legs had not stopped my joy-felt excitement as I lost myself in my deluded fulfilment. Alas all was now to end.

On hearing broken glass and the sound of shouting, Alison pulled away from me.

'What's that noise Scotty?'

Scott is my surname. My first name is Anthony and apart from the staff no one ever used that at school.

'Someone having fun?' I tentatively replied hoping she might bite the answer and return to my arms and, most importantly, my hand.

'No, I think it's more than that.'

'More than that?' I was losing her and probably my one chance to ever feel a female breast again!

'Do you think so?'

'Yes, I'm going to have a look… come on!'

'Have a look.' The words echoed in my mind. I felt in my back pocket and pulled out my squashed and shattered glasses. I would not be looking at anything.

I sat and listened for what seemed like minutes unable to make my mind up as to what to do next. If I followed Alison

I would undoubtedly fall over at least 5 million times and walk into the hardest people in the school who would punch me relentlessly. As I thought these 'happy' thoughts Wicko emerged from the 'display' room with his girlfriend. I could just make out they were totally naked and I heard Michelle screaming 'FIRE!!!' Several other people filed out of the same room in various states of attire. The thought crossed through my mind that if only Alison and I had gone in that room too who knows what I might have gotten hold of.

I realised I had to make a move but felt scared to do so. In the distance the sound of sirens began to fill the air. Clearly I was going to be in a lot of trouble and as fear overtook me I felt trapped by my own inability to see and my wish that none of what I was experiencing was really happening. The smoke was beginning to get rather overpowering and I was gradually getting in to a panic when, from the 'display' room, a dark solitary figure emerged. His arms were full of papers and he made his way towards me. I squinted my eyes and saw it was Steve.

'Hello mate,' he said in a calm and caring voice, 'what are you still doing here?'

He was totally unfazed by all the noise and commotion.

'I've broken my glasses,' I mumbled, ' and I wasn't quite sure what to do!'

'Well let's get you out of here shall we?' he said softly, taking my arm and pulling me upwards. He kicked out some windows from behind me and we squeezed through the hole ripping our clothes as we went. We ran all the way back to his house and did not stop to consider the damage.

In that moment in time Steve had probably saved my life. We would be best friends forever.

We were, of course, all in trouble. Thankfully no one had been too hurt, but there was the damage, extensive damage, to school property. The police picked us up from our houses later that night much to the total lack of amusement from our parents. Why they couldn't just see the irony of it all with 'good' kids causing such damage I do not know.

Thankfully the obliging caretaker took all the real blame. His house was found to have an incredible selection of pornography that had nothing to do with us and for fear of scandal it was easy to blame him for egging us on and setting up the party for his own financial gain. As a further stroke of luck it also quickly became apparent he was actually behind the beer sales.

Thank god that the summer holidays had arrived and whilst we were never going to be given any responsibility at school again, we were allowed back in to complete our sixth form studies. I have no idea how, although it did transpire that Wicko's Mum had once been very close to the Head of Governors.

After friendship groundings like the greenhouse experiment, Steve and I had stayed close throughout the years. Sure, we had gone our separate ways, me to Sheffield to study and Steve to deliver letters for Her Majesties Post Office, but we always found time to see each other. Now I was back in town permanently, a little like those Thin Lizzy boys but without the band, a hit single, any kind of instrument, no real accent and certainly no posse of screaming girls wanting to rip off our clothes.

Home that night at last from work after a day that had seen me share a bus with a demented old dear, meet the two beauties Magenta and Coco, and get ripped off by my comedian car mechanic, I was still in a state of triumph thanks to the wonders of Oasis. Now to tell Stevie. I picked up the phone and waited for his kindly tones.

'Steve, my boy, how does the land lie in the Isles of The North.'

'Oh hello mate, how's it going?'

'How's it going?' To be asked this by your best mate is one of the nicest things that can happen. It is the beginning of one of those conversations that will go on for ages and cover everything and nothing. Afterwards if you tried to think about what you had talked about for all that length of time you would be unable to recite most of it and almost certainly fail to make it in anyway interesting to a third party. It was private talk between you and your friend. The best of its kind as you used the power of conversation purely for the sake of being able to talk.

The years had not changed Steve. He had become a young man with remarkably quite a few Post Office responsibilities but to me he was the same. He was his own man, unmoved by how others had sort to mould him. This was exactly why my question to him meant he was perfect for the job I had him lined up for.

'Yea, good mate, very good. Now then I have some exciting news for you.'

'Really?'

'Yea, really. Have you heard of Oasis?'

'The girls clothes shop?'

'No.'

'That place in the desert where you get, erm, you get, something important!'

'You don't know what you get do you?'

'No.'

'You get water!'

'Is that all. No beer, women, general excitement?'

'Possibly those too'

'Oh, OK. Anyway is that it?'

'No. It's a new Band.'

'Oh yea?'

'You have heard of them haven't you?'

'I have, yes, though no tunes yet. Should I be lending them my ear?'

'Oh yes, indeed, yes indeed my dear friend! They are the future and they are everywhere! I want you to go to a music shop first thing tomorrow and buy their album and then call me tomorrow tonight.'

'Buy the album?' Steve was notoriously tight with money. The burning down of the greenhouse had taught him early in life that money can be lost as quickly as it is made and is almost always harder to make back the second time.

'Yes mate, trust me.'

'Oh, OK.' One of the beauties of Steve is that he has always done just about anything I have asked him to do. Whether out of trust, desire to keep me happy, or simply to shut me up I have never really known. It made me happy though.

'Just one question, why am I buying the album?'

'Because it is going to inspire you' I said, sounding like some Sunday morning preacher.

'To do what?'

'To be in a band mate, our very own band!'

'Cool,' replied Steve, and as he did I could see in my mind his smile and hear his heartbeat quicken with excitement.

'Call me tomorrow, yea?'

'Alright mate. You got it!'

With that we replaced our receivers and I hoped Oasis would hit him like they had hit me. I couldn't wait until tomorrow night and him ringing me with his thoughts. Patience has never been a strong point.

3

My brother.

The thing about Keith is that whoever meets him is in awe of him. Of course I know him better than almost anyone, and I am still his biggest fan. Then again he is my big and only brother. Three years older, and that really did make all the difference, so how could I be anything other than somewhat mystically entranced by him. It wasn't in a way that meant I wanted or needed to be like him because in fact we are very different people. For example his dress sense means he is a man destined in mid to later years to wear his trouser waistline too high, as though the heightened cloth will somehow act as a corset or, indeed, add some warmth to the male nipple area. He will love this when the time arrives and see it as an obvious addition to his ability to add humour to his aura. I would never want a high trouser line but I did want to be near that heightened belted waist. You see with him there has always been something that I could not touch. Partly it's the simple fact that he popped out three years earlier me, technically it is closer to four years, and this is experience in years I will never catch up on. In turn this just led to him carrying an air of experience of life that I can never close in on because of the age difference. In reality this is probably not the case at all, but in my head it most definitely is. Younger brother syndrome is what it is. It's a gap I or any other younger brother will never breach.

Keith had played bass guitar for several years and at the moment was showing twice weekly down at the local evangelical church as part of their musical worship band. Church life was part of my family's upbringing. From being born, and probably before that even, we went to church religiously three times every Sunday. As we got older we went at least once in the week as well and, when feeling particularly keen, three nights in the week. The ritual was a mystery to all my friends and, indeed, to me. It was almost like a science fiction movie where we were taken away by other beings on set times each week, only to be returned safe and sound to get on with being normal.

I believed in God, as did most of my friends I guess. It was just that in my case, as opposed to most people, my parents were incredibly good attendees of a local church and, as their children, we all became incredibly good regular attendees too. To be honest, being part of church was no big deal to me, at least the church I went to. The people were all nice and friendly and most of the time it was like a really good club. As I have gotten older I have become amazed by the similarities between a good old working mans club and our church, bar, I grant you, the hard drinking and heavy smoking and the occasional fights and the full on petting. We had regular turns come to entertain us, lots of juicy gossip, interesting hats, away days to Mablethorpe and live music. It is a comparison I have not mentioned to my father for fear of causing offence. No, church life may not have been for my school pals but I liked it! Besides anything I had lots of church friends all of whom were in the same boat as us in that their parents were also really faithful followers. This safety in numbers meant that we never saw ourselves as weird because that would mean we were all weird! In turn our non-attendee pals had their own strange quirky habits such as scouts or swimming club or paper rounds or dancing class and so on. I guess my going to church made me more tolerant. Why would I pick on someone who was doing something different when I was clearly in the stand out club already? Yes, being the neighbourhood evangelical made me more socially accepting, not less so!

Our church too was not too heavy. Sure it talked about Hell and avoiding dark places, to the extent that shadows became something I avoided for fear of demons waiting to catch me and do whatever they would do with me. Also the regular covering of the end of the world meant that every time I came home from being out with my heathen pals late at night I was never sure whether my family would still be at home or not. I recognise that these things did not fill my childhood with peace. However the church also taught far more about love and care too. To me that was a pretty good balance and I didn't mind it too much. Heavy is as you carry it in your bag. My bag remained pretty light as a result.

Both Keith and my friends saw our Christian sideline as an eccentricity that we had become part of at birth. It wasn't a problem to us, and so why should it be a problem to them, after all it was not our fault. Going to church put us in the same bracket as children with national health glasses, a lisp, an unfortunate limp, a stutter, a European surname or really large ears. Given that Keith and I both wore the aforementioned glasses and went to church did stand us out for further abuse than most, but we were not to be avoided for we had no plague, as such. Rather we were generally humoured and accepted. On top of this we probably gave them hours of entertainment when they talked about us behind our backs. In short, our religious fervour was adding to their lives as well. God be praised.

Overall I am grateful for my friends understanding. Sure they occasionally teased me, but overall they were respectful of my predicament and understood that it could so easily, in another life, have been them. In the main they simply wrote into their mind social calendars that Sunday was not a day to call for Scotty. He was otherwise engaged with someone they better not mess with, and I don't just mean my father.

I should add that not all the people I ever came across were quite so stoical about it. I had nearly every Christian nickname possible awarded to me. 'Jesus', 'Sandal Wearer', 'Bible Basher', 'Holy Moses', 'Mary', 'The Immaculate Conception', 'Satan, 'Genesis' and, amongst many others, my personal favourite 'Brian.' Given, though, that all of my friends at church were in the same position, and of course so was my older most respected brother, I humoured people. This ability to smile in adversity was one that I was sure could only help in later life.

I stopped going regularly to church as soon as I could though popping in is always a pleasure. Keith continued going to church as often as possible. It suited his character, he's a fervent believer and he loves the music. I admired him for keeping the faith like this in a way I couldn't. It wasn't that I stopped believing in God. I do believe very much. I just needed a rest sooner than Keith.

The music of a modern church was surprisingly upbeat and imaginative. It wasn't The Rolling Stones, admitted, but it did have a beating heart championed by the likes of Grapevine and Chris Bowater, and Keith loved it. Listening to my brother play and more to the point watching him play was an experience that you would pay serious money for. You had to strip aside the veneer of that pounding bass line that Keith attached to any song / hymn he played, and see at the back of it the quality that was Keith. His base lines, just like him, were unique, that is to say not at all deft and unlikely to be played by anyone else. It was magical to listen to any song begin and know that he would hammer out the same set of notes but at a different pace. You had to respect that sort of imagination and cheek in anyone. It was a gift he had learnt from my father who played the piano and church organ, albeit not at the same time. Every song, and I mean every song, had the exact swing type quality attached to it, and was invariably played in the key of E sharp. It could have been Amazing Grace or one of Fryderyk Chopin's preludes. You would not have mistaken Dad was playing it and in E sharp!

Then of course there were Keith's facial expressions. As he played his guitar, his face reached contortion levels that, if you did not know him, you would think he was desperately trying to keep three weeks worth of food from coming out all at one go. Knowing his ability to be regular in the toilet, to the minute, I knew this not to be the case.

His eccentricity aside, Keith had important and vital qualities that were required for any band and I was determined to utilise them. First of all he was very funny. When we were little we used to go to my Mum and Dad's church and during a song by a little old lady wearing a pink smock, and a furry velvet hat that wouldn't have looked out of place on a rather grandiose hand warmer, I would feel Keith looking at me. I knew that if I caught his eye my resolve would be broken and I would laugh uncontrollably out loud. He had this ability and power over me. My only consolation would be that Mum would always believe me and give Keith the lion's share of the telling off when we were later in the privacy of our home. As the old singing dear reached a high note and you wondered whether the sound she was making meant she was about to die, I would accidentally forget the gaze that awaited me and I would turn to Keith to smile quietly at the bizarre sound we were again listening to. Imagine a dog howling at the moon, joined in unison by a few rum looking drunken bulls, and you are getting warm. I would look at him and his face would now be holding an expression of mixed pain and horror. Only I ever saw these faces, the ones he reserved for me to crack me up into pieces, and I would have no option but to let the laughter roll. I had no choice. In a vain and last desperate attempt to keep my dignity, I would try and stem the laughter by biting the inside of my cheeks, hard. As a result the laugh that was forcing its way into my mouth would cause my face to turn very red, and sweat to appear on my brow. I would then begin to choke and snot would inevitably come out of my nose. As I gasped to wipe away the embarrassment of the new arrival on my face I would then begin to laugh. It was normally a high-pitched muffled laugh as I held my mouth hard in to the inside of my elbow. People would look at me, and I would inevitably feel like I had let the old lady, still singing with gusto, down. I had, but it was really very, very funny.

Secondly, Keith was very reliable. If Keith began something he believed in, you knew he would never let you down. Keith is that fanatical person who you see in magazines and you wonder how they had such energy and focus. Think Forrest Gump and his running for three plus years and you are getting close to Keith's character. He is the one who you read about and think that sort of behaviour is not possible. Think about those articles about keep fit fanatics who run thirty miles every day, whatever the weather. Think about those people who follow diets religiously and lose 18 stones in three months. Or what about those business types who get up before they go to bed to exercise, do emails and practice some zen like routine before working a 28 hour day and then going out to party like wild animals. Its simply not normal behaviour is it! What is their problem? Resolve is their problem. They have it in abundance. That was my brother. He had it, I didn't. Keith once read that it was good to start the day with fruit. His house is now a fruit palace. Everyday starts with five bananas and three oranges and a bowl of nuts. Not once a week, not even just twice. Every day is the same and no day is different. Like our upbringing he follows his new code religiously. His bathroom is best avoided until an hour after his morning visit. He is a 'fad' man who once he has decided on the fad he believes in, he will never let it down. I hoped that he would add my Band idea as his new fad and that his resolve would be the band's route to stardom, or at least a gig or two.

Thirdly, and vitally, he had his own transport. A vital rule of any Band is that as many of you as possible must have your own transport. These vehicles will prove invaluable for the transferring of gear and fans to gigs around the country and, of course, ensure regular rehearsal attendance. Keith had his own car. It was an old Vauxhall Belmont in a sea blue/ rust colour. It was still alive and well despite many attempts to leave this car life and move on to a new life in the roads of the sky. The car too was one of Keith's 'fads' and he wasn't about to let it go because of the every other day mechanical failure. Despite the car looking, and often sounding, to the innocent bystander as a car that was on its last legs, and despite the fact that the car too probably considered that its time was near, Keith, and he is the important factor here, believed this car would live for many more years to come. He believed this as fact, therefore it was true and therefore it would happen. It was this simple in his mind, and it was this sort of thought pattern that gave the man real resolve. You could disagree with him, and, when faced with the prospect of getting in the car for any journey of length, I often did just that, but such negativity didn't matter to Keith. Rather in such moments he would look at me with that slightly mad expression reserved for crazy scientists and show dog owners to tell me I was the mad one. It was an expression that held a little smile, tinged with a strength and sureness of grounded thinking that made you quickly realise there was no reasoning on earth that could convince him that he may be misguided and you, despite your doubts, suddenly began to find faith.

Fourthly, and finally, he had his own bass guitar and amp and leads. A vital tip for any prospective band is that in looking for band members you look for people who have their own gear already in place. The ability to play can always come later, but find a musician without equipment and you have the luxury liner passengers without a boat. Rehearsals and gigs really are just not the same when the drummer is hitting tins with his drumsticks, and the bass player is humming loudly rather than playing his notes. Now in Keith's case I had to admit that his gear was not necessarily top drawer goods, after all his bass guitar had the rather dubious name of 'Hondo' which, in all honesty, sounded more like some sneaky little Red Indian scout than an instrument. However it made all the right noises (Keith noises) and that, at this early stage, was all that mattered.

I had told Steve that Keith would be the man to provide the solid bass support we needed for the Band but he had not been convinced.

'He's your brother,' he said matter of factly, 'I mean how can you seriously expect us to play in Band with the man who has spent the last ten plus years trying his best to avoid us?'

This was not quite the case. Older brothers had to be cool and so being seen in public with the little brother and his friends was simply not cool or acceptable. When there was nobody there who 'mattered' Keith had always been the best friend you could have wished for. Suddenly, left with little choice, Keith had allowed me into his Pandora box and to me as the little brother that was all that mattered. To Steve, as the shunned friend, he had obviously been expecting a lot more.

'Look Steve, trust me. Keith is the right man for the job. He will be fine with you once you get to know him.'

'How's that going to happen seeing that he's made an art form of constantly ignoring me?'

'Well, yes, admitted, but try and see that as an underlining of his ability to stick to whatever he commits to and you are well on the way. Besides I guarantee every time he snubbed us he was laughing on the inside. Look upon it as dark humour. That's what all the bands have got, you know, a dark side.'

'Darth Vader.'

'Yes, that's it! Think of Keith as Darth Vader…' and using my best Darth Vader voice '…the power of the dark side is ours Luke.'

Steve was not sure.

'Look let's go and listen to him play and then we will decide.'

'OK, but not at church.'

I was nodding my head apologetically.

'But you know I don't like church. They're going to ask me to start being nice again aren't they?'

I was still nodding, but now in a wilder manner, akin to me listening to an Iron Maiden track.

'It's not aimed just at you Northy.'

He shot me that sarcastic 'of course it isn't' look.

'Look we have to go to church so that you can hear him play.'

'Alright then, if we must. When are we going?'

'Tonight!'

So there we were, Steve and I, sat on the front pew and singing a rather jaunty little number along with a congregation that resembled shoppers you might find in any BHS or Littlewood's store on any given day of the week. Keith was trying his best not to look at us as we laughingly attempted to reach notes that we really should have avoided. I was getting my own back for years of him making me laugh at the 'wrong' time as he kept flashing that 'Paddington hard stare' that somehow big brothers master for all their siblings.

We looked somewhat out of place, wearing faded jeans and baggy tops. Steve, despite the inclement weather, refused to take off his sunglasses, hence giving the congregation the impression that he was either ignorant, a film star, ill, blind or all of these. Still we made up for any concern by singing along heartily in the Church's end of month 'Songs of Praise' meeting where they concentrated on the more popular numbers that even Steve had a grasp of from various trips to the altar over many years with me. Such trips were normally connected to him seeing one of the young ladies he thought might swoon at his feet or the fact that he had nothing else to do on that particular Sunday night.

After what seemed like twenty hymns, and a preacher spending an awful long time getting very worked up indeed, we found ourselves in front of Keith who was meticulously packing his equipment away with a care that would not have gone amiss in the operating theatre.

'Nice singing,' he said sarcastically.

'Nice playing Keith,' said Steve.

'Thanks. It was a good meeting wasn't it?'

This was, I think, a test. Surely even Keith must have found old hell and gusto boy too much too, but Keith was searching for where our respect lay.

'Brilliant!' declared Steve suitably quickly and without hesitation, 'a real blood buster sermon there!'

Keith laughed. I laughed knowing that I now could laugh.

'They should get him on TV Keith,' Steve continued, 'he would be good after the watershed!'

The two were speaking. It was a first. The omens were good.

'Keith,' it was time for me to set up the moment that would out us on the road to stardom, 'Let us get to the point. You know that I bought that Oasis album and we both loved it.'

We did. We had both loved it. Apart from the Beatles, the Oasis album was the first musical experience we had both fallen in love with. Keith had actually spent money on his own copy. All three of us had now played the album non-stop. We woke up with it, took it through our day, returned home with it, and went to bed with it. The music had become our new best friend and lover all in one go. We were believers in the excitement of the music that Oasis had delivered.

'Well, it's made me think,' I continued,

'Goodness,' Keith said with just a little too much sarcasm.

'We should do something massive with our lives, you know grasp the nettle…'

'Take the bull by the horns, the monkey by the balls, the lady by the nipples…' Steve was taking the piss, but it was funny. Keith was interested. I could always tell when he was interested. His eyes lit up and the corner of his lips suggested a smile.

'And so I thought we, that is you, me and Steve…'

I paused, waiting to see if the mention of him potentially doing something with Steve included had been a bridge of a suggestion too far.

'Yes?' said Keith impatiently, knowing what was coming but making me work for it.

'Well, that you, me and Steve…'

'That we could start a band,' said Steve.

We were all quiet, the words taken out of my mouth by Steve, and not seeming to make any sense at all. Why on earth would Keith want to spend any length of time with his younger brother and his strange friend in a band?

Keith looked at me first, and then turned his attention to Steve. Steve looked down at his feet.

'Boys, and I call you boys because that is what you are, I would love to be in the band, that is my band, of course. When do we start?'

4

So there we were. The Band was born.

Now to find a drummer who could hold drumsticks, preferably not look too ugly and at least look competent, with transport. Then to rehearse and work hard, finding gigs to have something to work towards. Finally and crucially we had the small matter of finding a band name that would make us a stand out name on every hoarding board across the US of A, or at least Mansfield...

Having Keith on board was key to finding answers. It is important first of all to understand what Keith does because his occupation, and how he performs this occupation, would lead us to our drummer. Keith, and it will come as absolutely no surprise to you the reader, is a teacher. To many of his students though he was much more than just a teacher; he was a god. They talked about him, they talked to him and they talked around him. He was the subject of so many 'would you like to kiss him and oh so much more' discussions that quite simply meant he was almost worshipped. He was a tall dark chap with Mediterranean looks that bought so many young impressionable teenagers to their drooling worst, or best, depending how you viewed it. To the boys particularly he was one of them. He would play football with them, talk to them and listen to them. He was the cool teacher who was part of the crowd and, as a result, will be one they remember fondly around their pint pots and vodka bottles in years to come.

Back all that up with hard work and integrity and Keith was a teacher that both parents and school heads could also love. He was a model teacher, a dream professional, and a perfect magnet for fans that would love to follow his new band. Some teachers have what you can only call ' it.' Keith has it in spades.

This fantastic level of respect was there then to be milked, and we decided that we were to do the milking for all it was worth. The first 'cow' to be squeezed was our requirement for a drummer and the school band had the perfect answer. His name was Joe. He was in the sixth form, 17 years of age (18 if anyone asked), and as reliable as they come. His looks were not going to pull the girls in by the shed load and we accepted that his character was not going to enrapture the listeners of Radio One. However, he had the natural gift of rhythm and, crucially, parents that had spoilt him endlessly and bought him the most incredible Premier drum kit. It was a drum kit that I, as singer of the band, would be proud to stand in front of.

Singer. Since being little I had shown abilities in two areas, well obviously there were many other areas that time and the space in this book, and indeed many books, a full library of them, no, many libraries, do not allow me to delve into. So, for the purposes of this book, my first ability of the two mentioned was that of being able to tell a story. I could make something up easily and endlessly. By the age of three I could hold an audience and recite a made up story of murder, mystery, and suspense. This ability put me in good stead to gild the lily on many occasions, and, being in a band, this ability would be priceless.

My other ability was my sweet little voice and my constant desire to be the centre of attention. Mum used to stand me at the front of the room in family gatherings and ask me to perform. I loved it. I would enlist my brother as a fellow lead comedian, although not quite as lead as me. My two younger sisters, Susan and Anne, would be there as the outlying support actors; there to give that vital addition of a person running wildly on to stage and shouting something like "your horse is here sir!" Usually they would also insist on putting in an angel performance at some point and, of course, being the caring brother I would let them have their moment. Besides I have found that there is nothing better than an older audience likes more than a pair of little ones dressed up as angels. Their appearance would soften the hearts and ensure I would not get told off for some of the more risky material that I had given Keith to perform throughout the show. To me the naked Shepherd in the nativity scene is one of history's lost treasures, but alas my great aunts and uncles were not as enlightened as I would have hoped. Some might say this was connected to the fact that Keith had reached puberty three years before I did. All I know was that it made me laugh. A lot. An awful lot.

A few years on and my voice had now developed into a husky mix of manliness that was ready to be shared with a much wider audience than just me and my bathroom mirror, and indeed every other mirror that had the fortune, or misfortune, of receiving one of my impromptu performances. I guess that I should also perhaps point out that the other minor 'main' reason I was to sing was that Steve and Keith were both close to being tone deaf. They could hum a tune but you wouldn't thank them for doing so.

44

And so the band was formed! Within weeks from the 'church meeting,' a meeting of minds that may well have bus tours go and visit the building in years to come, we were having practices. The first few were extremely loud affairs. Joe's mum had very kindly, given it was golden boy Mr Scott who was playing bass, offered her living room, her very large living room, as our practice venue. They lived just out in the country and only a few houses surrounded them so we would struggle to disturb anyone. The living room, in particular, had a lovely view across the surrounding fields and a loving little brook that made its way joyously round the bottom of the garden on its happy little journey.

We would arrive at Joe's house all wearing 'shades' whatever the weather, and leather jackets that made us look like the coolest lads ever, or most stupid ever depending on your cool viewpoint barometer. Judging by the looks from the neighbours who were lucky enough to witness the start of a legendary band, they clearly felt we looked stupid.

We would then try to keep looking cool as we dragged our old, and extremely heavy amps, into his house whilst sweating like pigs in an overcrowded sty in the height of a very hot summer. Joe's two mad and very smelly massive dogs would greet us by jumping up to our faces and washing us with their bad breath and slop. One of them, the strong and well-endowed male, would then make love to Keith's speaker for the whole of the practice. This was of course a delightful and awe-inspiring sight that still haunts me today. The dogs never seemed to mind the music, correction commotion, that we cascaded around the house and surrounding area, albeit one of them was in a continual state of sexual fusion with a speaker. No doubt the dog is now in dog counselling, trying to work out why music has a dreadful effect on him, causing him to come over all frisky whenever he hears tunes escape from the radio.

After a month and a bit of full on practice we were becoming a tad more bearable to the naked ear. We had all been playing for some years, just not together, and although my rhythm guitar playing was our weakest link we quickly began to get an understanding, which simply meant that we now knew how to play badly in unison. Of course being rock gods in the making we all played miles too loudly, especially Steve who always played as though the whole of Wembley was listening to him. Keith, after only the second practice, took to wearing earplugs. This was partly to protect his hearing but also I believe to then also be able to play louder. Steve's hearing had long since been neglected, as he had spent night after night in clubs around the area glued to the speakers. As for Joe, well he was the drummer and, as with any other drummer I have met, he was almost totally deaf anyway. I tried earplugs but then could not hear the music or my vocals making my singing turn into a greater form of gibberish than it usually was. Instead, everything echoed around my head and I felt like I was swimming under water listening to everything in an out of body experience. I decided to leave earplugs alone for a while.

We aimed from the outset to master that Oasis type sound but at the same time to line it with our own unmistakable edge, the edge not only being our musical limits! Still after several practices of belting out 'Live Forever', 'Supersonic' and 'Rock and Roll Star,' we were clearly getting somewhere. It was then that we received a visit from an officer from the Environmental Health. It was not a pleasant evening, and the heavy rain and cold north-westerly wind had not made his one-hour attempt to make himself heard at the door likely to endear him to our cause. Some people have no sense of humour and, whilst it is said some faces tell a thousand stories, his told only one! During any practice Joe's parents would always go out (cowards) and we would close all the curtains so as not to let the world see what awaited them. It is also true to say that we were still a little shy and decided the curtain closing would let the rock gods come out in private and keep the embarrassment out.

On this particular night the sex mad dog had been a little too vigorous in his endeavours and Keith's amp had fallen off the back of the six foot tall speaker (one that he had found at the back of a flea shop and probably pre-dated rock and roll), and landed on the sofa where the other dog was busy cleaning itself in ways that I could never describe. Joe had dropped his sticks and sprinted over to see if both the dogs were still alive. Alas they were. It was at that moment we heard a banging that sounded like a sledgehammer bashing against the front door. We knew we were going to be popular but had not expected this sort of response quite so soon. Joe had made his way to the door through the smoke filled room (Steve managed to work his way through a packet of cigarettes each practice) and had found this poor little official with wide red eyes, dribble falling from his chin, and in a foul mood. Not quite the fan we had been expecting to attract at this early stage. He had forcefully handed over to Joe a letter and then run off to his car without even a comment on the musical experience he had no doubt enjoyed. Charming. Apparently there had been, unbelievably, five separate complaints about the noise over the short period that we had been practising. Now given that Joe only had four neighbours you had to conclude that the fifth complaint was someone from within the house. I think it may have been Joe. We would have to move on to a new practice venue to hone our unmistakable sounds.

Over the next few weeks we tried several pubs, all-eager to take our £10 room fee and our money for the drinks we drunk and crisps and nuts and pork scratchings that we ate. However they were also most eager to keep their other punters happy and insisted on us keeping our noise down below a level that meant Joe had to use brushes and mats, and Steve and Keith had to put their ears up to their amps to hear just what they were doing. For my ears it was luxury, but for the music it was not working.

Eventually we found a pub in Mansfield Woodhouse, our treasured birthplace, that was so empty on any Monday to Thursday we chose, that they were delighted to have the business regardless of any amount of noise we made.

We loved Mansfield Woodhouse. It held a special place in all our hearts. It is difficult to explain this special concept to outsiders. The casual observer would probably find it difficult to see past the badly disguised coal tips, the rotting industrial back drop, the run down estates, the boarded up shop windows, the stray mangy hounds that hogged the kerbs, the litter, the Midlands weather, and the general lack of obvious entertainment. To us though, the charm of our birthplace was Mansfield Woodhouse itself. It had nothing to prove to us because, in being there for us as we grew up, it had done that already. Look behind the façade of decay and you found beautiful old cottages hidden down lanes and behind decrepit shop fronts. In these cottages you found people of great character who had seen life at the coal edge and knew hardship and how to have fun to battle it. Talking to them made you kind of more full, more balanced. I would forever seek out characters because here, in my birthplace, I had grown up with them.

For a new arrival to the area I could clearly see that they might struggle with what was not obvious beauty. However, how do you put a price on the pub that served you your first drink, the park where you stole your first kiss, the field where you scored your first goal and the school that saw your first fight? You cannot. It was true that the High Street of Woodhouse was not full of modern choice but it had always had everything that we had ever wanted from our hometown. You would start at the bottom with the famous 'Crosby's' off licence (the 'offy') that served me sweets from an age of 5. I would walk past it everyday firstly on my way to St Edmunds Primary School and then, six years later, on my way to Manor Comprehensive.

Then, as you walked up the High Street were the scary pubs for stranger older types. These were generally best avoided unless going in for a dare or to contemplate death. We would always walk straight by these. Next, heaven awaited in the form of the most incredible bakers with beautiful fresh bread, smells and gorgeous little cakes that my mother would buy every Thursday. She had always done this for her children, despite our family's lack of funds, for us to devour at tea as a special treat. Often she would go without, happy to see us enjoying our little feast.

Past this to Cascade's, which was the carpet shop where Keith had his first job and nearly sliced off one of his fingers in a dreadful Stanley knife accident. The finger was saved but his job was not. Carlisle's sports shop was next with old Mr Carlisle having always been ancient ever since I first cast my eyes on him. Goodness knows what age he was but he always looked the same to me. It was his shop that supplied me, and all the kids in Woodhouse, with our PE and games kit from the age of 5 and upward. I would go in with my mother, amazed by the man who had so much sports equipment under his ownership in such a small shop. It was just like meeting the shopkeeper in Mr Benn.

You may have noticed the thread of me going everywhere as a child with my mother. In classic Cancerian mode I have always been devoted and ever grateful to my parents but especially my mother. What is there to say except she has never ever let me down, not even once. She has always been my number one fan when there was often not even anything to get excited about. It's difficult to underline how important a Mother's love matters, but in this respect alone I know that my life has been built on solid structures because of this one unmistakeable truth of her love for me. It is a love that all her children felt. We were the lucky ones.

After Carlisle's you come to the old Methodist church where my granny attended each week for an old dears' get together and sing song. It was one of those cute churches that actually had a place in the community. It smelt of polished wood and egg and cress sandwiches. Meeting Grandma there to walk back with her up the Rec steps and home was one of life's great pleasures, not just because I got her to myself for awhile but also because I got fed lots of home made cake! It was a church that was used for lots of things. Weddings, funerals, parties, speakers, tea parties, scout meetings, flag bearing, flower competitions and so on. Everyone in Woodhouse at some point in his or her life would go there for something.

Then the Co-op. This flagship high street superstore had once paid my mother her part time wages when she returned to work after having the fourth of her children. It was also part of the chain that employed my dear and hard working father to be an electrician. I therefore gave it due respect and therefore refused to steal sweets from there. Where were you if you didn't have scruples?

Halfway up your walk up the High Street and now you arrived at Mecca, The Angel Public House. This was the venue that decided to let me in from the age of 15, turning a blind eye to the obvious, and supplied Steve and me with the hallowed drink of beer. I fully appreciate that in writing this, The Angel sounds dreadful too for its lack of care for the youth and the road to drunkenness. I get that and saw the results of many kids, including us, getting rat arsed. However I can also say it was more than that. Here we met, chatted, laughed and planned our lives. Sure it was about the drinking, but it was also about the journey and in our story of our lives, it mattered. It was here that Steve and I drank with so many of our clan. Names that could go on forever, names like the great Paul Gamble, Alan, Rob, Jonesy, Smed, Leper, Dicko, Jono, Marshall, Moodie, Dean, Frank. Just names in a book but legends in our minds. The list is endless and I really could go on forever.

After that you arrived at Newton's Butchers, the place that my school pal's Dad owned and worked hard supplying pies to the whole of the area. I didn't like it. I had never gotten over a visit to the abattoir as part of a school trip at the age of 10. I kid you not. This really did happen. You can imagine that for some the experience was the most amazing and exciting thing ever. For others, like me, I never got over it.

Then the Army Store that had, during our surly youth, kitted Steve and I out. The clothes were cheap and offered that look that was different unless of course you were in the forces and living on an army camp which was something that Steve and I had no intention of doing. Looking like Robert De Niro from The Deer Hunter was one thing, but being anywhere near live ammunition and a nasty sergeant was quite another. I imagined often that the streets of Mansfield were probably akin to some sort of battle front and, indeed, that the army boys were probably sent into Mansfield on a Friday night by way of combat training.

Winsons Chemist followed where Wicko had bought condoms and Steve and I had bought combs and after-shave in the hope that in the fullness of time these may lead to us needing to buy condoms. And then, at the top of the High

Street and in all its glory, was the Portland Arms, the pub that now offered us refuge for our rehearsals. Around the corner you had the Doctors where I had spent many a happy hour trying to convince GP after GP that I had a complaint that meant I really should be off school for a whole term or even year or even for ever. There too was the library where a little Anthony Scott went with his fellow five-year-old students to choose his first reading book.

Then the hallowed ground of the Turner Hall that was home to the theatre productions of my Primary School 'St Edmunds,' and where I gave a stunning performance as 'Kojak' in a school production of the nativity play. My primary school was a trailblazer in modern productions of an old theme. Later I went on to put on my own productions including that of a King whose sole aim was to hang everyone. I gave Keith a major role within the play that was pivotal to the success of my own role. He was 'Fleabag' the palace servant.

Finally you reached the village church 'St Edmunds.' It was an Anglican church that had always given me a warm glow whenever I went anywhere near it. Sometimes churches feel so cold and impersonal but 'our' church was special because it had been the church I had gone to with my little friends from primary school. Its stained glass windows, the pews that would play havoc with piles, the heavy flagstones, long draped battle torn and weather weary flags and lists of important local and long since gone people all tore into our senses. Further the chiselled tributes to the fallen and to the deity that instructed us to respect our lives and to live better ones. Outside the old and ancient gravestones tried valiantly to stay standing tall, though many were now falling apart as age ripped away at the sanctity of respectability on death and reputations faded away into the history of time. The place where babes were christened, marriages were consecrated and the dead were remembered. Yes this was the centre of our community at those most critical of conjunctures.

And that walk up the hub of our part of our world is the summary of that hard to explain special feeling. This is the point of Mansfield Woodhouse to us and no matter what it becomes, those memories are ingrained on our minds forever.

Choosing a name for the band was as messy as trying to find a suitable rehearsal site. There we were, after another stunning rehearsal at the Portland Arms where we were actually getting quite good, sat round a little mahogany table on broken round wobbly stools that should really have made their way on to a bonfire. Joe had gone off to meet his girlfriend (the lightweight), and the three of us were sweltering in the glow of playing six songs that Steve and I had actually written ourselves. If only we had a name we would be almost ready for a gig.

'If Oasis can get away with a girlie shop name, then so can we!'

This was Steve's reasoning in a vain attempt to get Keith and I to name ourselves after his choice of band name 'Monsoon.' We had already banded around every shop name going and had even walked the shops in Nottingham and written down the shop names to digest later. We had paid special attention to all girl shops names, in honour to Oasis of course, and to all lingerie shops because bras fascinated us. Also Steve suggested that the individual lingerie brand names might give us the inspiration we needed. Why is it that the assistants in these shops do not take kindly to young men fingering their lingerie? We did not find a suitable / workable name but we had hours of entertainment.

'I would rather steer clear of girl shop names…' Keith, the voice of reason, '…What we need is something different, something that will hit the listener as they see the poster.'

'A wanted poster saying 'Catch those Woodhouse bandits'?'
I was trying to be helpful.

'No, really what we should do is take a concept and make
it work through the name.'

'Cool, concept name!' said Steve and I together. Concepts
had been what had made the 70's the 70's. Bands had built
their whole careers on concepts. You just had to look at the
Beatles leading the way with Sergeant Pepper and the birth
that gave to in the 70's of Pink Floyd with The Dark Side
of the Moon or The Wall, The Who with Quadrophenia, or
Bowie with The Rise and Fall of Ziggy Stardust. A concept
name could be our short cut to the top. I went on…

'Why don't we have a name that has something to do with
a body part?' I offered with amusement.

'Like willy?'

Steve was with me.

'Or The Intestine Band? How about The Inner Ear, The
Anal Canal, The Pulse…' he added.

Keith was beginning to laugh uncontrollably. If Steve went
on much longer Keith would inevitably break wind. He always
did. Steve continued,

'The Circumcised, The Ovaries, The Poo, Indigestion
Bites, Blood Shot Eye Ball…'

Sure enough Keith trumped very loudly. The Bar Lady
shot us a look and I glanced at the ceiling in a vain effort to
appear oblivious to the resonating second slice of wind that
ripped through the air.

The laughter subsided and a name suddenly came to me.

'I've got it!'

'Herpes?' Steve was on a role.

'Wide Eyed.'

Silence.

'Wide Eyed Wonder' said Keith.

It was perfect. It was a name that offered everything. The Wide suggested excitement, the Eye was the concept, and Keith's Wonder was what we hoped people would feel having heard us play.

'I like it, I really, really like it,' declared a satisfied Keith.

Steve joined in.

'Think of the backdrop of a massive eye that's all lit up.'

I took it further,

'Think of the T shirts, the posters, the album covers, the underpants, the thongs!'

'Band bras!' shouted Steve to the top of his voice as he stood on his chair and blew a kiss to the blushing Bar Lady.

We were away. We had a name and our own songs. Now we were ready for our first gig and the road to stardom that would undoubtedly open up. Possibly, maybe, perhaps! Now there was a name anything was possible.

5

Working in a Bank was never going to be inspirational for a potential rock god. I had worked for the NatWest for the last two years since leaving Hallam University. I had been interviewed by a beautiful girl and I, being wonderfully unaware of what a real job would be like, imagined that all the female bank staff would look the same. It was a reasonable line of thought based on no research whatsoever other than that which my eyes had beheld in that interview in a high rise office in Nottingham where glass seemed to be everywhere causing me to squint at her as though looking through the beach sun to a mermaid. Clearly research was never going to be a strong point for me! I remember her telling me in very excited terms all about the bank and its history, its concept for the future and why young men like me were perfect to find the fast route to success. It was all well and good except I was only thinking about the fast way to success through to her clearly many charms. The key to my error was that I really should have been listening to her and not imagining long lazy days staring at beautiful women, as they bent up and down picking up cash bags and such like.

At one point during the interview the young lady, who was called Amanda, lovely Amanda, noticed me accidentally looking at her legs. I knew I had been spotted and I was not sure whether to simply ask her out or whether to try and bluff my way out. Just what is interview etiquette on this rather tricky issue? To ask her out could have blown the job and so bluffing was the only hope!

'Amanda,' I said, looking her firmly in the eye, 'discussing detailed fiscal policy of any country is difficult enough at any stage, but to concentrate on doing so, and the role I hope to play within this fine establishment of one of the leading banks in the country, is so difficult when concentration is hard to hold.'

Amanda looked a little flustered and my next line needed to be good.

'You see the floor here should be beautiful!'

She leaned forward to look at the floor, her blouse fell forward too and I caught a glimpse of a world I could happily live in. I went on,

'Let me explain! Before University I helped at a local restoration shop where floors like this were to die for and yet,' and here I began to put a little anger muted by sadness into my voice, 'these wonderful tiles have been allowed to go to a position of almost no return. I've just been staring at them, wondering if you would mind me mentioning them, because details matter and your outstanding overview of what the bank could do for me does not match the way they have let these once beautiful decorative tiles deteriorate!'

I managed to just pull my eyes away from my new world as Amanda looked up at me from under her soul dirtying fringe, which had fallen over her eyes creating a cheeky minx of a look.

We held each other's gaze.

'Amanda,' I declared, 'you must give me the name of your Premises Manager. I can help him get this put right!'

She looked at me and gave me a most beautiful smile.

'Of course I will Anthony,'

She paused, looking a little uncomfortable, and I waited for her to ask me to leave.

'After the interview Anthony, do you think, and I hope you won't think of me as cheeky, but would you, could you, spare a few hours over a drink and tell me a little more about floor tile restoration?'

'Amanda, but of course! It would be my absolute and lasting pleasure!'

For the first few months of my chosen career I felt my life had turned a bright and positive corner. After three years of being in debt and living in a house with friends who did not smell very nice and never offered to clean my room or do my washing, I was now back at home. My Mother had resumed where we had left off with a vigour towards looking after me that was awe-inspiring. It was like having the staff of a royal household all at my disposal with all of them being called Mum. I was now 'earning' actual money, and more money than I needed. Having spent three years having no cash at all this was a wonderful relief. Of course my Mother only accepted a paltry weekly sum as board money and she invariably gave me that back with phrases like 'buy yourself something nice' and so I had nothing else to do with it all than spend and spend it. My CD collection grew at speed and I purchased the most beautiful Denon CD player to play my new tunes on. My wardrobe took on the look of a sleek young man with Prada suits for day and designer Diesel gear for night. Having been a Top Shop / Asda Man, if I was lucky, for three years and counting, this was a welcome change.

After a year of working for the Bank, when they assumed they had tied me in with their work ethic chains, they even took it upon itself to provide me with a company car. It had been part of the contract but was still a welcome addition. The Band had just started and the car would be rather handy. A company car! To an ex and broke student this really was manna from heaven territory. The car became my stallion and I was its white shining knight riding through the day with an air of invincibility and prowess. Or not. In fact the car was a little Ford Escort with an 1100 engine and with absolutely no frills and certainly no spills. It was however a reliable and comfortable ride, which in truth were refinements I had not been used to with my old car that had neither of these rather significant benefits. It also had, and this was crucial, a mighty fine stereo which I used to maximum effect.

When I started working for the Bank as a management trainee they inundated my mind with lots of things they thought I should know at course after course. Very wise I am sure. This was to prepare me for the future management and career progression they had mapped out for me at a speed matched only by modern day rockets. For me the daily routine of lecture after lecture took me back to dull college days that I thought were behind me. Out of the classroom, though, I was simply delighted to be visiting quality hotels around the country without it costing me a penny. I met lots of people, many of whom who were admittedly banker types and best avoided, but quite a few who were wonderful bright young things who just wanted to have fun. This did have the negative aspect of giving me hope that there would be many people like this within the Bank. Of course there were not.

After three months the honeymoon was over and I began the journey that awaits so many unfortunate souls, namely completing on a day-to-day basis a serious job. Given my frivolous nature this was to prove a most difficult transition. I was sent in a POW sense of the word to the Regional Office close to my home, which was based in Nottingham. My first training position was assistant to the PA who reported directly into the Regional Director. The RD's name was a Mr Ross. He was a rather slight figure with a look of terror in his eyes that you were not sure he felt, or he wanted you to feel, or both. My time with him and his team did not go well. On top of my exceptionally poor time keeping which has plagued me all my life, the RD slowly began to realise that I did not have even a slight grasp on banking. My constant quizzical expressions as he talked through various items that for me may as well have been in a hitherto unknown alien language rather gave the game away.

Mr Ross decided that life at the sharp end was required and so after only six months at regional office I was transferred to experience real banking in my hometown branch. This was supposed to last for three months but a further six months later and I am still here. Still I have been promoted to an assistant manager in charge of the sales team and I have of course now been given my stallion. Gone are the days of taking my car to my local mechanic, and hearing his whimsical summary on the terminal condition of my car. In the end I gave him the car. I felt it was the least I could do after putting him through the humiliation of having to service such a heap. Saying he was grateful would be a push but he did kind of say thank you, that is to say he said goodbye.

My assent to the dizzy heights of assistant manager had not been an easy one. On my arrival at the branch the manager, a Mr Cook for whom the world tolled and he never heard the bell, took me in to his office and spent a whole hour describing the virtues of being a banker. He had decided, at the personal request of the RD, to 'bring out the best in me,' and felt that I would learn the most about banking by starting at the cutting edge. I had quipped 'Will I be making the money then?' and he had shot me a look that was meant to teach me some people are not on this earth to be spoken to. I made a mental note to never ask him out for a lunchtime drink and to never remark on his dashing good looks and his wonderful sense of humour.

I was taken to meet the chief cashier who had, to put it politely, a face of thunder. He was aged about 40 going on 708 and he was, remarkably, called Mr Wilde. Now to me people who have unfortunate surnames would be well advised to change them. Mr Wilde looked like he had spent his life coping badly with the humour that his name would have caused. Perhaps he had done so in honour of the original Wilde clan who had probably come to fame in the English Civil War in 1642. King Charles the 1st probably asked his generals who would be the right man to lead the defence of the monarchy and they, all being extremely frightened and knowing of this young fellow who had no sense but equally no fear, answered in unison 'Appoint Wilde, he's the man for the job.' Little did Charles know that his new general was called Wilde because by the very nature of the name he would do something really silly. Hence in 1645 at the crucial Battle of Naseby, when Cromwell's Roundhead's as the 'New Model Army' lay in waiting, did Wilde declare to his loyal troops.

'Those Roundhead fellows have got a soft underbelly and we simply need to get in there and put it up them. Follow my lead and shout in unison "You are foul youths nurtured on unnatural breasts from women who really should have known better!"'

The approach was crucially flawed and resulted in a punishing hammering in the field. As a result the Royalist resistance fell apart and three years later King Charles I faced a noble death. It is a recorded fact that one of Charles last utterances was,

'That fool Wilde. From now on let the name mean very silly.'

So there you have it. Here I was faced by a distant relative of that misguided general who would no doubt be rather silly, but he, being a Wilde, would carry on regardless, convinced that he was not at all wild but really rather clever. This was the nature of the Wilde's. This was why they never thought of changing their name but rather continued to pass it on from generation to generation. Very sweet indeed, although personally, I would have either changed my name to something like 'Van Stratasburger' or left the country to live with some hidden away and extremely wealthy Wilde.

On meeting me, Mr Wilde looked at me and instinctively I knew that he would make my life hell. I was to have a stint at being a real cashier and Mr Wilde took it upon himself to train me. I am convinced that training to join the Royal Marines, or indeed the Parliamentarians of the 17th century would have been easier. Over the next few weeks I learnt several things. Firstly, and perhaps one of the most disappointing realisations, was that there were no young well shaped cashiers to stare at all day. The odd young beauty did arrive on relief duties when we were short of staff and they helped me through the boredom with which I was plagued. They also ensured my cash error was bigger than ever with my short concentration span being shortened still further. In the main the cashiering staff of my branch had been on the till doing the same brain dead job every day for around five thousand years each. Some people deserve respect for such service where as this lot deserved deporting.

Secondly, I quickly realised that all my illusions of handling vast sums of cash were badly based. Money smells. It gets on your fingers and it takes ages to scrub out the aroma. Young men do not like having to spend hours scrubbing their hands. I would liken the smell of used money to that of used fish. Not pleasant, not sexy, not inspiring. Just, not!

Thirdly I learnt that people could be evil. Mr Wilde would spend two hours a day with me giving me personal cashier tuition in an effort to whip me in to shape. He would sit by me and watch me like a hawk, which had the best hawk eyes in the whole of the hawk kingdom. He would lean in to me and breathe on me on purpose. He had the breath of a mad dog and the deodorant failings of a skunk. It was not nice and he knew it.

Mr Wilde had crushing line after crushing line to deliver on my inability to deal with a till. It was not my fault that I was totally inept at doing something that he was obviously a master of. Git. Over my till was a sign that said 'Trainee cashier.' It was probably just a small sign, but in my mind it had taken on a life all of its own. I felt like it was a massive sign that was backed by a flashing neon red light that warned all clients to use the dumb ass and hopefully come away from the till with more change through a trainee cash error. As each customer stood in front of me, each one waiting for me to complete some inane task that could have been completed by a monkey on or off steroids, Wilde would offer helpful advice such as, 'Not too quick boy or you will make an error,' or 'Slow down boy or you will make an error,' or 'There you again boy, you've made another error!'

After several weeks of general bullying I began to mutter general insults under my breath each time he said anything to me. He was a little deaf and I took great pleasure in him saying 'Sorry, what did you say?' after I had just called him 'an utter wanker', or I had accused him of 'you smell like you've just soiled your pants!'

We were never going to be friends and I decided to add to my cashier inabilities by purposely handing out an extra £10 or £20 with bundles of cash. Occasionally a customer would watch me and say,

'Excuse me young man, I think you've given me too much.'

Of course I had bloody given them too much! By even turning up at my boring crappy job I was giving them way too much.

After balancing my till only twice in three months, and then topping this with the unfortunate error of filling the cash machine with the £20 pound notes in the £10 slot and vice versa, even Mr Wilde had decided enough was enough. Regional office held the chief cashier personally responsible for cash errors and Wilde was beginning to look very Wilde indeed in not being able to train a university boy to do a straightforward task.

One day, and without explanation or discussion, I was transferred on to the enquiries team. Surrounded by a nicer bunch of people, some of whom were even under the age of eighty, I actually began to find a little bit of a niche. Working on an enquiries team you actually do not need too much knowledge. Most of the time a customer approaches the enquiries desk with a question that has a blindingly obvious answer. Of course I was still getting things wrong but I was good at talking to people and selling them such things as loans and insurance covers when they had only come in to ask the way to Tesco. Given that the other staff were all similarly targeted, but had no interest in their jobs and would have preferred to sell oil to the Arab Prince's, I was a great success. Even Mr Cook, the Branch Manager, praised me in front of the other staff and passed his thoughts on to the dear Regional Director. In truth I think they were as relieved as I was to find something I could actually do. I had found my niche.

Soon I began to settle down and make the most of my days. The branch manager noted I was very good with my other team members and I was soon as amazed as anyone when they decided to make me team leader, and give me my assistant manager job that the graduate position had promised within two years of starting. I had made it!

The Bank also had one invaluable plus point for me and that was my salary. This was not lost on me and, as upset as the job did make me at times, I was determined to keep seeing it out and keep the pounds rolling in. The Bank had taken me on, to their credit, as a graduate. As a result I was meant to progress through various roles quickly until that beautiful glorious day when I made Chief Executive and was released with a huge pay-off having lost the bank loads of money through some hideous set of mistakes. Of course it had not taken long to realise that I wouldn't even make Chief Cashier but having started something banks were sticklers at trying to see it through. I had therefore remarkably continued to receive set pay rises and was now an assistant manager with the appropriate pay. Like the pyramids it just went to show that wonders really do never cease.

The promised new car had arrived with my new status and it had come just in time as my old car had been very upset at lumping around my guitar and amp. My dear parents and grandma were already very proud of my Banker status but the arrival of a car notched me up still further! Glorious really. And so, admitted, the job bored me to tears but for now impression was everything. I would continue with it as long as I could stomach it or, and much more to the point, until my rock star status saved me from ever having to darken the bank doors again.

6

'Get that fucking car out of that space or I'll move your nose off your fucking face.'

It was a warm March evening and Steve and I had arrived at the Mason Arms, a true drinking hole in Mansfield, for our first live gig. The gentleman who was now exchanging pleasantries with us, was in the car park of the afore mentioned pub. He was some sort of attendant in the extreme sense of 'some sort of.'

I thought about commenting on the young man's grasp of the English language, and that in his clear abilities he obviously had a skill for poetry that the world was definitely waiting for. Instead the only words I could manage were,

'Oh I'm sorry, is that a reserved space?'

The rather portly chap, who was aged around 25 to 60, had just come steaming out of the pub where we were to play our first gig and had met me getting out of my car. He had large muscles poking their heads out of his clothes and a shaved head with a delightful bit of dyed stubble remaining that showed the numbers 666 on one side. He was clothed in tight faded jeans and a body gripping T-shirt that allowed his tattooed forearms to show off the extensive wall of well thought through artwork. Steve was with me in the car, which only added to my ability to say too much on every occasion.

My question had the effect of stunning the man as though we were boxing and I had caught him with a surprise right hook. Clearly he was not used to conversation. After a wonderful 20-second interlude during which confusion passed over his face, fear passed over Steve's face, and terror passed over mine as I realised the potential downfall in talking back to an obviously inebriated local thug, I decided wisely to back down.

I got back in to my car, started the engine and waved to my new friend. I parked in the next space along, which was also free. Steve had whispered that perhaps we should park at the bottom of the car park or maybe even the road but, given that we had enough musical gear to carry to the pub to give even a fit man six hernias, I felt I would dice with death a little more and hoped the man / animal would not mind.

I got out the car, walked up to the man and offered him my hand,

'Anthony Scott, with the Band Wide Eyed Wonder for tonight's charity gig.'

He began to laugh and, pushing aside my hand took me by the body and gave me a bear hug. It hurt rather a lot and as he contortioned my body out of shape my head unnaturally found itself facing the car. I looked at Steve, only to find him crouching down on the front seat of the car with his hands over his head. Brave as ever he was clearly expecting the worst.

The man pushed me back and, still laughing, explained.

'I was saving these spaces for the Bands so you can move back to that one if you want.'

I smiled. How kind this man had become! Steve sat up in the car.

'Look, no worries man. The car is fine there.' He waved to Steve who waved back a little too effeminately for my liking. The man continued,

'Sorry man if I upset you.'

'Of course not!' I lied with ease. 'I knew we would be friends!'

'Cool, no harm done then. Nutter's the name. Nutter by name and nutter by nature.'

Nutter took my hand and shook it with a firmness that would probably affect my guitar playing and anything else I had in mind for my right hand. He went on,

'I tell you what man I cannot wait to hear your stuff. When I heard you had decided to play for us I thought fuck me...'

The prospect of that thought went through my head and I felt a little uneasy. I then wondered what he meant by 'hearing' we were playing. Perhaps he had a soft spot for new bands.

Steve had now gotten out of his hiding place and had joined me as though nothing had happened. Nutter looked him in the eye,

'Yea man, sorry about the aggression. I'm not into aggression per se unless the situation demands it. If that is the case then all bets are off man. I have no choice but to let my other side come out and get heavy. I have to use it dude, I have no choice.'

Sorrow filled his eyes and I felt sure he was about to cry.

'If I can keep myself from violence though, I do! I keep myself and my feelings wrapped up like a babe in a blanket.'

'That must be hard,' Steve was empathising, 'holding back your feelings.'

I hoped the sarcasm would be lost on Nutter.

'No, not really. I just save it for the next ill advised bastard who decides to cross me.'

Steve and I both laughed heartily, and yet nervously at the same time. Nutter didn't seem to notice. He took Steve's hand and Steve winced accordingly.

'Can I help you with your gear?'

A difficult question. On the one hand Nutter would probably not treat the equipment with the care required. On the other hand we didn't want to offend him particularly after just making friends. Besides anything else it was all far too heavy and the help would put off the undoubted bad back that would follow. I accepted,

'That would be very cool man.'

'Yea thanks man,' Steve joined in the conversation. You will notice the liberal use of the terms 'cool' and 'man', which we never used on any other occasion other than on Band things when we used them far too much. I don't know why we did it, we just did. It was all rather silly but bizarrely perfectly natural. Man.

Our first gig had been obtained by Keith over a beer at the Red, his drinking local, with a longhaired hippie/rock type who was organising a music charity night to raise funds for Greenpeace. The two of them were old school chums and had remained drinking friends. 'Shark', real name Paul Cooke, worked at Mansfield's Bandwagon studios where he was one of the sound engineers. This was actually part of a front for his efforts to put his Band, 'The Wild Things', on the alternative music map. They had enjoyed modest success and the local papers held them in some esteem. I could not see it myself but a contact was a contact and that was all there was to it.

Apparently 'Shark' had happily agreed to launch 'new talent' at the annual Greenpeace benefit gig. Keith told us in fact it was the first time a brand new band had been allowed to play the gig, and we felt consequently suitably pumped up to do ourselves justice. Shark was confident that there would be people there of importance. Keith didn't push him on who these people might be, but he felt Shark was referring to the hallowed A&R scouts who could sign you up over night and make you into rock stars in under a month or some such time period.

'Do you think by important people he was referring to the mayor?' I ventured at a practice when Keith relayed the good news causing him to give me one of those cutting looks that I was so used to at work. Steve took on the theme,

'Or doctors or dentists, or other such professional types, after all they are all vitally important.'

'What about our Dad? Now he is important. Mind you if he sees me in a smoke filled pub that serves alcohol I suspect he will not be able to see the art for what it is.'

Dad had not agreed with our newfound initiative. He was a man of strong Christian principles that did not include the right for a young man to express himself in rock music, and definitely not to take that music into a pub, or den of iniquity as he called it. Mind you with the Mason Arms he had a point!

'Look lads,' Keith had adopted that fatherly tone which meant a speech was coming, 'this gig is our big break. People will be there and they will be hearing Wide Eyed Wonder for the first time...'

'God help them!' Joe was as positive a force as ever. I had known him now for three months and still hadn't been able to have a conversation with him past obvious pleasantries such as 'How was your day?' 'Nice weather today!' and 'Have a nice day?' and other such day referring comments.

Still he could play the drums and that was what we needed for now. Whether or not he actually liked the stuff we had written was not necessarily important and almost certainly best avoided as a subject. Keith went on in true Churchillian mode.

'Let's all make sure we bring at least 10 people each...' Keith paused to catch a reaction. Steve and I were busy thinking through whether or not we dare invite anyone to see us. It wasn't because we did not believe in our music because we did; after all it was Steve and I who were writing it. It was more because the setting was not what we had in mind. The gig was to be at the Mason Arms pub so called because I suspect a mason, or perhaps a person called Mason, had once kept a lot of illegal weapons there. It was that sort of place.

Steve and I once went there by accident during our early drinking days. The pub was a strange mix full of rocker types with appropriate dark clothing and on the other hand old men who obviously did not have a home but all slept and lived there. We had walked into the pub and begun to walk towards the bar when a punch had been thrown in front of us and a rather hefty man had fallen across our path. Another large gentleman then arrived and promptly started to kick the face of the man on the ground. For a young and immature 17 year old this was all far too much and I was sick on the spot all over the man on the floor. It had the effect of stopping the fight immediately and would have had the effect of me losing my teeth had the landlord not arrived and suggested we leave quickly. I have never left a place with such speed since. If by perchance the British Athletic 100 metre sprint management had been passing by the pub at that time, a long shot I know, but please just go with the idea, then my whole career could have been so different. I can see myself now on Parkinson as he asked me just how did I get my big break. I would smile, rock back in my chair and fall over. Then, embarrassment dealt with and nose bleed stemmed, I would climb back into the chair, careful not to tip it back, and launch into my sick story with extra made up details for the fun of it and the nation would smile with me.

The Mason Arms therefore did not hold good memories and there was nothing to suggest it had improved as a venue. Keith seemed to sense our anxiety.

'Look I know it's not the ideal venue…'

'Ideal! I would rather play at your Dad's church than play at the Mason Arms!' Steve was only half joking.

'Commendable I'm sure, and I shall pass on your sentiments to Dad, but the church is not the place to launch our future.'

'How about the launderette?' I offered,

'Woolworth's?' Steve quipped,

'The cemetery?' offered Joe, cheerful as ever,

'Now listen. The Mason Arms will have a different crowd in on the night. It's a charity event for Greenpeace. How peaceful do you want? If we take our people we will ensure support and if there are A&R there, and I have it on good authority that there will be, they will see our support and see we have a following.'

'How can we have a following when we haven't played yet?' A truthful, if not rather negative comment, and once again coming from the effervescent Joe. I was caught between nodding in agreement with Joe and shaking my head in amazement at his lack of faith. I looked to Steve for a lead only to see he had shot his head down. He was probably laughing and hiding the grin from Keith's view.

'They won't know that!' Keith almost shouted this out as though he had just been incredibly clever. He went on, 'the beauty of the music business is that nobody knows. It's all a con. Look at Oasis. They blag their way into a gig, force themselves on to the billing, and who should be there but the boss of Creation Records. Mark my words. Our music is fantastic…'

Keith always had a belief in my ability that defied explanation. Perhaps it was the plays and sketches I had written when I was younger that had begun an admiration in my abilities as an artist. Perhaps the parts I had asked him to play such as 'Fleabag' the servant' had caused an irreparable medical condition. Perhaps the songs actually were good.

'…we could be part of the future of music. We just need a break and this could be it.'

We were inspired. It was our first gig and already it looked so easy. 10 friends, I could bring 20!

So, here we were, and whilst Nutter was not necessarily the opening we had expected to our future fame and fortune it was no matter. We made our way in to the pub, which had not changed from our last shortened visit. Nutter waltzed straight through the busy bar like a well-trained lead Ballerina from the Royal Russian National Ballet Theatre Company. He carried my amp like a prized possession that no one would dare to take from his grasp. It was as though the amp had become his 'Odette' in a performance of 'Sleeping Beauty.' Nutter graced the stage as he danced in a manner that any Prince Siegfried would have been proud of. I know I was. He seemed to be heading towards a door in the far corner of the bar.

'Where the hell is he going?' Steve's bemused voice was asking the question I was not going to relay to Nutter. If he wanted to take us through to some back room then that was fine by me. I had my baggy combats on and they were not easy to get off due to around the twenty-five buttons used to fasten them up. Steve on the other hand had some tight leathers on that would surely be more attractive to Nutter if he wanted a bit of pre gig fun.

Through the door and up a rather thin staircase we mercifully arrived at the venue for the evening. A massive Greenpeace banner greeted us at the top of the stairs where there was a foyer manned by interesting scruffy types wearing seal printed type T shirts, at least I assumed they were seals. I guess they could have been whales or perhaps even goldfish. I would probably discount my latter suggestion given that I do not think 'Save the Goldfish' is a current Greenpeace venture although judging by the state of my neighbour's pond it really should be.

We walked in to the hall, which was rather dark and small. 'Close knit' would be the positive definition Keith would put on it later.

Keith was already there with Joe and they were busy setting up.

'Hello boys!' I called, and Keith turned with his usual grinning face, which told me that he saw the evening as holding tremendous potential for extreme comedy and success.

'What do you think?' he spluttered as he pointed around the room as though he was extolling the virtues of the Sistine Chapel. 'Is this not one of the great music venues of the country? Are we not the luckiest Band alive? Would you not agree that this is a perfect place for violence to break out for no apparent reason? ' Still he laughed and I knew that he knew the evening could hold disaster. When he was like this I never knew whether to just laugh along with him or fear for my health or both. Inevitably Steve and I fell into the laughter that Keith's giggles always produced.

Nutter had disappeared and left us with the clarion call of 'get fucking ready man to kick some fucking musical ass!' How pleasant.

'When are we on?' I ventured.

'Where are the lions?' Steve added, with suitable sarcasm in his voice.

'We are on second.' Keith declared.

'Who's on first? The Beatles?' I was genuinely interested. Which other collection of idiots had decided to play a gig that could lead to a spell in hospital and all their gear being ruined

'Sycamore.'

Steve and I burst out laughing. Keith put his finger to his lips and nodded towards the tree types we had walked past at the door.

'They are all part of the group…'

We all nodded seriously.

'…and their name is a play on a tree name, mixed with how they feel about tree cutting types attacking their trees.'

Keith was smirking throughout his wonderful explanation. I stopped nodding my head quite so vigorously in order that I didn't pass out.

'Perhaps they have a sister band called J'Oak?' I ventured.

The gig was to have the three bands each setting up in front of the other. As Sycamore finished, they would move their gear to the side and we would unleash the noise of the future. The Wild Things, a Thin Lizzy covers band, were on last and would have to cope with the now heavily drunken and chaotic crowd as they bravely tried to bring the evening to a fitting crescendo of an ending. Due to these strict arrangements, and the time constraints we had, it quickly transpired that we were not to be able to have a sound check. Frank, the sound engineer who from the look of him must have come straight back from the grave especially to be with us for the evening, assured us that this would not be a problem as he had handled this sort of thing on many occasions. The drummer and guitarists would be in charge of their own sound and volume because the small venue did not merit them being miked up. He would handle the vocals through the microphones set up for that purpose. I explained our line up to Frank.

'Will you be wanting a little reverb on the main vocal?' he asked me. In fact Frank was paying me a marvellous compliment in asking me a technical musical question about an issue I knew so little about. I thought about asking him what reverb did exactly, but I realised this would show up my musical ignorance. I decided to be decisive.

'Yes, absolutely! Who wouldn't want a little reburb!'

'Reverb,' prompted Steve

'Yes, reverb, absolutely!'

'A lot of reverb or a little?' Frank asked. Was Frank teasing me in his thick local Mansfield accent or giving me the credibility my combat pants deserved? I decided to bring him into the decision-making.

'Well Frank, it's a small venue.'

'True, after all I understand you are used to playing much larger venues.'

I caught Keith's eye as his head shot down and he let out a stifled laugh. I began to understand how we had got our first gig by lying about our experience. Nutter's over the top keenness was making sense! I had to go along with it.

'Well of course larger venues offer their own problems.'

'Such as when you played the Reading festival?' Frank ventured. My colour deepened as though I had just had the day on a Canary Island beach drinking for England and without sun protection.

'That's right man, Reading caused us all sorts of challenges.' I nodded my head as I agreed with Frank, realising the depth of the lie that Keith had created to get us in to the gig. It was time to finish my conversation and kill Keith.

'Look Frank, you are obviously a very experienced sound engineer and I think in a situation like this you need to just do what you think is right.'

'To fit in with your sound like?'

'Yea, cool man, fit in with the vibe.'

'Vibe, aye I'll fit in with the vibe.'

I doubted he would and at the same time wondered why I had added 'vibe' to my list of in words used only for band occasions. I took Keith towards the back of the room.

'What are you doing?'

He was laughing.

'I mean what if someone finds out?'

'Finds out what? That we didn't play Reading? Of course we did.'

'We did?'

'Bob…'

He called me Bob as a term of affection due to the fact that my second name is Robert. It amused him and, to be fair, the rest of the family.

'Bob, if we believe it, then everyone else will too. We just need to go with the flow.'

'You mean like heaven?'

'Exactly!'

I was confused. On the one hand I knew that blagging was a way of life, everyone did it. All the managers at work blagged all the time, particularly those higher up the career tree. It seemed to me that anyone who had anything had, at some time, made up something to get it and my own recent sales career was built on it! It was the real world we lived in and clearly we were simply doing what everyone else was doing. On the other hand we had never even played a gig and we didn't even know how we would fare under the spotlight of stardom. If Keith was building us up too much then we could have an almighty fall. At that point Keith's friend Shark walked up to us,

'Hey dudes, cool to see you.'

'Hello Shark…' Keith greeted the Greenpeace champion with a friendly bear hug 'This is our Bob.'

'Our Bob' had not been the way I had thought I would be introduced to the event's organiser. I made a mental note to discuss this with Keith as clearly I wanted it sorted before we played Wembley stadium. Shark gave me a sharp hug that caused me to almost bring back my dinner which had been a rather hearty affair with Mother wanting to make sure I would not be caught short for the big event.

'Pleased to meet you Shark,' I managed to say after he had let go of me.

'Pleased to meet me! Man, I'm the lucky one. Keith has told me all about the way you held that Reading crowd captive.'

I shrugged my shoulders with due nonchalance and smiled encouragingly. Keith laughed accordingly. Shark continued,

'Listen man, I know this is a much smaller crowd for you but just go with the flow man.'

'Yea, sure man, I'm on the vibe.'

As I said this I winked and cocked my head. He did the same to me.

'Listen guys have a good one. Must dash, people to see.'

We both nodded. Shark disappeared. I turned back to Keith.

'I don't mind you blagging but I wish you'd told us.'

'And you wouldn't have minded?'

'Of course I would have minded, but I would have liked the choice of whether to mind or not. Anyway you told us that you had told Shark we were a new Band.'

'Well I did, sort of.'

'Sort of?'

'Yea, well we are new in the sense that we are not old.'

'I see.'

Keith smiled.

'If only you did.'

I looked at him. I suspected that Keith had spun the Wide Eyed Wonder story a whole lot more. I thought back to Nutter's earlier greeting and the expectation level for our performance and began to wonder how many more people were expecting the next Oasis. I decided this was not the time to worry and certainly not the time to tell Steve who would probably literally wet his pants. I would tell him everything after what I hoped would be a trouble free first gig.

With 20 minutes to go to the start of the gig, the venue was filling up nicely. A lot of our friends had arrived and the excitement levels were building. Steve was talking to Nutter who had taken up a position on the door. I watched Nutter taking admission monies and casually dropping some of it in to his own tight jeans pockets. Would Greenpeace be getting this money I wondered? Would you take your girlfriend to Warsop Vale for a night out? Clearly not! I doubted very much that someone would be taking that up with him.

Joe's girlfriend had arrived and the two of them sat next to his drum kit like a mother defensively looking over her baby. They were not ones for mixing.

Keith and I were talking to our 'fans'. This was our first experience of people coming to listen to our music and I was really enjoying it. I guess the term fans is a little too strong given that they were actually friends who had never heard our music and had really only come to support us probably out of sympathy and to drink as much as possible. I doubted very much that many of them would have visited the Mason Arms for a social drink before, and I knew that most would be itching to leave the venue as soon as they could. In fact most of them would also be itching because they would undoubtedly have picked up more than just the musical vibe from the venue. It was fantastic though to be faced with questions about our music, our songs, our next gigs and our plans. It all began to make the dream of being in a proper band turn into a reality and it was a reality that I now wanted so badly.

Sycamore made their way to the stage and we nodded our heads to them in a knowing 'we are in a band too' way. They were dressed in dark clothes and all four of them had long greasy hair that they peered through into the audience. Two of them even had burning cigarettes poking out through their hair. I suspected they didn't really care about the fire hazard they were creating.

The crowd applauded politely as the band took up their instruments and the lead singer made his way to the microphone. He switched it on and the feedback caused most people to cover their ears as the squeal filled the room. Indeed given its volume I suspect the whole of Mansfield was forced to take evasive action! As the feedback subsided with the sound 'engineer' getting the balances right, the singer shouted something in to the mic. I think he said 'Mine's a fucking large one,' but I could not be sure. He may equally have said 'Wife's a cooking an onion.' I guess the actual words were not important, more the aggression and tone of the voice. Here my English Teacher would have been telling us to look for change in tone, flight of intonation, the pitch accent and other such prosodic properties of the syllables of the words... The guitarist then hit his strings and for the next 30 minutes my ears were terrorised with a sound that I could only liken to a cacophony of strangled animals, all joining together in a chorus of terror and all stood at the same time next to my ears. My English Teacher would have likened the experience to 'bloody shite.'

As Sycamore 'played' I looked at Keith and Steve, and the many friends who had come to support us. We were all unsure whether to smile or run from the room. More worryingly were the numerous grunge types who had emerged from the walls and made their way to the front of the room. They swayed and moved and made little whooping noises as though they were in the throes of an ecstasy that you would gladly pay good money for. As the throbbing built its way into the front of my head I began to wonder how the grunge types would appreciate our own blend of pop/ rock. I doubted that they would still be making their little whooping noises but as long as they were polite then that would be fine. I then began to think of the word 'polite' and put that at the side of the pub that we were now in. A new terror began to build in my mind and I quickly put these new thoughts to the back of my head. It's fair to say at this point that the back of my mind was now so full that it was spilling out into the garden of my mind. I needed another beer…

Sycamore finished their set with a lovely little number entitled 'Death will come.' It was a fair point and one made all the more certain and somewhat appetising by having to listen to their music. The Goths gathered in a group in front of the lead guitarist and lapped up each note. They were in seventh heaven. As the band left the stage the crowd applauded loudly, some because they had loved the set and some because they were thrilled it had finished.

I made my way to the front and at this point the nerves began to reach a new level. I picked up my guitar and the strap gave way. In truth no one probably noticed. The crowd were refilling their glasses in readiness to listen to us. To me though it felt like everyone was secretly casting a glance in my direction, watching to see how I would perform. I looked at Keith who smiled in that wonderful way that showed he was having a great adventure. His smile gave me heart and I forgave him for setting me up.

'Come on Anth, let's give them something to listen to.'

His voice was not laced with anything other than this was a time to stand up and be counted. I nodded. We had some great songs, some fantastic songs. Steve had worked out some incredible guitar pieces and the tunes were ready to be played. I looked at Steve. He was just checking his guitar tuning. He had already checked my guitar as he always did. I turned to Joe. He was simply sat waiting.

'Are you OK Joe, up for the gig?'

'Yea.'

That was it. Our conversation for the evening. I suspected the Oasis boys had a little more banter flowing around the band. Then I thought of Liam and Noel and realised they probably didn't at all. Steve came up to me.

'OK matey I'm ready. This is the moment we've been waiting for.'

He was right. It was for moments like this that best mates live for.

'Yea Steve, let's do it.'

I looked to the audience. Many friends had come and they had pushed their way to the front. I caught the eye of Chloe, Steve's girlfriend, and she put her thumbs up and gave me a massive smile. I noticed a girl next to her who I had not seen before. Chloe was an art student at Nottingham studying graphic design. The girl next to her was whispering something into her ear and they were both looking in my direction. Whoever she was, she was a dream waiting to happen. I looked forward to introducing myself after the gig. I was already beginning to see that the benefits of being a rock star could not be understated.

I looked at Keith, then to Steve, and then to Joe. They were all ready. I looked to the back of the hall and Frank gave me the thumbs up. I nodded back. The lights in the room went down and the spotlights were turned on. Now it was our turn. I walked to the microphone and turned it on. Of course it screeched and I waited for Frank to adjust the volume. The noise subsided and the crowd waited. My mouth was dry and for a moment all words left my head. Steve, sensing my nerves, turned on his guitar and the buzzing hiss caused the hairs on the back of my neck to stand to attention. He nodded to Keith and Joe and then launched in to the introduction for our first song, 'Take you there.' As his notes rang out into the hall and we all instinctively joined in, my heart was lifted and I suddenly felt so tall. This was our Band, our song, and our crowd. It was perfect. I launched in to the first lines,

'Woke up this morning, ran my fingers through my hair
Looked at the time and said just isn't fair…'

This was a rock song with a tune in which my words sort to lambaste society for caging me into a suit within which I did not belong. It was written by me, about me, and for me. It was my song and it meant so much to me because I could own it in a way I could never embrace anything at work,

'… Every day just doesn't seem to change
Got to get out because here I can't remain…'

As I sang I squinted out at the crowd. The lights burned into my eyes but I could make out some people jumping up and down. They included some of Sycamore's crowd. This was perfect. Into the chorus,

'Well let me take you there, you know just where,
Well let me take you there, you know just where…'

Steve and I were now singing in unison, his guitar notes filling the whole room and me.

'And it goes on and on and on it goes, the future's here and it get so strong
And it goes on and on and on it goes, the futures here and it gets so
Oh oh oh, it gets so strong
Oh oh oh it gets so strong…'

I glanced at Steve. He was jumping around like a deranged idiot, in charge of his guitar, lost in the song. I looked at Keith. He always played with his eyes closed, his face full of an expression that suggested he was just about to give birth. I thought about turning around to look at Joe but realised that the cramped conditions and my nerves would probably result in me falling over!

'Take you there' was played through, the guitar solo in the middle, note perfect. We drew the song to its ending, all of us releasing a final crescendo that made the room shake. The crowd erupted into noise so loud that all I could do in response was laugh. This was so much more than anything I had ever experienced before.

'Thank you, thank you' I shouted. The crowd called for more.

We were ready with much more and Steve set the notes rolling for the introduction for 'Shooting Star', another rock/pop anthem with a big chorus, a fantastic guitar riff. We were on a role.

To turn to two of your closest friends and see the fulfilment of a lifetime dream being met is one of the most beautiful things anyone could ever wish to see. Keith's head was now moving up and down in time with the music. It was glorious! Steve and I had taken to playing to the audience. Steve had played the lead solo to the third song, 'Looking for a Reason', on top of a table. In this song I didn't play and during the guitar solo I jumped down into the crowd to jump up and down with them. The lead solo had been repeated three times. No one seemed to mind.

As I sang our fourth song 'Showtime', another fast song that, in truth, was a direct rip off of U2's 'Angel of Harlem,' I let my mind wander to the local paper headlines that would greet our performance. I knew a lot of the local press were here because the Greenpeace gig was quite a big local event. I began to think about my answers to questions thrown at me by the CHAD, the Recorder, The Evening Post and the Observer (not THE Observer but rather the Ashfield local!).

It was then that I noticed the fight that had broken out towards the front of the gig and to my right, in front of Steve. We backed off and continued to play as four or five people, none of whom I recognised, began to kick each other as hard as possible. Then down the middle of the crowd a further disturbance erupted. I can only describe this as the effect of a tractor driving through the people and tossing them aside. It was of course 'Nutter', arriving to sort things out.

We continued to play, partially because we didn't know what else to do, and partially because if we had finished we could have drawn unwarranted attention to ourselves. This was unthinkable. As we repeated the closing chorus to 'Showtime' for the fourth time, and my fingers began to ache from paying the same chord progression over and over again, the fight had erupted into a blood bath. The majority of the audience had wisely filed out of the back of the room and down I suspected into the safety of the bar. I realised at this point that even Frank, our trusty sound engineer, had left his position for safer climes. I knew he had gone because as people had left the venue you were pretty much left with your sound, which had fewer people to absorb it. As a result everything was now far too loud and feedback was banging off every surface. I began to think about our escape.

At this point a young man was thrown past me at speed and Joe's drumming almost simultaneously stopped. As I turned I tripped over the young man's legs and landed on top of him. His head had gone straight through the bass drum. Most of the cymbals, very expensive cymbals at that, had been scattered and lay in various states of disarray all over the floor.

I turned to see that Nutter had picked one up and was using it to finish off the few people who were still standing. I turned back to Joe who was shouting something or other about what was he going to tell his Mum. I let that thought pass through my head without dwelling on it. Clearly more trouble was brewing.

Steve was by this stage hidden behind his amp, clutching his beloved guitar close into his chest. I turned to Keith and saw he was remarkably just casually leaning against the far wall, holding his guitar in a pose that reminded me of an old Stuart Sutcliffe photograph, and still smiling.

As the police arrived, and 20 or so young men were escorted out to the vans awaiting them, the four of us gathered up our equipment.

'My mum's going to kill me,' said Joe, over and over again. It was like a sad mantra that was not leading the young man to a relaxed state of his mind.

Steve, Keith and I looked at each other. There was a pause, we all smiled, and then we laughed and laughed. We had tasted something so good and we were hooked. Playing our music was the coolest thing in the world and we had truly arrived.

7

'Joe's resigned'

It was Steve on the telephone with news that I had expected. His mother had picked him up from the Mason Arms gig as soon as we had finished. She had given Joe a right ear full whilst the three of us kept a safe distance. Joe had sheepishly made his way back towards us and said he would not be staying for a drink after all. We all helped Joe carry out his gear, half of which was now ruined. His mother gave us all very dirty looks and the omens for Wide Eyed Wonder maintaining their original line up were not good.

'Doesn't he realise we had such a good night?' I reasoned with my usual simplistic overview.

'I know!' replied Steve, 'not to mention the fact that our place at the rock table of heaven is currently being set by Elvis and his sidekick Lennon due to the fact that there are already A&R people fighting to hear us,'

'They are?!' I asked with excitement.

'What do you think?' Steve replied with a little curled up sarcasm in his voice.

'Oh' I replied, the little breeze of happiness wind well and truly removed from my Wide Eyed Wonder sails. I thought of Joe, his continual whining and obvious inability to stand up to his mother after the minor issue of having his expensive drum kit knocked from pillar to post by some lager louts. Why were some people not able to see the bright side?

'Fair enough.' I said, my voice upbeat now. 'I don't really blame him. What can you do when tragedy happens? You just have to blame the parents!'

I had spent the night enjoying, no basking, in the glow of the praise we had enjoyed from the people who had come to the gig. Admittedly most of them were keen that we chose future venues a little bit more carefully, but in terms of our material, they were over the moon.

I was particularly taken by the comments, or should I say looks, of Chloe's friend from college who I had spotted just before we played,

'You played like Rock Stars, like you meant it. You know? You looked like you really wanted to be there, like you were made to be there!'

She had spoken in tones like I would imagine an angel would use. She certainly looked like an angel although there were parts of her that I was particularly interested in that would probably not be appropriate if I was addressing an actual angel. Her name was Annabella Jones. Now there's a name to knock you for six eh! She had long voluptuous blonde hair that flowed down her slender body and framed her in such a way that she looked like a classic beautiful model in my latest GQ magazine. Her eyes were like diamonds from Tiffany and her lips were like ripe cherry tomatoes from the Harrods food department, a particular food favourite of mine. As she spoke

I looked far too intently at her lips and imagined sucking on them. Suck, suck, and suck. Mmmmm… Her high cheekbones pushed out in such a way as to suggest I should climb up on them and swing from side to side like a happy little child on a playground in summer. I was hooked, snared, caught, captive and entrapped all in one go. She would undoubtedly get me in trouble because I wanted to see her again in a more intimate way far too badly.

'You liked us then?' I asked, as calmly as possible.

'Yea, I thought you were pretty cool.'

'Pretty cool' 'pretty cool' 'PRETTY MIGHTY DAMN FINE COOL!!!!!!!!!' The words echoed through my head as though someone had told me I had won a million pounds.

'What did you think about the…' I wanted to ask about my singing but didn't know how.

'About your singing?'

She asked what I was thinking! How did she do that?

'Well yea, if you like. What did you think about my singing? Did it hurt your ears?'

'No more than you'd think'

I looked at her, not knowing whether to laugh or pretend to cry. Thankfully she laughed

'No, stupid, I thought your singing was great. You reminded me of Crispin Hunt actually.'

'Really!' I asked having no idea who this fine Crispin was.

'Yea you did. Really.'

'Well, rare praise indeed,' I said, not missing a beat and making a mental note to research this young man later. He would probably turn out to be a failed opera singer, but no matter, she seemed keen.

She paused, a beautiful pause into which I threw my gaze at her lips waiting for more words to wash over my puppy like eyes.

'You were all great,' she said.

We were all sat together downstairs in the bar. There was Keith, Steve and I, Chloe and Annabella, and loads of friends. There were also quite a lot of sixth form students from Keith's school. There must have been 50 of us crowded around tables, delighted in the buzz of the evening. The gig had been abandoned by orders of the police and the Wild Hearts had been unable to play. The glories and the spoils then were left for us. Loads of people, half of whom I had never met before in my life, were coming up to me and telling me we were brilliant. It was the sort of praise I had never experienced before. It was fantastic. Could I get used to this? Is the Pope a Catholic? People were telling us they had never heard a local band sound so good. I could hear Steve being told his guitar playing was awesome. Some people told me they had wished they had seen us at the Reading festival. I wish I had. One even told me he had seen us at the Reading festival and we were even better than then. How nice. It was like inverted blagging coming back to us.

On top of all this new incredible attention I found myself now sat in front of a modern day Greek goddess. The evening really could not have got any better. She whispered something into Chloe's ear, oh fortunate of ears, most blessed of ears, ears that should never be washed and definitely never be syringed. Then the two of them stood up. I looked up at them.

'Off to the ladies? If so can I come as well?' What a comedian I imagined I was. I even laughed as I said it. Chloe replied,

'No, Annabella's boyfriend is picking her up in the car park. Don't worry I'll be back in a moment.'

My eyes must have betrayed my absolute disappointment. How could this girl already have a boyfriend? How could the world deal me such a cruel and terrible blow? Annabella looked at me.

'It was nice meeting you, very nice,' she said.

I tried to gather myself together,

'Oh ta very much…'

I was using my Beatles Paul McCartney voice for no particular reason other than to hide my embarrassment.

'Will you come and watch us play next time?' I said, far too desperately

She smiled. In my head I screamed 'Please say YES, please say YES!!!'

'Of course. Try and keep me away!'

With that she turned and went and I, I sat in a dream like trance, my bubble well and truly burst with the biggest of pricks. Keith then burped as loud as he could, Steve belched back, and I re-joined the party.

'Wild sod,' offered Steve

'What?' I asked

'You know what. You made a fool of yourself again'

'Did I?'

'Always'

'Bugger'

'Exactly.'

'What next then?' I asked the table, moving attention away from my crashing fall.

'Yea, when are you playing again?' It was one of Keith's sixth formers, all of who were incredibly enthusiastic for the band. The thought crossed my mind that perhaps Keith had paid them some money but at that point I wouldn't have really minded if he had.

'Well I am delighted to say that we have secured a string of excellent gigs'

Keith was taking centre stage. It was true that he and Steve had lined up some very good gigs in venues that I was quite surprised about. He had used a tape a friend had made for us at a practice in which we had mercifully not played at volumes akin to those of jet fighter engines. It actually wasn't too bad, after all it had managed to get us in to play several local pubs which we would use to build our local following. These included the Plough, Stockwells, Early Doors, Harveys, and the Woodpecker. Go Wide Eyed Wonder!

We were then to travel further afield including gigs in Leicester, Derby, Stoke, and of course Nottingham. I realised that the combined blagging talents of Steve and Keith were a match for anyone, and after the night's performance, I felt confident we could play and impress.

As Keith told his audience about the forthcoming gigs he handed out printed A4 sheets with our gig list. On the bottom of all the lists was an application to join our fan club, which apparently already had 200 people on the mailing list. Given that it wasn't even set up this was a fantastic achievement! You had to play to people's strengths. I was good at writing and OK it appeared at performing. Keith was fantastic at organisation. In armed combat he would have been an amazing sergeant major, organising the troops and ensuring their success.

As Chloe arrived back at the table, Keith and Steve were making their way around the pub, with a few helpful students helping them, handing out gig lists. I turned to Chloe who had a marvellous grin on her face.

'And you would be smiling at?' I asked, without needing to ask the question

'You, obviously!'

'And that would be because?'

'Of your fantastic dribbling effort.'

'Was it that obvious?'

'I am afraid it was.'

I had known Chloe now for six years. She had been drawn to Steve's coolness just as I was and having met him they had stayed together. I think I loved her almost as much as Steve did. Our ability to actually get a girlfriend had developed during our sixth form days. It was just after our greenhouse debacle when we had needed to hatch new and clever plans to meet eligible girls. I was then in my contact lenses and my confidence had grown to new levels. Who would have thought that two thin pieces of plastic hidden on my eyes would change my life? I was actually beginning to look more normal and even a little inviting as shown by the interest I was receiving from the odd female with eyesight issues of her own. Sadly Alison, the girl from the burnt down greenhouse, had long since decided I was too dangerous for her, which was sort of a backhanded compliment for me really. She still glanced lovingly at me when I saw her around, a glance I could now see with me wearing my contacts. It was a look that encapsulated what could have been had my furtive hands been allowed to explore her hidden secrets just that little bit longer in that greenhouse of hot desires.

Wicko had piled on the pounds in the sixth form but was still a hit with the ladies. He just looked so much older and more mature than the rest of us. His hairy chest was now legendary and in true mature fashion was already starting to lose some of his hair, which he compensated by growing a magnificent moustache. He was one of the first to get an income in play, adding still further to his allure, with his mother getting him an evening job at the Civic Theatre, Mansfield's play house. Wicko was in charge of the lighting booth, which controlled the house lights and the two spotlights for the stage. When his fellow spotlight operator was off ill or on holiday I got the chance to join Wicko and operate my very own spotlight. Many an 'actor' was suitably unimpressed with my spotlight aim as the stage manager's voice would boom in to our lighting box 'SPOTLIGHT 2 ON THE FAIRY' and I would light up the left hand curtain instead.

Steve had lost some of his awkwardness and was developing an attractiveness in an interesting and different sort of way. He had taken to dyeing his hair with a whole collection of colours including bright red and jet black. This had the effect of scaring a lot of people off as at that point in small town Mansfield Woodhouse the glam punk style of bands like Dogs D'Amour or Hanoi Rocks was as alien to us as, well, an alien itself. I think this move towards being more 'out there' from Steve purely because he wanted to for himself brought me closer to him. I thought he was so cool for being so different in that he listened to some bizarre music and he did things how he wanted to. The two of us though were connected through our times together, our easy comedy and our love of The Beatles and Dylan.

Wicko got us the break that also happened to lead to Steve meeting Chloe. Big Country, a wonderful Scottish Band with chipper music, were touring, and they had included for some reason known only to their tour manager the Mansfield leisure centre in their itinerary. Decent sized bands coming to Mansfield happened very irregularly so the local excitement as the date approached built to an extent that Big Country did not usually receive. They must have thought when they arrived that they had suddenly become massive over night, only to get to their next gig and be deflated accordingly.

We were enrolled to be bouncers, not because of our muscular disposition because we didn't have any, but because Wicko's mum was one of the people in charge and we would all get £10 and free entrance. Trouble was not expected. We knew the leisure centre well. Wicko and I played 5 a side football there. Steve and I played badminton there. Steve did not play football at all. I think he was worried about getting his tender bone shaped legs hurt. He was probably right. Out of clothes he did look like he could easily snap.

We arrived one hour before the gig as requested and reported in to the chief bouncer who was a rather large local gentleman with individual muscles larger than my head. He looked at us and literally laughed.

'To be honest lads, no offence meant, but I don't think we will be putting you three in front of the stage.'

This was a relief. The thought of asking people to please not try and force their way past me on to the stage was one I had not been relishing.

'You can all go on the door and collect tickets as people arrive.'

We all said thank you in far too polite a fashion and far too many times to add to our lack of bouncer credibility and then, seeing the big fella was tiring of our gratitude, sped away to the door. Chloe was one of the first people we let in and Steve, on taking her ticket, offered to personally escort her and her friend to a 'safe' place in the hall from which to view the event. Steve was a man immediately entranced by young love and we didn't see him again all evening.

And so, six years on, Chloe and Steve were still an item. Having met so young they had experienced their ups and downs with little breaks along the way, but they were still together.

'Who is she?' I asked Chloe, whilst doing a panting dog impression

'She is one of my best friends from college. She's on the fine art course.'

'Do you think she would let me pose naked for her?'

'Do you want to put her off for good?'

I gave Chloe my Paddington hard stare perfected from years of receiving the same look from my brother. I went on,

'Is the boyfriend six foot four with the body of an Olympian, and a Porsche, and a brilliant job, and fantastic personality, and is he loved by women the world over?'

'I am afraid he is most of those.'

'And the bits he isn't? I asked hopefully

'I believe the personality is a bit on the wanting side.'

'Oh...'

I paused, rather dumbstruck. Clearly this was a lost cause. Chloe interjected,

'But she does like you.'

Trumpet noises filled my head. SHE, yes SHE, did like me!!

'Oh really!' I exclaimed in my Sean Connery deep Scottish drawl.

Hope. Where there is hope there is always a way, possibly, perhaps, maybe, maybe not.

Chloe went on,

'Her boyfriend is called Callum McCore.'

'Oooo, Callum McCore. Look at me with my trendy little name!'

I was now using my best ladies voice, which was of course lifted from Monty Python. Michael Palin would have been so proud.

'And what does Callum McCore do, the big halfwit?'

'He runs his own gym in Nottingham, down Hockley. You might have seen it, it's called...'

'Wimps corner?' I ventured.

'No, The Gym'

'Original.'

I was grumpy now. Runs his own gym! Bastard.

'And yes, he is tall, he is very attractive, and yes he does drive a Porsche.'

Double and treble bastard! I already hated this man.

'Is he boz eyed'? I ventured

Chloe shook her head, laughing.

'Walks with an inexcusable limp?'

Chloe again shook her head.

'Has a third nipple, a third eye, an extremely so hard to find Willy, BO, 12 toes, hairy cheeks, an inexcusable weeing his pants problem. What about yellow teeth, black teeth, greasy hair, extremely long nose hair, stinky feet, big and gigantic spots all over his messy excuse for a face?'

Steve came over to join in the fun. He had assumed we were having fun with Chloe laughing so much and did not realise the desperate heartache I had been trying my best not to face up to.

'What's all this frivolity, has Anthony shown you his willy?'

'At least I've got one, unlike you!' I retorted in true school ground fashion. 'Did you know Chloe that Steve had to have his willy surgically fastened at Wilkinson's! If you inspect it closely, and I suspect you never have, you will notice it is actually hose tubing from the garden section'

'It is not,' laughed Steve, 'it's from the household goods section. Garden tubing was too expensive.'

After we had finished giggling Chloe told Steve the reason for her laughter and my woes,

'He wants to make out with Annabella.'

Steve laughed out loud and for a little too long than was polite.

'Not a chance mate. Her boyfriends, what's his name Chloe? Callum?'

Chloe nodded.

'He's got a Porsche, he's massive, and he's quite an attractive fella.'

I was now pouting in little child mode. Steve was laughing far too loudly but then stopped abruptly. I turned to where he was looking and saw some extremely large and aggressive types giving us the eye that told us to turn the laughter down or face immediate death. I turned again to Chloe.

'So, you don't fancy my chances?'

'Well I've not known Annabella for too long. We started doing some modules together this year. I really like her and it's not something she has said directly, but, I think, reading between the lines, she is not totally happy with Callum.'

'Why?'

'I don't know. As I say it's not really that she's said as much, but I just sense there is something not quite right'

Result! OK, potential result, that is the start of a result. At least there was no foregone conclusion here. I, yes I, had a chance!

'You've not told her where I work have you?'

Steve butted in.

'You mean that you are a wanker banker!'

I nodded to Steve, thanking him for his contribution. Chloe went on,

'She did ask me where you worked and I did tell her, sorry!'

'Don't say sorry! It's not an illness you know. I get good money!'

'Not as much as a guy with a Porsche.' Steve was again being helpful. I returned the favour and helpfully kicked his shin. Chloe again offered hope,

'She asked me quite a lot about you actually as we were waiting for Callum. I think she sees something in you she really likes.'

'Comic face always good for a laugh?' offered Steve.

'What did you tell her?' I asked in an extremely needy voice.

'That I have known you for ages and that you are funny, sweet, and talented.'

'You lied then.' said Steve. I offered him my 'say anything else and I will hit you' look. It wasn't a particularly menacing look and I really should work on it.

'That's good, isn't it?' I asked them both, hopefully.

Steve and Chloe both nodded, Steve of course with a sarcastic smile and totally over the top nod.

'Is sweet good?' I asked, nervously.

Again they both nodded.

'Will she come to our next gig?'

Chloe nodded and Steve promptly laughed and laughed.

And so here I was, after the magic of the night before, learning that with a week to go to our next gig, and my next potential meeting with my Greek goddess, our drummer had resigned.

'What are we going to do Steve, I mean the next gig, it's in a week!'

'Fear not, I have a solution.'

'You do?'

Steve and Keith were both excellent at finding solutions.

'You know my neighbour?'

'The one with the rats?'

'No, the other one, the student.'

'Oh yes, I met him at your house the other month. Thin chap, looks like he hasn't eaten for a few months. Smells a bit like a student as I remember, quite a lot actually.'

'That's the one. His name is Tim, although everyone calls him Tricks, and guess what he plays?'

'The harmonica?'

'No.'

'The paper comb?'

'No.'

'The didgeridoo?'

'Possibly, but he is a drummer.'

'Really?'

'Really. He was at the Mason Arms gig and he thought we were fantastic. I was round there the other night and he said it was a shame we had such a great drummer because he played too'

'Has he got his own kit then?'

'Yea.'

'Have you seen it?'

'No, but I'm sure it will be fine.'

This was quite exciting. Joe had been a good drummer, sure, but we had never got on. A new drummer could be a mate too!

'Have you mentioned it to Keith?'

'Yea and he's up for practising with Tricks as soon as possible.'

'OK, let's do it. I never got on with Joe anyway.'

'You don't say!'

Five minutes later Steve called back and it was all arranged. We were to practise for the next four nights at a studio called 'Blubber Biscuits' in the fine City of Nottingham, which Tricks had recommended. He was already making his mark and that had to be a good sign. We would be ready for our next gig after all.

8

As Keith picked me up in his fabulous Vauxhall Belmont, which continued to amaze modern science by still being on the road, we were extremely excited. Our first gig had been a resounding success. We had already gathered 50 people on to our mailing list, all from the Mason Arms gig. Adding these to the imaginary 200, we had therefore amassed over 500 on the list already! It was this sort of reasoning that most small businesses of the entrepreneur variety are built on, the sort of sums that make Britain proud.

So many people, remarkably, were asking about the next gigs and we felt things were really taking off. On top of this we were about to take on a new drummer who sounded genuinely enthusiastic about the material we were writing. This sort of attitude would be so refreshing. No more looking across the practice room to a drummer with the face of Eey-ore, but rather a more hopeful band member that may look like Piglet!

Added further to our sense of optimism was the fact that for the first time we were to practise in real studio. I was already thinking Abbey Road, Trident, Sunset Sound and other such legendary establishments that guided our musical stars to the top of our great musical trees. Using a proper rehearsal suite would give us a real sense of professionalism and make us feel still further that we were on that star glittered road to rock stardom. Blubber Biscuits, the studio, was located in Nottingham just before the BBC studios. We pulled up in high spirits and viewed the large ancient looking building that had once been a clothing factory but now looked rather deserted.

'Now then Bob can you see a sign for the studio?'

We had arrived at this point having followed the instructions that Steve had given us, which wasn't necessarily the best way to get anywhere.

'There's Steve's car. Just pull in down the bottom Keith. Steve said to park here and then ring on the bell on the ground floor door which is over there I would guess.'

We pulled up, and the Belmont came to its customary abrupt stop as the engine cut out. I got out the car to be greeted by the oil and petrol smell that I had grown accustomed to. Keith began to attach the three car locks he had to various bits of the car. Of course why he bothered was part of the entertainment that is my brother. The car is the sort of car that you actually would want stealing for the tiny bit of insurance money that you would get. Still it always amused Keith and me as he fastened first the handbrake lock, then the steering lock, and finally the clutch lock. Keith would chuckle away as each lock was fastened, amused with the knowledge that what he was doing was totally ridiculous. This was, of course, the whole point!

I found a set of doorbells at the side of a large door at the bottom of the street and sure enough one of them said in scribbled writing, with a few musical notes 'artistically' drawn around it, 'Blubber Biscuits Sound Studio.' It wasn't Abbey Road but at least we were here!

I rang the bell and then went off to help Keith with the gear. We arrived back at the door to find Steve waiting for us with a large smile on his face.

'Evening boys.' He radiated a real happiness and excitement all across his face.

'Hello mate,' I said

'Well if it isn't our triumphant guitarist,' Keith gave Steve a wonderful big grin, 'the girls at school can't wait to see you again.'

'Really!?'

Steve had been quite a hit with all the sixth formers, the lads taken with his dazzling guitar skills, the girls attracted to his dyed and long jet black hair, as well as his long thin legs that were covered in tight black leather trousers. These were his pride and joy. The girls had been somewhat circumspect with their admiration with Chloe being there but Steve gladly received their appreciation.

'Do they want any pants as keepsakes?'

Steve began to undo his jeans.

'Not at this stage, I think photos would be acceptable though, and indeed a good start.'

'OK I shall have some done tomorrow.'

As we talked we gathered all the gear at the door and then began to carry it down to our rehearsal room for the night. I asked about our new drummer.

'Is Tricks here yet?

Steve smiled. I thought there was something else that had been amusing him. I enquired further.

'He is OK isn't he?'

'Yea, of course he is! I brought him down with me, his car's knackered or something.'

A drummer without a car is rather like having a HGV driver without a lorry. Still I let that pass.

'Just don't expect too much of his kit. I think the best way to describe it is that it will do the job.'

Keith and I exchanged glances. For Keith especially, things in the Band had to be right. Before buying any product, be it a new stereo or a new brand of beans, Keith would question many people long and hard. He would read up on all the facts available. He would be informed. Once the decision was made, Keith could clearly say that he was prepared. He did not like others to not take the same trouble and be unprepared, and as regards matters to do with the band this mind-set was even more critical. I sensed trouble.

As soon as we had launched the Band he had bought himself a new bass guitar, although not of course before he had literally toured the country to find the right guitar for him at the price that he was willing to pay. He would sit in the music booth for hours playing each note with a circumspection that would make an aircraft engineer proud. The music shop that had finally secured the deal had actually let Keith have the guitar for an unbelievable discount, no doubt in an effort to get him away from the shop. Fair play to them! You had to hand it to shop owners for protecting their sanity at the expense of simple profit.

For Keith the Band had to be a perfect well-oiled machine. A drum kit that would not do the job would be a real problem for him because the Band meant so much to him and he could not afford to be let down by the obvious things. To be honest it would be a problem for me too. I had long since been affected by my brother's requirement for high standards. He had taught me from being tiny that my trying my best in things that were important to him was not to be questioned. Failure here would see his natural disappointment in me, and I, as his adoring little brother, could not stomach such emotions. His disappointment was my failure and so my failure was not going to happen. It wasn't so much that it bothered me that I had not come to his standard, because remarkably I had developed a strong enough mind to sometimes disagree with his standards, it was more that I hated to see him upset. I always had.

It didn't matter that the car he drove was really only just, at a push of the imagination, road worthy. To Keith the car was not an issue because it amused him to keep it the way it was. Keith chose the things he needed in his own mind to be right and his decision was, in his own mind, final. Nothing anyone could say would change his mind. This made him unique and very difficult for an outsider to read. All I knew was that he was my big brother and if he wanted something to be changed then I felt that pressure like nobody else. The fact that he was upset meant that all was not well in the world and if all was not well I was uneasy. It was all part of the unending circle that was my relationship with my brother.

So, with heavy thoughts of what the night now might hold for me, we had walked down what seemed like several floors of wide industrial steps into a basement area that was effectively a chill out reception area for the bands. My arms felt somewhat stretched as I dropped my amp on to the floor. The smell in the air was a mixture of damp and a sweet pungent smell, which I kind of liked.

'Steve, that's a nice smell. What brand of men's toiletry will that be?'

Steve cut me short with a look that told me the occupants might take offence to me referring to 'nice' smells. Clearly this was not the done thing. I understood immediately, I thought, and kept quiet.

All was quiet in the reception area and Steve led us through a door and down yet more steps into the bottom studio. The dampness was not only in the air but also all over the walls and floor and ceiling. It showed itself in a selection of mould colours and peeling paint. Delightful. It was the sort of place that mothers everywhere would envisage student flats to be like. I longed for the earlier sweet smell from upstairs or any smell really rather than the one I was currently inhaling.

Tricks who I recognised immediately was setting his rather basic drum kit up. It was an old Premier model that had undoubtedly seen better days. Still it all looked as though it was all there, which was about the one positive thing I could have said. Joe had collected an immaculate collection of cymbals that were so perfect and, and here I am demonstrating my lack of knowledge on drumming gear, so very shiny. Tricks' cymbals looked as though they had seen both 20th century world wars having been used as giant serving plates and lived to tell the tale. They were probably used by the Royal Cumbrians in some earlier 19th century campaign in the Sudan as a shield of some kind. Then, in later years, they had been melted down into cymbals for the army band to bash together in Empire celebrations. Eventually, and just as had befallen the Empire, the cymbals had shrunk, and now found their way on to Tricks' kit. As we walked into the room he straightened up to greet us.

'Hey guys, cool to see you. Hope you like the studio, isn't it groovy?'

'Yea, erm, cool!' I answered, somewhat thrown by the cool surf speak that we normally reserved for when the Band was in the public domain. Keith went over to Tricks and shook hands. I suspect Keith used his extra firm grip.

'Very pleased to meet you Tricks.'

It was a solemn moment given, I suspect, for Keith to establish the pack, and I think Tricks was somewhat overpowered by this formal greeting. He spluttered out,

'Yea, cool man. Hey, the other night, you were kickin', you were slaying the chicks man, and you were hot, hot, hot!'

There was a tiny awkward pause and I looked hard into my brain for any more cool speak words I knew that hadn't already been used to try and join in as Tricks was looking right at me. I glanced at Steve who had turned away to the wall with a massive grin on his face. I knew we would laugh about this introduction for years to come.

'Well it's great, erm cool that is, to have you with us Tricks,' I said, grasping the nettle of friendship in both hands. 'We can't tell you how great, erm cool, it is to have a drummer who actually likes the stuff we are playing and says as much.'

'Like it! Hey guys, you dudes are so far out I can't even see the surf man! I said to Stevie wizard fingers here from the opening note the other night you guys were diggin', you were cutting holes in the mind, grooving the highway of another world man! You had that crowd by the balls and then you squeezed even harder. Testicular delight boys, testicular delight.'

Rare praise indeed, at least I think it was. Keith took over. He could see from my facial expression that I was struggling with just being so pleased to hear our new drummer being so very positive, and at the same time struggling not to laugh at the very different language I was so not used to hearing.

'Nice kit Tricks.' He delivered the line in classic dead pan mode.

I turned to the wall wanting to die with laughter. Keith had said that on purpose, knowing the effect it would have on Steve and myself and yet knowing he could keep a straight face. I managed to splutter out,

'I'm just off to the loo.'

And Steve added,

'Me too!'

And the two of us fell out of the room, ran upstairs, and laughed far too loudly. After our mirth subsided enough for us to speak, Steve reasoned,

'Look Anthony, I know he's a little different to us, but he loves the music.'

I looked at Steve, a large merry smile all over my face.

'He can play the drums as well,' he added to shore up his defence of our new drummer.

'Are you sure?'

'Yes.'

At this Steve burst out laughing again. I stopped smiling.

'Steve!' I said, sternly. 'If there was one thing we definitely needed it was a drummer who can play.'

'No, really, he can play. You made me laugh. Tricks played his kit for me at home the other night and I thought he was really good. He's not a rock drummer admitted, but he's got a real cool softer touch.'

'Oh I see; you were attracted by his softer touch?'

'Well of course, who wouldn't be? Seriously though, I think his drumming will suit the Band because it sits with the music and doesn't take it over like Joe's sometimes did.'

I had to agree with this. Joe would get so carried away that I felt like my whole body was vibrating and shaking with the beat he was banging out. I think he was using his drum kit as a sort of therapy tool. Perhaps he hit it so hard as a way of fighting back against something in his personal life that he couldn't actually stand up against. Perhaps he just had a heavy touch. Perhaps he had exceptionally heavy arms and whenever he lifted them up they automatically came crashing down in an involuntary act of vandalism. Whatever the reason I had to agree that a softer stroke on the drums, as well as a very positive attitude, more than made up for a somewhat hard to understand use of the English language and a drum kit that was not up to the standard of our beloved Oasis.

'Look, if you think he is the right man then that's fine by me.'

'I do.'

'Well I've only got one thing to say to that.'

We looked at each other and repeated over and over like schoolchildren in brat mode,

'COOL, COOL, COOL!'

9

Six practices, four local gigs and three weeks later we found ourselves on the road to our first gig 'out' of our area. Things were going well. Tricks had settled into the Band really well and was an immediate hit with our growing fan base. The mailing list had grown to an improbable 750, that is 389 people really and a list that included my complete family, from my little sisters to my Grandma and Great Auntie. Let it not be said that Wide Eyed Wonder were not prepared to appeal to all comers. We were a band for the people and of the people!

Tricks had pleasingly proven himself very adept at talking to complete strangers, one of my absolute weak points, and signing them up for the mailing list. His clever use of language was not proving the handicap I had feared. In fact people seemed somewhat mesmerised by it. Our student following were particularly taken with it and could now be heard using Tricks phrases themselves. In short he was becoming something of an icon.

As regards my new found and only love, I had seen Annabella only once during this period. She had come down to the last gig we had done which was three days earlier in Mansfield at the Stockwells pub, which incidentally is based on Stockwell gate. I wonder if you had a pub on Puberty Street, would you automatically call it The Puberty Public Arms? What about Constipation Road, Come Street, or Windy Row? The pub names would be legendary. In fact I reckon this could be a winner. You would have busloads of tourists from all over the world coming to see, and drink, from these watering holes. Councils take note! This idea could save your town.

Annabella had again come to the gig with Chloe, arriving just before we were due on stage. I say stage when in fact a more precise definition would have been ledge or, at a push, a step.

'Can I get you a drink?' I ventured as soon as she arrived.

'Mine's a G&T,' offered Chloe.

'And I'll have another pint,' joined in Steve.

'A red wine please,' smiled Annabella.

Going to a bar such as this in Mansfield and asking for a G&T and a glass of red wine, just before you are due to play a rock gig, seriously affects your Indy credentials. Still I was prepared to lose all credibility for the sake of impressing Annabella, and of course my old friend Chloe. I would of course state loudly that the drinks were for 'LADIES', just so that punters around me were clear.

Since the Mason Arms gig I had thought of little else than the band and Annabella. I had convinced myself that there was hope with Annabella, after all Little Knob, which was another of the many fetching and, I felt, particularly accurate nickname I had given to her boyfriend, was not in a band such as my good self. I had reasoned that he was clearly not the most artistic of fellows and it was within this glitch that I planned my success. If Annabella could be won I felt it would be by seeing the artistic pop star type man she really wanted, not the bulky large rich type she was currently saddled with. Why choose money over artistic temperament I reasoned? Paying the mortgage, I grant you. The bills of course, the holidays maybe, and, I suppose, money comes in useful for weekends away, the theatre, the cinema, leisure in general and being clothed like a princess and not a pauper. Then there is the dream house, the expensive holidays, the private jet and the remote Caribbean island. However, and crucially, would money buy happiness? It might help, yes, but would it fill the heart? Point proven. Perhaps. Perhaps not.

I returned with the drinks, and Chloe and Steve kindly gave us a little space for the two of us to talk on our own.

'Thanks for coming,' I ventured with a playful smile, 'I was hoping you would come and see us play again.'

'How could I miss seeing one of the area's main attractions'?

'You mean like the town's shopping centre, or the open air bus station, or the market, or the viaduct?'

'Yes, all those.'

'Or the Town Hall, or the taxi rank, or the big roads, or the viaduct again?'

'Enough already!' Annabella replied, laughing in a way that told me I wanted this girl more than new Diesel jeans, or better still second hand extremely worn Levi ones with a tight arse and slight flare, which were really in at the moment.

A little silence. I was worryingly reverting to schoolboy shyness. Annabella just stood there and smiled at me. I felt she knew I liked her and she waited, looking quite happy letting me make the moves. I pinched myself into action,

'I understand you are an artist then?' A rather limp little question but it was the best I could muster.

'I'm a student of art, yes.'

'And being a student doesn't make you an artist?'

Annabella offered me another of those heart wilting smiles. I carried on,

'I bet you're brilliant, in fact I bet you are the best on your course. Do you do nudes?'

We had been talking for only a few minutes and I had already fallen into talking about nudity. Still she was an artist and perhaps it was OK to ask.

'All day every Wednesday.'

'ALL DAY!!! Oooh err madam'

Appearing to look like a complete Philistine was not the impression I was trying to make. My unending and accidental roll of words just seemed to come so naturally. Sometimes I know I am a complete and utter wanker.

'Why, are you interested in modelling?' She asked with a rather wicked little smile.

A rather dangerous little question I thought. Of course she must have been joking with me and so I responded,

'Interested? I really am, yea. It would be great exposure for the band!"

'You're on then.'

BUGGER! The hole I had just walked into had been dug all by myself. There was no one else to blame. I had gone and hired an industrial digger and removed earth to reveal an eye-catching hole of massive proportions. I had even filled it thereafter with some sort of sewage and then just closed my eyes and jumped straight into it! I had to rescue the situation.

'You're joking, right?'

She smiled widely.

'You're not joking are you…'

She shook her head softly causing her hair to flutter.

'Will it just be you and me?' A wonderful cheeky reply I thought. I was beginning to warm up. This girl was so hot

I could feel my lips burning with anticipation. It was a cold April night and Annabella had arrived with a long black faux leather coat on. Underneath she wore casual jeans and a tight white top. I was trying my best to not let my eyes wander to inspect the tight white top and the delights which so obviously lay below but it was proving increasingly difficult.

'Well, it will be just you, me, and a few other students and a lecturer. What do you think?'

She looked at me with a cheeky twinkle in her eyes and I realised, with dread, that she was perfectly serious. I immediately thought of her boyfriend, that he too must have modelled at her class. My heart dropped as I thought of the Adonis Little Knob, who in truth probably had an awfully large one, posing for the group with an ease at the size of his everything. I was filled with dread at the inadequate physique I had in comparison. Of course here I am not referring to the size of my own willy which I should mention at this point is larger than the Eiffel Tower when at its peak of sexual excitement. Kind of. In fact in general I am not in a bad shape at all. In fact I look pretty darned good, particularly if viewed from 25 yards through clouded spectacles that are cracked across both lenses and are shaded against the sun that is full on to the eyes of the viewer. I was therefore not unhappy with my body. I was simply not confident to compare it with Mr Universe, Callum McCore in a nudist art class that included the ideal love of my life.

As my face clouded with my thoughts Annabella carried on,

'We are encouraged to use friends as actual models rather than just impersonal models. It's much more fun.'

'Fun' was not the word I wanted to hear in conjunction with the suggestion I do some nude modelling. Excitement would have been a more suitable word, or perhaps amazement, awe, privilege or inspiring. Words that I would not feel were appropriate would have been giggle, snigger, joke material or eye sensitive. 'Fun' filled that middle ground that hinted at the possibility of me causing amusement rather than invoking a sense of awe.

'Besides,' as Annabella talked she was cheeky, serious and sexy all at the same time 'as you say, it will be great exposure for the band. Think of the press publicity, 'lead singer has also done some nude modelling."

I was thinking more in terms of 'Lead singer of Wide Eyed Wonder is anything but wide.'

Annabella went on. She was on a roll whilst I was on a downward spiral.

'And besides anything else,' and here Annabella's face filled with a beautiful big smile 'I bet you look great in the nude.'

As she said this I realised my mouth was wide open and beer was dribbling down my chin. I also became aware that my little man had become somewhat excited and was on its way to that Eiffel Tower state I mentioned earlier. Thankfully I was wearing some baggy combat trousers and, whilst pulling in my stomach and groin area in, I hoped I was hiding my excitement. Of course it is never easy to keep a giant hidden, but I think I managed it.

I wanted to now say 'no' to this modelling request, knowing that tremendous embarrassment could be mine, but with this exceptionally leading conversation I found myself uttering the immortal words,

'I will.'

Annabella laughed,

'I'm not asking for your hand in marriage!' she said.

'Not yet,' I replied with a twinkle in my eye and a determination to get my own back.

She looked at me, caught between I did not know what.

A little silence again. I had overstepped what I could and could not say. Bugger again. Ah well, in for a penny and all that.

'Well I am already looking forward to my first nude modelling assignment,' I said, eager to atone and to not let her consider she had just made a big mistake in asking me to model.

'Well that's fantastic,' she said, the smile returning to her face. 'Give me a ring in the week and we can arrange times.'

'But I haven't got your number,' I replied, whilst offering my dopey dog look.

She lifted eyeliner out of her pocket and, lifting up my T-shirt, she wrote her telephone number across my stomach. I had only just got my nether regions under control, which was just as well.

'I should be able to get you in to model in about three or four weeks, if that's alright?'

'Three weeks!' I choked, 'could we not make it three years giving me time to get down the gym and find a muscle or two?'

'You'll be fine. Think of it as another live show. I've seen you perform live and you're brilliant.'

Unfortunately flattery gets anyone everywhere with me.

'Alright, I can't wait.' I lied wonderfully well. I had no idea why I had agreed to this shocking experience except that the girl I wanted had asked me to do it and consequently I had to say yes. It would also be one of those experiences that I knew would cause immense laughter with my friends. It would keep us going for ages. Perhaps I could get them to model too although the thought of unleashing 'The North's already developing beer belly on unsuspecting students was perhaps a little unfair. Mind you I understand that the challenge of drawing light and shade is one of the main criteria in still life. With Steve, his beer shaped stomach at the side of his otherwise thin physique would give plenty of light and shade practice.

'If I come straight from work can I keep my suit on?' I asked.

Annabella laughed.

'What about my shirt? My boxers? I know, what about my socks, just my socks?'

Steve and Chloe came back to us, both wearing large knowing smiles.

'Well Bob,'

I gave Steve an especially hard stare, 'Bob' really was not the nickname I wanted Annabella to know me by and was one that Steve never used. Steve corrected himself 'Anthony, erm, my dear pal, it is time to go on and give this audience a life changing experience.'

'Why, did you bring the lubrication and Marvin music?'

'Erm, no, I forgot.'

'Well let's just go and play some rock music instead shall we?'

I looked up to the front of the pub to see Keith and Tricks all ready to begin. The lads had very kindly left me alone to talk.

Annabella gave me a cheeky smile and proudly announced, 'Anthony's agreed to so some nude modelling at college.'

I noticed two things here. Firstly Annabella had said my name with such a lightness of touch that I found immediately quite moving. The way she said it made it sound almost European and therefore exotic. She had made my name unique to her, which I thought was incredibly cute. Next thing you know, and by natural definition, she would be using my toothbrush. Secondly I noticed that rather than the uncontrollable laughter I had expected from Steve and Chloe, instead they actually looked a little frightened for me.

Steve looked at me, incredulous at my nerve.

'Really?'

Chloe and Steve just stood there burning their stares into me. I looked at them both and laughed nervously.

'Really! Why not? Think of the press for the Band 'Lead singer is a nude model."

'Or 'Lead singer is a wanker."

'Steve,' it was Chloe, using her fine telling off voice, 'I think it's very brave of you Anthony though perhaps a little forward,' she had added with the political sensitivity of a John Prescott line.

'Thank you,' I answered, weakly.

Steve walked off to the stage, chuckling loudly as he did so. I turned to see him whispering to Keith who in turn looked down towards me and began to laugh. I turned back to Annabella.

'I'll see you in a bit, yea?'

'I'm afraid not. I have to go in half an hour. Callum's picking me up because I've got an early start in the morning.'

'Oh, Callum.' My heart dropped. I had managed to put him out of my mind.

'But you are going to call me next week?' she asked.

My heart bounced back up. She had written her number on my body!!!

'Yes, yes, and double yes.'

I kissed both ladies on the cheek and turned to the stage to see the band in fits of laughter. My new predicament was, of course, very funny.

And so, three nights later, we were driving down to Leicester for our first gig away from our area and, perhaps most scarily, no fans were making the journey with us. We had achieved much in such a short space of time and our new fan base had been very supportive. Keith and Steve had managed to book us in for quite a few 'big' gigs out of the area in the months ahead and so we decided this first one, at a local pub in Leicester, would be best served by us going alone. We would save our support for the gigs that mattered.

Steve had got this gig at a pub called 'The Royal Mail.' It was a little out of the middle of the town and next to Leicester's main Post Office sorting centre. Steve had spotted the pub a few weeks earlier on a visit to the said sorting office and asked the landlord if he fancied having a top 'up and coming band' on at his pub (Wide Eyed Wonder in case you were wondering!). The landlord had been over the moon to be offered such a high calibre act and had readily agreed. He had even provided Steve and his friends who were with him at the time with a free round in recognition of the top night of entertainment that would follow.

I was driving down as ever with Keith in his high quality Belmont as we followed Steve in his smooth black BMW with the laid back Tricks, who incidentally was still having problems with his car. In fact since we had met Tricks he had been unable to get his car working at all. Still Steve didn't seem to mind and we assumed the drummer motor would perk up as the warmer weather arrived.

As we drove through the centre of Leicester we were quite excited at this new phase to our campaign. Tonight we would play for people who didn't even know us. It would be a true test of our songs' ability to stand up in the public domain. We worked our way across a very interesting road layout that would have taxed the mind of Einstein at his peak. Eventually, as the shops died out and the streets became a little bit quieter, we arrived.

The Royal Mail was situated on the corner of a back street set back off the main road. Apart from a few flats there was no

residential property to be seen and very little sign of life at all.
I hopefully assumed that it was the sort of place where people
came from miles around to experience the vibe of a lively pub
and crucially live rock music. Keith and I stepped out of our
car to meet the grinning Steve.

'Here we are lads, what do you think?'

'You look like you've come up trumps here Steve' said
Keith, laughing, 'Is it going to be buzzing as much inside as
it is outside?'

'Oooh definitely.'

I was a little concerned at the content of the conversation.
Surely we hadn't come all this way to play to a small crowd.
Still it was only 7.00pm and we had arrived in plenty of time to
set up our gear and sound system. There was many an ample
hour for the crowds to arrive. As we made our way into the
pub, our arms breaking with the weight of the prehistoric PA
which Keith had got for only £30 from a second hand local
'music' shop but that still sounded amazing and better than
anything he had tested out at literally thirty plus music shops,
we were met by a small grinning bearded man who had the
look of a wild snarling dog. In fact he had little bits of saliva
rolling down through his beard to match the picture. Add to
this the bits of crisps and other such crumbs, this was certainly
a beard to try and forget.

'Good evening gents,' he growled, and, turning to Steve,
'these are the boys then Steve?'

My heart dropped as I realised that this would be the
landlord. The evening from hell awaited and as I glanced at
Keith's smiling eyes I knew that he had known all along.

'Yes Arthur, that's right. This is Bob, our lead singer.'

'Pleasure to meet you Arthur,' I offered my hand and, as he
took it, I realised the dreadful error I had made. His grip was
warm and clammy and he held my hand for what seemed like

five minutes. I could clearly feel several lumps on his warm palm that were probably some sort of wart or open sore. Nice.

'Lovely to meet the face of the future of British music Bob.'

Fantastic. This small little wet wolf like man was already calling me Bob. It really was not the rock and roll image I wanted to present to the world. 'Q Magazine get an exclusive interview with Bob,' was not the headline that I felt would pull in the masses or one that I would have framed.

Steve and Keith were purposely quiet as Arthur held my hand and looked into my face. I don't know what he was looking for, but I found myself blushing under his intense gaze. As Keith eventually began to laugh out loud and Arthur's steadfast attention was broken, I blurted out,

'It's Anthony, actually, my name is Anthony.'

'That's right Arthur,' said Steve, cheerfully, 'Bob is just his middle name gone wrong.'

Thank you for that Steve, I thought. Mental note made for later which read, 'destroy Steve's car, and, perhaps for good measure, his life as well.'

Steve introduced the other members of the Band.

'And this laughing hyena is Keith.'

'Oh delighted Keith, I've heard so much about you.'

'Really?'

'Yes. You know ever since Steve told me about your ability with the women'

'The women?'

'Yes,' went on Arthur, 'and I have to say that I still don't understand how you managed to have that thing with those girls whilst you were trying to play live.'

We all broke into fits of laughter, Arthur too as he assumed we were laughing at the remembrance of the evening in question. To the rest of us we knew Steve had spun possibly his largest story ever, no doubt aided by the friends who were with him at the time and the drink that was so obviously flowing. Arthur was the perfect sponge to soak it all in.

'And this is Tricks,' said Steve.

'Hey man, dig that groove brother,' offered our drummer.

The two of them shook hands. Tricks' face showed suitable alarm as Arthur's wet grip tightened on his own smooth hands that had possibly never seen a day of actual hard labour.

'Well Arthur,' Steve announced, rescuing Tricks, 'we better get set up. Where do you want us?'

'In what way?' he asked, with a scary grin on his face. We all laughed, perhaps a little nervously.

'Only joking lads. I am as straight as a fit, young man's spine. There's about as much chance of me making an approach on you as there is of me shagging Elle Macpherson.'

Absolutely no chance there then and a certain amount of relief swept through the Band. Arthur showed us to a raised corner area where we would play and we set about getting ready. Tricks and I spent the next five minutes scrubbing our hands in the toilet. Such clean living boys! `We then spent about the next half an hour of lumping in gear and setting up enough wires to light and warm a minor city such as Lincoln. We were ready for our sound check.

Tricks stick's clicked 1,2,3,4, and we were away with 'Take You There.' As we played I looked around at the guys and I realised something important. I had often thought about big nights entertaining thousands but this wasn't the only reason I had started the band. Just being here, laughing, playing a venue I would never have come to, this was just so amazing. I guess it didn't really matter whether we played Nottingham's Rock City or Leicester's Royal Mail. The buzz of playing a song and being together meant so much to us that this moment, this time, was fantastic. I hoped, no matter what, that we would always keep this. It had a certain kind of magic that was boxed up right there for me.

As we drew to the end of the song Arthur and another man who had appeared at the side of him at the bar, applauded for all they were worth. The buzz of the guitars faded off into the pub and we could hear Arthur shouting,

'Bravo lads, fantastic.'

We joined him at the bar.

'I can't tell you how good it is to hear such loud shattering sounds. It takes me back to my days down the coalmines and working on the pit face. How I miss those dirty deafening machines.'

Rare praise indeed!

'Well lads, let me introduce you…' Arthur turned to the man who had joined him 'to my lovely wife Barbara.'

It was a woman. The man was a woman. In fact as I peered closely through the long curly hair that covered the dark hairy chin I could just make out it possibly was a female. There were lumps coming out all over from the woman's clothing and I suspected some of these probably related to Barbara's female parts.

'And…' Arthur went on 'hands off lads. This one's all mine.'

'Quite right Arthur,' Steve proclaimed.

'Wouldn't dream of it Arthur,' I said, seeing Keith's shoulders move up and down to the side of me as he put his head down and tried to quench the giggles that so obviously wanted to come out.

'You lucky dog Arthur,' said Tricks in a wonderful deadpan tone that sent Steve and Keith running out of the pub to laugh freely without embarrassing our new friend. As I listened you could hear wolf like noises filling the night air. I hoped Arthur didn't realise what the noise was.

One hour later and the pub boasted an audience of eight, including Arthur and Barbara. We were still sat at the bar waiting for people to arrive and realising at the same time that it was unlikely we would be adding too many to our fan base, although this wouldn't stop Keith pretending we had picked up another 50 or so names.

'Quite a busy night then Arthur.' It was Tricks; thrilled to be in the middle of this comedy scene we had created for ourselves.

'Well not really lads,' clearly the art of irony was somewhat lost on the barman, 'but its not too bad for a Tuesday.'

'What's it normally like then?' I whispered to Steve, 'two old men with flat caps and sixteen whippets!'

Arthur looked at his watch.

'Well lads, it's 9 o'clock. I think its time we heard you for real, time indeed for Leicester to hear the sound of the future.'

You had to give it to Arthur. He had looked out into his empty pub and had seen Leicester waiting. Remarkable. Here was a visionary who would not have been out of place within the Kennedy backroom staff of the 60's. Well, when I say out of place…

Steve, Keith and Tricks made their way to the stage and did their final checks. Steve as always checked my guitar whilst I made sure the sound system was ready to go. I then made my back to the bar to await the boy's nod at which time I would make my grand entrance. As the Band did their stuff Arthur went off to fetch his daughter.

'She's really been looking forward to this,' he said as his grinning face disappeared down the dark passage that sat menacingly to the side of the bar. I knew a rare sight awaited me. I looked around the pub. Two more people had arrived to swell the audience. Looking at them it was though part of the cast from 'The Valley of the Damned' had called in for a pint.

We had picked a venue to receive our first away from home gig that was a place set aside for the more unusual members of society. How apt, then, that we were playing! As I gazed at the faces of our audience I saw faces that were, as an artist might state, interesting. A painter would call them unique and unusual. Steve would call them 'hilarious', Tricks would call them 'kickin different, stroke, frightening man.' I myself wondered if in fact Leicester was a port city and that these people had been shipped in from all over the world by way of some unusual exhibition. Women or men, I could not tell.

'And this is our daughter Anthony,' It was Arthur, happily arrived with his pride and joy, 'her name is Esmay.'

Esmay was a picture of delight, her long green hair matching her coloured eyes and lips which were also in shades of green, her chubby cheeks folding over on to her spot infested chin. She was wearing green velour that looked like it had been used for black out curtains in the war. She looked at least a size 28 and I suspected weighed around 25 stones. As you know though you should never ask a woman her weight and so I didn't.

'Hello Esmay, thanks for coming down to listen to us,' I said.

'I've not come down, I've come up.' She chuckled to herself rather loudly. Her voice was very deep and quite scary.

'Really, how nice. Come up from the cellar?'

'That's right Anthony,' chimed in Arthur, 'our Esmay loves the cellar don't you love. Anyway I'll leave you two to get acquainted whilst I serve all these punters. I tell you what Anthony, you have brought in the crowd tonight. When you are big and famous, don't think I will forget this kindness!' Good old Arthur! Mind you to be fair to him fresh punters had arrived. Several new weird looking types were crowding the bar with a look of thirst that may well have been as easily satisfied by blood as beer. I turned back to the delightful Esmay.

'What sort of music do you like?' I asked, trying to sound not too interested but at the same time, polite.

'I like Devil music.'

'Oh, good.' A remarkable evening of entertainment was taking on a new level.

'And that would be?'

'Really good!'

'Right, but what sort of sound is that?'

'Really bad!'

'Yes, right, OK,' I was struggling here, 'but what particular bands do you like?'

'Thrash fast Metal and hip hop country.'

The connection was not immediately obvious although I had to admit it was one with certain merits. Both were horrible and both were listened to by people with strange looks on their faces and strange attire on their bodies. The audience was beginning to make sense. We had walked into a devil's cauldron and we were going to be boiled alive and sucked free of all our blood. Still, it beat being at home and watching Coronation Street. Now to do something really evil,

'Well Esmay that is remarkable because,' as I spoke Esmay's eyes widened. She leaned forward on the bar and her low cut dress revealed far more than I deserved. I couldn't think of anything I had done so particularly wrong as to merit such a sight. Urgent action was required and I had that action well and ready lined up to deliver.

'Do you see our bass player over there.'

Esmay cast her dark all encompassing eyes over to the stage where Keith had just completed his tuning check.

'The tall one with lovely dark looks?' she asked, in a somewhat playful tone.

'What a wonderful description, he will like that!' She had bitten. 'Well Keith likes exactly the same music as you.'

'No!!!' As she declared this in an extremely loud and excited voice, she pushed me playfully on my chest with the force of a mad ox escaping the clutches of its killer. I went flying off my stool and into the lap of a large building type who was just settling in to drinking his first pint of the night. As his drink went all over him, and indeed all over me too, I saw the look that I hated so much, that of violence deciding how to be violent. I saw the method of pain chosen click in his eyes, and his left hand rise in the air to no doubt punch my face a lot.

Thankfully Esmay caught his arm.

'Now come on Donny,' Donny, I ask you! 'It was my fault, not dear Anthony's.'

Dear Anthony, it could be the start of my agony aunt role.

'Go on darling,' Esmay was talking to me, 'get off Donny's lap before he kills you.'

She was laughing as she said this. Unfortunately Donny was not following suit, although he had at least decided to not hit me. Esmay looked at me and simply said,

'I'll sort Donny out. You go and play, play like there's no tomorrow,' her voice was rising to a crescendo pitch, and she called to me as though she was auditioning for some Shakespearian tragedy. Looking around the Royal Mail I knew that in fact I was taking part in a more modern version of a Shakespearian tragedy. This must be being filmed somewhere. This had to be a set up! She went on

'Play like you mean it Anthony, leave no part of the music untouched, Let the vibe have your soul Anthony, let it have your soul!''

I ran to the stage and picked up my guitar.

'What's all that about?' the ever observant Steve had seen me in trouble. He had not admittedly jumped to my aid but surely he would have done if called upon to do so.

'Arthur's daughter has arrived.'

'The one with the green sack on?'

'That's the one.'

We looked out to her and saw that she was waving to Keith and blowing kisses in his direction. Unwisely, Keith was waving and blowing kisses back! How amusing.

I turned to the rest of the band.

'Well lads, I know the crowd isn't quite what we expected,' I looked at Steve 'that is, not what most of us expected, but we are here now and we should just play like normal.'

'Yea, it's good practice if nothing else, and who knows there might be loads more people yet to arrive!' Good old Keith, ever the optimist.

'So let's do it. Keep to the original song list.'

I turned to the mic.

'Hello Leicester…' Steve laughed out loud, Arthur clapped out loud, Donny wolf whistled out loud, Keith trumped out loud.

'We are Wide Eyed Wonder and we hope you like our music.'

Steve piled into the start of 'Take You There,' and we were away. As we played our opening song I looked at the audience as I always did, challenging them with our music and eager to gauge their reaction. Arthur, Barbara and dear Esmay were swaying to the music with their hands in the air. Donny and his exceptionally hard looking two friends just sat very still, each trying to out do each other in giving me the dead eye. I decided to not look in their direction ever again. Two old boys at the back were dancing with their dogs (not imagery but actually dancing with their four legged friends), and everyone else (i.e. the other fifteen or so strange types) seemed to be tapping their feet and even clapping their hands wildly out of time.

As we finished the song, warm applause greeted us from all angles, apart from Donny and his compatriots. Killjoys!

'Do you do Black Sabbath?'

It was Arthur from the bar.

'Yes, what about Bucks Fizz?'

That was a friend of Donny's.

'Or Horse Shit?'

I couldn't tell who that was but they were either taking the piss or knew of a band I had never heard of. I decided to give him, or indeed her, the benefit and continued.

'This next song is called 'I Want To Be Me."

'I wouldn't!' shouted Donny. The audience laughed. I smiled back.

Steve's stinging opening chords filled the pub and got my adrenaline going. I didn't care if these people liked us or not. I had written this song after a particularly dreadful day at work, which had started badly and had gone downhill from there. First of all my boss, Mr Cook, had been heading out for his first appointment of the day out of the branch, and had seen me just pulling out of my street heading for work. It was 9.15 in the morning and he had blown out of the water my excuse of heavy traffic and an awful road accident. He had looked at his wristwatch as our eyes met and I knew cross words awaited. I had run into work fifteen minutes later to be met by a queue at enquiries, equivalent to the population of France. All of them wanted to grumble about something or other and sales were not the menu of the day. At 11.45, just before I was due to take lunch and respite from the morning, Fooky Cooky, my lovely little nick name for the boss, had called me in to his office for a good dressing down.

'You have to set an example Anthony. You are the Bank's future and the other staff look to you for their lead,' I hoped this was not the case because my job would undoubtedly soon be gone if it was.

'Do you see what you are doing Anthony, do you?'

I assured him I did. I promised it would never ever happen again and in fact I had only been late that morning because of my mother's illness and my looking after her by making a cooked breakfast. Total fabrication of course but it seemed to soften him a little. He even sent her some flowers.

My dinner hour was cancelled and I traipsed back down to enquiries for more abuse. The afternoon had continued in much the same vein with the notable highlight being a customer getting hold of Mr Wilde and threatening to punch his lights out. This would have normally been high entertainment except that on this occasion the customer actually carried out his threat and it was very nasty indeed. I piled in to the fray to pull the man off Wildey only to receive a blow to my groin that bought immediate tears by the bucket load to my eyes. The police had arrived, closely followed by the ambulance, and both the mad customer and Mr Wilde were carried away. I spent the rest of the afternoon sat in one position at enquiries, unable to physically leave my position as I awaited the less than pleasurable throbbing from my groin area to go away. The bag of frozen peas that one of my colleagues had gotten for me helped. Alas the constant stream of staff coming over to enquiries to laugh at me did not!

By the time I arrived home, I had resolved to resign from the Bank and travel the world and leave everything and everybody behind. 'I Want To Be Me' was the result of my depression and the light I saw in a new beginning for a new me.

It was our second song in and we went for it.

'And I looked out into my world, and I said come look at me

I refuse to be what you want, to be what you want to be;

Be a Rock Star straight from London, be a boy fresh out of school

Shout as loud as I can manage, try and break every rule.'

Out of the corner of my eye I noticed Donny stand up. I went on,

'All I ever wanted was to make you see. All I ever needed was it all.'

Donny was walking towards us. Death, or at least a certain amount of maiming, undoubtedly awaited. The thought flicked through my mind that perhaps I should vacate the stage and exit left but somehow I felt unable to do anything but carry on,

'I want to be me, I want to be free, I want to be breaking down your doors,

I want to be me, I want to be free, I want it all.'

Donny was now directly in front of Steve. I cast a glance towards him as I repeated the chorus and to my amazement I saw him smiling and giving Steve the thumbs up. Steve, who had a cigarette falling out of the side of his mouth, simply winked back and continued to play like the rock guitar god he had become.

We carried on with the song. The second verse, the chorus, the big brassy tart of a guitar solo, the repeated chorus and the banging and rocking ending. As we finished Donny just stood there clapping and shouting to Steve,

'Fuckin shit 'ot guitar man. Shit 'ot!'

It was remarkable. A man who I thought signalled certain death for at least one of us, i.e. me, was a convert to the cause. I had witnessed a modern day miracle and if that was not enough to convert a non-believer I don't know what else could.

As the rest of the gig went on more people did arrive at the pub. These were normal people out for a normal night. Something in us was connecting with something in them. It was incredible that our music was touching people. How cool is that! It was the Oasis effect, that of hearing a tune and its words, and it actually affecting you.

When I heard Rock and Roll Star for the first time I had never heard of Oasis or seen a photo of Oasis. It was just a song that the evening session on Radio One was playing. I heard it and it blew me away. I didn't initially make out all the words, but there was something about Liam's voice and Noel's guitar riffs that just broke me apart.

'Tonight, I'm a rock and roll star,' had sneered Liam, two fingers majestically raised to the world. And he was, even before he was famous, he really was a rock and roll star because he believed what he sang, and I believed it too.

If you could create that buzz in a person, then you had something special. Tonight we had done exactly that and I was proud, so proud.

As we had finished playing that night, at the Royal Mail, around 40 people were listening and the place was cooking. This was partially due to the heat that had been created and the sweat of very smelly people, the band now included, filling the room. There was also an atmosphere though of something that had been created, a feeling, a moment in time. All four of us had really enjoyed ourselves and this had obviously come through to the crowd. People came up to us afterwards to ask us about our songs, look at our gear, talk about our inspiration. We got another thirty names added to our mailing list. That is of course 90 at least in Keith's mathematical terms.

'Loved that slow song,' It was Esmay, a wonderful smile sliding across her exceptionally large face as she cornered me by the bar.

'Thank you, I wrote it a few weeks ago. It was the first time we have played it live.'

The song was called 'I Need You,' and was written in honour of my new found love, Annabella Jones.

'It's about a girl you love isn't it?'

I nodded obediently.

'Does she know?'

'Sorry?'

'That you need her, stupid.'

Esmay slapped me on the side of the arm sending a stinging sensation through my upper body.

'Yea, I think she does, although, perhaps she wishes I didn't.'

'I don't think so sexy!' Esmay smiled, kissed my cheek, and turned and walked away to find Keith and to find out about the rest of her life.

Later that evening, as I sat at a petrol station waiting for the RAC to arrive and take us home, I felt elated and yet stupid at the same time. We were waiting for the recovery vehicle because the Belmont had stopped for no apparent reason about half a mile away from the service station. Given the gear in the car, and the fact that Keith made me push because he had to steer the vehicle, and I use the term vehicle in the loosest terms, I was now well and truly knackered.

Part of me felt so cool that me and my band were making people listen, and these people loved what we were doing and wanted a piece of us. Part of me though felt like a fraud. I was just one of them, and in truth in many ways they were better than me. Here I was with my clever words and a band, showing the world what I could do and that I could break out of the mould. I looked at other people and thought 'I am making a difference' and deep down thought how clever that made me. These people, though, were real people with their own aspirations and I felt a new respect as I realised a crucial fact: It was me that had the need to be in a band, not them, me that had to write these songs, not them. It was me then, with the addiction, not them. I wasn't so clever after all.

'Keith?' I asked, as the cold continued to bite into my legs from the cloudless chilly night. He had called the RAC over an hour before but still they had not arrived. Apparently a lot of pregnant women and OAPs had decided to choose the same night to break down and as we were two healthy men, broken down on the side of a busy road, we were lower down on the list of priorities.

'Yes Bob?'

We had been silent for a few moments each lost in our thoughts of the night.

'What will we do if we make it?'

'Well, get a few hours kip and make sure we get into work el pronto I suppose.'

'No, stupid, what do we do if the band makes it?'

'Oh. I see.'

Keith paused, his brain turning over. If I listened hard enough I could hear it clicking. After all it probably was a machine.

'Well Bob, I guess we will just give it our best shot and see how it goes.'

'But do you think we'll like it?'

'Like it! We'll love it. Think about it, no more boring job! We will be free to do what we want to do. We will be recording our own stuff, playing it live, going all over the world.'

It was a mad, mad dream without any cap of reality. If it all worked out and it was all really that good it would be perfect. Why should we think about the bad things now, just think about the good things!

'But it doesn't seem fair.'

'What doesn't?'

'Well, look at Oasis. They have made it and then there are lots of other people like us striving for the dream and we might not get all that, you know, not make it.'

'But don't you see, Oasis made it and that means we are living the dream too.'

'We are?'

'We are. When we hear their songs on the radio we are hearing our songs on the radio, when we see them performing we are seeing a bit of ourselves performing too. Bob, bands like Oasis are an extension of the people.'

Good old Keith, ever the preacher, and me ever the converted. I smiled.

'That's great Keith. I hope we make it too. That would be great, really would be fantastic.'

We were quiet again, each thinking about what we had just said.

'Keith?'

'Yes Bob?'

'And what if we don't make it, won't we have let all the people who like us down by not building their dream?'

'No, I don't think so. Tonight they saw a Band that believed in what they played. Regardless of anything they will remember that.'

'I hope so. That would be good.'

I noticed in the mirror the distance flashing lights of a recovery van, or was it an ice cream van looking to cash in on the early morning trade at the side of motorways? I squinted my eyes to extend my sight just that little bit further but I squinted a little too much because they were closed and I could see nothing. Opening them a little I could make out the beautiful letters RAC. We were saved.

'Keith?'

Keith turned to me, his eyes full of life.

'Don't ever sell the Belmont will you, not ever.'

'No Bob, not ever.'

10

The next day I pulled my way into work having had only three hours sleep after our very eventful evening's entertainment. Everyone was their normal banker like self, thrilled to be dealing with those life changing problems like cancelling Direct Debits, amending Standing Orders, ordering foreign currency and opening new bank accounts. Dizzy and heights comes to mind. Most days, however, I considered the shallow depths of my job and was amazed at how I had fallen so badly into such an ill-fitting career. Still I was on a new wavelength now and with the Band taking off and the sexy Annabella awaiting my ever-widening charms, the world was a much brighter place. At 11.00am I excused myself from enquiries saying I had a very important errand to fulfil for the Chief Cashier Mr Wilde. Instead I cleverly slipped off down the banking hall and barricaded myself into the bottom interview room. Here I could happily hide for a few moments, and make my earth shattering impression on Annabella over the telephone.

As I looked at the number which I had so carefully copied on to paper prior to my sweat dripping performance at Stockwells the other night, I realised that I didn't even know if Annabella lived with Little Knob, or with other students, or on her own, or even with her parents. All I knew was that it was a Nottingham number because of the dialling code. I was fantastically unprepared then, but still tapped in the numbers on the phone; this was, after all, my destiny. After a few seconds the numbers connected and the phone started to ring. One ring, two rings, three rings. After sixteen rings, not that I was counting of course, I had just about decided to put the phone down. My heart was beating faster than if I had run round the whole of Mansfield 212 times with a washing machine strapped to my back. Grumpiness had added to this uncomfortable feeling and I considered my destiny was to not get through when, miracle of miracles, it was picked up.

'Hello.'

It was a man's voice, short of politeness and a little shrill I noticed, and my heart dropped. Annabella must live with Little Knob and he was there with her and her things. The only minor consolation was the wonderful, effeminate and high-pitched voice that he was using. I had not expected this wonderful twist, and where I would normally have replaced the receiver without saying another word, I decided to talk to the fellow.

'Yes, hello. My name is Anthony. You don't know me, we haven't met, but I know Annabella very well indeed.'

'How nice for you. So do I.'

Excellent. The young man was obviously riled. I decided to go on and upset him still further,

'Well I'm glad you do. I don't know how long you've known her, but it seems to me like I have known her all my life.'

'Well I am delighted for you I'm sure. Judging from the sound of you I suspect Annabella is less so!'

He was being a smart arse. No doubt I deserved it! Never mind, I would carry on regardless,

'When I was talking to Annabella the other night, and we entered into the small wee hours, as we often do, I just thought to myself, am I not the luckiest man in the world to be here with this beautiful woman.'

'How nice for you. In fact how nice for you both. Now is there any point to your call or can I go now and carry on with my day?'

I was getting no wild or desperate response from Little Knob. Perhaps it was his way to give off an air of not caring, laissez faire and all that. Well he wasn't going to put me off. I had come too far now and I was intent on staying in the driving seat. I went on,

'Yes, indeed, of course there is a point. With us not talking before, I just thought it important to let you know how well I know Annabella and indeed how I got her number.'

'Right…I see… How did you get her number?'

He had bitten. Happy miracle of miracles!

'Well, it was as she gazed into my eyes and stroked the inside of my muscular legs, I got the feeling that she really liked me. It was then that she wrote her number on my strong manly thigh, the ones I was just talking about, and she asked me to call. So hence here I am! So how do you feel about that eh?' I was done. Delivery of our love that technically was still unrequited but no need for Little Knob to know this.

'Er, whatever. You do sound somewhat weird so I suspect you are one of her arty friends on drugs or something. Have you been sniffing something?' he asked with a little irritation laced with minor concern in his voice.

'I have a little cold if that's what you mean,' I replied defensively.

'And you sound croaky,' he added, his voice sounding less manly by the second.

'Well, I was singing last night,' I replied and immediately wondered why I had let this piece of information out without adding the line that I was a rock star of the learner capacity.

'Well ask your Mother to make you comfortable and have a day off work dear'

Dear?! This conversation really wasn't going as I had intended. The door then opened to the office with Mr Wilde giving me a dead eye. I put my hand over the receiver and mouthed the words 'private call' and shot him a look back. I was getting braver with him as the band and my career had taken off in tandem and my confidence had grown.

'Is she there?' I asked abruptly.

'Erm, no she is not here. Who are you anyway?'

He sounded very upset now, which was, of course, superb. Obviously the thought of his beloved in another man's arms was too much for the little skunk. I guessed she perhaps wasn't out at all. He carried on,

'She's out every day, all day, at college. You seem to know so much about her so I suspect you knew she went to college, yes?'

'Oh yes indeed. I know so much. I am a man endowed with knowledge.'

'And little else I guess?'

Well really! The cheek of it all! Mind you I had been very forward and he was entitled to be a little upset. He went on,

'Well as you know then, she's doing her arty farty things and is rarely back here before tea time.'

Priceless. Little Knob obviously had real problems with her artistic nature saying something so crude and philistine fitting as 'arty farty.'

'Actually Callum, I think she is a very talented artist with a bright future ahead of her.'

'Well I'm glad you do Anthony. You are obviously a man, and if you don't mind I will use that term in a very loose sense, a man who respects Annabella and her art. I have to say your description of her writing something on your thigh was somewhat vomit inducing, as is your general demeanour on the phone. Using the name Callum explains a lot. I have similar views on that little toad too.'

Stunned silence. I had made myself, as I did so often and indeed did it so well, look a complete and utter twat.

'I see… So you would be?'

'Well that's not really any of your business, is it? I could be her secret lover, her possessive brother, her sugar daddy, her lesbian toy.'

All were possibilities I did not wish to consider at this point as I found myself sinking lower on my chair. 'Not' Little Knob went on,

'I could even be a burglar who you have so rudely interrupted whilst I try to strip the house bare. As a result of your general tone I am now a very upset burglar who will have to vent his frustration on the house in question by various bits of rude graffiti and unsightly deposits!'

'I see, fair point.'

I didn't see at all and I saw no fairness in the embarrassment I felt.

'WHO AM I?' he was shouting now. I thought about telling him rage was a sure way to high blood pressure and an early grave, but reasoned this would only add to his anger. He went on,

'I live here with Annabella. We are housemates. I regularly see her with and without clothes on, and I can confirm it is a pleasure to share those views and her company.'

'I see.'

I still did not see. If only I could. That particular naked view was the precise one I was aiming to get a look at myself. I did not like the tone this girlie voiced man was taking and I decided to bring our conversation to a much-needed ending.

'Well, erm, erm, and your name would be?'

'I am Leslie, Annabella's housemate. We rent the house together.'

Relief of relief's! Not Little Knob was in fact a girl with a deep voice. Of course she would and could see Annabella in the buff. They were both girls and so why not!

I smiled to myself safe with the realisation that Annabella did not live with Callum. I congratulated myself in knowing all along that Leslie's voice had sounded a little funny. Perhaps she was a drama student. Now was the time to put things right and so I offered the hand of friendship to Leslie over the phone.

'Oh I see, I didn't know Annabella shared her house with another girl or should I say, lady. I am so sorry for the confusion. How nice to get to talk to you Leslie. I do hope I have not caused any offence and that we can be good friends.'

'Leslie is a name for both genders.'

Leslie was being a little abrupt still. How strange when I was using such conciliatory tones. There was a short silence and then she added,

'I suggest you think on that, you little shit.'

With that the phone line went dead and, as I saw Mr Wilde poking his badly broken nose on the glass of the office, steam filling around his conker, I realised that Leslie was of course a man.

Later that evening Annabella called. She had thankfully found my telephone gaff very amusing, although she said that Leslie would need time, perhaps months or even years, to get over the offence.

'Next time you call I suggest you ring after 6 when I should be in. I don't think Leslie would speak to you at all.'

'Fair enough. I totally understand. I am so sorry.'

'Don't be silly. It's fine. I have been laughing all night since getting back.'

'Oh, OK. Glad to be of service!'

'And I understand Anthony that you have quite a vivid imagination.'

A little pang of terror arose as I thought for a moment she might be a mind reader and see all the depraved thoughts I had been having about her.

'Vivid?' I murmured, hoping some drunken bravado had not made its way back to her sweet ears.

'Yes, you know, the run down you gave Leslie on our friendship. I hadn't realised we had been getting on quite so well.'

In moments like these, which were happening far too often at the moment, I would wish for the ground to open up and a hole appear where I could just go and hide until all the bad things went away. Thankfully, being on the telephone, she could not see the fiery bright red colour that filled my face.

'Oh, that! Well, yes, quite. I really am so dreadfully sorry. I guess I was trying to be smart and ended up looking rather spectacularly stupid. Sorry again, I really am. Of late I don't know what's come over me.' I really didn't!

She laughed, a beautiful sweet laugh of a sexy woman who I was falling madly in love with. I didn't even know her and yet I already knew all I ever needed to know.

'Are we still friends?' I asked with my sweetest little voice.

'We might be.'

It was a cheeky playful voice. I was possibly home and maybe even dry.

'What about lovers?'

'Anthony!'

'Mad crazed lovers running around the world throwing our arms wide open and breathing in everything we see.'

'You are forward aren't you?'

'Only where you are concerned Annabella.'

'Now you're reverting to chat up lines but I don't mind because I like you. You are different.'

SHE LIKES ME. The most beautiful words in the world and I knew I was actually getting somewhere. There was hope!

Everyone told me I was different but I knew what most people where actually saying was, 'you are very strange and whilst I don't mind being your acquaintance, I think we will leave it at that.' Annabella was surely not saying that. Here was an open gate asking to be pushed well and truly wide open! She was saying I was different and she liked me. 'There is a God', my head screamed, 'there is a meaning to life, there is more to my day than the one sweet surprise of what toy may be in an un-opened cereal packet of a strange looking plastic figure or a special book on jungles or such like.'

'And I have a date for your sitting.'

Oh dear! How quick the journey changes from the rocket to the moon, to the depth charges to sink my submarine.

'How nice.'

'Someone has dropped out for next Wednesday's afternoon session, so I've been able to fit you in much sooner.'

Silence.

'Anthony, that will be alright won't it? I've already passed your name on but I can let them down if you want?'

I knew then that if Annabella asked me anything I would always end up doing it. Her voice meant I had no choice.

'Problem?' My voice was tight and I coughed to clear it, 'no problem, no absolutely not. I was just scratching an itch thing, which stopped me from replying immediately. The itch was on my neck, not somewhere like my bum, in case you were wondering.' I was rambling like a lunatic. 'Anyway, what time do you want me there and where am I coming to?'

'Well firstly thanks for the bum itch thing. A lovely picture!'

'No problem.'

'The session starts at 2, so I thought if you could meet me in the Student Union at say 1.30, we could have a quick drink, give you some Dutch courage to numb the fear factor, and then get on with it.'

'Fear factor. Hah! I laugh at fear factors!'

'So you don't need a drink then?'

'Well, if you insist. Perhaps just 6 or 7 vodkas and then lead me to the action!''

'Cool. Will you have time to have a drink after?' she asked, breezily.

Time! For a drink! Afterwards! The words wafted through my brain like a rich treble espresso coffee stimulating my senses. I would try and answer as calmly as possible,

'Of course I will, that would be great.'

'I thought I could buy dinner too, by way of a thank you, if that's OK with you?'

OK WITH ME! Dinner! This was getting better and better. Next stop bring me the honeymoon suite and the champagne on ice!

'Oh, sure. All the better. I really can't wait.'

'Wednesday then?' she said, clearly bringing the conversation to a close with me trying to reel her back in.

'Yea, Wednesday. Oh, and Annabella?'

'Yes sweetie.'

Sweetie! This girl was warming to me.

'It will be alright won't it?' I had to ask her if the modelling thing had disaster written all over it.

'Anthony we are drawing people all the time. Men, women, big, small. You are just, in the nicest way, another model. No one knows you. Don't worry. It'll be cool.'

'Right, OK. And how many are in the class?'

I was thinking perhaps 15 to 20, tops.

'Well its a double class on Wednesdays, so about 60 in the main studio so don't worry.'

Worry! Why worry. I was only going to take off all my clothes in front of 60 complete strangers who included the girl I was trying to impress. I would probably be so terrified that my willy would shrink up into my body and I would forever be known as the Mansfield eunuch. No doubt I would make the local press but for all the wrong reasons! Double, treble and bloody times a hundred drat!

We said our goodbyes with me being as upbeat as I could and I was left with the conflicting feelings of terror and satisfaction. Still taking a day off work had a nice ring to it, and the evening with Annabella had an even better feel to it. All I had to do between now and then was not think about the modelling session a single moment and then it would just creep up on me from behind, like a nasty little surprise that just happens and then is gone. It would be just like that jab thing I had in my first year at Comprehensive. I had gone to school that day in simple good faith, no idea that one of my letters to my parents had instructed them of the dreadful event that would enfold later that morning. Mum assured me later that she had told me and that I had taken the acceptance note back in to my form tutor and handed it in. My dad and brother just laughed uncontrollably. All I knew was that at 11 o'clock we were filed out of our classroom to join a long queue. The whispers began and before I knew it I was alone with a so-called nurse who asked me to just take off my school shirt. I thought she was a little forward and then, before you could say "what the fuck are you doing with that thing!' she had finished her dirty work and it was all over.

A short sharp pain was always for a reason. She would be my reason.

11

Thursday night and another practice waited. We had only lasted in Blubber Biscuits for a month because as much as anything our health had deteriorated. We had all quickly developed ridiculous and deep chesty coughs; although in Tricks' case it may be that he had always had this. We decided to find more professional and affluent surroundings. Magnet Studios were one of the 'in' studios in the area and we had managed to get a regular slot for every Thursday from eight to eleven p.m. Unlike Blubber Biscuits, Magnet did not smell of damp and was not accessed by having to walk several miles of stairs until you reached the practice studio.

On top of the damp, we had grown rather tired of Blubber Biscuits after several unwelcome occurrences. Firstly the studio had promised quality personal amplification equipment to be in all the rooms. In fact all there was was two extremely old mikes plugged into an even older PA. The damp in the rooms did not help the aged equipment work any better. On the third practice there I had suffered throughout the evening from an electrical shock from the mic. Every time my lips caught it I would be wounded, dreadfully I might add, by the pang of live electricity, which is never a good thing when you are trying to find yourself in a band practice. After two hours of singing with increasing terror, which meant I was getting further away from the mic and hence the band not being able to hear me, Keith and I went to find assistance. After hunting for five minutes for someone from the hidden staff to help us, all we had managed to find was a drugged up young student who didn't seem to have any understanding of where he was, never mind where he was working.

'The microphone is not working,' I said.

'He will be in later,' the youth replied.

'Who will be in later?' Keith asked.

'The man who knows what to do with the gear!' responded the young man, looking at me like I was stupid.

Keith and I exchanged glances. Clearly we would have to take matters into our own hands. I looked our host for the night straight in the eye hoping my directness would bring him to his senses and out of the floating haze we had found him in.

'Where do you keep the microphones?' I asked. It was simple question yet one that seemed to send him into a bout of hilarity as he whispered to himself something or other. We were getting nowhere.

Keith decided to look in the cupboard in the office for himself and sure enough found some spare microphones of differing quality. We left the muttering student type to his own devices, and returned to the rehearsal room to find Steve and Tricks smoking. They both seemed incredibly chilled and I thought how nice it was that they were so relaxed with one another, after all they had not known each for that long. It was almost enough to make me want to start smoking, particularly the brand they must have been using because it was so sweet and unlike the stuff Steve normally smoked.

Keith set everything up and asked me to try again. As I put my lips up to the microphone I was reminded of being on school camp at the age of 10. I had seen, possibly for the first time, an electric cattle fence, and I only understood what it did by touching it. It hurt. A lot! I was having exactly the same nervous twitch as I very tentatively went up to the new mic, hoping against hope that it wouldn't hurt this time. Once again I was sadly disappointed as the electric pang sent a pain through my head.

'I have a sparkling idea!' declared Keith in that unmistakable teacher's voice that he had always mastered so well, 'we can fasten a cloth over the mic and you won't feel the shock.

Magically he produced said two cloth from his massive kit bag.

'What would you be using this for normally?' I grinned at him awaiting the reply.

'Well you never know when something might need dusting,' he smiled back. He knew he was rather like a mad hatter but the amusement of it kept him and all of us very amused indeed. He went ahead setting up the anti-electric shock security blanket. Perhaps he could patent this for all crap rehearsal studios in the country. He could make a fortune! I turned to Steve expecting to see him smiling at Keith. Instead I saw he was now in a lateral position on the floor. He was inhaling from his cigarette in a long slow manner, and then gently blowing the smoke into the air in little puffs of cloud. In fact the room was getting quite smoky and I was feeling a little light headed myself.

'Steve, do you want to try your mic now?' Keith asked

'Yea man, that's a sure thing,' he said in a slow drawl. He was not only getting on so well with Tricks, but he was even beginning to sound like him.

Remarkably the cloths worked, and we got on with our practice, but the warning signs that the studio was not the professional unit we had been led to believe, were plainly there.

Three weeks later, and the drugs raid that led to our arrest confirmed my suspicions that it was not only us that found the studio a little shifty. We were all released without charge, although Steve and Tricks were both given warnings about smoking. I thought it was good that the police took the dangers of smoking so seriously, after all not only could it kill you, but it could also be a real fire hazard in small-enclosed spaces. Steve told me afterwards that this was why they had been cautioned because, as the police had told them, if they had dropped one cigarette by accident the whole place could have gone up. Steve told me he had learnt a valuable lesson that night, and one that he would probably never forget.

The studio was temporarily closed down and, thankfully, we fell on our feet with Magnet. It was run by a chap called Rob who had the air of a man who had been there and done that, 'that' being anything you cared to think about. He was a very entertaining man and we would spend at least forty-five minutes each week hanging out with him. He was, by profession, a drummer, and had decided to start his own studio after experiencing so many disappointments in other studios in and around the area when he had been in bands. He was still only in his mid thirties but had decided that whilst being a world famous musician may have passed him by, he could still set something up that would help others. What a man.

The studio boasted four very well equipped rooms with not only all the quality PA equipment you could need but also all the musical equipment you could need to. This suited Tricks down to the ground as he could hire drums and not have to carry his own kit in and out of the studio for every practice.

This Thursday we were working on a new song called 'I think it's all over.' I had written it because it seemed to me that so many relationships begin to break down simply because people are not right for each other and that shouldn't really be a problem. To my simple little mind if X and Y, or A and B if you will, were not seeing eye to eye it would mostly not be because X, or A, were doing anything particularly bad. I reasoned that relationships often began because people were attracted to one another. After getting to know each other, you might realise that the other person was a nut case or some other small issue and a need for hiding would be required. No problem you would think and yet breaking up was hardly ever a simple step. This was my clarion call for people to see life more simply. A small drop in the ocean I hear you say, but as my Uncle Stuart used to say, without the drop where is the goal?

The song was my simple little effort to put some perspective into the problem.

'It's not about looking, it's not about cookin' (the live version
    had fuckin')
It's not about Friday night
It's not about you then it's not about me, so let's not have a
    fight.
And you say what you want, but not what you mean
And the truth lies in between
I wish I could say that we'll make it some day but that's not
    quite what I mean
And I think it's all over
I think it's all gone away
I think it's all over, gone away
Don't you ask yourself the question, don't you see the reason
    why

We're so different and you know it, and you only stop and cry
And I'm holding out my honesty, you're sticking out your pride
When the truth is lying naked and to me it's no surprise
And I think it's all over
I think it's all gone away
I think it's all over, gone away

I was finding writing the songs for the band remarkably easy. Having started writing, this had led to a release of something from within me and now I couldn't stop. Half of my songs were pants but the other half had something. I knew if the band liked them then we could do something really positive with them. Steve would take my simple tune and add to it the Wonder sound, his own little magic that he created with his guitar. In effect he would make what was a naked sound from my stuttering guitar playing, into a full sound that made the song complete. Being in this band was a sum of its parts. We needed each other.

We had been working on the song for after about an hour when Keith suggested he and Tricks have half an hour just playing together to get the back line tight. We left them to it and Steve and I went in to the lounge to chill. We got a beer each from the fridge handing over our cash to Rob who was on the phone with his feet nonchalantly stretched out on the desk in front of him, and then sat down on two well-worn sofas away from a rather strange looking band that were also taking a break. They all looked like Iggy Pop and played like him too.

'Chloe alright?' I enquired.

'Marvellous.'

'Cat OK?'

'Super.'

'House?'

'Steady.'

'Car?'

'Sound.'

'Willy?'

'Asleep.'

We both nodded in agreement as though we had just muttered some ancient immortal code. Perhaps we had.

'Any news on your modelling session Anthony?' Steve asked the question with the broadest grin that told me he knew full well that tomorrow was my D-Day.

'Well, as I suspect you know full well, tomorrow is my date with the artists and boy what a treat they have in store for them.'

'Exactly. Are you OK about it then?'

'OK? Of course not! I'm shit scared! I've been trying to avoid thinking about it. Every time the thoughts start to rise inside my head I try and to imagine it's a film and I have yet to watch it and must not think about it as it will spoil the surprise!'

'So, it's driving you mad then?'

'Basically, and in a nutshell, I'm truly terrified! Still, at least I have a clear reason for my madness.'

'Ah, the lovely, soon to be whisked off her feet in a flurry of passion, Annabella.'

'You're confident then?' I asked him, keen to swoop on his positive words.

'Of course!' he added, then seeing my unease added 'and you're not?'

'Well I don't know what to think. It's another subject I try to dream away. I mean for all I know she might be in love with Callum.'

'Or falling in love with you, just like me.'

'You mean you're only just falling in love with me?'

'Mate, the point I am making is that every day is a fresh day to fall in love with you again and again.'

'Fair point.'

'Fair point indeed.'

We both smiled, lost in our little world of strange and wondrous conversation.

After a while Steve asked,

'Do you think the students canvasses will be big enough to get all of you on?'

'Oh yes, just. I'm not planning on the General being enlarged so hopefully they will have just about enough room.'

'And what about your hairy chest?'

'My hairy chest?'

'Yes. Well every one knows that models are normally smooth, totally smooth and covered in baby oil.'

'It's not a porn movie I'm starring in Steve, just a drawing session, all quite innocent.'

'Well I know, but as much as I know you are proud of your hairy chest, perhaps the smooth approach will be more acceptable.'

Steve was actually being serious, which was a little worrying. The thought had already crossed my mind that for some girls a hairy chest is not the preferred option. Still it was only a drawing session and I assumed that the majority of their models were hardly the types to get carried away with their looks. This was a student modelling session and not a GQ photo shoot! I had tried to not get into the detail and was trying to approach this whole thing with the view that I just needed to grin and bear it (bare it all in fact), and then get on with my life. Steve carried on,

'You know I bet the majority of their models are the young and beautiful, you know beautiful young nubile student bodies, all of them looking to get a little extra cash to add to their paltry grants, and in the process get themselves noticed.'

'Don't be silly. Surely not?'

'No really! This sort of thing is for people to show off.'

'How do you know?' I asked, fear in my voice now.

'Well it's obvious. What about the likes of Annabella's boyfriend? I bet he's modelled just to show off, perhaps even just to get the ladies going, and I bet you he's as smooth as an apple.'

My heart dropped. What if Steve was right? I didn't have a problem with my body, in fact I thought I was OK, but up against the likes of Callum, who was surely a walking heart throb, well I had already felt inadequate and now felt quite the disaster.

'Well if you're trying to be encouraging Steve, believe you me you are not.'

'You agreed to do it you crazy git.'

'I know.'

'Nobody forced you.'

'Once again, I know!'

'You can still back out.'

'I can't. I could not let Annabella down. Besides this is my one big chance to make a play for her. She's promised to take me for dinner afterwards!'

'And if this is a minor or even major disaster do you think you will feel like dinner?'

'Well, perhaps. That's a chance I am prepared to take.'

We paused, Steve smiling at my predicament, and me considering what he had said.

'What's wrong with my body anyway?'

I had posed the question a little too loudly and the Iggy characters all looked our way. They had probably closeted us all as raving homosexuals anyway and this outburst would have simply confirmed their suspicions.

'Nothing. I think you're perfectly lovely,' replied Steve, purposely extra loudly for comic effect. The comedy was lost on our audience.

'Well then?'

'I just think that if you insist on modelling then perhaps you should shed the hairy chest for the occasion.'

I considered his argument and agreed.

'I'll shave it off.'

'You can't do that.'

'Why not?'

'It'll be spiky.'

'Straightaway?'

'Well no, but by the time you and Annabella are alone.'

His eyes twinkled and his grin worked its way around the side of his head. He went on,

'Although I accept, as you do, that this is unlikely! However, what about an unsightly shaving rash?'

'Shaving rash?'

'Yea, don't you remember what your chin looked like the first time you shaved it? I bet it was like the floor of an abattoir.'

'I see. Of course you're right. Well what's to be done?'

'Waxing.'

'Waxing!' I had almost screamed my response. Thankfully the Iggy types were making their way into their rehearsal room, although they still had time to shoot me rather disdainful looks and one pointed at me and laughed.

'Yes, it's easy. Chloe's friend Danniel has it done all the time and he says its fine.'

Danniel was one of Chloe's friends and a jolly nice chap. He owned and ran a beauty place in Nottingham. Surely he would not lie about such a thing.

'Oh. I always thought that would kill.'

'Well it would but apparently they put some sort of wax on, hence the name waxing, and this has the dual purpose, I believe, of dulling the nerve ends on the skin so that you hardly feel a thing, as well as getting the hairs ready to come off easily.'

'You know far too much about this Steve.'

'Too much time listening to Chloe and Danniel rattle on I'm afraid. Apparently, according to Danniel, the waxing lasts for a few weeks before any hairs begin to show again. Chloe goes to his salon to have her legs done. She has done for ages and they are super smooth afterwards with no unsightly rash!'

'Really?'

'Really.'

'And you are sure about the limited pain?'

'Sure.'

'Positive?'

'Yes matie, absolutely. Why would Chloe go if it hurt that much?'

'Oh, right. Makes sense. Do you think he could squeeze me in tomorrow morning prior to the unveiling to end all unveilings?'

'Ring him, I know his number.'

And so I did. I used Rob's pay phone to the side of his office so as not to be overheard for obvious credibility reasons and rang Danniel. The phone rang three times and then the unmistakable camp voice of the very pleasant salon owner answered.

'Hello Danniel, it's Anthony, Steve's friend.'

I had known Danniel for a few years now, seeing him down town drinking or at various parties. I explained the situation and Danniel said he would be thrilled to sort me out in the morning at around 10.

'How long will we take do you think?' I asked nervously anticipating about 10 minutes maximum.

'Oh only about 30 minutes or so.'

'Great!' I lied, trying to think how he could possibly fill 30 minutes doing something so simple. 'Steve assures me it won't hurt.'

'Well of course Steve has never had it done, but it won't hurt for long.'

'For long?' The phrase bothered me.

'No pain no gain Anthony.'

'Right.'

'Ten in the morning then?'

'Right.'

And so there it was, my appointment with Satan.

12

The day started well. I had phoned in sick and thankfully Mr Wilde had not been available to take the call. In his senior position it was his privileged place to take all the calls from staff needing to take the day off due to illness. The experience was not a pleasant one and many a home relationship suffered because no one in the household wanted the job of phoning in and having to explain matters to the ogre that was Mr Wilde.

The day before I had already done the groundwork in preparation for my grand illness deceit. All day I had been letting it be known that I was feeling increasingly nauseous. I even refused to eat the sandwiches that my mother had so lovingly made for my lunch, and instead made it clear all I needed was some fresh air to try and blow my poorly tummy away. Thirty minutes later, and the visit to the upstairs Co-op Café and its lovely dinner safely deposited inside me, I returned to work in a worse state than ever. Mr Wilde had simply offered me a dirty look as he saw Sylvia, one of the older and more reliable cashiers, sitting me down behind the chief cashier screen and wafting cooling air on to my sweaty brow with a brochure made into a temporary fan. Amusingly the brochure she had chosen was on income protection against long-term illness, which given my projected health was clearly where I was going! At many people's request I had reluctantly left work just after 4 so as to avoid passing on the illness. How nice of everyone concerned! I had spent my extra hour at home messing around on my guitar all at the bank's expense.

So the next day I left the message that my stomach was again playing up and that my mother thought it best to stay in bed. Happily the Wilde man was in a meeting so I told Eileen, Mr Wilde's unfortunate right hand woman, that I would therefore be tucked up all day and not contactable as everyone in the house was going out and of course I would be unable to get to the phone once settled in bed. Eileen, who had quite a soft spot for me, told me not to worry about a thing and to take all the days off I needed. I assured her that I should be back the next day as all I was really concerned with was being the team member I strived to be everyday. Eileen was touched by my strong work ethic, but she told me in no uncertain terms not to rush back as it is so important to give your body time to rest. Apparently her sister had experienced a similar bug back in the middle ages and she had made the classic mistake of rushing back. As a result the world had ended and only restarted when her sister had at last recovered after a trip to the seaside. 'Had I considered a trip to the coast?' she had asked in a voice laced with deep concern. I told her I would consider the idea if this illness did not lift and with that thanked her and made my goodbyes. Convinced then that I should in fact take the week off, if not the whole year, I replaced the phone on the handset with a huge grin on my face and left my house for Nottingham.

I was of course a little concerned about the modelling session, but I felt comfortable with the whole thing being a giggle experience to share with the boys for many years to come. I reasoned that Annabella had been right when she said it would look good on the band CV. I could think of no other current rock star that was renowned as a naked artists' model and consequently kept running through the sort of things I would say about my modelling days in the many future interviews to come. I even thought about the poses I could hold during future magazine shoots, and the locations across the world that I could insist on going to before de-robing myself again and again. Skegness the following weekend could be my first shoot…

First though was the 'minor' irritation of a chest wax. I arrived at Danniel's salon, 'The Body', at ten minutes to ten and parked just a little down the road. I didn't want anyone seeing my car outside a beauty salon. Mind you I wondered if this was the sort of place and thing the band would have to get used to as we toured the world and were pampered by make up and hair consultants for shoot after interview after filming after tour. I was lost in my band world quite a lot at the moment and clearly had too much time on my hands!

Danniel met me as soon as I arrived and made me a coffee. Thankfully the place was quiet with just a few people in having their hair done. The salon was one of those very trendy affairs with well thought through lighting and glass bricks and Perspex everywhere.

'Nice place,' I offered.

'Thank you,' Danniel replied, 'I'm very proud of it.'

I was relieved when Danniel told me the waxing suite was upstairs in the beauty parlour, not that I had envisaged being 'done' in the middle of the hairdressers, but none the less it was a comfort to think I was away from the main entrance.

Danniel insisted I went up the stairs first and I couldn't help but feel the intense eyes that followed my bottom.

'Will you be doing the waxing yourself Danniel?' I asked, hoping that I didn't have to undress in front of him, whilst at the same time looking forward to telling Steve and Keith that I had done exactly that.

'No, not me Anthony, I'm far too squeamish for that! I leave that sort of thing to my staff. I really don't like to see people's eyes water.'

Mmm. It was pain that he had mentioned last night, and now he was talking about eyes watering this morning. I thought about backing out but then remembered all Steve and I had talked about and how easy he had made it all sound. Besides if Chloe could come and have her legs done then surely I could come and have my chest waxed. After all there wasn't too much of the old chest fluff to move anyway. It would be fine!

We arrived in the beauty parlour, which was also quiet. I had obviously picked the right time to come and be 'done.' Danniel introduced me to one of his staff called Rupert and told me he would be doing the necessary. How nice. I noticed Rupert gazing longingly at Danniel and I wondered if they were lovers.

Rupert asked me to follow him, and the three of us made our way down to a side room. I couldn't help but feel that the beauty parlour was a cross between a very smart looking private hospital, with its clean and clinical nature pervading throughout, mixed with a hammer house of horrors type of place with its very stark look suggesting that there was something sinister hiding beneath the exterior. Perhaps this was a room where the boys took people and turned them into something else such as a wild beast. I wondered what Rupert would turn me into given half a chance.

The room we were now in was apparently, and pleasantly I felt, used specifically for waxing. This reminded me of the castles I had visited where there were very specific rooms set aside for quite specific tortures. This room, decorated in a lime green colour with large canvassed paintings taking up the majority of the windowless walls, had a cushioned table covered in clean white towels in the middle and at the side of this, looking oh so innocent, a steel trolley on wheels with a brightly shining deep stainless steel container on top. This seemed to be giving off a little steam and a sweet smell. I assumed it was the soothing wax that would help me get through the procedure.

The three of us exchanged pleasantries whilst I finished off my coffee, which I was, of course, trying to spin out to be allowable for an entry for the Guinness Book of Records in being the longest time ever taken to drink a cup of coffee. I couldn't help but begin to feel a faint dread banging in my chest. 'No turning back now,' I repeated in my head over and over again.

The coffee inevitably and eventually drained out of my cup and down my throat, and with that bang went the excuse I had been holding on to for not getting on with things. Rupert straightaway asked me, no told me, to take off my shirt and loosen my trousers. For a moment I thought about Steve's smiling face and a hidden camera that must be filming the whole event. Clearly this was all, in fact, a practical joke and soon I would be re-living the whole experience with millions on a Saturday night programme entitled 'This man is very silly.' I again reasoned that I had come this far and there really was no turning back now. I looked to Danniel with a slightly concerned look, and he simply smiled back at me and said,

'Now come on Anthony, don't be shy.'

I smiled and replied,

'Why would I be shy with you Danniel? I've always wanted to strip off for you.'

As Danniel's big grin smiled at me with, I felt, a new and fresh regard, I took off my shirt and turned to hang it up on the coat hangers provided in the corner of the room. Danniel, curiosity fulfilled, and perhaps fulfilled too quickly I felt, turned to go.

'I'll leave you two to get on then and see you in a little while Anthony, OK?'

'Yes, fine thanks. Thank you for squeezing me in Danniel.'

Danniel smiled at me and gave me a look that I was not used to receiving from a male.

'It would be my pleasure Anthony.'

I was torn between feeling a little weird in being seduced by a man, to being proud in the fact that he had massaged my ego. Danniel left and Rupert asked me, rather curtly I felt, to lie down on the treatment bed. I dutifully obeyed and stretched out on top of the rather uncomfortable slab that was to be my immediate destiny.

'Have you known Danniel long?' he almost demanded.

'Oh yes, ages really. He's a good friend of Steve, my best mate.'

'And is he gay?'

I laughed far too loud and far too quickly, and then immediately realised the grave insult I had unwittingly created. I tried to splutter out a response that would cover up my embarrassment.

'He, and I, are not gay, but we have gay friends, all of whom we like, although not physically. Not that I don't find any of them attractive, I mean, I do, but not in an 'I'd like to get your clothes off' way which, incidentally, is fine by me. Although not with me, but by me, in as much as I think it's cool! '

'I see.' Clearly he did not.

I went on,

'Having said all that, perhaps Steve is gay and he's not told me?'

'Oh you'd know, just like you noticed Danniel shooting you that look as he left. He's got a boyfriend already you know.'

'And is that you?' I asked in a way to build him up and give him major kudos even if it was not him. In fact this was another major clanger and now Rupert didn't even answer me. Obviously he was not Danniel's boyfriend and this was not something he would have wanted me to notice or assume. He finished stirring the wax potion, which he was to utilise on my bared chest.

'Well Anthony,' he put far too much emphasis on my name for my liking, 'have you had a wax done before?'

'Never.'

'And do you know what it entails?'

'Well I believe you put the wax on my chest and it numbs the area somewhat. Then you put some paper on it and whip it off with the hairs attached. It sounds like it must be painful doesn't it?'

'It is,' he said with a wicked grin on his face. 'Numbs the pain…' he muttered with a little high-pitched giggle.

Oh dear.

'Is it very painful?'

Rupert looked in my eyes,

'Not for long, relatively speaking of course.'

'Relative to?' I asked, hopefully

'Amputation,' he replied, without any hint of humour in his ever increasing, harrowing voice.

Oh dear, oh dear, oh dear! Alarm bells rang louder than the bells ringing in a bell tower with you physically having your head taped to the biggest bell. Now was the time to make my excuses and run, run like I have never run before. I closed my eyes and swallowed deeply. I was aware that my pulse was racing and sweat was beginning to pour from all sorts of regions. This was my moment of truth and I would just have to bear it like a man. This, of course, was the problem. I was a man.

Rupert spread a little wax on the lower part of my chest. It was quite hot and made me jump a little.

'Now just relax. If you tense up it will make the whole thing a lot harder. There's not too much hair here and it shouldn't take me more than ten to fifteen minutes OK?' I sensed he was being kind to me, which was also a worry.

'Fine,' I smiled encouragingly as though I didn't have a care in the world. I was generally good at giving the right impression even if I didn't actually have a clue; after all I'd made a career out of this at the bank to date. In this case I really did not have a clue at all. Still Rupert had referred to only a little hair, and whilst he had mentioned ten to fifteen tortuous minutes, my confidence began to build. How bad, after all, could it be?

Rupert spread a strip of waxing paper out on the already applied wax and smoothed it out flat, rather like you might smooth down a piece of sellotape across the back of an important envelope that you didn't want to come accidentally undone.

And then it happened. Without warning and in one swift movement, he whipped it off.

I don't think in my life I had ever known such immediate pain. It was rather like the afore mentioned time I had the TB jab at school and the nurse had said 'It won't hurt.' Of course it did. It killed. The difference here was that each hair that was pulled involuntarily out was equivalent to one of those needles, with the pain being amplified accordingly. I opened my mouth to scream but no noise would come. I could not tell you whether this was because of embarrassment, or because my vocal chords were too scared themselves to allow a noise to come out in case their time was to come.

Rupert carried on regardless, rhythmically applying more wax and pushing another strip down. Within seconds it was pulled off and again I grimaced in agony, holding my eyes tightly shut and with my hands gripping for grim death the side of the couch.

Rupert began whistling 'The Power of Love.'

'Everything alright?' he asked in angelic tones that failed miserably to hide the delight he was undoubtedly having in introducing me to medieval torture.

'Yes,' I spitted out through gritted teeth.

'Much more to do?' I enquired.

'Oh yes, still quite a lot to do,' Rupert replied, in the most upbeat voice he had used the whole time I had been with him.

'Super,' I hissed.

As each strip was pulled away, my clammy hands gripping on to the sides of the table for dear life, I counted the number of times I would physically have to hit Steve. Then I counted the number of days after that I would refuse to talk to him. Then I counted the number of times I would refer to him in live gigs as 'Please give up your appreciation of Steve, our lead guitarist, who incidentally is openly frank about his cross dressing and would be thrilled to talk to any of you about it after the gig.'

Eventually Rupert mercifully informed me that it was all done and that all that was left was for him to smooth on some cream to take the soreness away.

'You have come up rather red Anthony, but I must say it is nice to see this well kept chest all out in the open.'

I opened my eyes, which had remained tightly shut throughout the proceedings. I looked down at Rupert's handiwork to see all my hairs gone and replaced, instead, with red stripes. These were not just little bits of red gently glowing through my skin, but rather a glowing of the beacon variety that a lost at sea sailor could use to attract attention. This was not quite the fetching look I had been aiming for, and of course not the look I had wanted to show to my soon to be student admirers.

'When will the redness go?' I enquired hopefully.

'In its deep brightness? Well, in about an hour or so.'

'Or so?'

'Well with you being a virgin wax client, it may take a little longer.'

I didn't like the use of the word 'virgin,' coupled with the longing way he looked me up and down as he said it.

'I shouldn't worry sweetie,' he added, 'it should go off soon.'

'Good' I replied without believing him.

'Though it will remain red for some time. Just not as red. It's normal. Don't worry! You will be pleased when you look tomorrow.'

'LOOK TOMORROW!!!' I screamed in my head whilst letting the words actually drip out in a mournful way.

'Seriously Anthony, from a distance you will look grand by lunch. I will apply a soothing cream now and this helps hugely. It's rather miraculous really. Let nature just take its course.'

As he applied the soothing cream he took far too long a reasonable time in smoothing his hands over my chest, saying nothing as he did so, though I noticed his eyes were closed and he had a little cheeky smile on his lips. In return I could not find words to say either. Miraculously after a while the soothing cream did begin to dull the searing pain and I began to relax from the hyper sense of tension I had gotten myself into and enjoy the massage biting into the pain, albeit that

169

it was being administered by a man who had only minutes earlier been thrilled to see me in said pain. After a few minutes, Rupert's smoothing hands began to rub in cream far lower than was necessary. Thankfully I had not been sent to sleep by the stinging sensations radiating themselves like super fine laser guns on my chest. The cream was good, but not that good! Realising Rupert's intentions were probably far from pure I jumped up off the table muttering,

'Thank you Rupert, most kind I am sure!' I gave him my Paddington hard stare look that told him taking liberties was not something I approved of, 'seriously, thank you very much for your help. It has been an experience I shall never forget.'

'Me neither,' he replied, grinning. 'Are you sure you don't want the cream rubbing in a little bit more? You seemed to be quite enjoying the effect.'

'No, thank you for asking. Kind offer I'm sure. I'm fine, just fine and dandy.' I was getting dressed very quickly indeed. I fastened my shirt up to the neck and tucked it into my trousers by way of showing my newfound admirer that my chest was now off limits. I was immediately struck by the heat radiating under my shirt and had to undo the top three buttons and pull the shirt out. He was loving this. Donkey!

He opened the door for me and walked with me to the counter for payment.

'Thank you for calling Anthony. That will be £35 please'

£35 for torture.

'Is that all?' I asked with as much sarcasm as I could push through the pain that was again shouting at me from my chest. Rupert just looked back at me and smiled an annoyingly large smile. He had enjoyed himself immensely.

I handed over my hard earned cash and said,

'I suppose that some people might pay good money for that as enjoyment?'

'I suppose they might.'

'Would you like our bonus card for points back on future visits? He asked me in a highly charged sarcastic voice.

'I shall pass on that thank you. No offence.'

'None taken.'

My card was handed back.

'Well Rupert, thank you for a most warming experience. I shall remember it, as I shall you, forever.'

'You are welcome. Any friend of Danniel's is a friend of mine. Have a nice day and come back soon!'

Have a nice day! Who did he think he was? In my books he was a sadist. Pure and simple.

I wandered down the stairs to be met by Danniel.

'Everything go well Anthony?'

'Fine thank you Danniel' I lied, again, 'No worries at all. It was quite satisfactory. Almost a pleasure. I shall look forward to coming back soon,' I trotted out, trying my best to be as upbeat as I could and mask the uncomfortable now nuclear heat that seemed to be coming from my chest area.

Danniel was very pleased with my response and gave me a farewell hug that pressed far too hard on to my sore chest, not to mention my groin. I said my goodbyes and left to find the nearest sports shop. After buying some swimming shorts I got back to my car and drove to the nearest public swimming baths where I lay in the larger and cooler pool for a full hour to soothe my aching chest. Never has the word bliss been created for a more perfect moment.

One hour later and with my chest was a much less shade of red than it had been. I had also taken the trouble of calling in to a chemist and had applied some fake tan. Having never done this before I was faced with the dilemma of how much to apply. Knowing my predicament of not wanting to look like a robin, I decided a liberal application was the order of the day. Also, I realised that if only my chest looked brown I would look silly. Therefore I used the whole tube on any parts of my body I could reach including, of course, my face. By the end of the exercise my hands looked like I had been making chocolate Easter eggs by shaping them myself! The tub had promised that the tan cream would fade into a natural look within a few hours and so, confident in the instructions, I made my way to my car to get to the modelling session.

I parked my chariot in the car park for visitors having been turned away from the student car park by a weedy looking gentleman who was using his position of car park attendant as a way of making up for his small and inadequate frame. He had watched me pull in to the car park, watched me park in a space that was easy to find, given that half of the car park was empty, and watched me get out of the car and lock it up. As I had strode manfully away from the car on a mission with destiny I was hailed by a rather squeaky loud pitched voice,

'Excuse me sir!'

I turned to look for the person who owned the squeak only for him to sneak up on me from behind with a cunning stealth that would have been well received in the SAS. He was wearing with great pride his local authority car park attendant attire that was in a rather tasteful green in honour, I think you will find, of that great local legend Robin Hood.

'You can't park that there sir!' he said with both clear assertiveness and authority. He exercised his little power base well.

I turned to look in the direction he was pointing, which he was doing whilst holding a wonderfully bemused expression that would have suited Neville Chamberlain when he came back from Hitler's Germany to tell us Mr H was actually quite a nice fellow who meant no harm after all.

'Park what?'

'Your car sir,' he had just about reached me, 'you cannot, under any circumstances, park your car there.'

'Oh, my car! I see,' I replied, with far too much sarcasm in my voice.

He was now stood directly in front of me, purposely blocking my path from out of the car park.

'I suggest you remove it immediately before I have to take matters further.'

'And that would mean?'

'A car lock, a tow away, and a £100 fine.'

'I see.' He really had delivered this last line with an authority that the Sheriff of Nottingham would have been proud of. Incidentally this position is still in existence today, but when referring to this little chap sounding like the Sheriff I am of course referring to the Sheriff of old that proved such a thorn in the side of our dear Robin Hood.

I decided to use the voice of reason in an effort to get round the little fellow.

'Look, I am visiting the art department whereupon I will be doing a spot of modelling for the students there.'

The man laughed. I let that go. I went on,

'I am already a little late for my appointment…' (I wasn't at all) '…and I really do not want to have to tell the Head of the Department who, incidentally, is a personal friend and on the car parking committee…' (total fabrication of course) '… that it was you that made me late.'

I sensed my argument had won the day. The fellow's face had drained of colour and I felt the killer card played had been the one about the car parks committee.

He looked me up and down and then began to laugh, again!

'I've heard some excuses in my time.'

'Excuses?' I lamely said.

'Yes, excuses, but I think this one about takes the biscuit. Do you know what I think?'

'Erm, no.'

'I think you are a little late for an appointment of some sort.'

'Really?' I offered.

'Yes, really. As for you doing a spot of modelling I am sure they are not that desperate.'

'Well really!' I said with feeling. The man had insulted my name and my looks. 'If that's the attitude you are going to take I will gladly move my car from your smelly little car park.'

'Yes, you do that young man!'

I began to stride off to my car as the man held his position, a big powerful winning grin filling his fat spot filled face, not that he had any spots but in my mind's eye I was now placing them all over him.

'And don't think you've heard the last of this' I shouted, tripping on a kerb as I had turned to shout to him. Picking myself up I heard his laughter echoing around the car park. I decided to let him have his day and that it was now best to concentrate on getting to my car in one piece without tripping again or walking in to something.

Ten minutes later I eventually parked in the rammed visitor's section of the car park and, now running a few minutes late, ran around to the student bar. Annabella was there along with what seemed like six million friends. She saw me come through the door and walked towards me. We met half way between the door and the bar and she put her arms around me and kissed my cheek. She then held me at arm's length and looked closely at me,

'Are you wearing fake tan?' she asked with amusement in her voice.

'Erm, yes, a little,' I said, embarrassment spreading through my whole body but especially in my face where it buzzed like an 'on air' light. 'I thought I should wear something a little exotic for the occasion,' I said, my voice trailing out like a lost schoolboy.

'Exotic! Well you do look a little Egyptian, our very own Anthony of Arabia.'

She was laughing as she said this so I decided to try and laugh along whilst sobbing inconsolably inside whilst muttering 'I've never used the damned stuff before.' She saw my eyes and leaned over to me and whispered,

'It's OK Anthony, you look lovely. It's all fine.'

I smiled and my worries and upsets moved to the back of my mind as Annabella led me to her group of friends and introduced me,

'This is Anthony everybody, our nude model for the afternoon session, and fantastic lead singer of the soon to be world famous pop group Wide Eyed Wonder.'

After several nice to meet you's I downed the pint of Guinness and the two shots of whisky that were already waiting for me. Rather too soon the clock ticked around to ten minutes to two and Annabella led me to the studio. I was feeling pretty buoyant at this point fuelled with me having looked at Annabella in great detail and the alcohol. We got to the room and she showed me where I would stand or sit or lie down, and explained how I simply needed to change my pose when asked to do so. Easy.

Students were already filing in to the studio and taking their places. Annabella saw my now worried expression as I looked at the people coming in.

'Just forget about the people and think about the buzz.'

'OK, forget about the people and think about the buzz,' I repeated like an obedient child.

'It will all be over before you know it,' she added.

'Right, before I know it.' I said, trying to sound as convinced as I could. 'Where do I change?'

'Just behind you.'

I turned to see a door that was open. It led through to a little room in the corner of the studio behind the platform area for the model.

'Get your clothes off and put on one of the robes.' Annabella instructed. 'When the lecturer is ready for you, which will be after about ten minutes of instructing the students, she will call you out. When she does, take off your robe and come on to the platform here. Unless she tells you otherwise assume a position of your choosing...' we both exchanged a naughty glance '... and straightaway we will all be drawing.'

'Right,' I reasoned in my head that I must be seriously mad.

'Don't worry. We only have a limited amount of time on each pose and don't have the time to admire the view.'

'Or otherwise?'

'There would of course be a stampede Anthony. Anyway I promise not to tell anyone if your willy is super teeny.'

She laughed cheekily and kissed my cheek, turning then to go and find her position. Her comment about my manhood was less than helpful. In fact it was somewhat terrifying.

I made my way behind the divider and began to undress and at the same time sulk. What if my willy was small compared to you know who's? I would personally, if asked, not that I ever was, have described it as normal. Being a man you often regularly showered with other guys after many sports activities. I felt I compared fine but had not actually had a 'how big is yours' discussion. Time bloody wasted I saw now! I couldn't help thinking about Little Knob and realised that my competition probably meant I wasn't even in the running.

Perhaps this was Annabella's way of weeding out the weedies and perhaps my previous view about my decent sized member was in fact seriously mis-placed.

I began to undress and realised, to my horror, that my red chest was still red, though to be fair it was now a brown red. When I say brown, I mean a very tacky looking cheap fake tan brown. I went to the mirror, a handy full length mirror in the corner of the room, only to see my body was all covered in the cheap fake brown tan colour, part from, of course, the parts I had not been able to reach. Disaster was clearly looming. I rushed to the sink and rubbed water and soap into my skin. The effect was immediately slightly better and so I took to scrubbing my whole body. After rubbing far too vigorously I realised that the old problem that had followed me all day of a red glow on my chest, was now being repeated all over my body. I decided to stop and take a breather. I could hear the students all talking and laughing and wondered if this was all being screened out to them on some live feed!

I stopped to take stock of my situation and addressed myself with positives around me looking not too bad after all and to get over my fears. This was a big moment for me and not one to mess up any further. No, confidence was needed! After a few minutes I heard the lecturer arrive and my heart dropped again as I heard her begin her afternoon address to the soon to be giggling art students. I sat down depressed by my brown and red body and potentially not big enough willy. What could I do to make this right?

In a split second I made a decision. I was determined to create the right impression about my willy size, after all everyone knows the saying 'its the first impression that counts. I decided therefore to partake in a little fantasising. Annabella had said I had 10 minutes and so if I had a few sexual thoughts, I considered, I could get my little man appropriately larger and give the students more of an eyeful for their palettes. Admittedly I ran the slight risk that I might be a little too large for public show but the way I saw it I could fantasise for two minutes and then let the 'General' soften off for the next few minutes prior to my curtain call. Easy.

I closed my eyes and thought back to that night I had talked to Annabella at the Stockwell's gig in Mansfield. Her breasts had looked magnificent and I thought about me just looking at them right there in front of her and her knowing and seeing exactly what I was doing. As I imagined the smooth contours that framed her beautiful blessings of love, my little man sprang into action and became the unleashed monster that lurked so playfully down below. It was at that moment that the lecturer's voice broke into my thoughts and I could hear her saying that one of Annabella's friends had kindly filled the gap that had been left by the withdrawal of that afternoon's lined up model and then, much earlier than I had expected, or had time simply flown by, she announced,

'Right Anthony, if you would like to come out and assume your first position of your choice.'

Now to walk at this point and assume any position could have, and probably would have, seen me arrested. Certainly Annabella would have had nothing more to do with me. I looked down in horror at my enlarged friend and compatriot poking his wonderful head out of the now unfastened robe. There was no doubt that I had nothing to fear now on a size front other than it was that size that had to disappear and fast. I decided to try and think about nasty things to take any feelings of passion out of my body quick. I thought about a butcher's shop windows, Halfords, burning my finger on a hot stove, getting hit very hard by a large ugly gentleman, service station forecourts. Mistake! The service station in my mind had a gorgeous assistant and she was looking proudly in my mind at my willy.

Sweat began to take over my body as I panicked madly. The lecturer kindly called again,

'Anthony. When you are ready please.'

This was an epic disaster. I had to act even faster. Spinning round I caught sight of the sink. Fantastic. All I had to do was run some cold water over my willy and it would soon shoot down to normal size. I turned the tap on at full throttle to get the coldest water out it could manage. Lifting myself over the edge of the basin I thrust my willy into the water's spray and breathed with ease as the coldness began to take effect. As a pathetic smile filled my face, which was from a mixture of delight and relief, I turned my head to see the lecturer, mouth wide open, staring at me.

'Cleanliness…' I announced without hesitation or any hint of embarrassment '…is, as you know, next to godliness.'

And with this I wiped my self dry with a towel that was mercifully next to the sink, and then strode past her, letting the robe fall off my shoulders, and taking my position on the catwalk of art. The lecturer, obviously a little off balance from the wonders she had just taken in, followed me out and strode into the room to address her art students. I looked above their heads as though peering at something that had caught my eye towards the back of the room, wondering desperately what on earth I was supposed to do now.

'Now then Anthony,' it was the lecturer, 'please just take up any pose you please.'

I had thought through this the night before and considered the positions I would take if asked that would best set off my natural beauty. Hiding outside the room though was not an option and so I simply stood there in the position I was already holding, gazing across the room in a stance that I thought would have benefited a classical Michelangelo painting.

'Yes Anthony, when you are ready, please do take a position.'

'This is my first position,' I replied in a disdainful voice that made the room laugh.

'Oh, I see' she replied, 'then class please draw what you see.'

She was at the front of the class as she said this and was therefore right in front of me. I thought I heard her mutter under her breath 'If you can see it!' but I let that pass deciding that the earlier shock I had caused was worthy of a snide comment.

Over the next hour I was asked to pose in sixteen positions. I had tried standing looking graceful and meaningful, and then contrasted this with a mean and menacing pose. I had laid flat on the floor, and then on my side, and then my back, and then my front. I had turned my back to the class and held my arms by my side, then folded them around my chest, and then held them high in the air. This last position also raised quite a few laughs. By the end of this first session I was knackered. I would never have thought that staying still could be so draining. The class stopped for a short break to have refreshments and visits to the loo. I retired to the back room and pulled on my robe. Annabella came in straightaway.

'You're doing really well' she said, a big beaming smile giving me confidence.

'Oh good.'

'In fact you're doing really, really well.'

'Really?' I said, 'I'm only doing it for you of course.'

Annabella smiled at me with a face that I could not read. She was obviously pleased I was there but I was not sure how pleased.

'Here have a drink,' she said. She handed me a coke, which I opened and took a small sip.

'I'd better not have too much because I'll be wanting to wee my pants,' I said.

'You're not wearing pants!'

'Good point.'

'Mind you we haven't been asked to paint a nude having a wee yet.'

'Well, I shall just keep it as a surprise,' I laughed, 'in fact it will be my final masterpiece!'

We laughed together as the image of me weeing unannounced crossed our minds.

'Annabella?'

'Yes?'

'How bad does the fake tan look?'

'Honestly?'

'Erm, no, not honestly.'

'Well in that case, what fake tan? Have you been on holiday?'

'OK, I get the picture! I'll tell you all about it later. Will this next session be as hard?'

'Oh no,' she said, her impressive cheekbones highlighting her face, 'for this next bit you simply sit in one position and we do different drawings of you.'

'And then that's it?'

'Yes.'

'Great. Bloody great!'

I heard the class taking their seats and Annabella said,

'Just enjoy it Anthony, you're doing fine, really good. Remember, you're on stage, performing.'

With that she leaned over to me and kissed my cheek, her soft perfume filling my nostrils.

One hour later I was again fully dressed and emerging from behind the changing area to be met by a highly delighted Annabella.

'You were fantastic, a natural.'

She took me in her arms and gave me a most wonderful kiss on the lips. The day was beginning to make sense once again.

'Why thank you. I kind of enjoyed it; I really did.'

'You've amazed yourself, yea?'

'Yea, I did. I know it's not the same, but once I got over the initial shock it just became like a performance with the Band.'

'Except without clothes.'

'Yes, true. Perhaps we could do a naked band gig?'

'It would bring in the fans.'

'And the police.'

Annabella was looking at me with eyes that were wide with life. They were the most alive eyes I had ever seen and I wanted to dive into them to see what on earth made them so bright.

'Come on then…' Annabella said, breaking me out of the spell, 'let me take you for the very well deserved meal I promised you.'

We went in to the Student Union to say a few goodbyes first. Loads of people who I had never met were coming up to me. They all wanted to talk about my modelling session, where I'd been on holiday and then the Band. It was promotion of the highest order and it had cost the Band nothing other than my dignity. Perhaps I could arrange a Band nude session as a follow up. I thought of Steve and decided this was exactly what I should do by way of retribution.

I distributed several flyers for our next Nottingham gig, flyers that Keith had armed me with for this very opportunity. Everyone I spoke to said they would be coming. The gig was our biggest to date being at the world famous Rock City in the heart of Nottingham. The list of who had played here over the years pretty much incorporated the world's greatest rock stars, and Wide Eyed Wonder were set to be added to the list. No one would be able to take this away from us and we were suitably proud and excited. Steve had obtained it by the use of perfect blagging and interesting use of made up facts. Apparently we had just pulled out of a tour backing The Verve because the money wasn't right. Quite right too! If the promoters were going to be tight wads then we were not going to play ball. Also, apparently, we were laying down tracks for Creation boss Alan McGhee after he had heard us play in London. Why not! For Alan I would pretty much lay down just about anything.

We were fast learning that the music business works on hearsay and rumour, no matter how misinformed or badly placed. The more Steve blagged, and it was an ability he was born and blessed with, the more people got interested in Wide Eyed Wonder. We had taken to recording ourselves during practices using some of Rob's excellent recording gear. We needed these recordings to send out to A&R and radio people who had begun to call us. The A&R were from smaller labels, most of them fairly local and of no interest to us other than the vibe they were creating. Local radio stations also responded positively to us, underlining the fact that the rumours and hearsay we had created about ourselves were beginning to create its own publicity. We were like a snowball pushed from the top of a steep hill, or at least a slight incline.

And so, amazing as it was, we had got in to Rock City and were to play on a Thursday in June, which was their student night. BBC Radio Nottingham had asked us to go into their studios on the previous Saturday night to the gig to do an interview for the legendary Dean Jackson on The Beat. This was a very popular pop programme and one of the few that BBC Radio Nottingham had credibility for with a younger audience. On the same show Dean would not only be interviewing us but he would also be talking to

Dodgy who were playing live that night at Rock City. I was telling anyone who would listen about this, and it further enhanced our reputation in anybody's mind that cared to listen.

After a few well-earned drinks, and having made lots of new friends, Annabella made our apologies and we left.

'Are you taking me away to have your pleasure madam?' I cheekily asked, lost in a wonderful sense of care free happiness that had taken over my whole body since it had realised the hard part of the day was done. For the rest of this day, at least, it knew I would no longer be forcing it to endure new pains and take on new colours in the name of art.

'Of course,' she smiled, her eyes twinkling in response to my forwardness, 'I thought we would go to a new eatery that's just opened in Hockley. It's called 'That Cafe Bar' and I've heard good things about it, and on top of that, you pay for your meal the time when you arrive, so if we get there before six it's a cheap meal too.'

'Perfect,' I replied with unhidden glee.

'Yea, perfect.'

Walking away from the university together and down in to town felt so good. I kept stealing glances at people as they walked by us, eager to see people looking at us, thinking of us as a couple. Annabella seemed so very relaxed, in easy control.

'What did you really think then?' I asked, unable to hide the question any longer.

'To your modelling?'

I nodded in over the top fashion, looking as though my neck was loose and held only by elastic. Annabella laughed,

'You must get that neck seen to.'

'Too late. They've fitted springs you know.'

'I told you already; I thought you were a natural. You did really well.'

As she talked to me she looked at me, ensuring that I knew she really meant what she was saying.

'Although at the beginning,' she added, 'you had me scared. I thought you weren't coming out.'

I laughed, nervously.

'I said to Anna, our lecturer, that I would go and get you but she insisted.'

My heart dropped into my nether regions as I thought of Annabella arriving back stage to see me with my nether regions sprawled over a sink. The day had been kind to me after all.

'Oh, I was just a little scared.'

This got a huge result, indeed a hat trick to Scotty as Annabella's beautiful blue eyes lit up at my vulnerability. I went on, eager to add to my score.

'It was my first time in the nude for a group greater than ten men in a shower together and I was nervous, as much as anything, at getting out the little, erm I should say, big, general for the troops.'

More giggles all round.

'You were fine, you looked lovely.'

Lovely. The word went round my head. My mum called plants and old ladies lovely. On the other hand, one of our Bank Business Mangers was also called Lovely. There again lovely was a lovely word. I thought of Little Knob and, before I knew it, the words came stuttering out of my mouth,

'Up to Callum's high standards?'

'Well I think you are very nice in every way. Comparing you with Callum is not for me to do. If you want I could ask him if he would mind you looking him over, for comparison purposes of course.'

I had over stepped the mark. Asking about Callum when I had not even found out how the two of them got on was both unfair and ill timed. Annabella had taken it in her stride but I regretted the question immediately.

We crossed Lower Parliament Street at the busy pedestrian crossing outside of the Victoria Centre. Nottingham was still teeming with lustful shoppers just catching the closing few minutes of retail therapy, or torture dependant on your point of view, and workers streaming home for their social lives to continue after the rude interruption of a capitalist trick. In the middle of this busy city I walked, as lost and as found as all these other people. The movement of life, the energy of all that was around me, was like a potion that I drank right now as though it was champagne because I was walking on young love. It filled me inside and moved me forward, and I wanted to get things back on track. I turned to Annabella,

'I'm sorry for asking about Callum, it really wasn't fair and was a little stupid on my part.'

'That's OK. You can ask about anybody. I don't have to answer.'

True enough, but she had.

'It's just that…' I stumbled over my words, not wishing to tell her I liked her, albeit that this was a fact that she would have obviously known. I just didn't want to start a ball rolling that actually had nowhere to roll to. What if Annabella liked me for my company but was madly in love with Callum. I had thought through this many times before tonight, about his car, his prospects, his money. She was, though, always so pleased to see me and I thought that she liked me.

'What?' she asked quietly.

We had arrived on Broad Street and there at the bottom was That Cafe Bar. We stopped outside. Annabella had caught me lost in thought.

'It doesn't matter.' I replied in as upbeat manner as I could manage.

'Are you sure?'

It was the wrong question from Annabella. She was supposed to say at that point 'Of course it matters. Tell me everything. Open out your heart and I will be there for you' etc etc etc.

'Of course I'm sure.' I gave her a big 'Scotty' special smile by way of underlying my fine state of mind.

We went in to the Bar and took our table. Annabella ordered a large glass of red wine and I ordered a bottle of Peroni. She then excused herself to do whatever women do in the rest room for a period that either suggested they needed a long and arduous emptying of their bowels or that they were decorating the restroom with their eyeliner or that they were measuring the length of the unrolled toilet paper. Whatever Annabella was doing, and it could have been any of the afore mentioned activities or any number of other events, I was left for a few moments to take in my newfound surroundings.

It really was a fabulous little place, an Aladdin's cave. The walls were painted in a soft terracotta paint with sheets of aluminium figures and imaginative woodcarvings adorning the walls. There were a few people in already, mostly students here for the cheaper food option for the early eaters. The music was up beat and funky.

Annabella came back and we ordered our food. I went for the blackened tuna whilst she settled for the veggie curry. That Café bar was a fabulous place and it felt good to be there. Steve would love this.

'So you've not been here before?' I asked.

'No, I haven't. It's not been open that long. I know a couple of people who worked on kitting it out, you know students, and they've kept telling me to get down. I can't wait to tell them I've been and to come back with my friends.'

'Like Chloe or Callum?' There I was again, asking about Callum despite only ten minutes earlier apologising for asking about him. I was living on death wish row and I really needed to move. Still Annabella, to her credit, didn't seem to mind.

'I would come with Chloe; she would love it, but not Callum. He's not really into this sort of place. He likes to go somewhere where the bill matches his car.'

'Right, I see' And I did see. Given the state of my old car, prior to getting the company chariot, I knew exactly how Callum felt because I felt exactly opposite. I ate at the cheapest places imaginable because they matched my budget, which was indeed in line with the quality of my car. Still to hear about Callum not wanting to go to places Annabella wanted to go to was sweet music to my ears. I decided to spend the rest of the evening in court jester mode with Annabella being my court.

Five hours of delicious conversation followed, mixed with mouth-watering food in a place that was made for this evening. We didn't talk about Callum. I avoided the subject that remained an unanswered series of questions shouting out at the back of my brain. Annabella told me about her upbringing, her brother and sister, her wider family, which seemed to encompass the whole of the United Kingdom, and her many friends. She told me of her love for art but that this art was a confusion for her, offering no clear career path but rather a seemingly unending list of possibilities. I told her about my banking choice and the one option it gave me of boredom!

Annabella told me she often found it impossible to settle on anything. 'Fingers in many pies' she said. I thought about her finger in my pie. I smiled widely.

I told her about my family, my friends, my hopes and dreams. I found it so easy to open up. Being with Annabella just seemed so straightforward making me feel I could just be myself.

As eleven o'clock came and went, I looked at my watch and was amazed on two accounts. First of all it was still working. I had been having trouble with it ever since I found out it actually wasn't water proof to 50 metres. In fact it wasn't ever waterproof to half a metre and had been badly affected in the swimming pool earlier in the day. Secondly I could not believe the time.

'It's gone eleven!' I declared in an amazed tone that suggested I had found a secret treasure that had been lost to civilisation since the beginning of the world when Adam had said to Eve, 'Hide the core my love, no one will ever know.'

'Is it really? A little late for you' Annabella smiled in that all encompassing way I had noticed she possessed that was both captivating and beguiling at the same time.

'Late? Not at all. I have the whole night for you mapped out!'

She laughed at that!

'Well, and sadly, I had better make a move. Anthony it has been a wonderful day!'

I loved the way she said my name, in her way. She made it sound so full and it all came out so languidly like anything special should do. This was a girl who did things in her way and I loved that.

'Thank you for asking me out,' I said, happily.

'You did so very well earlier and I was very proud of you.'

'I'll be back next week!' I replied, this time with a big grin across my face.

'And your idea about doing the whole Band is fantastic!' The boys would probably kill me for this but I couldn't help it. Think of the publicity, the waxing and the obvious unfortunate events that would be ours. No longer my own little adventure, but one shared with my best buddies!

'Where are you parked?' I asked, not yet giving up on the evening but hoping to spin it out even further.'

'Oh that's all right thank you. Callum's gym is just at the top of Broad Street. He's there till late tonight and so I told him I'd meet him there. He knows I'm eating with a friend.'

I was crestfallen, heartbroken, a child whose apple had been stolen by a big fat wolf with yellow teeth and smelly breath. I was a footballer who has just had his career best goal, which he scored having taken the ball by five players and then volleyed it in to the top corner from 25 yards, taken away from him as it was disallowed for offside. Annabella could not fail to see my crushing misery.

'Anthony, I really have had the best night I have had for a long time. I hope we can do it again some time soon, really soon.'

I looked at her. My eyes had surely never looked so dopey.

'I would love to. How about tomorrow? No, I know, how about in another hour?'

She laughed. I laughed. She looked straight at me,

'Look, I know we haven't talked about me and Callum all night.'

'Have we not? I hadn't realised.'

We both smiled and both knew we had purposely sidestepped the big lump of lard that was Callum. Annabella went on.

'I have known Callum for a long time and whilst I can't tell you I am madly in love with him, I can't tell you I am about to stop seeing him.'

'What are you saying Annabella?' Not that I really wanted to know because it sounded like I was about to receive a cooling off notice.

'Just that I want you to know tonight has been very special to me. You have made me laugh and feel very special. I haven't enjoyed an evening so much for such a long time and this should mean a lot to you. It does to me. I do, though, have a boyfriend at the moment. I know you like me and I do want you to know I like you too, but that's all there can be for now.'

'For now?'

'Yes, for now.'

'Is it that obvious how much I like you Annabella?'

'Well yes, I am very intuitive but in your case seeing that you liked me would have been possible for a blind man.'

'Not that I am obvious or anything' I said this with a little hurt in my voice.

'You have been very sweet.'

'So this isn't a push off?'

'No, it's just me being honest. I would love to see you again but you need to know that at this moment I am still seeing someone.'

'But you might not be soon?'

'I don't know, I really don't know.'

Annabella's eyes wandered off to the few people who were still in the bar. We had arrived at the beginning of the evening and were still here after most people had come and gone. I looked at this lovely girl lost in her thoughts, her feelings confused. I knew I must try and lighten the evening, otherwise we would end it on a down note and that would never do. I just had to ask a few more questions and so I did.

'Well I can't say I'm sorry to have made you have second thoughts,' I said, 'I mean you were probably having them anyway.'

Annabella's eyes returned to me,

'I was, a little. Being with Callum has always been so easy. He does his thing and I do mine. We both have a lot of space and that's been bad and good at the same time. It's suited us and we have existed together quite comfortably'

'Comfortable like an old slipper or a really nice new bra?' I asked and she gave nothing back. Hearing her talk about her and Callum was uncomfortable for me, but I needed to know a little more if I could. Annabella went on,

'But to walk away from Callum is asking a lot and I can't do that just yet.'

'Sure, Annabella, of course you can't. I understand, really I do.' I said, lamely. I reasoned that I must find another response.

'Can we see each other when you can and see how we get on?' I asked.

'I'd like that.'

'I'd like that too. In fact I'd love it,' I added.

She smiled.

'I'd write a book about I,' I continued, 'make a film about it!'

Now I had her laughing. A better way to end the evening!

We asked for the bill and Annabella insisted on paying as promised in honour of my performance.

'I'll get the bill next time, when we go to the chippy on everything's a pound night!' I said as we headed out on to the street and then stood facing each other on the pavement.

Annabella then leaned over to me and kissed me on the cheek.

'Call me at the weekend, yes?' she said.

'Of course. Oh and thank you,' I replied.

'For what?'

'For letting me get to know you. For letting me say your name over and over in my head a thousand times a day.'

She took my face in her hands and kissed me on my lips. She then stepped away, smiled, and began to walk up the road to her boyfriend's gym. I stood glued to the spot, lost in the kiss I had received and the perfume that rested on my cheeks from her hands.

I shouted after her,

'Annabella.'

She turned.

'I'll show you mine if you'll show me yours.'

I could see her smile in the dark. She walked back to me.

'I've seen yours!' she said, 'Ring me soon.'

'In five minutes?'

'Not that soon! Oh and Anthony,'

'Yes?'

'Next time you have a chest wax, I suggest you give your skin a little bit longer to recover before showing it to everyone.'

She was laughing as she said this to me.

'You knew?'

'You were a little red and shiny.'

'Badly?'

'Not that anyone would have known.'

'Really?'

'No, not really, of course not really. You were attracting planes with your bright chest!"

She laughed, blew me a kiss, turned, and went.

'Bugger,' I said under my breath, 'Bugger, bastard, bugger!'

13

Tricks was a strange mixture. On the one hand you would look at him and straight away wonder about his personal hygiene. He had all the classic hallmarks of an unkempt student that spent rather too much time partying and not anywhere near enough time in the bathroom. You couldn't help but notice that for starters he did smell a little; not in a stinky been living out on the streets for several weeks' way, but rather in few days' way. His hair was invariably rather greasy and not at all glossy and shiny like those ladies in shampoo adverts. His clothes never looked like they had seen or even heard of an iron, though to be fair to him he didn't have my Mother to help out there. His footwear consisted it seemed of one pair of converse that had almost definitely been the original Chuck Taylor trainers from the 1930's because they did look that old. On the other hand I often saw him rubbing some powder around his gums in an attempt, no doubt, to keep his mouth fresh and his gums healthy so teeth hygiene was obviously important to him.

He was a very amiable fellow who would definitely have been well suited to the surf beaches of the world was it not for his lack of interest in anything that involved physical activity. Why he had chosen drumming was a mystery to me although as he sat in his smoke induced haze, smoking that brand of cigarette that sent him on a high, somehow he went together with drumming so well. He was a laid back drummer, never one to quicken the pace of a song but rather a follower of the beat. I often thought that we must be the only Rock and Roll Band ever to be led by the beat of the bass guitar and not the beat of a drum. He was still brilliant in his own way and I kind of loved that.

Often in a gig or a practice I would turn to Tricks for a response to the music. If it was early on he would look up at me and smile crazily, rather like a mad bad cowboy in a spaghetti western who is just about to draw in a one against 20-gun fight, knowing the odds were hopelessly stacked against him but not giving a flying thought to such trivialities. If I looked at him towards the end of a practice or a gig he would not be able to look up. He looked like a man who had just been on three back to back marathons with a massive rucksack of boulders fastened to his back. Sweat would have overtaken his body, his glasses long gone having slipped off his ears and down his nose, his body soaked through with his clothes looking as though someone had just tipped seventeen buckets of steaming water on to him. For 30 minutes he was brilliant. For the next 30 he was holding on to dear life.

Tricks was not an extrovert drummer. He didn't toss his sticks high into the air and catch them in his bottom whilst continuing to play the same beat with new drumsticks in his mouth. He was, though, interesting to watch. He would move his head up and down to the beat of the music, his shoulders moving madly as if some large east European ladies were giving him a massage to remember. He did keep the beat and he was entertaining to people who came to see us and this was what made him a good drummer and who knows if he got fit, a great drummer.

'Groovy venue man.'

It was early June and we had just arrived at Leicester's 'The Charlotte.' Tricks was admiring the tight stage and darkened hall that would soon be brimming over with excited students who were arriving to watch the up and coming newly signed band Octopus. We were one of the support bands. Steve had told the promoter that we were the best new Band in the Midlands, (of course), and that we were to play three major festivals that summer, as well as being lined up by 10 different record labels to sign us up for one of the biggest deals of the year. He was getting his blagging off to such a fine art that we actually believed the hype ourselves. All of us told the same stories to our friends and families though mine were watered down and Steve's were embellished even further! The effect though was like Chinese whispers as I would often get stopped and asked about something that I had first heard Steve mutter in some dark corner only for it to be replayed to me at some new extraordinary level!

The deciding factor for the promoter at The Charlotte though, as was almost always the case for this sort of venue, was how many people were we to bring to the gig to drink their alcohol and make their profit. As always Steve was suitably elaborate telling the promoter that we were to bring a full 50-seater coach down with us. That sort of promise, if it was believed, was normally enough to get you in to most small to medium size venues. The Charlotte was a well-known music venue across the country and was used regularly for the up and coming newly signed Bands as a springboard to bigger and greater things, hence the arrival of Octopus for the night's gig, but even so it still valued paying punters so the promise of 50 new ones form out of town was enough for most promoters to put up with the blagging no matter how extreme.

Needless to say we did not have a 50-seater coach arriving that night. I had seen a few on the motorway on the way down but none that I could specifically say were coming down with us for the gig. We had been quite busy playing local gigs and building up our following, which had grown substantially. The mailing list actually did now boast 900 real people's names (1500 if anyone asked) and we had genuine fans following us from gig to gig. With a huge Nottingham Rock City gig only ten nights away it was important to save their enthusiasm for the big one so this was a gig on the list but not one we had pushed separately.

A few cars of students from the mighty fine Eastwood Comprehensive would be coming to The Charlotte and this would be fine. We were now confident enough to make up any story so as to get us into a gig knowing that our music would do the talking and any lack of paying punters could be blamed on any number of reasons. If the worst scenario was that a venue did not ask us back then there were many other venues to take their place. The nice thing about a venue like the Charlotte was that because of the type of Bands they had on, it was a venue ideally suited to the student community and, providing the Band playing had achieved limited success, the venue would be brimming over. The lack therefore of our bus would not even be noticed. Brilliant.

We set up and sound checked at our allotted time. We were to be the first on for the night and therefore the last to sound check. It was rarely fun doing a sound check, particularly at a venue like the Charlotte where there were so many people milling around doing their own thing yet earwigging to the bands in set up mode. The main Band would be walking around as though they were already world famous, their management complaining about anything that might take away from their Band. On this particular night our sound check was interrupted on several occasions by the sound engineer having to keep updating the requests from Octopus for different things they wanted incorporating into their set. On the third interruption with us trying to start our sound check once again, I put down my guitar and strode purposefully to the back of the room. Here the sound engineer was trying desperately to remain calm as management and band members of Octopus surrounded him in a typically aggressive manner akin to a Premiership football team surrounding the referee after a decision went against them.

'And on the third chorus let's lift the echo until it sounds almost surreal,' said the lead singer.

'Right,' replied the stressed out sound engineer.

'But not too surreal,' offered the far from polite tour manager.

'Right,' replied the soon to freak out sound engineer.

'And don't forget on the final number that my guitar needs to cut in and across the whole piece in a wowy sort of all encompassing wall of sound way.' This was the lead guitarist who threw in his ridiculous request as though no one else mattered. To be fair, they probably didn't.

'Right,' replied the ever-paler sound engineer.

'But not too across,' threw in the tour manager in a way you might throw in a grenade into an enemy bunker.

'Right,' replied the now bored to tears sound engineer.

It was interesting listening to the discussions because as anyone who plays a gig this size knows, the sound engineer will do none of what you have asked him to do. He will simply do what he always does, that being his own thing. These discussions between band and sound engineer are part of the natural two-way process where the band are putting the sound engineer in his place and letting him know who is boss. The engineer has in return one of his hands under the table and is making rude gestures to them. As they ask for each slight change to the sound, he smiles mildly at them whilst thinking to himself 'You absolute and total wanker.'

Enough was enough.

'Excuse me.'

No one even looked at me. That really pissed me off.

'FIRE!' I shouted sufficiently loudly for everyone to turn around.

'FIRE IN THE BACK ROOM! It's a real hot fire with real nasty flame things!'

This was where the main band Octopus had placed all their ridiculous amount of shiny new gear, which they had no doubt purchased on credit with their first cheque from the record company. They all fell over themselves to get to the room. I watched them sprint away and then turned back to the engineer who was quickly gathering his own things to save his own life from the dreadful inferno that awaited us. As he glanced at me he saw I was laughing and a knowing recognition of relief and then acceptance filled his face.

'Now can we finish our sound check?' I asked in a smug and self-satisfied voice.

He laughed. The giggle would ensure he gave our small set some concentration, which in this venue would be concentration enough.

'Yea sure man, good stunt. You had me going for a while though man, but it was worth it to upset those wankers.'

'You're very welcome.'

I made my way back to the Band as the Octopus guys filed out of the non-existent fire room. I smiled accordingly. They did not smile back. Their manager was heading straight for me as I veered to the right and ducked past several people before jumping up on to the stage. I picked up my guitar, the sound engineer gave us the all clear, and we thundered into 'I Want To Be Me.'

We had never shrunk from playing our music live. We believed in it and the only way we knew how to play it was 'in your face.' Our attitude matched our music perfectly and it hit the listener therefore both in their ears and their eyes. Seeing other bands often so far up their own bottoms that you could only hope they bathed regularly and thoroughly, filled us with a sense of us against the world. We wanted nothing to do with doing something the same way as everyone else but rather to do whatever we wanted in the way that we wanted to do it. This probably came through to anyone who cared to watch and listen as though we were up our own bottoms too, but that thought had happily not occurred to me.

And so we played our Indy rock tune at a volume far too loud for the small gathering, we did so with a swagger born out of frustration. You could see the other two bands suitably worried and filling up with feelings of inadequacy and within moments we had finished the song, placed down our instruments and promptly left the room without a glance backwards to get some ale down us prior to playing.

'So Bob, what's the song list' said Keith.

I thought to myself that the sooner he left teaching the better. He has always been so good at issuing orders, assuming the mantle of an army brigadier from Her Majesty's fine British forces. Since becoming a teacher, his ability to issue edicts had reached new heights; indeed the other three of us in the band lived in fear of him catching us out. He literally gave the Band homework to do, little tasks that he had carefully assembled at home for us. If we got the task wrong or, worse still, we forgot to do it all together, then we would feel the wrath of teacher Mr Scott just as we had done when we had got stuff wrong at school. The guilty party would literally sneak in to the class (practice or gig) after everyone else had arrived in a vain hope that Miss Uppity (Keith) might have forgotten what she asked you to do. Just like Miss Uppity, Keith never forgot. Elephant. Unlike Miss Uppity, Keith did not wear a bra or suspenders or a see through top whilst teaching the class with the sunlight coming from behind her left shoulder, making this experience with Keith then far less enjoyable.

He had dished out Band duties unannounced and uninvited at a practice a few months earlier. He told us that each of us, by taking on these simple and yet effective tasks, would feel even more the fulfilment of being in the Band. When he talked in the assured positive manner he had perfected over many years of practice we all fell in line behind his every command. He was our organisational leader, an inspiration, and a pain in the arse.

Steve was on gig getting duties and PR. It was his natural forte. He had no problem at all in ringing anyone up and lying through his back teeth. At times this ability did not always help the band and we often found ourselves having to question Steve more closely in order to find out the true extent of a venue's pitfalls.

Tricks was given getting mailing list names duties. His ability to talk to anyone without any embarrassment at all and not walk away until they filled out the piece of paper pushed in front of them was almost poetry to watch. At every gig he would walk in to the crowd with his mail shot sheets and return an hour later with loads filled in.

Keith pronounced himself as administrative co-ordinator. Effectively he was the Field Marshall of the piece. He prepared all our flyers, updated our mail shot list, kept our gig lists plus he booked our practices and gave us all lists with inspiration quotes to make the appropriate entries in our diaries. If the band didn't work out it would be no problem for Keith in terms of a future career. He was a headmaster in the making, and very proud of it.

I was given two simple duties. Firstly I was to write songs and write songs and write songs. I would take them to a practice and they would magically either work or be dismissed. I would play the band a song, just me and my guitar, having handed out to them a photocopied sheet with the words and chords for the new piece. If they liked it we would play it and, after a few ropey takes, the song would take on a life of its own. It gave us all a real buzz of value and of being a true band. They needed my songs, but I needed them to make the pieces turn into our sound. Early on when I brought songs in that they did not like I would feel offended and not be sure what to do with the rejection, occasionally re-working one and bringing it back in a few weeks later only to be caught out by Steve who never missed a trick on songs. After a while we had more than enough for two sets and it became less important having lots of songs and more important to have the best songs and so I worked harder and we got better.

Secondly, and this job never received the attention to detail it should have done, I was given the job of preparing the song list for each gig. This was an exercise I normally completed in 30 seconds at the photocopier at work just prior to leaving. Occasionally I forgot all together.

'I have it here,' I declared in a way that suggested it was I that had discovered the whereabouts of the Titanic. Keith gave me a look of a satisfied tutor with the performance of his charge. I felt, as I always felt when I received that look, so extremely relieved.

I set about explaining the list and the choice thereof with renewed eagerness having received the blessed nod of approval from my glorious leader.

'Now as you know we only have a 20 minute slot so I thought hit them between the eyes.'

'Right on man. You're one cool dude!'

I nodded at Tricks, grateful for his kind support and delighted with his continued insistence on using a language that Scooby Doo would have expected from Shaggy.

'So let's kick in, and I mean a Shearer kick boys, with 'I Want to be Me.' Steve,'

Steve was looking at me, half wanting to laugh out loud at my fine performance and yet half entrapped by the zest with which I was delivering instructions.

'Yes?' He nodded ridiculously, almost making me laugh and fall foul of my watching teacher.

'Hit the intro really hard.'

'Yea, right in their fuckin' mashed up faces man,' said Tricks.

Tricks was really switched on tonight. I noticed as he smiled that his teeth, if anything, were getting browner despite the white powder I kept seeing him rubbing into his gums. Even Steve seemed to have joined in with the teeth brigade club as I saw them both doing it whilst we were setting up. I knew that Keith flossed and I was getting quite concerned about my own lack of over the top dental hygiene. All I did was brush my teeth, strenuously I might add, once in the morning and once at night. I made a mental note to ask Steve about his views, and indeed what he was using, later. I went on,

'Then straight into 'Shooting Star,' again keeping it really up.'

Keith was smiling in such a way that suggested he might have just pooed in his pants. Pride really is a wonderful thing.

'Keeping it really up is no problem to me Anth,' offered a happy Steve, only to have a 'keep it quiet' glare from head teacher Keith.

'Then on to 'Long Way to Fall.''

'It will be man if that big dude of a promoter realises we don't have a bus coming after all. It will be goodbye Mister Happy and hello Mister Grumpy and 'have you met my big bouncers?''

Tricks was making a fair point. I hadn't considered this unfortunate potential ending to our evening, assuming that with all the people that would pile in to the venue our little lie wouldn't be noticed. I noticed Steve giving Tricks a hard stare and realised that something must be wrong.

'Steve?'

'Yes?'

'What's Tricks saying?'

'That there are people expected, as always!'

'Yea, I know,' Steve was looking highly uncomfortable and I know something was amiss, 'but what is the promoter really expecting?'

'I don't know! Ask him yourself…'

'Steve?'

The voice of Keith cut in rather like Badger interrupting a conversation between Toad and Rat in the Wind in the Willows. Steve laughed a little nervously and I realised that he had once again gilded the lily a little too golden and in so doing omitted to tell us of a minor matter that could lead to physical punishment.

'Well it's only a small point really,' he began.

Tricks spluttered on his beer.

'It's just that everyone who goes in has to say which Band, if any, they have come with.'

'Right. I see' and of course I did see. We were doomed.

'So the promoter knows which Bands brought who.'

We were all quiet. Tricks laughed.

'Have you seen the fuckin' size of those bouncers?'

We turned to see some rather hefty looking chaps take their positions on the doors. We were due on stage in 45 minutes. There was no way of making a quick getaway, as our gear was at the back of the stage and we would not be able to get it all out until the end. It was time for Keith to take over.

'OK. Everyone keep calm. Bob, will you kindly finish the list.'

'Right. OK. Erm, the list. Where was I?'

'Long Way to Fall,' replied Keith with a prompting a small child to read tone.

'Yes, after the appropriate 'Long Way to Fall,''

'Or should that be run?'

Steve offering the funny at the most inopportune time I felt. Tricks just laughed. He never seemed to mind being in a precarious position or indeed ever seem to be in any state of anxiety ever. I was never too good at facing the prospect of pain and did not laugh. Rather my insides began to feel like I needed to get to a chemist and fast.

'We will go into 'Hold on tight,'' I forced out.

'Yes that really is a classic fighting tool' said Steve.

I looked at Keith who bizarrely was beginning to laugh uncontrollably.

'And then finish with 'Alright for Now.''

'Or All Fight for Now,' suggested Steve. That was it, the sign for Keith to trump so loudly that half the pub heard. He had always had the habit that when he laughed so hard, wind came out of as many openings as it could find. To be fair the trumps were rarely smelly ones, but none the less not the sort of thing that one would use to necessarily impress a crowded pub. Once Keith and the others began to laugh I laughed too. I couldn't help it. I could never help it.

Within the next half hour, three cars worth of students had arrived from Keith's school led by our chief number one fan Richard, top sixth form student and chief rounder upper of loads of support for the Band. Three minutes later all eighteen of us were out on the streets handing out flyers and telling people to say they had come to listen to Wide Eyed Wonder. I would have never dared ask people who had travelled forty miles to go straight outside and hand out flyers. Keith knew no shame. In fact the students didn't mind at all. It was as though he had suggested that outside was free beer and the students followed him, which was quite simply remarkable.

One hour later having performed an electric set we were being interviewed back stage, which in this case meant on the fire escape behind the stage, by a reporter from Leicester's local newspaper 'The Mercury.' The reporter had with him a most lovely young photographer of the female variety who was taking lots of photographs from just about every conceivable angle. It was funny with the band and attention. Keith would always start interviews and then leave Steve and I to take over and glow in the energy we were still feeling from the performance and just talk. Tricks on the other hand just sat wherever he could, lit up and tried to get his breath back.

'You were fantastic tonight and the crowd obviously loved you,' the reporter clearly had the gift of saying the right thing at the right time. Flattery for a start out band is really the best way of getting close to them. 'Now could you tell me a little bit about the Band and what you are up to at the moment.'

'Well,' it was Steve, 'at the moment I am rather taken with your beautiful photographer.'

She smiled at his cheek as I laughed at his nerve. What a man!

'Is it girls, then, that inspire you with the Band?' asked the reporter as though a new thread and take to this old 'new band' story might be forming in his mind.

'No.' Keith said in considered tones 'It is the Art.'

'The Art?' The reporter repeated hopefully.

'Yes. The Art.'

'What sort of art?'

'I am speaking holistically of course! The music we play is in truth a way of taking the whole of what is in us, and presenting it in a music art form for others to interpret as they will. All of it, if you will, is art.'

This was priceless! He was presenting like a lecturer with statements of facts and I had no idea what he was talking about. We were all struggling with the word holistically and not sure whether Keith was taking the preverbal or being serious.

'I can honestly say', said the reporter, 'that I have never interviewed a band who have used the word holistically!'

We were all quiet. What more could be said? Tricks was too knackered, Steve was too distracted, and I was too confused. As for Keith, well Keith had said enough. The reporter tried to change tack.

'What did you think to The Charlotte?'

It was my turn.

'I think she is lovely.'

'So do I,' said Steve as he continued to gaze longingly at our clicking new friend.

'Have you been here before?'

'If only,' said Steve as the photographer got very close shots of him.

The reporter was a little perturbed, but not too much. Clearly he was used to talking to Bands who rarely made, and probably had, very little sense. He then asked the key question, which is the question that means Keith turns into official list man.

'And where do you play next?'

It was the sort of question that meant Keith could produce all his photocopied lists of forthcoming gigs and events. It was the sort of question that in short he was born to answer. It was his 'manna from heaven moment and he walked the man over to a table and produced reams of paperwork. He gave me one of his looks that meant come over and look interested, which I duly did, and he then proceeded to tell the man, who was called John, everything about the band.

In fact we did have quite a lot coming up. Keith and Steve had been busy in booking lots for us to do. There was our interview with Radio Nottingham on Saturday followed by our gig on Rock City's Disco 2000 stage on Student night the following Thursday. We then had a run of five local gigs before making our way down to the Big Smoke to play 'The Orange Club' on an August Saturday night in London. We had set up a real bus trip for that one, and hoped that it would be the gig that the A&R of the world would take note and sign us up. Steve, with the help of a friend of Keith's in London, had blagged us magnificently on to a Saturday night showcase for new bands. We couldn't wait.

Clearly the reporter was most impressed as he told us we would be getting a fantastic review in the paper and he promised to send us a copy himself.

Steve by this point had deepened relations with the photographer who apparently was freelance and was called Julie. They were snogging passionately by the fire escape door, Steve's hands on her bottom, which was clothed in a short little thin red leather skirt. Her hands in return were running through his grease filled bleached hair. Goodness knows what she would find.

Tricks was stood to the side of them in a wonderment state, staring at the couple's embraces and Julie's bottom as he gripped the camera he had obviously been told not to drop. I could see the headline now: 'Perverted drummer is Wide Eyed at Guitarist's naughty behaviour.'

Interview finished I went over to Steve and began to squeeze his bottom too!

'Are you staying here Steve?' I enquired in as sweet a voice as I could muster. The young couple stopped kissing and turned to me.

'Anthony, I will just be a moment. Julie and I are going to exchange details.'

'Right… details?'

'Yes. You know, photo information and so on.'

'Right! Actually Julie when we have gone, you could perhaps get a few naked shots as well of Steve.'

'Yes, I guess I could.'

She was serious. He was horrified.

'We're all going up stairs to that alternative venue. Do come when you are ready, yea?'

'Oh yea!' said Julie with a massive smile as she gripped Steve's right hand and put it back to her derriere.

We left Steve and made our way to the room at the top of The Charlotte. Apparently the Charlotte always ran on new band night an alternative evening where people were welcome to bring their own songs or poetry or favourite pieces they just wanted to share. This was culture for us! In Mansfield the nearest you would get to an evening like this would be a trip down to Field Mill (the home of the mighty Mansfield Town FC) where you would hear all sorts of verse put majestically to well thought through tunes.

Yes, a spell of culture to end the evening would do very nicely thank you! It all sounded extremely full of wonderful potential for a good giggle and the production of lots of future stories to tell.

The three of us walked, or in Tricks' case was led as the mixture of alcohol, teeth rubbing and tiredness took over, into the upstairs crowded room. We made our way past several punters to order drinks at the bar. As we placed our order I looked around and saw the most fascinating selection of people. A few looked normal in as much as they would have happily fitted in to my daytime world of bankers and customers. The rest would not. They looked like people with a story to tell in the right place to tell it. The hair cuts, the colours of hair, the crazy clothes, the piercings and the tattoos. It is worth mentioning that in Mansfield we were somewhat sheltered from what was really happening in the outside world. Yes we had seen the major musical movements over the past few decades with mods, punks, new romantics aplenty. However the versions we saw were more often than not a local take on a national theme. Place this with the fact that in the main whatever form of fashion was on show in Mansfield was invariably in a limited number. You may see a gaggle of punks, you would not see a whole gang of them. Too many together all at once would have been an affront to the harder lads in town and an inevitable stand off would have ensued. A beating would have taken place and normal order would have been installed. It wasn't pleasant but it was the way it was in small town parochial England. To get out and see more freedom was blissful.

Steve, of course, had been one of the few to choose to stand out to look different and in his time he took a fair few beatings for the trouble. It was all part of being in a more local northern town setting. Here in the big smoke of a big student city, with a much more varied ethnic base and a wide selection of musical tastes on offer, anything became more acceptable and this venue showed that. For me the opportunity to smell this breath of fresh air was wonderful. The band had really opened up the door for all of us to step out of our limited world into one full of colour and vibrancy. It was a trip from black and white to colour.

In the corner of the bar on a slightly raised platform were two stools and two microphones. There was at this moment a lull in proceedings with no one performing. Two guitars, battered and bruised by years of play, sat by the wall waiting to be picked up and befriended. There was no music in the air, at least not music that had traditional notes. Rather the room was filled with the wonderful sound of people sharing stories with people. There were loud voices, outlandish laughter, and the gentle hum of idle chatter. It was fabulous.

Keith passed me my pint of black nectar and we turned to see a man take the stage.

'Welcome to the second part of our evening. Thank you again to those who did stuff in the first part. It was really cool, yea.'

I turned to look at Tricks who was obviously entranced by where we were. I suspected the people here would speak his language and I immediately felt stupid. Who was the smart one? Almost certainly Tricks.

'For those of you who have just joined us, and perhaps not even been here before, anyone can come to the stage and do whatever they want. You are all welcome. The only rule is that you keep it under ten minutes and that you are not abusive to other people who are here. If they are not here then fuck them all you want too, right?'

Big laughter.

'Now to start us off is Billy with a song. Please put your hands together for Billy.'

Polite applause. Billy, who looked very much like a band member from The Levellers, came to the stage and, picking up a guitar, addressed the audience.

'Thanks for giving me the clap.'

Gentle laughter.

'And I mean you Carl!'

Lots of laughing.

'I'm going to sing one of my new songs. It's a gentle song called 'Rain.'' I hope you like it.'

As I listened to Billy playing his song I was struck by the fact that unlike my Band, which was all about being big and loud and hopefully famous, this guy was simply here in a little unknown place playing to a few friends. I didn't know if he had aspirations to play Wembley stadium but I somehow thought he probably did not. I felt a little ashamed, indeed embarrassed, by my constant connection to success being measured only in terms of how well known the band would get. Mental note – try to stop being a wanker!

Three minutes later and Billy had quietly finished his song and disappeared back into the crowd. The compère again took the stage.

'Thanks Billy. That was really cool. As always, thanks a lot man.'

I realised my mouth was wide open. I simply could not take in the fact that I was here with people who were simply here to be together and for no other reason that I could see than to be together. I knew that in all honesty I had come up to the room in the hope that I would be able to crib a story that I could use for many months to come to laugh at their expense. My shame was not going away, it was building. I decided to file these feelings away in my brain for now, marked under the section 'try to not be like that again.'

'And now to Sarah with, I believe, a poem.'

Applause made its way around the room as a lady made her way to the stage. She was quite small and dainty. She was, as so many here were, in hippie gear with lots of beads around her neck and on her wrists. Her hair was dark, long, and beautiful. Her face was soft and her eyes large and bright. Her cheeks were high and her smile sweet.

'Thanks Tom,' she said.

My feelings of shame were being replaced by awkwardness. It was as though we had stumbled across a special place where all the people knew each other in a unique way. Their meeting was one of self-expression without taking advantage over one another. We were outsiders and probably had no place here. And yet the room had not been barred to us and no one had looked at me in an aggressive or unwelcoming manner. Sarah went on,

'As some of you know I recently lost my brother, Tim, to AIDS. Those of us who knew him all miss him.'

There was a pause, a gentle quiet moment as people took in what she was saying. It was strange. It was a heavy emotional thing that was happening but without it feeling threatening. Sarah continued,

'And yet somehow the way he was, the way he lived, the things he said. They are all with me all the time and they comfort me.'

Sarah stopped to wipe away a tear from her cheek.

'It's OK Sarah. Take your time. We're with you.'

It was someone from the crowd, a lady's voice. I could not see who. It was just a friendly voice that gave her friend strength. They really were there with her! It was like being in an episode of The Waltons, and yet all I felt was the embarrassment of being my own personal dick head.

'I just know how much Tim loved to be here and with tonight being, well would have been, his birthday, I just wanted to read one of his favourite pieces of poetry.'

She stopped just for a moment to gather her thoughts. I looked at this young lady and floods of emotion ran through my body. There was nothing to say to either Keith or Tricks. We were each in our own way caught up and transfixed by what we were experiencing. I glanced at Keith. He was smiling. Something about his look told me he felt at home here. Somehow this made me feel worse as I imagined he felt more at home here because he too was a far nicer person than I. I filed this thought in my brain too, but this time in the section marked 'try to be different.' I thought of my family and friends and how I had not known pain like Sarah was feeling. I felt humbled and empty.

'The poem is called Morte D'Arthur and it is written by Alfred Tennyson as most of you will know (I didn't…) and I shall read some of it, not all of it I promise!'

Gentle laughter flowed around the room like a healing balm.

'So all day long the noise of battle rolled
Among the mountains by the winter sea;
Until King Arthur's table, man by man,
Had fallen in Lyonnesse about their Lord,
King Arthur: then, because his wound was deep,
The bold Sir Bedivere uplifted him,
Sir Bedivere, the last of all his knights,
And bore him to a chapel nigh the field,
A broken chancel with a broken cross,
That stood on a dark strait of barren land.
On one side lay the Ocean, and on one
Lay a great water, and the moon was full.
Then spake King Arthur to Sir Bedivere:
'The sequel of to-day unsolders all
The goodliest fellowship of famous knights
Whereof this world holds records. I think that we
Shall never more, at any future time,

Delight our souls with talk of knightly deeds,
Walking about the gardens and the halls
Of Camelot, as in the days that were.
I perish by this people which I made, –
Tho' Merlin swear that I should come again
To rule once more-but let what will be, be,
I am so deeply smitten thro' the helm
That without help I cannot last till morn.
Thou therefore take my brand Excalibur,
Which was my pride: for thou rememberest how
In those old days, one summer noon, an arm
Rose up from out the bossom of the lake,
Clothed in white Steveite, mystic, wonderful,
Holding the sword-and how I rowed across
And took it, and have worn it, like a King:
And, wheresoever I am sung or told
In aftertime, this also shall be known:
Not now delay not: take Excalibur,
And fling him far into the middle mere:
Watch what thou seest, and lightly bring me word."

Sarah paused, a natural break in Lord Tennyson's telling of Arthur's last moments. The poem was clearly synonymous not only as Tim's favourite poem, but also of his own passing away and what it meant to those he had left.

As Sarah had read she had done so with a clarity and feeling that moved me. Her voice took me back in my memories to warm winter nights when I had stolen my mother from my greedy family who all wanted and needed her to themselves too. By some magical twist of fate I found myself resting in her arms as she read to me, her soft voice causing my heart to warm and my eyes to shut.

Sarah carried on,

'For those of you who don't know the poem, Sir Bedivere leaves King Arthur to throw Excalibur into the lake.'

Sarah stopped and laughed.

'Is this taking any of you back to English Literature days at school?'

'Yea, my teacher was fucking gorgeous too,' shouted someone from the crowd.

Laughter exploded. It was that nervous kind of laughter where you can't help but laugh but you are not sure if you should have done. Sarah coloured up a little.

'Well for those of you with less happy memories I apologise. Anyway Sir Bedivere goes to throw Excalibur into the lake but finds himself unable to throw such a beautiful sword away. He doesn't understand. Twice he returns to King Arthur and twice King Arthur scolds him, seeing right through him. The third time Sir Bedivere throws Excalibur into the lake and again the same mystical arm rises out of the water. He goes back to King Arthur and tells him what he has seen and he then helps the dying King to the water's edge where a barge with three Queens awaits them. Sir Bedivere helps his King onto the barge and the three Queens comfort him. You know in this poem I am very much Sir Bedivere, not wanting my brother to go, not understanding that he had to. Let me read the last pieces.'

She pushed her right hand through her hair, pushing it around her ear. In that moment I swear I have never seen a more beautiful woman in my life. The radiance of inner beauty was far too much for me and I realised a tear had fallen down my cheek. I suddenly felt incredibly embarrassed only to find an arm come around my shoulder. I turned to Keith. His face was empty of him. He smiled at me and turned to the stage. I took a deep breath and did the same.

She continued.

'Then loudly cried the bold Sir Bedivere,
'Ah! My Lord Arthur, wither shall I go?
Where shall I hide my forehead and my eyes?
For now I see the true old times are dead,
When every morning brought a noble chance,
And every chance brought out a noble knight.
Such times have been not since the light that led
The holy Elders with the gift of myrrh.
But now the whole ROUND TABLE is dissolved
Which was an image of the mighty world;
And I, the last, go forth companionless,
And the days darken round me, and the years,
Among new men, strange faces, other minds,'
And slowly answered Arthur from the barge:
'The old order changeth, yielding place to new,
And God fulfils himself in many ways,
Lest one good custom shall corrupt the world.
Comfort thyself: what comfort is in me?
I have lived my life, and that which I have done
May he within himself make pure! but thou,
If thou shoulst never see my face again,
Pray for my soul. More things are wrought by prayer
Than this world dreams of. Wherefore, let thy voice
Rise like a fountain for me night and day.
For what are men better than sheep and goats
That nourish a blind life without the brain,
If, knowing God, they lift not hands of prayer
Both for themselves and those who call them friend?
For so the whole round earth is every way
Bound by gold chains about the feet of God.
But now farewell. I am going a long way
With these thou seest-if indeed I go-
(For all my mind is clouded with a doubt)

To the island-valley of Avilion;
Where falls not hail, or rain, or any snow,
Nor ever wind blows loudly; but it lies
Deep meadowed, happy, fair with orchard lawns
And bowery hollows crowned with Summer Sea,
Where I will heal me of my grievous wound.'
So said he, and the barge with oar and sail
Moved from the brink, like some full-breasted swan
That, fluting a wild carol ere her death,
Ruffles her pure cold plume, and takes the flood
With swarthy webs. Long stood Sir Bedivere
Revolving many memories, till the hull
Looked one black dot against the verge of dawn,
And on the mere the wailing died away.'

As Sarah had read, tears had gently and willingly fallen down her cheeks. She didn't stop to wipe them away. She just read.

As she finished she simply closed the book from which she was reading and walked back into the crowd rather like King Arthur's boat disappearing into the Lake. I could not see the group she was with, they were sat in the far corner of the room away from me. I did see an arm go around her and her head fall to rest on the shoulder of the person who had comforted her.

I turned to Keith who nodded to me and gently smiled. We then turned to look for Tricks who had found a chair and was fast asleep.

'Philistine,' muttered Keith.

'Tricks the Philistine. That really suits.'

I woke him up and the three of us made our way down stairs to find Steve. He was in the main room with the sixth formers who had come down to listen.

'Octopus any good?' I enquired.

'No idea matey,' replied Steve, 'I was busy elsewhere.'

'Busy, you say?'

'Yea, real busy!'

We both smiled. I had been having a deep touching moment upstairs, and he had been having a deep touching moment downstairs. Priceless.

14

The week flew by, as of course it would when you were looking forward to being interviewed on the radio for the first time. Compare these exciting thoughts with my day to day routine of absolute boredom and you begin to understand how difficult I was finding it to go to my day job with the contrast between night and day becoming far too great. By day I would find myself talking to customers about such wide ranging and exciting topics such as opening bank accounts, buying home insurance, cancelling direct debits and ordering foreign currency. I would find myself having out of body experiences with my physical body sat uttering words that meant nothing and my mind being absolutely caught in the night to come. My life was quickly speeding towards one of extremes and the cracks were becoming far too visible. My week days were not filled with body fluid making excitement, but my evenings and weekends were coming alive. I was living two lives, one to provide the pound notes, and the other to spend them.

On the night of the big BBC interview the band met up at the rather earthy Firkin pub in Nottingham, which was just next to the studios. We had decided that the best way to steady our nerves and consider some of the awe inspiring things we would say in the interview was to drink a fair amount of thought inspiring alcohol. Perhaps not the most cunning plan in history and almost certainly not one that would have won a great war, but it was the only plan we could come up with that fit into our timetable.

'I think I might talk about the size of my willy.' Steve, at his most thoughtful, would almost inevitably fall back on to thoughts about his dearest and closest friend.

'How you can't find it and you need help?' I replied, without hesitation.

'No! How people the world over talk about his many attributes'

'His?'

'Yes. He is a he.'

'That's nice,' I said, smiling and wondering what Keith would have to say to inspire us when he arrived back from the bar with fresh bottles of nectar.

'Or the size of your spliff, man,' interjected Tricks with a crooked smile.

'Yo dude, good call, though keep that sort of talk down,' Steve offered, nodding towards the approaching bass player and very aware that Keith would not like talk of drugs at this crucial point.

I offered Tricks a little smile and he caught it, wrapped it worryingly in warmth and gave me one back.

Silence settled over our little gathering and now the great man spoke. He looked at us all over the bottles of fresh beer, overfilling ashtray and bags of crisps that filled the table, and he began his Churchillian speech that would send us into the interview as men with a mission. Churchill was in fact a real hero of Keith's. He had read loads of books about him, watched films and documentaries around him, and, I suspected, practised in front of a mirror to be like him. I could imagine him addressing his girlfriend during a sexual encounter. He would start along the lines of,

'No one can guarantee success in bed, but only deserve it. Never give in, never give in, never, never, never, never – in nothing, great or small, large or petty…'

His girlfriend would look at him with longing eyes, showing through her look the passions that he had caused to take over her body. He would look back at her and, as he pulled down his trousers to reveal his bright red extra tight jockey pants which were from a selection of three for a pound from 'Dickie Dirts', he would say,

'I have nothing to offer but blood, toil, tears, and sweat.'

And she would shed a tear at the very excitement and prospect of such an advance.

They would then embrace and do what came naturally. Hours, or perhaps minutes, or perhaps an hour and a few minutes later, the two of them would be lying back on their love nest of joy when Keith would stand up and deliver the fine lines of,

'This is not the end. It is not even the beginning of the end. But it is, perhaps, the end of the beginning.'

His girlfriend would begin to applaud, and the sixth formers from his class at school who had been brought around to observe would also applaud and cheer loudly. The camera crew from BBC 'Look North' who Keith had invited to see Woodhouse life for themselves would sing 'For he's a jolly good fellow', and the neighbours who Keith always liked to keep very involved would look to one another and smile knowingly whilst Mrs Warren would hand out slices of Coffee and Walnut cake baked only the night before. Yes, Keith was a triumph of the modern day man.

And so it came to pass, here at The Firkin, that a fresh speech began. He looked at each one of us slowly and individually across the smoke filled table. Being with Tricks and Steve meant that an almost smog like atmosphere followed us wherever we went. It was like living constantly in Dickensian19th century London, or in fact in a small room with a boiling kettle that was very smelly.

'Tonight boys we get our big chance to address the youth of today.'

The youth of today. You had to hand it to Keith. He was an evangelist in the making.

'They will be having their Saturday tea, many making preparations for their evening's entertainment, when on their radio will come news of the most exciting thing to hit Nottingham.'

'Debenhams?' ventured Steve.

'The roads?' I offered.

'Spliffs man,' grinned Tricks who promptly received a kick on his shin from Steve under the table.

Keith nodded to us all in the same way that a dog owner would smile at the little puppy who had for the first time gone to the door to be let out to do its business rather than do it all over the floor in the living room.

'Yes brothers in arms, tonight we will address the youth of today and our address will be our future...'

His adopted Churchillian voice now slowed for extra depth of feeling as he now eased into his flow. As always with Keith he was half joking and yet half serious at the same time. He spoke with a grin but his message was deathly serious. Miss his seriousness and risk a Paddington hard stare.

'... And when Dean, that number one disc jockey from the Beeb, asks about our plans I want us to be honest and to the point...'

'Honest?' repeated Steve with a confused look. It was not something he was good at with gilding the lily being his main forte.

'...We are the future. Wide Eyed Wonder are the way.'

'You've stolen that line, but it's very good' proffered Steve.

'Hear, hear,' I said, pounding the table.

'Right on!' added Tricks.

Keith carried on, letting our little comments happily fill the role of bit part player in a performance at the side of a master. We were the supporting occasional bongo player. He was the lead cello. He, yes Keith, was Jacqueline du Pre! We were Cyril Brown from Bognor Regis.

'But remember, whatever you do, do not go quiet on the radio because people cannot see you when you smile, they cannot hear you when you grin, your stylish clothes choice is lost on them, your designer hairstyles a waste of time. No, remember at all times my precious little parakeets, that on the radio they need to hear you, lots of you, because it is your voice and your music that will clothe their impression of you as they sit by that warm box at home called a radio listening to you as they eat their pre clubbing fill up.'

Keith sat back in his chair, a big grin on his face and we set down our beer and clapped in recognition of another great speech. We were being told that we were the future and we bathed in the glow of it all.

We arrived at the studio, as requested, at 7.00 p.m. having had far too much to drink and being definitely in the post giddy stage. The die was cast. Dean's delightful right hand anchor woman, Emma, came to let us in to the building personally. At this time of the night there was no entry via the main doors. Access was by a back door and using the intercom direct up to the studios.

As we walked together up the stairs we could hear Dodgy being interviewed live on air.

'Will we get to meet Dodgy Emma?' I asked as we walked into the studio waiting area.

'Dodgy?' replied Emma, seemingly oblivious to the fact that they were live on air now.

'They are on the radio now?' I ventured, not wanting to make her look silly given that she was just about to brief us before our big interview.

She laughed in a 'you really are sweet' way and informed me,

'Big Bands don't normally come in. We usually go to them with recording gear and do the interview in some hotel or back stage rehearsal room. It's generally only local people that we have in 'live.'' She said this in a way that suggested everyone knew this sort of thing and I nodded in a way that suggested that I knew in fact that every band did things this way. She smiled back at me in a way that told me I didn't know anything but she thought it was cute that I tried to give the impression that I knew something.

'Right lads Dean will come out to you in a few minutes and say 'Hi.' He will talk through the interview and then give you around 10 minutes to get yourselves ready whilst he plays a couple of records. Then he will call you in and you will be on 'live.''

'As in 'live?'' I checked.

'Yes, as in 'live,'' Emma smiled. She had a nice smile, a very pleasing making me feel better about life smile.

'I will leave you to do what you need to do then guys and Dean will be back for you in a mo!'

With that she turned on her heels and made her way off to the studio, closely followed by some interested eyes finding more than just her smile rather pleasing.

'What a lovely smile,' I said as she disappeared into the night like a welcomed dream.

'You do make me laugh,' said Steve, smiling himself broadly as he did so.

'Yea,' added Tricks, 'I mean, smile!' he delivered as though it was the biggest one liner ever causing him and Steve to begin to splutter like schoolchildren.

'Now then lads, to order!' Keith, as always, called us back to focus. 'Caffeine is needed to settle our wobbly brains!'

We quickly set to try and work out the coffee machine. After the far than sensible amount of alcohol consumed we needed the wake up call that caffeine could provide. We exchanged little jokes and acted around like naughty schoolboys waiting to be called into the headmaster's office. Within five minutes Dean came out of his studio and introduced himself. He was pretty much as I had imagined, cool, pleasant and kind. This all boded well! He wrote down each of our names together with our role in the Band on a sticky label, which we applied to our chests. This would ensure he knew who each of us were during the interview and which one of us he needed to address questions to during the interview. I suspected he had not had to do this with Dodgy but decided that was fair enough. He told us not to be nervous.

'Don't be nervous.'

To be ourselves,

'Be yourselves.'

To enjoy it,

'Enjoy it.'

And not to swear because it was live and this was, after all, the BBC and he would get in lots of trouble and we would never be invited back again,

'(all that).'

'Enjoy yourselves guys,' Dean added, clearly coming to the final few words he would have for us before leaving us to stew in our nerves, 'we will look after you! I have my engineer, the fabulous Alan Clifford, in the other room and he will make sure your voices are loud and clear and heard by the listening hordes! So all is good, OK?'

We all nodded extravagantly. The listening hordes had a quite a ring to it.

Dean left us then to play the last few records before we made our way onto the airwaves. It was fantastic to hear him say on the radio,

'In just a few minutes we will be hearing live from the most exciting Band in the area. You have probably heard of them because they have been making heads turn in both the local and the UK wide music community. They are, of course, Wide Eyed Wonder and they will actually be here live on The Beat at BBC studios here on Radio Nottingham.'

It sent an incredible tingle through the body to hear yourself mentioned on the radio. It was just amazing and we all exchanged huge grins.

Keith issued his last few instructions including a suggestion to Tricks that if he didn't feel he could talk without swearing that he perhaps should try not to speak at all. Tricks just smiled and said,

'Fuckin' cool dude.'

Then we heard Dean announce,

'Here is Oasis, a Band that I know have had a big impact on our next guests. The track is called 'Live Forever' and after that we will have Wide Eyed Wonder live in the studio.'

'Live Forever' started and Emma came out of the studio to fetch us and take us back in with her and get us seated and ready. Dean was sat behind his desk with all sorts of switches and lights everywhere. CD cases were piled high all around him and his desk was covered in papers. Across from him were four chairs and on the edge of his desk in front of the chairs was a big microphone with one of those black woolly jumper type coverings.

'Now then guys,' it was Dean addressing us as DJ to Band, 'when the track finishes I shall introduce you one by one. Just say Hi to the listeners. When you speak please do lean into the mic so that we can make sure you are clear and heard by everyone. OK?'

We all nodded in unison like obedient little Westland terriers, all lined up and preened to perfection for their big show at Crufts.

'OK!' we replied.

'Live Forever' came to an end and Dean announced,

'That was Live Forever by Oasis, a Band who continue to make all the music news headlines and a band who have influenced lots of people. Here in the studio I am delighted to say that I have with me a local Band who are also gaining headlines and are some of those people who Oasis have very much influenced. We are delighted to have these guys with us tonight, Wide Eyed Wonder, welcome to the studios of the BBC.'

We all muttered out some sort of greeting apart from Keith who leaned, as instructed, into the microphone and said a very firm and very loud,

'HELLO DEAN.'

'Let me introduce you all. Firstly we have the bass player, and interestingly with the Oasis connection the first brother of this band, Keith.'

'HELLO DEAN.'

'Next to him we have the second brother and the lead singer of the Band, Anthony.'

'Hi,' I managed in a far too soft voice causing Dean to smile at me and motion to us all to speak out louder and clearer.

'Next to Anthony is the lead guitarist and backing vocals of Steve.'

'Alright,' declared Steve loudly and easily.

'And then last, but by no means least, the drummer with the great name, Tricks.'

'Yea man,' said Tricks. You could hear his grin through his voice.

'Now then guys. You have only been on the circuit for a few months and yet everyone is talking about you. Why?'

I was thinking of a suitable answer. I could see Steve was doing the same. I have no idea what Tricks was thinking. A simple question had caused my mind to become a wilderness for any words. An empty wind rushed across the desert of my brain and I realised that being interviewed on the radio had all the potential for me to look like a donkey! Thankfully Keith needed no time to think as he leaned easily into the mic and spoke.

'Well Dean it's because we are doing what the people want. We are a real band, playing to real people, real tunes.'

'Yea man,' added Tricks, 'we rock. We Fu...'

'...fully understand how people feel,' interrupted Keith, whilst shooting a look to Steve to keep Tricks in order. It was rather like asking Steve to keep his willy in his pants when faced by women who found him attractive. It simply could not happen.

Dean had a little smile on his face that may have been hiding a 'What a bunch of wankers' thought. Then again he could have been suffering from wind or perhaps he really was interested in us and found us amusing. I hoped it was the latter because I rather liked him and his show. He seemed a real nice fella and I hoped that Tricks could keep all foul and abusive language in check so that Dean would keep his job forever!

'Now I mentioned the Oasis connection. First of all you like the Band a lot, and then two of you are brothers just like the Oasis brothers.'

Dean was addressing the whole Band but Keith leapt in to answer. Once again he leaned into the microphone like a well-trained seal at a sanctuary pooping up to catch perfectly the food.

'That's right Dean. We respect them Dean. We respect what they have done. Their music flies in the face of all the techno grunge stuff that is out there. It says a simple message that doesn't allow itself to be tainted by those people in marketing and in the media. With the songs that Anthony writes...'

Anthony! Why include me. He was doing perfectly alright on his own. There really was no need to encourage Dean to come and get me involved. I pinched him hard.

'...We are doing the same. Our music though is better.'

'Better than Oasis?' remarked Dean in an incredulous voice that he could have used in asking us 'Is the world really round and, by the way, does night always follow day?'

'Yea man. We rock. We fu...'

'... fully rock,' jumped in Steve in his new found role of covering over Tricks swearing without Dean or the listener realising what was happening. Keith just stared ahead, Tricks and his lack of control was not going to put him off kilter though I suspected he may kill him later.

'And so you write the songs Anthony and these songs, are they better than those written by the Gallaghers?' asked Dean continuing to use a voice of utter disbelief which was fair enough as clearly what Keith had said was plainly ridiculous. I shot my dear brother a bothered glance only to see him grinning back at me in a proud, 'he's my brother,' sort of way.

'Well Dean, our music is from the East Midlands and not from the streets of Manchester so that's got to be in our favour!'

Dean smiled widely at this. I had delivered a killer line and my dear brother sat back nodding his head in agreement rather like the cabinet sat behind the PM at Prime Minster's question time.

'And the process of writing these tunes of the Midlands is what?' Dean asked warmly.

'Well, I write the tune and the words and then Steve adds all the gloss. He makes what I write turn into Wide Eyed Wonder material.'

'And where does your inspiration come from?'

A cunning question and far too deep for me given the lager and Guinness I had just consumed.

'Erm, everywhere. Everything. I write about things that are around me, things that are like Keith was saying real things. I haven't got round to writing about Keith's wind problems but I will soon.'

We all laughed and Tricks could be heard saying,

'This is fuckin' shit cool man, fuckin' shit cool.'

Whilst Steve could be heard covering over this with,

'Funkin sheer cool man, funkin sheer cool.'

I could see Emma looking very perplexed and worried but thankfully Dean hadn't caught on. It was then I realised that Tricks was more out of his head than normal, which was really saying something. He was on an all time roller coaster of a high, and live on the radio on our first big broadcast was not necessarily the place he needed to be.

'And so would you say, as your brother has said, that you are better than Oasis?'

Now there was a loaded question! Of course we weren't better than Oasis. How could you be better than to what I considered to be the best? Keith had been caught up in the moment and his pride in the band and me, and committed the must not do media heresy of saying something that was plainly not the case and that people would hear and think we were jumped up egotistical monsters. I looked at Tricks and realised that we probably were.

'Yea, why not!' I said, in a faltering, stumbling affirmation that showed I didn't really mean it, just in case Liam was listening and he might want to hit me, but was a yes nonetheless that would encourage people to come and find out for themselves.

'So guys what's next? Tell us what's coming up. What are you going to throw up that is going to turn the head of the music industry.'

I think it was the phrase 'coming up', although it may have been the more classic line which followed of 'throw up', that caused Tricks to be exceptionally sick. It sort of came out in one big line across the desk and all over Dean. I don't know what it sounded like on the radio but to me I heard a gurgling sort of noise first followed by the classic throw up cry.

I considered running out of the studio straightaway and hiding somewhere, but I found myself strangely unable to move. It was as though we were having a dream like experience that couldn't really be happening and I was literally stuck to my seat by the most super of glues. I turned firstly to a very stunned looking Steve who in turn was looking across to a grief stricken Emma. Dean was just sat startled, Trick's discharge covering his head and body. I noticed a little drip just thinking about whether to fall off the end of his nose or not, and I was tempted to lean over the table and just wipe it off for him and sat considering the small gesture by way of easing the pitiful situation. My attention was then yanked back to Keith who in a classic World War II like operation that Churchill would have indeed been proud of, had seized the initiative and was actually announcing our up and coming dates. The nerve was something to behold. A gentle smile could be seen at the side of his lips as he spoke to the nation,

'Well Dean, the big news is that on Thursday we are at Nottingham's prime venue Rock City, so listeners don't miss out but be there and see us all in a blaze of glory. We will be taking names there for our bus trip to London on Saturday August the 11th where we will be playing one of the capitals premier music venues for new bands 'The Orange Club.' If you want tickets please call on Mansfield 01623 328419…'

As Keith was speaking Dean had slowly stood up and left the studio. He had said nothing, utter and total shock taking away his vocal ability. I remained fastened to my seat, now probably out of fear of moving and not thankfully because some of Tricks' spray had reached my chair. Emma had also left the studio and I could see her busily setting up another desk in an adjoining studio.

Tricks was bent over double holding his stomach and murmuring 'fuck me, fuck me man…'

He was probably murmuring loud enough for the listeners to hear him, which in turn began to bring a little smile to my face.

Steve turned to me and said, simply,

'In a few days we will be able to just laugh about this.'

I smiled encouragingly. At least we couldn't be arrested for one of us being sick. Keith carried on with our gig list and forthcoming events and reasons why the listeners lives would be enriched by following us. I could see Emma switching on buttons and I suspected Keith had only seconds before his fine display would be cut.

'Keith,' I said, interrupting his flow, 'What are your thoughts on the wider issues of music, for instance where do you stand on playing music in public lifts.'

He laughed. I went on,

'In fact, let me bring in Steve here. Steve, what are your thoughts on women?'

'In general?'

'No, in the Mansfield General Hospital.'

'Isn't that shut?'

'Yes, but before it shut, what did you think to the women at the General?'

'I thought they were dreamy. They had lovely see through nurse like uniforms…'

'All of them, or just the nurses?'

'In my eyes, all of them.'

'OK. Thank you Steve. And Tricks, where do you stand on sharing things in public, like for instance food?'

Tricks remained bent over but the listener if they listened carefully, and I am sure they were by now listening very carefully, could have just heard him utter the immortal line,

'I'm fuckin cooked man. Give me air, get me air'

'Thank you Tricks' I responded, in classic interviewing type person voice. 'And so Keith, before we hand back to Dean, just remind the listener of all those gig dates.'

'Thank you Anthony. Of course.'

And he did. Every last detail. Just as he was describing the bus in its minutiae for our London trip, including the velour seats and the silver rimmed ash trays, 'Return of the Space Cowboy' cut across him. So ended our fine first visit to a Radio station. We sprinted out of the studios without waiting to talk through the interview with Dean, and then out into the night laughing uncontrollably.

The CHAD, Mansfield's fine local newspaper, ran the headline 'Band in Disgrace' on the front page and pages four and five in a PR pouring like manna from music heaven. The article covered all the major points in fantastic detail from all the parties concerned. Dean's team tried to be as diplomatic as possible, after all, the episode had future rock and roll stars written all over it and everyone was talking about it. Dean was quoted as saying 'The lad obviously had a poorly stomach.'

It was a quote that was taken straight from the diplomatic diploma course studied, no doubt, at BBC HQ.

Emma was quoted as saying 'They were a little bit out of control.' That was more like it. The station chief was not diplomatic in any way. Of course we had not even met him but he made it clear in his three paragraphs of quotes that he knew us only too well. He said that we were all extremely drunk and that from the moment we had arrived it was obvious that we were going to be trouble. This was not at all true as we had arrived with the intention of being fabulous, although, and to be fair to the fat controller, Tricks was so far gone that you could have safely said he was off his trolley and looking back most definitely going to be trouble…

The cheeky executive went on to say that we were so far out of control that they had to call security to have us ejected from the building. As regards to being out of control I think he was referring to when we took over the show but then again what could we do? They were a man down with Dean unable to speak and suffering from shock plus needing to freshen up in the bathroom. We were simply doing what anybody would have done by filling in for him. It is worth noting that we did this totally gratis and would not be claiming our financial right in carrying out DJ duties live on the radio. As for calling security, as soon as we realised they had regained control of the show from the other studio, we had done a runner through the same door we had arrived. We never saw any hard looking security types coming to do their worse and exert their authority. Just as well really as it would undoubtedly have made us all ill!

The report included a quote from a local councillor who said that young bands often incited this sort of behaviour. He said that the young people of today would be better off avoiding the sort of fair that bands like Wide Eyed Wonder had to offer. Had he even seen us? I suspected not, unless he had worked in a former life in the council within the environment team and he had been forced to call, on a wet and miserable night, to ask a band to turn down their act.

On Keith's advice Tricks simply lied. He was correctly quoted by saying,

'I had been feeling very down dude in my stomach area for over a week, but man I just felt I had to be at my first time on rockin' radio. I was so excited man, but then my illness took over. To the main man Deano, I am just so sorry man. If you are reading this article I want you to know you are a happening guy and I don't want you to let this affect what you do. I would love to meet you and apologise to you personally man.'

It was a heart-rending quote that disguised the fact that he had in fact been hopelessly drunk and as high as a very high thing.

The interviewer had met my mother coming out of work from the Kings Mill hospital where she was a medical secretary. I have no idea how they knew she worked there, although it was the local paper with local reporters and therefore people who knew local people. She was beautifully quoted as saying,

'My boys wouldn't do anything of the sort.'

The wonderful mother type point here is that she really believed we would not. She had not caught any of the interview because we had deliberately not told her we would be on radio for fear of some poor language coming out. Therefore Mother was able to truly take her position of butter not in a thousand years melting in our mouths!'

There was a lovely picture of mum on the front page with her simply smiling sweetly for the cameraman. There was an ambulance behind her and a few nurses walking through the hospitals main entrance. The photo had a warm feeling about it which in any other scenario would have been reason enough for mother, I felt, to be proud of the photo. Instead it added somewhat to her own misgivings about the Band. As for my Dad, well he kept his own council and said nothing though his face over dinner that night, lasagne and a salad consisting almost entirely of iceberg lettuce, was one that clearly said it would take some time to get over this.

I was asked by the press for my version of events and I decided to be simple and direct,

'It was really wonderful of Dean to let us have a go at taking over the show. That entire sick story is clearly far too incredible to be true isn't it? Wide Eyed Wonder are the coolest Band around so make sure you catch us at Rock City on Thursday.'

Keith, who was with me when we were questioned by the CHAD reporter, added to my fine comments by saying,

'I enjoyed it so much that I can't wait for Dean and the gang to invite us back. What a guy! I hope that all DJ's are like Dean.'

Steve said, when phoned out of the blue by the intrepid CHAD reporter,

'Radio show? What radio show? I haven't even been on a radio show.'

Priceless.

The large picture of the four of us, taken after our Leicester Charlotte gig by Steve's little pal, was incredible advertising for us. I thought we looked great. Better still, the story was picked up by the NME and The Daily Mirror with little snippets of joy being relayed across their inner need to fill pages. PR genius! By the time Thursday night would arrive we would be the toast of every music type person in the area and we knew we were in for a very busy night at Rock City. For Tricks, being sick had never felt so good. It was a marketing dream made in heaven and we intended to milk it for all it was worth. We would be like cow hands at the udders of the world's greatest milk giving cow. This cow was there to be squeezed and yes sir, we were going to squeeze this baby for all she was worth!

15

I saw Annabella again on the Tuesday night. We had talked on the phone twice since our dinner together. They were long chats that seemed to go on forever. Our conversations were flowing really well with me constantly interjecting to try to make her laugh as much as possible. I told her all about the Band and my ridiculous job. Annabella told me she did not think my job was ridiculous but rather normal. I told her I did not want to be normal. She told me I would be many things in my life, one of which she made clear would never be normal. She talked about her course and how busy she was and what she hoped for. I told her she was brilliant and would be the most famous artist ever. She told me I hadn't even seen her work and that my kind words were never going to come true. I told her I would like to see everything to form my own judgement on her wares and she told me not to be cheeky. The thing was that in talking to Annabella all I wanted to do was to be cheeky.

'Let me be cheeky,' I asked, solemnly.

'No,' she replied, sweetly.

'Can I squeeze your breasts?' I asked, quietly in my brain, which came out as,

'Fair enough…'

Our busy schedules allowed us at last to get together and we met once again at That Cafe Bar. I had called ahead and asked them to set aside the same table thinking the touch a romantic one. I arrived before her with a single rose greeting me for company in the middle of the table as I sat looking at the fabulously painted walls. The artists had literally painted figures all along the sides that stood besides me in different electrifying poses that caught the eye. The paintings were in vibrant reds and oranges that blended in perfectly with the wooden floors and the big in your face mirrors. I sat giving each names and thinking about the big gig to come.

I had arrived five minutes early and Annabella arrived fashionably ten minutes late. We kissed, a quick meeting of our lips that sent a pulse all the way down to my nether regions.

'Sorry I'm late,' she said.

'Are you late?'

She smiled.

'Well bugger me backwards with a large cucumber. I really didn't notice. Admitted I have been here all day, but no matter. You are here now.'

We ordered our food, both going for spicy little numbers to add to the spice that I wanted to have away with her later. We exchanged a little general chitchat as we worked through the little bit of embarrassment of only our second proper 'date.' Not that it was a date, officially that is. Of course to me it was an out and out date. It was as much of a date as the dates in date and walnut cake. It was a real big brassy tart of a date. For Annabella I imagined it was more of a meeting a friend as far as my boyfriend needs to know meal. She was treading carefully and I understood that. I didn't like it, but I understood. Simple really given that Callum was probably 17 feet tall and weighed in at 68 stone of pure muscle, and probably not one for taking the news of this dalliance with much delight. If he turned out to be a violent type I was in trouble as fighting had never been my strong point.

It was true that I had mastered taking a punch after years of being terrorised by my brother. He adored using the top of my arm as a punch bag, or my thigh as something to be kneed very heavily. Giving me a dead arm, or leg, or dead anything really, was one of his favourite pastimes and I would punch back with my younger arms, only to be punched back even harder by older stronger blows. It was a totally uneven contest and I had therefore learnt very early on, probably from the age of a few days, that fighting back brought a swift hurtful response usually culminating in me hiding somewhere safe until Keith had gone out to do whatever he went out to do. By the time I had grown up and I was big enough to fight back against my older sibling, he had gone on to other things and revenge was not a dish to be served at all.

Perhaps someday all that locked up terror and need to avenge will come out of me in a fit of rage. I might be in a Safeway store, for instance, at the cheese counter and suddenly for no reason go mad when asking for blue cheese, despite the fact that I hate the stuff, and lo and behold they've just run out! That could be the final straw and I explode in a fit of expletives that see me carried out of the store by a large security man who once worked for the Met. 'Banged up for Cheese!' will be the headline in the local CHAD newspaper.

Perhaps revenge might not be so sweet after all. Even the mystery to me that was Callum McCore might take a more pragmatic view and not wish to kill me. He may reason that Annabella and I were clearly more suited to one another than his own involvement. He may also prefer another relationship himself and this may be the perfect opportunity to get him off the hook and release him from the chains of a not working relationship. On the other hand he may view me as a lying, snivelling little shit who, if he could see me now, with my angelic smile and happy eyes, would find interesting and unusual ways to alter my appearance. I guess you just couldn't second-guess the great Callum McCore. All I could do was to try pretend it didn't matter and in my great dreamscape carry on as though all that mattered in the world was this perfect moment. Delusion ever was and ever is.

As the wine came and we relaxed in each other's company the conversation just flowed so wonderfully well. We put the world to rights and laughed about it all as we did so. If only world leaders could take a leaf out of our book, albeit that would also entail them all wanting to sleep with other! And yet throughout the evening one subject kept coming back to haunt me like a really scary ghost who comes back to haunt you despite the fact that you ask him nicely not to. His presence cast a shadow upon me, as though I was sat at the side of a massive tower, and the sun was directly the other side of the tower casting an almighty and freezing cold shade over my whole body.

Annabella had just finished telling me about how her and her friends had spent the afternoon messing around in the dark room. As she had done so I had gazed at her imagining my lips upon everything I could see and then all of a sudden I was pulled out of my beautiful dream by the thought of Little Knob Callum McCore. I could stand it no more. I had to get the bottom of how she was feeling about me and 'him.'

'Has Callum modelled for you?'

'At college?' Annabella answered quickly, perfectly relaxed, and seemingly not at all worried by me bringing up the subject of the boyfriend.

'Anywhere?' I spluttered not really wanting to hear any other answer than no he has not because he is so square.

'Not at college…'

I smiled.

'…But quite a lot at home, or at the gym.'

My head screamed with a noise akin to a police siren. Alright, enough already I thought. However that wasn't enough. I needed to know more. I tried to remain looking unfazed and relaxed. I said,

'Oh that's nice.'

Annabella smiled. How did she manage to read me so easily? To look into my thoughts and to know me.

'Anthony…'

'No it's OK,' I interrupted, 'I shouldn't have asked.'

'No you should.'

'No I should not. I don't want you to have to pick because I know he has you and I…' I paused, wondering what I could say, '…don't want to lose you because I've only just found you, and…'

Annabella reached over the table and took my hand and tears annoyingly filled my eyes for no apparent reason.

'…I really like you Annabella… I do.'

Annabella smiled at me and stroked my hand.

'I know you do and I like you, a lot. You must know I do, don't you?'

I smiled. I had been here before, dumped by a girl who thought I was nice, but also thought I was as mad as a mad thing. I am. That's my problem. People didn't really know what to make of me. They like me to be a fool, to be around, but as for someone spending too long with me it was like asking someone to go into the lion's cage with a lion who has a personality crisis.

I braced myself, ready for the inevitable line that would send me back into the world without her.

'Callum and I have been together for three years,' Annabella said.

'Nice,' I replied with no enthusiasm.

'Listen Anthony, I want to tell you everything so that you know where we stand. Is that OK?'

She was being serious so I gave her my serious face back and replied,

'Yea sure, sure it is. Sorry.' A pause filled the air. Silence waited for me to speak again. 'Seriously, I am sorry. I do want to listen, for you to feel comfortable to talk without me being stupid, as always. Well when I say always, not always, that is, not now.'

I looked at her soft red lips as she began to speak about how she met Callum. I wondered whether she was about to tell me her history with little knob because she wanted to keep seeing me or because she was about to tell me she couldn't see me again. Her big blue eyes, her soft high and sexy cheekbones. I didn't want to listen and yet, like that same macabre interest that causes you to be unable to not look at an accident as you drive by the ambulances and accompanying crowd, I had to.

'I was young and he was…'

'A sheep farmer?'

Annabella gave me a look that told me she was very serious and a further ill-timed interruption would not be well received.

'Sorry. Please go on. I won't interrupt again. Promise. Cross my heart, hope to wee myself.'

Annabella smiled. I had apologised enough for her to go on, thankfully having made her smile too.

'He was 25 and gorgeous.'

GORGEOUS!!!!!!!! As starting statements went on the getting the blood boiling front, this was up there with the Pharaoh saying to Moses 'No you can't leave Egypt!' I changed the word gorgeous automatically in my brain to read nauseous, after all it almost rhymed and Callum was most definitely causing me to feel pretty sick!

'He drove a red sports car and I was just a young girl. We met at a club in Nottingham. I was dancing away and then suddenly this really attractive man appears and danced with me like an angel. He can really move, you know?'

I did not know. I am the worst of dancers, my arms and legs go in different directions, all four of them. I have zero timing. Bugger.

'…I was blown away. We danced, we talked and we got on really well. It was fantastic. I had never met anyone like him and I thought I had fallen in love, there and then.'

'He was a lucky, lucky man.'

'And still is.'

'Certainly is. He is the luckiest man in the world.'

I declared this statement with a fervour that surprised even me. I liked this girl perhaps even more than I thought, and it was already loads. I had met and known lots of girls, some of whom I had gone out with and some of whom I had really liked, but not like this. This was lust and wonderment and respect and excitement all rolled into one. Perhaps this was even, dare I even think it, the early onset of love?

Annabella smiled. Ever since I had met her the normal rules of being slow to show my hand and keeping my cool had gone out of the window.

'I don't normally gush so easily you know,' I suggested, trying to hide the truth in my voice.

'Are you sure, you little charmer?'

Of course she knew exactly where I was coming from!

'To be honest Annabella I have never ever been so hopeless at hiding my feelings…'

The truth was out! I smiled and I felt I saw Annabella blush.

'You don't mind do you?' I asked.

'Of course not…'

She paused, weighing up her words. She was so good at this. Carefully deciding what to give to me, knowing that I would be carried by her words, and therefore being extra careful in exactly what she said to me.

'I like you saying all the nice things you say to me. I like it a lot.'

There was a small silence that sat between us like an extra comfy pillow that you fall on to at the end of a long day. Whatever she was to tell me about her and Callum I would just have to grin and bear it.

'Shall I continue?' she asked in a soft voice.

I nodded, holding her gaze, desperately trying to separate what I felt for her from what she was telling me.

'College came and I moved in with Callum. For a while it was really good but then things changed.'

Dinner arrived and I ordered more drinks. Between mouthfuls of glorious food Annabella told me how her and little knob had grown apart to the extent that she had moved in with her friend, and of course my friend now, Leslie. She and Callum had not yet grown far enough apart to break up. They remained 'an item.'

'So how are you both now?' I asked as matter of factly as I could manage.

'OK. We are always OK. Nothing more, nothing less.'

'And do you want more than what you have with 'him?''

'Of course…' There was a pause, an 'Annabella is thinking' pause.

'…Are you the man to give me more?'

Shock question! The mouthful of beer, which had been lovingly lowered into my mouth, now choked in my throat. Annabella went on,

'I know I am being cheeky. I have probably had far too much too drink and I probably shouldn't have said that.'

'Oh but you should, you really should!'

I looked at her, her eyes shining, and her lips ready to kiss.

'I would love to be with you Annabella.'

For a moment she held my gaze and for a short space of time the two of us were together. Then she looked away.

'I'm sorry Anthony, this isn't right. I am still seeing Callum and I need to sort out how I feel about him first.'

'You don't,' I joked.

'I do,' replied Annabella, seriously.

'You do,' I conceded.

'Listen Annabella, you don't have to make a decision now. I am not asking you too. I want to see you, but I am happy to wait, thrilled in fact.'

Annabella smiled. I had delivered the right answer!

'Take all the time you want as long as you can decide in about five minutes,' I added.

A worried look flashed across her face until she realised I was being silly. Of course I wanted her now but it would be wrong to push her.

'Thank you,' she said, simply.

The night went on. We talked and talked. Callum was now a non-subject. I knew, that is thought I knew, that this was falling on my side.

We finished with our coffees allowing the sobering effect of caffeine to hit home as we talked about the excitement of the big gig at Rock City. Annabella was to bring her camera and be our official photographer for the night.

At 12 o'clock we said goodbye to the staff and stepped out into the cool evening air. It was a clear night, although the Nottingham lights created a glare that went a long way towards hiding the stars above.

'I'll see you Thursday then,' I said in as carefree a manner as I could manage.

I leaned forward and kissed her warm cheek, the smell of her perfume on her neck filling me with desire. She suddenly took hold of me and held me tightly. I wrapped my arms around her and waited. We stood like that for a few minutes.

'Are you OK?' I whispered.

'I don't know…' she croaked '… I am OK here, with you.'

With that she leaned up and kissed me, a short soft kiss on my lips. She then stepped away.

'That was nice. I shall see you on Thursday.'

'Yea, Thursday.' I stood there happy, content.

I waited until Annabella was out of sight and then went to find my car. Things were looking well and truly up.

16

4 o'clock Thursday afternoon, and Keith picked me up from the Scotty homestead for the biggest gig to date. A few years earlier he had left the family estates, a small yet sweet three-bed semi with a postage stamp garden, to set up a new home where he could forge his own identity away from the family who he had loved but from whom he now needed space. He had moved one street away.

We lived on Catherine Avenue, a tree lined leafy slice of Mansfield Woodhouse. We were fortunate to have one of the three trees right outside our house although the annual sap loss from the sycamore meant we could rarely see out of the car window throughout the summer. A small price to pay for the honour of a sycamore tree, after all it had biblical references and, as a child, I thought this made us very grand indeed.

My dear, if not somewhat overbearing, brother and I had grown up with our two younger sisters, Anne and Susan, at this very house. It had been my mother's house since she was born and before that had been her granddad's house. Indeed she had been quite literally brought into this earth in this house and I had the honour of being the only one of the children to follow her into our world in the same way. It was a warm house with stories to tell and feelings that hugged you and made you feel you belonged. It was also a warm house because, as the older bigger boys, we got the larger and warmer South West facing bedroom in which we had a lovely single bed each. The girls got the only room that wasn't warm, this being the much smaller Northeast facing corner room with bunk beds that somehow Father had managed to squeeze in. Consequently when the winter winds shook our house it was the girls' tiny room on the back that meant each needed 28 hot water bottles to avoid frostbite. Keith and I on the other hand lay on our beds in simple multi coloured striped pyjama bottoms from the Coop humming Hawaiian theme tunes and dreaming of the sun.

Mansfield is in the East Midlands and was very much in the centre of the coal mining community. The stretch of this industry touched all of us in the area whether or not we were directly employed by it because it was so huge and so important financially. Being brought up in a pit town that was quite literally rushing towards its end without any of us knowing it had been fascinating. We were all, as youngsters, set to become involved with the mines in some way or other because it offered so many options regardless of intelligence or background. Of course you could be a miner and earn a small fortune if you got face work, or you could get an apprenticeship in engineering or technical drawing or management or finance or accounts or pretty much most things. The pits were more than getting coal out of the ground and much more about educating a poorly educated east midlands town. As we got older the nightmare scenario had happened as the pits began to cut back on staff and the inevitability of closures hit the area like a damp blanket darkening our spirits. Other jobs had to be looked at, other futures considered but recovery would take generations. How much of that was considered by those in authority is an interesting question and yet the highlight on our areas became one of outrage as miners fought one another and the authorities. The moral high ground was lost and public opinion faded into the sea of the north south divide.

My town had much going for it despite its relatively poor economic outlook. There was always good banter and friendliness that welcomed one another into each other's houses. What we were not overflowing with was culture with such wonders as art and ballet and orchestra being left to the big cities, which back in the day seemed a long way away despite Nottingham being only 12 miles away and Sheffield 24. This to most of us may as well have been London. It was a bus journey away and there was no direct bus apart from the National Express. This cost an arm and most possibly a leg, and the same bus firm went on to London so why not go the whole hog!

Yes, culture was lacking in the centre of our fine town with Mansfield not attracting the RSC, the Tate exhibitions or Royal National Ballet. We did however have the Mansfield Palace Theatre, the ABC Cinema and the Museum so all was not lost especially if stuffed animals was your thing! And yet, to a large extent I, and my wonderful friends, were cast out to be cultural heathens, and we were! The closest I got to real art was the wondrous finding that the school library contained many illustrated art books and I began an interest with the Italian Renaissance period and its fascination with nudity. I considered shortly that if this was art then it was the career for me until I then discovered I could not draw. At that stage I had not understood that in modern art this was probably a distinct advantage and instead I had decided to concentrate on other areas.

Education in general in the UK was not a sure fire way to Oxbridge and sadly the option to go there simply did not happen in our school. I had heard of the fine establishments of Oxford and Cambridge, Harvard and Stanford, but these were as accessible to me as becoming an astronaut. It may not have been the dark ages when I was at school but it might have well been. Surprisingly though I was pretty bright at school with a natural flair for maths and English. The former was a necessary evil that I found easy and just worked through, even being part of the additional maths group, which meant I got to hang out with the smart satchel brigade and pick up enormous rip from my pals. It was a price worth paying as I enjoyed the teasing for being smart! English though was what I enjoyed. I loved to read and to write and, besides anything, the English teaching department tended to employ the more interesting teaching staff. For a young boy at a comprehensive school anything that added excitement was a must have opportunity.

The major downside for me was following my brother through school. He had excelled in the sciences, subjects for which I had no interest. I would honestly have rather spent my time sand papering my bottom than listening to some teacher waffle on about atoms and body parts and ohms and experiments. It was all lost on me but not on the teaching staff who would ask the inevitable,

'You're Keith's brother, aren't you?' each teacher would exclaim with hearty expectancy on first meeting me, their keenness to have another Keith in their class.

'Yes I am.' I would reply, mustering up as much enthusiasm as I could manage.

'We shall expect great things from you then because if you

are anything like your brother you…' and at this point their eyes would go all watery and they would fix on to some imaginary far away thought, '…you will be a star pupil, a class leader.'

'Not a chance,' my mind would scream.

'I'll give it my best shot,' my mouth would say.

And then sure enough after the first parents' evening the dreadful truth of my inability to concentrate on anything scientific would come out. Inevitably from then on the teacher would drop all interest in me and move on to more worthy students. The wonders of the comprehensive cattle market system, where each pupil flies or drowns by their own interests and not their own ability, were not lost on me.

And so here I was, years later, being picked up by my big brother to go and play a gig in Nottingham at the biggest venue we had ever played, a venue that we could never have imagined that we would play. To us Rock City was a Zen like place with Mecca qualities for people with interest in real music and we, us normal little people, were going to play there.

We had been there for a few Thursdays since learning we were to play and the place was busy with students willing to get as drunk as quickly as they could. The smaller bands played down in the Disco 2000 room, which would squeeze in at a tight push a few hundred people. The trick was going to be attracting enough people into the gig venue and away from the main floor where the evening student entertainment was a fantastic dance party. The main floor was home for the big stage and the big bands. It was a large and impressive venue that on student nights was open forum for all.

We had loads of people coming and were confident that we would fill the downstairs Disco 2000, particularly after our recent press bonanza, but we still felt very nervous. This was new territory for us and we considered this as we drove through the heart of Mansfield and out up Nottingham Road towards the big city and our future.

'I've printed off a few flyers' Keith said, nodding towards two full boxes that were squeezed behind my seat. I twisted round and picked up a leaflet.

'The Next Oasis' it declared in large bold letters on top of a picture of us taken at Leicester's Charlotte, the same one that had so gracefully adorned the front of the CHAD after our radio interview. At the bottom it simply said 'Wide Eyed Wonder at Rock City Tonight.'

The flyers were in a bold orange printed by kind and unwitting courtesy of the school Keith worked at.

'Very nice,' I said, 'you are so very clever.'

'Well of course I know this information already, but all the same, thank you.'

'No, thank you.'

'Well thanks.'

'Don't mention it.'

'I won't.'

'Don't.'

'It would be wrong to.'

'You already have.'

'I have? Oh yes, I have. Good point. Please excuse the repetition.'

'So,' I declared loudly as we passed Derby Road College, an important marker as it meant we were leaving the safety of our town and going on to other places, 'this is it, the night we've been heading towards.'

'I guess it is Bob.'

The use of my shortened version of my middle name Robert never felt sweeter than when used by my brother in the right scenario, that is when declared in private!

'Have you brought your guitar?'

'I have.'

'Amp?'

'Aye!'

'Spare pants?'

'Three pairs.'

We paused, lost in little scary thoughts such as to how many times I might forget my words or how Keith might play the wrong introduction. He had done so on numerous occasions, each time convinced that everyone else was getting it wrong and carrying on regardless until it was so blindingly obvious that he was out of kilter with the rest of us. Even then he would be carrying on playing the wrong bloody tune until he had bent over to peer at the song list and realise he had made a mistake. He would then try a few bass notes to try and find the right one until eventually he would find the tune and play along as though it had all been part of the piece in the first place.

We had reached Larch Farm traffic lights at Ravenshead. This had for a long time been the posh part of our area bringing up the tone at the Joseph Whittaker Comprehensive in the large mining village, that is ex-mining village, of Rainworth. Of late though, the Gedling Borough Council had somehow adopted what had always seemed like part of our territory and had stuck up Borough of Gedling signs everywhere. I suspected they were very proud of themselves and their stupid little signs. I mean where the hell is Gedling?!

'Do you think we will be OK?' I asked Keith as Newstead Abbey's gates, the once grand home of Lord Byron, passed by on our right.

'Of course we will. Just be yourself.'

'A banker?' I enquired, half mischievously but half confused at what I actually was.

'You are not a banker.'

'Ah, you've been reading my appraisals haven't you.'

'Is it still not going too well?'

'No, it's going OK,' I said, nodding to myself. 'I think Mr Cook still wonders how on earth I got in but…' my mind wandered as it inevitably always did when I considered the dark and taxing question of how on earth I had found myself in a Bank at all.

'…oh you know, I'm doing OK but I'm just not settled.'

'Well that's good because if you were settled then you wouldn't be doing all this band stuff would you.'

'And neither would you.'

'Quite right.'

For Keith the Band was about the only thing that he could make sense of. He taught at a local comprehensive where the Headmistress would have kept a school of psychologists busy for months. The kids who were the mainstay of our fan base were at least an inspiration with which he could make sense.

For me the majority of my work colleagues would have been shocked and indeed frightened to be in the sort of crowds that listened to our music. It was the difference between them and me that made me feel so alone and out of it in my day job. The only reason I was so good at selling bank products was that it meant I could actively talk to real people every day about real things. Every time I met a customer I would spend more time talking about life, theirs and mine, than talking about anything to do with banking. The latter was just an ancillary but necessary part of our conversation that meant I would keep my job! I guess this made me more real to them because they were more than happy to sign up for loads of things. I could never understand why on sales training courses they spent days teaching you to be something you are not. Surely a fool could see that people see through the crap of sales banter. Apparently not.

Seven Mile House, the traditional halfway point between Mansfield and Nottingham came and went.

'When we are big and famous, will you still be the same?'

'Of course I will Bob. Same old Keith.'

'Will you still have so much wind or will you get treatment for it?'

Keith just smiled.

'Do you think Tricks will be alright tonight?' I was somewhat concerned about our drummer who was progressively getting more spaced out every time I saw him.

'It's the drink, right?' I asked. I think we both knew it was a deeper problem around what we knew to be 'drugs,' but because we had absolutely no understanding of what a drug even looked like, it was easier for the two of us to put this down to things we did understand.

'Yea, I'm sure it might be, possibly, maybe, perhaps.'

This was as close as Keith and I would ever get to understanding what went on in the mind of Tricks. He was a good guy. We knew that. He was very different to us. We knew that. He could play drums. We knew that. Of late though Tricks had begun to have mood swings. Not normal ups and downs related to a day's good and bad things, but real ups where the world offered him everything, and real downers where you were scared to even look at him. The good news was that whenever we gigged he was generally always on a high, but it concerned me that we were not getting closer as a band but rather growing further apart. I reasoned that long hours spent on a tour bus would need us to be close.

'He'll be fine tonight,' Keith reasoned. 'It's our biggest gig and he will be on a high.'

We let the subject go. It was easier to just assume the best and not consider things in too great a detail. I went on to a brighter subject.

'Northy boy is so excited about it. He must have rung me about 20 times this week'

'Yea, he's been ringing me too and e-mailing ridiculous suggestions for our attire this evening. He makes me laugh.'

'Me too.'

That was nice. I had brought Steve into Keith's life, and in turn Steve was making him laugh. What a good brother I am! We were now driving through Daybrook and Rock City waited for us. We would be there in 10 minutes from here.

'How many are coming tonight from school?'

'Well best estimates is about 100.'

'100!'

'Well the whole sixth form is up for it. Of course half of them are under age and I cannot be seen to be encouraging them to come, but I know most of them will give it a go.'

'Imagine that. These kids, most of whom I don't even know, are prepared to queue up and be turned away in the hope that they can get in tonight and listen to us.'

'I know. It's just brilliant.'

'They must think a lot about you.'

'They think a lot about the Band and most of that is down to you. It's your music.'

Keith always did this, made me feel proud of what I did, made me believe in what I wrote.

'I think as much as anything they love to listen to Steve.'

'I know. 'Northy, Northy, Northy.' He adores it when they chant like that. It's incredible.'

'Beautiful.'

We dropped down through Sherwood and then cut up through Hyson Green, the last part of the outskirts of the city over, and then down again and into the heart of it. Driving past Trent University I wound my window down and shouted from the car to passing students.

'It's us Wide Eyed Wonder. We're playing here tonight.'

Keith pipped his horn and waved regally to anyone who bothered to turn. We took a right and pulled up Talbot Street and then we were there, pulling into the Rock City car park. Tricks' borrowed Mum's car was already there, the boot was up and half his kit awaited collection. As we got out the trusty Belmont, Steve pulled into the car park, a large grin taking over his face. He jumped out his treasured black BMW and shouted,

'We are here, we are here!!'

We heartily slapped each other's backs in self-congratulatory satisfaction that we had blagged our way into a gig made in heaven. Unpacking our gear never felt so good with even this tedious task taking on new warmer meanings, after all we were carrying our gear into hallowed musical ground. Vole, the legendary Rock City soundman who looked like he lived in cave, met us at the door. We got signed in and were given special band wrist passes with Rock City on them that would allow us in and out all night. This simple thing made me feel like the coolest and luckiest man in the world! We were each allowed to put four names down on the guest list (guest list!) and then we made our way through to the Disco 2000 venue to sound check with the Volemeister. I did not know why Vole was called Vole. We had met him quickly a few weeks earlier and been introduced to him as an upcoming band who were due to play. He had been pleasant but he looked hard enough to not ask stupid questions and now was most certainly not the time to ask him where his name came from. He didn't particularly look like a vole although he was dark and his long hair could be said to be velvety and somewhat, perhaps, vole like in a vole like animal sort of way. Maybe I would ask Tricks to ask him later whilst I hid behind the speakers and watched for a response.

As we set up, and Vole began to connect cable after cable, Steve asked him about the Bands he did the sound for. Apparently Vole always did the sound for the Student night but other than that he was one of the main sound guys for the big bands. Each Band tended to want something different, some with a legion of their own soundmen, and others happy to rely on the local knowledge of our man Vole. He told us he had worked at Rock City for the last 12 years involved in doing the sound for just about every Band we cared to name. He was also a drummer and in fact we had heard his band practising down at Magnet. They were a rock band that made a lot of noise but did do in such an authoritative way that you found yourself, as Tricks had said, respecting the vibe, man. Tricks said as much to Vole as they set about mic'ing up his kit.

'Man,' stated Tricks in his unmistakable drawl, 'I respect your music because it kicks in with a real buzz. It makes me kinda woozy and touches my groove.'

'Well cheers man,' replied Vole with a smile that may have been from professional pleasure or possibly he was breaking wind or just general amusement at listening to Tricks. Maybe they even understood each other?

Tricks sound checked, as drummers always did, first. I never questioned the unchanging running order of a sound check. Firstly it was always Tricks. The drum sound check started somewhat monotonously. Bang, bang, bang, bang, bang and so on. Sometimes this would take 30 seconds but playing a decent venue, and especially here at Rock City with Tricks sound checking with a fellow drummer the banging, sorry sound checking of the individual drums, went on for a full 20 minutes. He then went on for a further 15 minutes going around and around his kit, sometimes playing the whole thing and sometimes individual drums. I did wonder how on earth Tricks was going to have the energy to play later after such an exhaustive sound check.

As they practised, and with the sure knowledge that it was the sledge hammering bass player to sound check next, Steve and I took a walk up to the empty main hall, which was hallowed ground for anybody who had a healthy respect for rock music.

'You know Steve,' I said as we walked out of Disco 2000 and turned to walk up the stairs to the main auditorium, 'this is something we have dreamt about.'

'I know. It's crazy isn't it.'

A few moments of silence sat around us as we climbed to the top of the stairs.

'And how do you feel?' I asked, the doors to a future we could only dream about there before us.

'Feel? I feel nervous, obviously!'

'Obviously.'

'And yet really calm, excited, full of energy. You know…'

We opened the doors and walked into the main hall, eerie in its silence and vast cavity of emptiness.

'…It's just that we've been best buddies for ages, and Keith with us now as well, and now we are here, together. It means everything,' Steve added in faltering, nervous language. This was a big night for us and we knew it.

I ran across the empty hall floor and jumped round and round in a fantastic expression of happiness and sheer elation. Steve had walked past me and had climbed on to the main stage. It was a wonderful stage that stretched far and wide and yet remained critically part of the hall and didn't threaten to over take it. This was the charm of Rock City, a venue big enough to bring big bands and yet small enough to remain accessible and real.

'Ladies and gentleman,' Steve shouted in mock announcement tone, 'please welcome, fresh from their major successful tour of America, our very own, indeed your very own, WIDE-EYED-WONDER!!!'

I applauded and attempted to wolf whistle. It was a hopeless effort seeing as I couldn't do it, but nonetheless it was a valiant try. Steve then made the wonderful lead guitar start to Take You There fall out of his lips and I jumped up and down at the front of the stage screaming 'Northy' in mock adoration.

As he skipped from one side of the stage to the other I let myself fall backwards to lie on the floor and gaze up to the light filled ceiling. My world was going round and round in my head. Tonight the band I loved, with two of my closest two buddies in the world by my side, would lay its dreams before an audience, and there in that audience would be the girl I wanted to embrace into my dreams.

Steve jumped off the stage and lay down beside me giggling at me lying on the floor and at him for joining me.

'I hope no one comes in,' he said, unusually conscious at what people might think.

'I hope someone does, after all we've got passes to be kings of the world for the night and I intend to use them.'

'You're right, in fact you are always right.'

'Apart from all those times I am not.'

'Absolutely, but let's not remember those dark times.'

We laughed. A lot.

'You know Steve, this is it. No matter how good it ever gets or doesn't get, no one can take it away from us that we have been here.'

'No one.'

I would have laid there for hours but Steve who was far more sensible than me pulled me to my feet.

'Come on Mr Rock Star. The amusement that is Keith's sound check awaits us.'

We made our way back down and sure enough the main man was on stage banging his way through his sound check routine. It wonderfully did not matter whether he was sound checking for Vole or some tiny non descript pub gig. He always had the same routine, albeit that this one was going to be a longer version of the same thing. He would work his way around his fret board in a plodding fashion that suggested he was more suited to playing in a Hillbilly Band than a cutting edge rock band of the 90's. Sometimes he would amuse us by playing through a church chorus and smiling like an engaging chimp at the wonder of the amusement spell that he cast over us. Always he would make us laugh, without fail. It was a gift. A giggle-giving gift.

Vole seemed to put up with Keith's antics with good grace and then mercifully called time. It was Steve's turn now and he was always primed for his turn, a cigarette lit in preparation, his sunglasses down from the top of his head and over his eyes. He made his way on to the stage and picked up his guitar, sliding it over his neck in a cool controlled manner that hid all the nerves I knew he felt. By this stage he had already drunk at least two pints and was well into his third. He loved to drink and I had noticed he was able to drink more and more, and do so with an ease that hid the amount he was actually drinking.

He launched into the start of 'Take You There,' feedback filling the air and causing me to cover my ears. Steve carried on regardless until he saw Vole waving wildly at him from the control section at the middle of the room.

'Turn the volume down on your amp Steve,' Vole shouted, a request that was tantamount to asking a Spurs fan to wear an Arsenal shirt. Grudgingly Steve turned down his amp a little, Vole probably realising that this was a battle he was not going to win. After a while he told Steve to use the volume that he was comfortable with from the stage and that he would only give a little volume from the main desk if the place was packed.

Then it was my turn, initially to check my rhythm guitar. I hated sound checking, but I particularly dreaded checking my guitar. My skill level was mediocre at best. As it sat at the back of the band during a performance its filler effect sounded fine but now, during a sound check, I felt again like the naked model laid bare to the world with all my faults so very plain to see.

I played through 'Hold on Tight' because it was a song that sounded OK even with my playing.

'Again please,' shouted Vole and I again begrudgingly replayed the piece.

'Again please.' AGAIN!! This man was like a top-notch torturer from a top notch-torturing place such as parents who make their young children go with them to DIY shops. I played the song this time with an over the top stage performance, smiling at my fellow band members as they gave me encouraging two finger salutes.

After that the embarrassment that was the vocal sound check began. I tended to start with the traditional 'One, two. One, two.' I would then progress on to a story usually based on fictional characters I just made up as I went along. On this occasion I didn't have the nerve to do anything other than make noises and sing a few notes.

'And a tune?' asked Vole, which given I was halfway through the scales seemed a little heartless. I sang 'Take You There' and spotted Steve pretending to take Tricks 'there' which kind of helped deflect the self awareness torture I was feeling.

'Thank you,' shouted Vole. It was weird hearing your voice be turned up and down, thrown loudly into the distance and then all of a sudden it would be cut off. Back and gone, reverb and clear, all part of the score of a band sound check. I imagined big bands had doubles for this kind of thing.

'OK Anthony…' my eyes looked up in the hope that my ordeal was over and then, there it was, '…that was great thank you.'

Bliss upon bliss! My least favourite bit of singing raw alone to a room of the band, the sound engineer and the bar staff was finally over! Glory be! Now it was Steve's turn to again take the stage and get his vocals right, a task that took mini moments it seemed to me and at last we were done. Vole asked us to make sure we were available for 9 o'clock.

'Where can we crash man?' asked Tricks as tiredness inevitably hit him. I suspected he was rarely active for more than two hours at a time and this three or four-hour stint seemed to have really knocked him out. He needed to climb into a quiet corner and do nothing for a while.

'In your dressing room if you like,' smiled Vole.

'Dressing room?' I repeated like a line thrown back in a ham half cut play.

We must have looked like excited school children because Vole picked up on our open jaws and seemed to want to father us all of a sudden.

'Yea, your dressing room boys. All our Bands get their own dressing room and rider no matter how big or small.'

Dressing room and rider. This was getting even better.

As Vole led us through a series of back stage doors and corridors we began to get the sense of walking in the footsteps of rock stars. Suede would have wandered around these very corridors. The Stone Roses too. It was all getting quite emotional.

'And…' Vole went on as he pushed open another door that led us into a large open area which would be the first point of entry for any bigger band and their gear from the car park,

'…seeing as you are the only band here tonight and I kind of like you already, you can have the number one dressing room.' NUMBER ONE DRESSING ROOM!!!! This was just getting better and better. What on earth could happen next? The room maybe filled with wonderful scantily dressed ladies wanting to massage my aching muscles? Maybe the Oasis boys would await us, having popped over to share their thoughts on how best to approach the evening.

'Now hang on there for a moment,' our glorious new friend said as he disappeared into a small room whilst we stood looking at each other with big grins on our faces. I gave Steve a big thumbs up whilst he did an impression of falling over having drunk yet another free can of beer from our rider which I suspected would actually consist of no more than four cans of Stella. We all just stood there taking in all that was around us, an area which was in fact just a large square unkempt lobby, but to us it was yet another part of the beginning of the future we longed for. Vole returned moments later with three crates of beer. THREE CRATES OF BEER! He had a happy grin on his face, which was that of a man who was proudly showing his young protégés both the ropes of the business that he was already so very much a part of, and also the riches that awaited them which clearly included lots of free booze!

'Now then,' he went on as he led us through yet another door and down a small corridor, 'there's plenty more beer for you already cooling in the fridge' he opened a door to a long room that had thread bare sofas all down one side of it. It had bad strip lighting, a large mirror and, just as he had said, plenty more beer.'

'And this is free beer?' checked the ever fiscally aware Steve.

'Of course it is. Drink as much as you want. Just don't take it into the main areas and don't tell anyone how much I've given you. I may have been overly generous!'

There was a strange smell hanging in the room. No doubt the cleaners had spent hours on trying to get rid of various stains and interesting marks left by the bands and their privileged fans that made it back stage. I noticed a small sink next to the fridge, which I noted could be useful for making tea. I would just need to find those teabags… I also noticed the walls were covered in graffiti and I looked forward to adding some of our own as the evening went on.

'So I'll leave you to it,' said Vole. We all just stood there, like school children on a camp trip having been shown to their quarters and just now waiting for the teacher to leave. Vole now turned, a grin on his face, as we all shouted thank you. We must have been the most polite band he had ever come across. No doubt, as he made his way back, a wry smile would have crossed his face as he thought of our please and thank you's! What can I say but we are what we are. I poked Keith in the back as Tricks and Steve pushed their way past me to make their way to the fridge. Vole shouted out,

'See you at nine and don't be late.'

I walked to the door to close it, and then turned back into the room and we all began to laugh. This was indeed the life. Being treated like a 'someone' who actually had talent and was therefore to be respected (!) was something we all rather liked and could definitely get used to. I knew that Vole was just another along the long line of people we would be expected to woo with our talents, but nonetheless to us he was an important person, an older hand, who showed us respect and was himself to be respected. It was rather like Luke Skywalker meeting Obi-Wan Kenobi or the young Bill Clinton meeting JFK, like minds skipping over the difference in ages to forge an impressive link that knew no bounds. OK I know I am overdoing it and of course Vole was in truth only a few years older than us but the point is still valid. Just. Perhaps. No, sure it is.

We tossed the beers around the changing room. Keith exchanged a giggle enhancing wind escape that meant we had to leave the room for a little while. On return Tricks collapsed into a sofa at the far end of the room with several beers nestling up to his chosen resting place and a pack of cigarettes open by his side.

'Does anyone want to eat?' I asked.

'I've got some food man,' Tricks tossed his head in the direction of his little rucksack sat by the fridge. I thought of the loaves and fishes story and wondered if Tricks would like to share his food. This thought was quickly followed by the obvious realisation that of course I would not want to eat what was in Tricks bag anyway as it would undoubtedly smell of, well, Tricks.

'A trip for food anyone?' I asked.

Keith and Steve both nodded, Steve bolting back his third can of beer since we had arrived in the room and pocketing two more for the journey, Keith picking up some flyers for us to hand out on our journey.

'Are you coming Tricks?' I asked.

'No dudes. I'll just chill here. Roseanna,' Tricks girlfriend and equally interesting character, 'is going to come through and we'll just hang in here.'

Roseanna had in fact just arrived and had gone to powder her nose, and no doubt other parts as well…

Tricks noticed us looking a little concerned at his exhausted state.

'Guys, I know I look as flaked as a snow flake right now, but give me a few magic mushroom moments and I'll be ready to give good juice.'

He winked at Steve, who straightaway looked down at his feet.

'Well, just you and Roseanna be good, yea?' Keith warned Tricks in a tone that hinted at a fall-out that nobody would want to witness.

'Oh we'll be good, big man.'

'Good at making babies?' offered Steve.

'Dude please. I know all about protection!'

'Sellotape on the end of your willy will not always work,' I said, 'and the proven long term medical problems of ripping it off after intercourse are now well documented.'

'Very funny man,' Tricks said this in a tired tone. He was clearly flagging.

'So you're OK here?' said Steve cutting in with a final voice of reason despite his estimated 6 pints already.

'Yea you go, but don't be too long and...' a big grin covering his sweat filled face as he added '...make sure you knock before coming back in the room.'

The thought of catching Tricks and Roseanna naked in a more than compromising position was terror enough to ensure we would not forget to knock with the loudest knock since knocking shops were first invented.

We walked back through the same labyrinth of mazy corridors that Vole had so expertly led us through getting lost only once on the way. We re-entered the Disco 2000 venue that would be the venue for our triumph that would follow in only a few hours and pushed open the back doors with an authority akin to John Wayne arriving at a salon in Rio Bravo. It was already seven thirty and we had arranged to meet our guests at the doors at a quarter to nine and so time was now at a premium.

We walked past the door staff that were increasing in number, there were five present now, and made our way down Talbot Street towards the town centre and food. Keith insisted that we hand out flyers to anyone who looked remotely like, a. They would like our music, and b. They would come to a venue like Rock City. This handing out of promotional material rather took away from our true desire to walk the streets like pop stars that had the world at their feet. I could not see that Oasis would do this or indeed that they had ever done this.

'Keith,' I reasoned, 'Can you really believe that Liam would have walked down the streets handing out flyers?'

'Possibly not Bob, but then again you don't either.'

It was a fair point. I walked down at the side of Steve and Keith who handed out flyers freely and happily. They were brilliant at it. It was if they had been to college and studied it, as though it was one of the gifts that God had given to them at birth. To watch them approach complete strangers and strike up a conversation into which they introduced the concept of the wondrous Wide Eyed Wonder made them the sort of material that the Jehovah's Witnesses would crave over. I, on the other hand partially saw this as an activity that the artistic and creative leader of the Band should not partake in for, of course, artistic reasons. The truth was that I was just plain embarrassed by it. It was a weird thing to me that I could happily stand in front of complete strangers and perform for them in the style of an Indy band singer, and yet here on the streets of Nottingham I found the prospect of simply handing out our inoffensive flyer a little scary. It bothered me that these strangers would not want to be approached. It didn't bother Keith and Steve at all. In fact it enthused them. The challenge was the carrot.

I therefore became the effective flyer carrier, occasionally springing into action when the mood took me, which was normally when guilt over took me, or when an attractive set of females became embroiled in conversation. At such a point I would join in the discussions as though this whole leaflet thing had been my idea from the off.

'Well I'm the lead guitarist,' Steve would normally say, 'and on stage I really am one of the finest things you could hope to see.'

'Like a piece of art developing before your very eyes,' Keith would volunteer.

'Yes Keith, art before your very eyes,' Steve would gleefully repeat.

Keith would move on to other passing punters not wanting to miss out on the free and ready trade that was so happily presenting itself and I would join Steve.

'These girls are thinking of coming tonight?' Steve would say by way of introduction with a gleam in his eye.

'Oh, cool. It's going to be really good tonight,' I would say sensibly, 'I'm Anthony, the lead singer.'

'And he is hot,' Steve would say, a statement that I would let pass with a knowing nod, dropping my head just slightly by way of mock embarrassment at my good friend's kind comments.

'Are you from Nottingham?' I would enquire, or Leicester or wherever else we were. At this stage the girls would either giggle accordingly, happily taking part in our shameless exhibition of a male plumage show, or on some rare occasions, i.e. nearly always, they would have made it clear they were not really interested at all by making their excuses and going on their way as quickly as they could to get away from the weirdo band types!

Often we would bump into a group of students and whilst some would wander off, others would hang around and chat and try and make some sense of us. It is fair to say that some girls in particular would be put off by our clothes. Steve and I both wore second hand black leather reefer jackets bought from the wonderful second hand clothing shop 'Daphne's Handbag.' The shop perched magnificently at the top of the main city graveyard and was situated as though it had taken some of the clothes from the trendier departed and was now selling them on for others to use. Many years of smells in said coats were added to by pub and gig smells so people probably smelt us arriving down wind long before they actually saw us.

We would both have on traditional trainers. Steve had always worn a pair of normal Puma's, white with a red dash. I would wear a pair of traditional Adidas trainers, white with red stripes down the side. The beautiful three stripes had somehow grabbed my attention as a child and, having fallen in love with them, I would find myself unable to wear another brand. Why, I am not really sure. I just liked the look and it was that simple. For a boy it is often like this. A brand becomes an attachment to the personality, an extension of who they wish to become, and who they think they are.

To add to his look, Steve would always wear for bigger gigs his leather trousers that looked as though they had been surgically fastened on to him. They were a throw back to his Glam rock and punk days. He would then tie it all together with a simple T-shirt and then, perched nicely on his now bleached blond head, his moody ray bans. Here on the streets he peered happily over them but in a gig they would be pulled tight over his eyes.

I would wear combat pants in classic faded khaki, and a simple T-shirt too. I would also wear sunglasses and in a gig would do so in exactly the same way as Steve. What other way was there? Beads rested nicely around both our necks. Steve wore several large and extravagant rings. I wore two. Both were grazed silver, one a simple large plain one and the other a smaller Celtic patterned ring. I liked the feeling of something Celtic on my ring. It felt right. Kind of connecting me with things from my past that I had little idea about but it just felt good.

Met by the two of us looking like we did, and listening to us telling them about the Band the way that we did was enough to either put a group of students off straightaway or to reel them in totally intrigued. Being in a Band was fun. It gave me something more than even the music. It gave me an identity and a way of life that I felt was totally me and, in turn, not at all like the version that had to work for a living. Small talk conversation would continue with Steve and I trying to collect as many giggles as possible. Our crossing of paths would end with the students who had bothered to stay and listen to us suggesting they might just make it to the gig. Sometimes they would. Sometimes they would not. Always it was worth the attempt!

The three of us eventually arrived at Broadway. We had a few precious moments now to chill before heading back for 'the big one.' Broadway was one of Steve and my favourite haunts. It had everything we wanted. It was first and foremost a film venue that offered both films and training in the making and study of films. It didn't just show the latest box office mush to come out of America's big film houses, some of which we loved admittedly, but also smaller stuff from all over the world that had never been made to make millions of dollars. This association with the underdog was one that we understood very well and very much associated with. On top of showing newer and often independent films, Broadway would also show old time classics. It was a place to go and hide and find yourself for a bit and for that alone it kind of mattered a lot.

Broadway, most vitally, had a most cool bar that was way ahead of anything else in Nottingham because it didn't try, it just was. It was certainly a bar that you could chill in, a place to truly relax. That was why were here now. Later on in the evening the bar would become awash with a mix of people who had been in the later showings of films, to people out in the town and just passing by, to others who were in the place to drink for the night. With such an eclectic mix the place, to Steve and I, was buzzing and inspiring. Another major positive was its food, simple yet effective with excellent and quick service. The drinks menu was wonderfully wide with over fifty different beers on offer as well as wines, spirits and juices. Heaven.

We had, however, never quite managed to win Keith round to the charms of Broadway. Keith liked his pubs to be simple and straightforward. He liked a pub to have a good beer smell, for at least one wall to adorn a darts board and for there to be the offering of pool in the corner. Better than that he liked a pub to be full of local people, in the establishment after a long day living their lives, and now together as a community to nurse one another's hopes and fears. This place was too much a mix of too many different things. He came to a bar to drink. He was not an artist. He didn't follow art and had no interest in it. As for the cinema he could see the point of blockbuster films with the unending talents of Bruce Willis or Steven Segal, but to him, art house stuff was surely just for the art community, whatever that was! This was their place, not his and he didn't like it one bit. It really was no use trying to explain to Keith that things could be varied and exciting. To him, life was black and white. He knew what he wanted and that was what he aimed for. The one proviso to this was if there was entertainment to be had, Keith wanted it. Here in the Broadway Keith did at least recognise that the people we saw and mixed with were interesting and entertaining and with that in mind he would put up with the 'arty farty' nature of the place, and just sit in the middle of it and laugh.

Drinks bought and food ordered we made our way to a table in the middle of the half full bar and sat down. The film slide projector threw its images on to the far wall opposite the bar. Each image was taken from a film that had been in a recent season, or was on, or was coming. These scenes were rarely from the more obvious Hollywood blockbusters, albeit a few were, but they were primarily from the smaller cult films such as Before Sunrise or older classics such as Breakfast at Tiffany's. The pictures conjured up still further the feeling that this was a place to sit and get lost, both in the feeling of the place and the atmosphere it so perfectly created. Keith would just make noises of dis-satisfaction as each image shot across the wall with the occasional reference of 'who the hell was that' or 'never seen her' or 'another pointless shot.' Steve and I would smile at the narration.

Normally at this point, that is drinks in front of us and food ordered, Keith would ask that I produce the song list to ensure it was fresh in all our minds and having sat down he did precisely that. Tonight's song list, unusually for us, had been put together at a practice several weeks before and we had been practising it solidly ever since. We had an hour set, which we expected to go on for a further fifteen minutes with encores. We would begin at 9.30pm and had to be finished by 10.45pm to give Vole time to clear the stage before letting Disco 2000 become the Disco venue for those who liked their music loud and thrashing. The majority of revellers would be upstairs in the main hall dancing to more mainstream Indy and pop music.

Keith took the list and looked at his two band colleagues across the table. He coughed, to clear his throat, and then addressed us in serious tones,

'OK boys tonight is the big one and I don't want either of you two going off on a strange tangent like you normally do…' he said this with a smile because the only person who went off on one in a gig was Keith. Occasionally during a song his bass fingers would be almost magically taken over and a thumping good tune from the Wonders would suddenly have a bass line

275

from a church chorus played in the background, instead of the one Keith had worked on for months. Old habits died hard!

'…Now then let's see.'

He placed the list in the middle of the table pushing aside the ashtray in Steve's direction, together with the candle, which was lit, and the single red rose that sat by its side.

'You can keep that,' he smiled.

We looked down together at our songs and breathed in the excitement they had given us, and the hope that they would move the feet and bodies of those listening in less than an hour and a half.

We had gone for a simple in your face list that would exhaust both ourselves and, we hoped, the crowd. It went as follows,

1. Take You There. An obvious starting point with a massive guitar introduction that made you want to jump up and down like a crazed animal. A chimp with fleas comes to mind. It also had the magical effect of making the four of us feel like rocking up our music straightaway. Steve and I had been practising one night at my house and we had listened before hand to Rock and Roll Star to inspire us. There was no other song introduction like it. Of course some might argue that Noel had simply stolen bits from bands like The Who and The Stones but they were wrong. For us Noel had created by his very self the sound of the 90's. When his guitar kicked in at the beginning of Rock and Roll Star you instantly knew that life could be better and that it was to be lived now. We could not hope to reproduce such absolute perfection but we came up with what we thought was a pretty amazing and fantastic guitar introduction that would launch us into a great song. The start of 'Take You There' never disappointed the Band or the crowd. It was the perfect appetizer before the main course.

2. Alright For Now. A true beauty and probably my finest moment to date. The chorus consisted of the classic words 'Round my house in the morning sun, I'm eating cornflakes and a chocolate bun, and I just want to be alright for now.' Admittedly not Geoffrey Chaucer but certainly a conversation starter. Steve had come up with another stunning big and bold guitar start, and a seamless middle sixteen lead guitar break to rival the haunting beauty of Noel's in Live Forever. If the crowd weren't wetting themselves at this point then we may as well finish and shut up shop and go home in sobbing mode. We were confident though.

3. Hold On Tight. A song about living for your dream with a jaunty tune that made you just want to bob up and down. It was our Columbia meets Twist and Shout.

4. Showtime. A tribute to U2's Angel of Harlem. Some might unfairly call it a rip off but to me it was always a tribute. The song moved and weaved its magic as it moved with an ever-quickening pace to its splendid finale. By its end I was always exhausted having rushed out lyrics faster than any other song we did. I called this song our Indy rapper number. A listener had recently called it 'this is shite!' as he shouted across to the band at the Fox & Hounds as we tried to draw the song to an end with dignity.

5. Hear The Words I'm Saying. By this stage we would be flying by the seats of our red hot pants. This was our version of Cigarettes and Alcohol. It said to the world that they might ask us to do all the things that they did, but on this occasion we were saying no way. It was my two-fingered tribute to the establishment that made me work a normal job that I loathed more than ever when I sang this song. I loved this song as much as anything because even I got to play a clever little bit on the guitar, perfectly simple so that I couldn't get it wrong despite playing the guitar with 10 thumbs.

6. I Need You. At this point in the gig we would be knackered and we needed a song to fall into. On this evening this would be our one rest and our one song that showed we had a soft side. I had written it not long after meeting Annabella. I could write into the song words I could not possibly speak out loud to her at this point in our relationship, which was still effectively just a friendship. She was in my mind everything I had ever wanted and this song opened my heart bare with such lines as 'From the first time that I saw you I knew that our love was meant to last, and from the first time, that I kissed you, I felt it move me deep inside, my love for you I'll never hide.' It was Romeo and Juliet poetry written by an inebriated Shakespeare's half brother, and with a middle guitar solo that showed Steve to be a master craftsman. Yes it was a song that would show our fans that we could slow it down with the best of them.

7. I Wanna Be Me. Cranked up back to speed of light and fantastic. This would bring us and our crowd straight back into the jump up and down like an idiot mode. It started with screeching guitar and drums and then straight into the line, 'And I looked out into my world and I said come look at me, I refuse to be what you want, to be what you want to be.' From chilled back classic straight back into two fingered salute.

8. I Believe. Now in flying position, this song just made you want to jump up and down. It pulled no particular punches. It was our Digsy's Dinner. It was never going to be a classic but it was great fun.

9. Last Bandit. Eating out of our hands now, I would step aside to let Steve and Keith enjoy themselves with a Dogs D'Amour song. I would at this point simply, in a classic role reversal, stage dive into the crowd and jump up and down with them whilst Steve belted out the lyrics in an angry tone with an effervescent tune.

10. Shooting Star. The crowd, now delirious, was ready to do anything! We would respond by ending on our crowd favourite and proven classic. It was our Rock and Roll star with the chorus oozing out the immortal words 'All I want is a bright guitar and the sun shining down on me, all I want is a Shooting Star and the world to look at me.'

Having left the stage to tumultuous applause mixed with the now pumping crowd screaming, we would go back stage to slap each other's backs in a manly exhibition of self-congratulationary support. In the background we would hear stamping of feet and rhythmic clapping of hands along to the crowd made lyrics of 'We want more, we want more!'

Keeping them waiting just long enough (too long sees some of the crowd leaving and too short catches some of the crowd stuck at the bar) we return back to the stage to an even more enthusiastic welcome than we ever thought possible. The boys all go first, probably to chants of 'Northy, Northy' as he slips on his sleek and mean looking Gibson guitar.

I would then emerge from the side door left, to the crowd's eye, and jump on to the stage making sure to not catch my foot and fall head first on to the mic stand. Many gigs had taught me that all disasters where possible and every precaution was worth taking. The crowd would kindly now whoop with delight as I made my way to my microphone and thanked the crowd. I would remind them, having been warned by Keith not to forget, that each and every one of the crowd could be on our mailing list. Forms were already littered around Rock City for this very purpose. I saw this as my Billy Graham moment and thought how my parents would see my abilities as wasted promoting a silly band when I could have been promoting something so much more fulfilling. The truth was that I hated having to promote anything and usually started my 'Join the mailing list' speech with the words 'Keith has asked me to not forget to mention…' This went down very well with so many of our fans who knew Keith as a teacher and those who had been taught by him knew only too well what it was like to be asked by him to do something. He would ask and ask and ask until you did it.

And then on to the two encores for the night.

Encore 1. Life Goes On. Both encores were songs that we had been doing since we started. This one was a simple rock anthem. It started simply with guitars and drums at one in rock unison. The lyrics kicked in with 'You say you want me, you don't know what you mean, the way you treat me, I think that it's obscene! You come as you please, in the day or night, abuse my time and think that that's alright.' Words with attitude that meant nothing in particular but at the same time meant everything to a young man trying to make sense of what he was doing. I sang it as though I was singing it to everyone who had ever had a go at me, and everyone, who I may have never even met, but if I did then those who would have had a go at me. The link carried on with 'Well in this life, just once or twice, a wish comes true, for me and you, and I say, Oh yea, Life Goes On!'

At this point in the song Steve would probably be down in the crowd playing crazy rock guitar. At different gigs he had played his guitar in different places with amazing control. He had perched on chairs, on tables, on amps. He had jumped off stages, jumped back on to them, laid down on his back, and let the crowd hit his strings. He was a genius and I loved him for it. So did our crowd.

And then the simple easy to follow and easy to sing along chorus of 'Alright life goes on, alright life goes on.' The song wasn't rocket science. It would never win a musical award. It was just get your head down and enjoy the music, and that suited us and our crowd just fine.

And, finally, our last song of the evening. It needed something a little anthemic, something for the crowd to take away with them. We would deliver this with 'Viewpoint.'

Encore 2. Viewpoint. There was only ever one song to finish our first gig at the legendary Rock City and that was this one. Steve and I had pretty much written it together. What would happen generally when we wrote pieces together was that Steve would come to my place and we would get set up in my bedroom with our acoustic guitars. Noise control was important given that my parents were already quite upset that their two sons were in a worldly band at all. As with when I took songs to practices I would generally have both the lyrics and the basic tune, but more often when Steve came round these songs were even more skeleton than normal. We would then work on this and Steve would get to grips with the song. Then he would begin to add the bits that I called 'Wide Eyed Wonder' bits. They were the little frills and edges that transported the songs from the simple little numbers I had put together in my bedroom, to songs that would actually weave their way into peoples' minds. Sure I came up with the majority of the song but it was Steve who turned it into a Wide Eyed Wonder song. Often though, we would simply mess around and jam for a while with bits of music that one of us had found on our guitars, and sometimes something might come out of it. Usually it was something that when we played again after a coffee break, or perhaps a break of a week or so, the song was actually not very good at all and we would let it go like a fisherman tossing his catch back into the river. Sometimes though, we struck gold, and that was what happened with Viewpoint. A simple song played over three chords it talked of a girl and of things going wrong for her and of her trying to make sense of them. It was my attempt to counter all the happy crappy pop songs of our time that said everything was so fine when for so many it so wasn't. 'There she was all sad and lonely; things just hadn't gone right for her. She missed the spring, she missed the summer, she felt like letting down her hair.' Keith played pretty much the same pumping bass line throughout the whole song and it worked incredibly well. Coming towards the end of the song the crowd were jumping and swaying together to the hypnotic beat of the tune. It was magical.

'So that's it then,' I said, looking at the song list.

'Yea, that's it,' said Steve proudly. 'We are going to rock like grannies on acid on rocking chairs.'

'You already are, with all that drink you've already had' I said to Steve. I was not unduly concerned because I was used to seeing him take down more alcohol in a night than I could drink in a week. He was knocking it back though big style tonight.

'Yea, you're right I think I'll have some of your coffee for a while.'

Our drinking habits were all so different. Steve could drink as much as he wanted when he wanted and still get away with it. I could drink up to say five bottles of beer, my favoured drink when performing, but after that I would fall over. Keith could happily drink two pints of lager and then a magical change would wash over him. After the third pint he would become a party animal without any co-ordination to aid him in his new drunk found fondness for being as loud and as crazy as possible. The drunk Keith was all the natural comedy he had in his personality thrown together without any natural temperance to keep a check on him. The problem was that this would last for thirty minutes at most before he would need to find a corner to sleep. Keith therefore knew he couldn't drink before a gig and so he didn't. His natural ability to show incredible self-restraint was a revelation.

So here in Broadway we sat with a different drink each. Steve had a pint of Stella. I had a cafetière with strong Colombian coffee to give me massive dose of jolt up caffeine. Keith had a pot of tea because, quite simply, he liked tea, a lot. Also he loved asking for a pot of tea wherever we went, and I mean wherever he went, because he knew it was very funny. A cup of tea would do, but he was always insistent that the staff got him a pot of tea! Normally they did!

Food arrived and again you could tell beforehand, if you knew us, who the food was for. Steve had a burger with chips. He hated anything that was not greasy. I had a Mediterranean salad. I adored salad and would eat it as often and as much as possible. Keith had nothing because he had already eaten sandwiches he had packed for himself during the sound check. Keith was not tight with his money. He has always been a most giving person and liberal with buying drinks at the bar. However his motto was always why spend money when there is money to be saved. If you were allowed to bring your own cans of lager into a pub then Keith would.

'Is Tricks going to be OK?' I asked.

'Apart from getting stuck in a rude sexual position with Roseanna you mean?' Keith laughed as he spluttered out this suggestion.

'You know Anthony you must try and talk to him a little more' It was Steve. He found it easy to get on with Tricks and it was clear that I was finding it progressively harder to relate to him.

'I do try,' I reasoned, 'but he is so different to us.'

'Yea, crazy man, you do my head in dude,' Keith offered helpfully in mock Tricks speak.

'You know it's not just how he speaks, it's how he is,' I said.

'Bone idle you mean,' Keith knew exactly what I meant. It was just that he found it easier to get on with Tricks than I did.

'Yea. He's not one if us,' I reasoned.

'But he never will be Anthony,' replied Steve, 'no one will be.'

'I know,' I said, in resigned acceptance that I must try and get closer to Tricks for the sake of the Band.

'He likes you and looks up to you,' Steve added as though this should encourage me further to take Tricks home and sleep with him.

'He doesn't, I know he doesn't.' Of late I had been getting bad vibes from Tricks. Nothing that I could pin down to any one situation exactly but just bad vibes.

'He does,' Steve went on, 'it's just that you are such a strong character and he finds it difficult to approach you.'

Keith nodded happily as he poured himself another cup of tea. He found these conversations very entertaining unless, of course, they were aimed at him. Steve was right to tell me that I was sometimes too forceful.

'Look I write strong tunes and lyrics. Some people will just have to put up with that,' I reasoned pretty lamely.

'Not the drummer,' responded Steve strongly, too strongly for my liking.

'I like him a lot Steve, I just don't get him? I will try, honest.'

'I bet you're not like this with Annabella,' said Keith with a big grin on his face.

'Oh darling,' he went on in full comedy fashion, 'you are such a sweet thing, what can I do for you? Stroke your ears? Comb your hair? Shave your legs?'

'I bet he's forceful when he needs to be,' suggested Steve in a sideways comment to Keith. I didn't at all like where this conversation had gone.

'OK, OK. I know I don't try hard enough when I don't get on with someone.'

'Replace that with 'try at all,'' said Steve.

'That's not fair,' I responded. 'When Tricks joined the band I got on with him just fine. Anyway you're the closest to him now and there's nothing wrong with you being the link.'

'The missing link,' said Keith to himself.

'I just want you to try harder,' Steve added, hurt in his voice.

'Oooh,' I said childishly, 'bossy!'

Steve hated it when I talked down to him. He always looked so hurt and vulnerable and I generally made up as soon as I had said something, usually with a comment on his favourite subject.

'So Northy boy, are you going to get those young ladies bouncing up and down tonight?'

His eyes brightened at the prospect of bouncing breasts and the Tricks subject was for now put out of our minds. We all knew that the gulf between the three of us and our drummer was becoming a problem and we had begun to talk about it. I had even suggested that we look for another drummer but both Steve and Keith had said this was foolish and counter productive. Tricks was well known to all our fans and many of them could associate with his student status.

Our conversation brightened and we finished our food and drinks in double quick time and then made our way hurriedly back to Rock City. It was just past 8.30pm and we just had time to get back, find Tricks hopefully in a clothed state, and then together sign our guests in on the front door.

We walked through the front doors proudly showing off our shiny passes to anyone who cared to look. It was far too obvious this was our first time, but we didn't really care. The novelty was everything! We made our way through Disco

2000, which already had some people in including some of our student fans from Eastwood Comprehensive. We stopped to say hello and Keith stayed for a while longer as Steve and I made our way back through the corridors to our dressing room. When we got to the door we found it locked. We knocked but there was no reply. Smiling knowingly at each other we pressed our ears up against the door to listen to naughty noises but there were none to hear.

'Perhaps Tricks has locked the door and gone somewhere,' said Steve.

'Yea, that seems a reasonable thing to do,' I said in a heavy sarcastic tome, 'except he didn't have a key!'

'Why?'

'There wasn't one in the door. I looked. There was a bolt lock though on the inside'

'Do you think he's alright?' Steve now nervously asked. 'Perhaps he's had too much to drink and fallen over and banged his head.

I looked at Steve and smiled. He laughed.

'I think the more likely explanation is that you know who arrived, they've drunk all the beer, and now they're flat out and dead to the world. An alcohol induced sleep is going to thrill Keith! He'll probably be out of it all night!'

'What are we going to do without a drummer?'

At times like this Steve's mind always went in to major negative nose-dive. I had been trying to learn over the years to minimise the information I gave to him on a need to know basis. Needless to say on this occasion I had failed miserably and set Steve's brain alarm bell ringing.

I knocked again. This time very loudly, but still to no avail. Keith arrived and Steve explained what was happening as I shouted, 'Tricks, are you alright?'

Keith was eyeing up the door for a break in.

'I'll kill him,' he was muttering as he walked into the adjoining changing room to see if there was another way in. Keith would put up with a lot but he hated anyone letting him down. I couldn't help but think that, at least as a side issue, if Tricks was sozzled inside then this would add a lot of clout to my 'Get Tricks Out Campaign.'

After further shouting and banging on the walls we heard some movement. We waited and a few seconds later, the door lock was slowly opened and Roseanna appeared at the door with her finger to her mouth in a 'be quiet you naughty boys' position.

'Tricks is having a little nap,' she said in a totally matter of fact way, 'I guess I must have dozed off with him.'

Roseanna was a small lady with a face that could smile at you sweetly or scare you half to death. She, like Tricks, was a student and, like her man, from the section of the student fraternal that assumed they were there for 3 or 4 years to get as wasted and as much in debt as possible. She, again like Tricks, constantly complained of the essays and assignments they were being set as though they had not signed up to their courses to do any work. Nothing was ever her fault but rather the fault of the world that now surrounded them. I imagined Roseanna's arrival a few moments after we left and to the drink and shag heaven that was in front of them. Neither would have thought about the short-term consequence of Tricks being knocked well and truly out but, true to form, and the reason I had begun to be very worried about him, they had pleased themselves only. Typical!

She, seemingly oblivious to our Paddington hard stares, gave us the sweetest little smile she could muster. Her blouse was noticeably fastened up incorrectly. Given the intensity of the smell of alcohol, which filled the room, I was surprised she had even been able to find one button. I thought about asking her if she would like Steve to help her fasten up correctly but thought better of it. Steve might snigger or there again, and more likely, he would run off, or, even more likely, hit me.

She looked at each of us in turn hoping, I felt, to catch a sympathetic look. Steve and I simply offered blankness. Keith offered the look of thunder. Seeing this Roseanna decided to return to the sanctuary of her lover at the back of the room who was, sure enough, asleep like a baby. At the side of the sofa were at least twenty empty cans and an ash try that looked like a group of 10 had been using it all night.

'We've only been gone about an hour,' I said, half marvelling at their beer and cigarette consumption, 'Have you had friends round?'

Roseanna flashed me a look that told me they had not and underlined the point that I would be better served shutting up. Charming!

'Has he taken anything?' Steve asked knowingly and Roseanna, after some hesitance when you could see her weighing up the consequences of divulging this information, nodded.

'The usual?' he enquired still further. Roseanna nodded again.

Interesting questions I thought and looked at Keith for a reaction. There was none. He was just staring at 'Idle Stupid Bollocks', the new name I had just given to Tricks in my mind, and probably sizing up how best to kill him and get rid of the body without anyone finding out. I immediately began to let loose the theory that possibly Steve and Tricks took more than painkillers for headaches but I was still struggling with the obstacles that Tricks wouldn't have the cash and Steve wouldn't have the need. Perhaps I was wrong on both accounts. On the other hand perhaps when Steve referred to 'anything' and 'the usual' he was referring to a sexual stimulant or to a bottle of Buxton spring water or to a milky bar each. I personally have always been a fan of milky bars finding them just the right side of sweet for my tastes. We were clearly swimming in new waters, or to be exact, Tricks was not set to be swimming anywhere soon. I decided not to ask further as to what Steve and Roseanna were actually talking about due to my obvious total and utter ignorance on the subject when Keith snarled in a controlled, yet exceptionally angry voice,

'What do you mean 'anything' and the usual'?' he was using his 'I am very mad at you' and 'As a result I am going to kill you' tone, which was hidden in his 'I am the teacher of your nightmares' voice. I hated it when he used that voice and so, by their expressions, did Steve and Roseanna. All of a sudden Steve had become part of the naughty group, which at any other time would have been very funny indeed. Now it wasn't. I stayed at the back of the room in the good group, which consisted of just myself. I felt at this point that it was important that I stayed particularly still and exceptionally quiet.

'So not only has he drunk in one hour more than he normally drinks in a whole week if he's lucky,' Keith voice was getting louder, 'but he's taken some bloody drugs as well!'

Keith was now not only shouting, but he was also swearing as well. This was the top of the serious tree for him. All, clearly, was not good. I stood shaking my head rather like Manuel would when he was agreeing with Basil Fawlty, but not having any real idea about the gravitas of what was actually being said.

'Well we may as well just go home then,' said Keith, with a finality that was very concerning. It was not like Keith to throw in the towel so easily.

I looked at Steve. During arguments or situations like this his eyes would become bloodshot and he would resemble a wounded dog. At this particular moment he looked more like a dog on the verge of suicide, a dog stood by the side of a busy morning session on the M1 motorway, musing over whether to go for it or not! He was looking at Keith, waiting for him to say something that would make everything OK again. Nothing was forthcoming.

Roseanna on the other hand had sat down next to her beloved and was stroking his hair. Tricks had moved on to his side and was now snoring quite loudly. A big grin covered his face as his magical dreams took him to a wonderland without Keith. I thought it was probably best that he stayed there for as long as he could.

Keith looked at his watch.

'Steve you go and sign everyone in.'

Steve smiled weakly. Keith was having pity on him and allowing him to leave the funeral parlour with a nice job to do instead. No longer would he have to stay and eye the deceased as Keith got to work in preparing for presentation before the burial service. Steve could now leave and return when the dark deeds had hopefully all been done.

'Can I…?' I started to ask if I could be excused too but realised that we needed to be there for each other in this our darkest of hours, 'help at all?'

Keith turned to me and smiled weakly. If I carried on like this, I reasoned, Keith might even present me with a good behaviour certificate at the end of the night. Of course such reasoning rested on the proviso that we would reach the end of the night safely. At this stage even this was looking unlikely.

Steve stopped at the door and asked bleakly.

'It will be alright won't it'?

'No,' said Keith far too quickly.

'Yes,' said the now very unpopular Roseanna, 'you are all worried about nothing. He's always like this.'

That I could believe.

Steve left us to sign our guests in. Keith had his girlfriend Cheryl and her sister to sign in. I had the wondrous Annabella and my youngest sister Susan to sign in. My other sister, Anne, was now up at college in Lincoln studying to be a teacher. How unlucky is that to have not one but two siblings becoming teachers. Even Susan, who was at college now, had begun to study childcare. Imagine the dinnertime conversations that flew so easily around the latest Education Minister who needed to be shot, the orderly queue we would have to form before we walked into dinner. Before we would begin our fine and hearty lunch we would have to endure grace for 5 minutes that seemed like five hours before eating and any sniggering would be punished by detention.

Steve was signing in Chloe and her beauty salon friend Danniel who I was sure would utilise no discretion whatsoever by whispering stories of my red beacon chest into Annabella's ear.

I wondered now, with woe overtaking my every thought, what Annabella's alternative photos of this night would now look like. Rather than 'Band on stage' it would be 'drummer is sick'. Rather than 'lead singer jumps into the crowd' it would be 'bass player arrested by police after brutal one sided and exceptionally violent fight.'

'Well why don't we just wake him?' I asked. It seemed the obvious thing to do and the funniest.

'Because he will be of no use whatsoever,' replied Keith firmly. It was a voice that suggested he knew for definite but I knew he didn't. He was just frightened that everything was going wrong on our biggest night yet. Keith and I didn't really understand the amounts of things some people could take and still somehow be alright. A few beers and we were anybody's. But people doing things like Tricks and we were totally clueless.

'Are you sure?' I asked in a respectful manner that I hoped Keith wouldn't find too challenging

'Well perhaps it's worth a go,' he offered.

'That's my boy,' I replied, as positively as possible.

In our desperation we walked over to the loving couple. Roseanna looked at us with the face that said she would handle it.

'He'll be fine,' she said confidently. 'Can we perhaps just leave him for a few more minutes, perhaps five minutes before?'

'NO!' we both said in a very loud voice and demanding tone that even made Roseanna jump.

'Oh, alright then,' she mumbled. She began to stroke his face and whisper 'come on sweetie, it's time to come back into the real world from your lovely little dreams.'

We waited as she soothingly ran her fingers down his cheeks waiting for the sleeping drug filled drunkard to awake. His face stretched into a bizarre contortion and I wondered if he had just come in his pants. I looked but he looked pretty dry down below. Mind you his dark and very stained trousers could probably hide a multitude of sins.

'Come on darling, the Band are waiting.' She shot us an accusing look as though we were the ones in the wrong. 'Why you can't just give him another half hour I don't know,' she muttered.

'Because he's going to need a lot more than 5 minutes to wake out of this stupor,' Keith was using his angry teacher's voice to great effect. Roseanna took what he said and began to push her lover's shoulders in a now more valiant attempt to wake him up. Tricks turned and made a deep grunting noise, his nose wriggling up and down like that of a little rabbit picking up the scent of a delicious carrot. We waited, watching his movements as though they were having a hypnotic effect on us. He gradually seemed to be waking up.

'Tricks, it's Keith, we need you to wake up,' said my dear brother in a loud and exceptionally stern voice.

He was stirring. Imagine coming out of the depths of wherever he had been to hear the tones of Keith suggesting death may be coming. Tricks seemed to lift up his head slightly. His body was wrestling with the prospect of enforced awakening or returning to the sleep goddess.

'Wake up!' Keith demanded now in a worrying screech.

The rhythm of his breathing changed and he pulled himself on to his back, his head now pushed forward by the back of the sofa. Keith pushed his way past Roseanna who was watching Tricks with worshipful adoration.

'Come on Tricks, time to come back.' Keith put his hands under his shoulders and pulled him into a more upright position. How he could put his hands under those armpits I did not know. Still we were desperate. Keith turned to me.

'Get some water Bob and lots of it.'

'Right,' I said turning to the sink. There were no glasses so I filled two empty beer cans with cold water and returned to sleeping beauty. Tricks was still asleep, dribble now making its way down his chin. Perhaps this was a photo we could get Annabella to take for the CHAD, our local newspaper, who would doubtless make great news out of this latest catastrophe to befall the band.

Keith took the water off me.

'Right then Tricks, it's time to wake up.' With that he emptied a beer can on his head and then vigorously rubbed his hands up and down his cheeks.

I heard voices in the corridor and turned to see Steve arrive with Annabella and Chloe at his side. All of them were looking very concerned although I could make out a slight smile on Steve's face. Cheeky bugger!

'Hello,' I said as cheerfully as possible, 'just a little hiccup on the band front. The drummer's out of it and we are due on stage in less than 30 minutes. Apart from that everything's fine.'

'It'll be OK,' said Chloe hopefully.

'Steve said he's only had a few drinks, right?' said Annabella with an encouraging smile.

'Steve's an idiot,' said Keith without pausing to look back at the arriving party.

'Probably not,' I said.

'Oh,' said Annabella.

'Oh dear,' said Chloe.

'Shit,' said Steve.

We all watched Keith who was now pinching Tricks' cheeks and shaking his head up and down at the same time.

'Wake up Tricks, wake up,' he was saying as desperation filled his voice.

'Now careful Keith. I think you might hurt him,' pleaded Roseanna who at last seemed to be seeing the depths of the situation that we now faced. Tricks was certainly making some encouraging movements now. Little gurgling noises were coming from his intestinal depths as his body at last began to stir back into life. The smile had now left his angelic 'I haven't done anything wrong guv'nor' face. Mind you this was not surprising given the rough treatment he was getting from the increasingly physical Keith.

'Right you bugger,' said Keith as he got the second can of water I had got for him, as teacher's precious pet, and poured it over his head. He then pulled his arm back and muttering 'desperate times call for desperate measures' he slapped Tricks hard across the face. In turn Roseanna slapped Keith across the face just before Keith could slap Tricks again with his other hand.

Tricks went flying into the side of the sofa and then bounced back up, his eyes springing open. Keith had fallen on to Tricks stomach holding his ear and shouting 'It hurts' whilst Roseanna clung to Keith's arms in a valiant effort to stop any more violence against her lover. Tricks now sprung forward with the joint impact of Keith and Roseanna and, with a grace that matched the situation, he was once again, following his marvellous performance at BBC Nottingham, violently sick. The trajectory was inevitably all over Keith.

We all groaned together as Keith pulled himself free from Roseanna's grasp, she was also covered in sick, and sent another loud slap across Tricks' other cheek. This one sent him banging onto the floor on top of his beloved Roseanna. Quite apt I thought given that this was probably the position they had assumed only an hour earlier. Keith turned and made his way towards us. We all pushed ourselves against the wall so as not to be touched by the sick that was now sliding off my brother.

'I'm going next door to get myself tidied up,' he declared as though nothing was wrong. There was a shower down the corridor and this was obviously Keith's immediate destination. 'Anthony you go and pacify Vole. Steve…' and at this point he had stopped directly in front of Steve. He wiped a little sick away from his right eye and gave Steve a hard stare that told him Keith thought he was particularly responsible for the events we had just witnessed. '…Steve, get him into shape and do not let me down.'

'Yes,' said Steve nervously with as much authority as he could muster, 'of course. Count on it.'

Keith left the room. I turned to Tricks who was making a low groaning noise whilst Roseanna held him close. If she held me that close I would groan as well. Probably much louder. In fact I may well howl like a wolf that had just found once more its howling voice after 10 years of being without it.

I turned to the girls. They were laughing. I hoped I could laugh later about it too.

45 minutes later, fifteen minutes later than we were due to start, we made our way on to the stage. Vole had been fantastic. He told me he had seen much worse and to not worry. It was after all he reasoned perfect rock and roll behaviour. Keith had of course had a shower. He had done so fully clothed in order to wash off all traces of Tricks. He had then spent ten minutes trying to dry his clothes on the toilet automatic hand dryer. Steve had force fed Tricks three black coffees and amazingly he came round. He was very apologetic. Keith would not talk to him, possibly ever again!

I talked to Tricks more than I had probably ever done so because I feared not to do so might make him too afraid to come out and play. I waffled on about his course, my work, the music, the night, his fine playing; in fact anything and everything that came to mind. Tricks just sat in a hypnotic state drinking more coffee and smiling sweetly.

Five minutes before we left our second changing room of the night, the first having been abandoned because of the smell Tricks had so magically created, I called the Band together. All our fans and well-wishers who had come back stage to wish us all the best were now front stage and waiting for our entry. This was to be our night. Fantastically one of Keith's old friends, Tom Brown, had come along and he was the bands Booking Officer for the London School of Economics. He could be important to us and had helped us get into the Orange Club. He was a good guy and there was no doubt that impressing him would open up many more doors for us especially in the hallowed musical turf of London. He had driven up especially to hear us. We had a show to give and we needed to do it well.

'OK guys,' I started, the three of them sat in front of me like children listening to their father. They really did look like someone had stolen their dummies. Steve wisely sat in the middle of Keith and Tricks.

I stood in front of them for effect rather like a general addressing his troops before a vital battle.

'Tonight we can do it. Tonight is our night. In fact…' and as I spoke I looked each one of them in the eye. This was not so easy in Tricks case given that his eyes were still roaming all over the place so I just looked at the centre of where the eye should be and hoped for the best, '…if tonight's little hiccups…'

Keith snorted. Tricks looked down.

'…if they are anything to go by then surely they show us that destiny is in our favour. By good rights Tricks should have been out for days.'

Tricks lifted his head and thought about arguing the days down to hours, but wisely thought better of it.

'Look,' I paused, wanting to get us all to understand what waited before us.

'Tonight, there are all sorts of people out there. Some of them, like Keith's friend from the LSE, could make a massive difference to the rest of our lives. Most of them are just here because they think we are brilliant. Others will be hearing us for the first time and will tell others about us. Let's not play for ourselves, let's play for them, our fans.'

'Yea,' said Steve, a smile beginning to show on his worried little face. So many times Steve would be to so many people the rock star, the guy who had his shit together and was prepared to be so different. I loved that side of him. Often though I would see straight through that and see the quiet hurt little boy who just wanted to find his place, his peace. So often he was like a rabbit who knew he would have to cross that busy road at some point and was just waiting for his time to be called. For now though I had given him the green light for the night. Tonight was not to be his turn to cross the busy road of life. Rather we could stay put and be a Prince.

Steve put his rock star glasses on and lit up another cigarette.

'Come on guys...' as he said this he put his arms around the two non speaking band members, '...let's go and fuckin' rock.'

And so we did. We hit the stage with a fresh determination that I had never felt before. It was like I had received new insight, a depth of knowledge. The band could speak to a multitude of people in a way that I could not even comprehend. Adversity had tried to face us down and instead we had come up smelling of roses, or in Tricks and Keith's case, of something not quite so sweet!

Walking into a packed venue was amazing. To hear each of your names called out, shouted out, screamed out, is pretty bewildering. You take it in and float on it. That night was just incredible.

Tricks held himself together amazingly well only having to leave the stage once to be sick. I told the crowd where he had gone and why and they loved us all the more for it.

Keith moved his head round all night to the music as though it was fastened to his body with a spring. His eyes remained tightly shut throughout each song, opening only at the end to receive the applause and cheers that shook the room. His bass playing was impeccable. His beat was massive.

Steve. Steve was a rock star. He played like a god. A burning cigarette just sat between his lips as he span round the stage. At points he jumped into the front of the crowd thrashing his guitar like a magician. He was immense. At one moment as we both sang the chorus to 'I wanna be me' the two of us looked at one another across the hot sweaty smoke filled stage. We laughed. It was this moment that we had longed all our lives for. No matter what else came in our lives, on and off stage, that moment would be with us forever. He was my brother too, probably more so, my wingman, my steady hand, my inspiration. We didn't need words; in that look we just knew.

As for me I just let myself go more than I had ever done so before. Egged on by a crowd who worshipped whatever we had to offer I jumped and screamed and laughed my way through the night. As the Band ended on the crescendo of Viewpoint my body had reached an all time high. I felt liberated and alive in a way I had never known before.

The crowd erupted. Wide Eyed Wonder had arrived.

17

What we did immediately after a gig varied greatly. Sometimes the only thing to do after a gig was get out of the place as quickly as possible. This normally happened when we played places away from home where our crowd was not there and the locals thought we were taking the piss. Steve's guitar exploits were not seen for the powerful display of musician ability that it was but rather a guitar player who should know his place and stand by his amp and just play. Similarly my jumping up and down was not seen as the performance of a pretty hip showman, but rather the performance of a deranged fool who was at best a moron and at worst a total tosser who was asking to be pulverised.

Sometimes a gig would be that good that we simply fell into our fans' arms and let them deliver plaudit after plaudit whilst drinking more and more beer and happily smiling in the face of life. Tonight, after the greatest gig ever, was one such night. As soon as we had finished so many people swamped the stage. We normally knew most of the faces at any gig but tonight was different. There were many new people that we simply did not know and they all just wanted to get a piece of us. It was a new and totally freaky experience for us. I exchanged looks with each of the guys. We were elated.

In the background the tone of the night shifted as the band music was replaced by the hard-core thrash metal music that would be home for students of that musical persuasion for the next four hours. For the rest of the crowd it was time to head upstairs to the main hall for an out and out student disco. Fifteen hundred students would simply spend the night getting as hot and sweaty as possible dancing, amongst many other things, to fantastic Indy pop and dance music.

We thanked those who had only come to listen to us and were now heading home. For those meeting us upstairs we promised we would be up as soon as we had packed away to party along with them. We shook hands and exchanged bear hugs and kisses with everyone who handed over a completed mailing list form. There were more handed in than any other gig we had played. As the crowd thinned and the blast of the heavier music kicked into my earlobes we made our way towards the entrance to the room and away from the now ear splitting noise. I thought of Annabella and wondered where she was. I noticed Chloe shouting into Steve's ear and I realised they were both looking at me. I looked to the back of the room and thought I saw Annabella making her way through the doorway towards me. Throughout the gig I had seen her at different times taking photographs. I wished myself to be her camera, thinking of her holding me that close to her face, her hands clasped around my body. Before we had played 'I Need You,' I had said,

'This next song is for someone who has recently come into my life and changed it.'

Annabella had just looked at me with an expression that I took to mean she wanted to be with me. I looked forward to talking to her after. As the gig had reached its crescendo I had lost sight and thought of her, but now she returned to fill my mind.

'Anthony.'

It was Steve, calling me out of my thoughts. I turned to him and hugged him.

'He's here,' Steve shouted into my ear, overcoming the noise of the music that had now taken over the airwaves. I stepped back.

'What?'

'He's here…Callum is here.'

The words began to sink into my brain as I turned to see Annabella just ten feet away from me with a tall athletic Callum McCore beside her. They were fighting their way through the crowd that was mixed between our crowd making their way out and the grunge gang making their way in. The two of them were not holding hands, which I thought was a good thing. He was here though which I knew to be a bad thing. I looked for Annabella's eyes but could not catch them. I needed to see if being with him made her happy.

'Keep cool,' Steve shouted, 'She'll be yours in time, just like I am yours my dear pal!'

He winked at me with that knowing cheeky look which he had mastered over many years of being Steve. He knew all about how I felt about Annabella. I had bored him on far too many occasions on the only subject separate to the Band that seemed to occupy all my waking thoughts.

Annabella was almost upon me. Keith clapped his broad arm around my shoulder just as Steve had turned away to talk to somebody else.

'Once again may I salute you. You were brilliant.' He smiled his words out like a ray of sunshine. I turned to him.

'And you were the best bass player in the history of bass players. Thank you.'

'No worries. You are absolutely right of course, and what a turn out Bob!'

He turned to see Annabella now almost in front of me and with a second glance he saw Callum behind her. Instinctively he turned away from the group of students and friends who were with him to be at my side. It was not in his locker to look menacing, but Keith automatically had an air of authority that people rarely challenged. It was his gift.

Annabella reached me and leaned over to kiss my cheek.

'He arrived out of the blue…' she whispered into my ear for only me to hear. Stepping back she made way for Callum and turned to him.

'This is Callum,' she said and, turning to me,

'This is Anthony…' and turning to Keith '… and this is Anthony's brother and fantastic bass player Keith'! With that she leaned over to Keith and gave him a warm hug.

Callum took my hand.

'Well done man, you were excellent.'

His tone was pleasant. His eyes seemed friendly enough. In fact he seemed quite annoyingly OK.

'Right…' I replied, somewhat dazed. I didn't know what he thought of me. I knew he knew about the Band because he had come to pick Annabella up from a gig in Mansfield. What I didn't know was if Annabella had talked to him about me as a person. I didn't know if he saw the Band, or any members within the Band, as a threat. I didn't even know how bothered he was about Annabella, perhaps he wasn't! In short I knew, as per normal, very little. What I did know was that Annabella deserved to be treated like the lady she was and he was not doing that. I thought all the abuse I could think with my brain crying out negativity about him, words that I could not share but that I was worried were emanating from me.

'Have you played here before?' he asked, again with a seemingly genuine interest in his voice. I considered his height and general physique and realised that saying 'the bigger they are the harder they fall' was obviously made up by a bitter little guy who had been beaten in on far too many occasions by bigger guys.

'Never,' I replied. I knew I should say more, make small talk, but I really couldn't be arsed. I didn't like him. Here he was, the man between Annabella and me. Why should I talk to him? Brave rock star bravado filled my head and I felt bigger and better than the man before me.

'Oh right,' he went on. Was he oblivious to the fact that I did not wish to talk to him? 'Well you must all be very pleased to be here.'

I smiled. It was an awkward smile. I suspected it looked like I was being the idiot that I was. It was not big of me and I was clearly not helping the awkward situation.

'It's a dream gig for us,' it was Keith, jumping in with conversation, trying to cover over my rudeness.

I glanced a look at Annabella. She glanced a look at me. There was something not quite right here. If only I could talk to her on her own without 'him.' I imagined 'him' sat at home on his own. There he was wearing a dress, a pink one with flowers on it, and eating a tub of ice cream whilst watching daytime TV. High heel shoes with tall pink stilettos graced his smelly feet. It was a happy vision that I wished he would just bugger off and fulfil.

'What time did you get here?' Keith asked his new found friend. Annabella now shot me another more urgent look and I read in her eyes that now was not the time to be ignorant. If Callum wanted to be my friend for the night then I needed to make myself available to be his friend in return. OK, time for serious head reflection! I began to reason that maybe he had come here to suss me out. He must by definition then still want Annabella. To be rude would mean trouble for Annabella and if I knew anything I knew I did not want that.

'Just toward the end of your set. I was just saying to Anthony here that I thought you were pretty amazing. It was like you must have played here lots of times.'

The noise around us was exceptionally loud and communication was by loud talking leaning into one another's personal space and shouting. The rest you just tried to lip-read.

'So you caught a few tunes then?' I asked, amazed at the friendliness I had injected into my voice. I noticed a small smile slip on to Annabella's face. I was doing the right thing.

'Yea, the last two or three,' he said, his smile retuning to mine.

'The last two or three!!!' I thought. He was taking the piss. If he thought anything of us he would know exactly how many songs he had caught.

'And they were all brilliant.'

'Oh right. Thanks a lot. It was a great crowd and that kind of helps really.'

'I've always wanted to be in a Band myself,' he went on. He actually seemed quite relaxed. That was perhaps a good thing I reasoned. If I kept him sweet then Annabella and I could keep seeing each other on the side and build up our friendship into outright lustful love, and then she could give old pleasant chops the big heave ho.

'Did you want to sing or play drums or guitar?' I asked. I found myself being actually interested in his reply.

'To play lead guitar like your friend. I used to play act playing a massive guitar solo at Wembley stadium in front of 50,000 people.'

'I bet that's not the only thing you used to play act in your bedroom,' I thought, wisely keeping my thoughts to myself. If someone could crack mind reading we would all be in trouble!

'Well I should introduce you to him,' I said.

'That would be great. I'd love to meet him and look at his guitar,' Callum said, almost sweetly.

I turned to my right where Steve had been and saw he was not there. I saw Chloe then walk through the side door from the maze of corridors through which we had to move our gear.

'Have you seen Steve?' I called.

Chloe walked over to us.

'Hello Callum.' She greeted him with a peck on his cheek. I noticed his left hand, the one Annabella could not see, rub up and down Chloe's back. 'Probably just a friendly gesture' said one voice in my head. 'Slimy bastard' said the other.

'What did you say?' Chloe called to me.

'I said where's Steve? Callum would like to meet him and talk guitars.'

'Oh right. He's through in the changing room with Tricks and about thirty of your fan club.'

'Are they all naked?' I asked.

'Obviously,' she replied.

'Do you want to go through and meet them?' I asked Callum, warming to my role of being a nice person to this lucky bastard who was clearly a nasty ungrateful git.

'I'd love to,' he replied, turning to Annabella.

'Well can you just wait for me whilst I get all my camera gear locked up in the car,' she said.

'Well why not meet us through in the changing room?' said Callum.

I thought about standing on my own with Callum whilst Annabella disappeared for five minutes and immediately agreed in my head that getting this donkey through to other people to talk to was the best for all concerned. Keith had returned to his group of admirers having ensured things were fine with his little brother and I hardly wished to be left with Callum on my own.

'Look you know where our changing room is,' I said to Annabella, with as much encouragement in my voice that I could manage, 'why don't you just come through when you're ready?'

'Well wouldn't you rather wait?' said Annabella with far too much concern in her voice for my liking.

'We'll be fine,' I said with bravado in my voice.

'Yea babe, it's good. We'll see you in the back, OK?' said Callum.

'Well if you're sure,' said Annabella.

I gave her as happy and as confident a smile as I could manage. In fact I curled the outsides of my mouth up so much it almost hurt!

'I'll come with you,' said Chloe to Annabella. I shot her a 'thanks for nothing' look. Just me and him then.

Annabella leaned over to Callum and kissed him on his cheek. My cheek hurt at the lack of a similar kiss. She smiled at us both and then turned to join Chloe. They disappeared into the crowd, which was now almost entirely made up of people from a sub culture I knew nothing about. The music was now reaching ear-bleeding levels as I turned to Callum and nodded towards the side door. We walked through and within an instant the door closing behind us shut out the majority of the noise.

It felt somewhat strange being in a back corridor with 'Little Knob.' In fact every nasty little name I had ever christened him with strangely drifted away as I realised now was probably a good time to just be nice.

'Just a few miles of corridors then Callum and we will be through to our majestic changing rooms.'

We walked along side by side and exchanged small talk.

'I hear you've had a few sickness problems tonight in the changing rooms,' he said to me.

'Yea,' I laughed, 'Annabella told you about our sick boy drummer then.'

'He sounds quite a handful.'

'Handful! There was a lot more than a handful came out of him tonight.'

'Yea I hear he gets sick quite a lot.'

'That's right,' I replied as we approached another door nearly half way by my reckoning to me getting rid of my association with Callum for the night. Still he was being remarkably pleasant I thought. Then he spoke with a coolness that made my heart almost stop,

'Probably having to look at your sad, ugly, bastard face.'

Callum walked quickly ahead of me and reached the door before me. He simply stood there, right in front of me, causing me to stop dead in my tracks. For a moment the words he had just spoken worked their way through my ears and into my brain. As the words 'bastard face' began to make their awful impact, a punch was unleashed and arrived at the side of my left eye. It was a quality punch suggesting, I reasoned as I flew through the air and into the sidewall, that he was right handed.

I looked up just in time to see his right boot moving quickly for my face. As I pulled my left arm up to protect myself I found myself thinking that he must be right footed too. The force of his kick seemed to split open two of the fingers on my left hand as it flew into my face, only partially protecting it. Something had to be done quickly I reasoned as his second kick from his left boot hit the top of my head. The force of the kick made me forget about whether or not he was right or left footed and I squirmed forward and caught his right boot that was coming in for the kill.

Off balance he majestically fell backwards allowing me time to pull myself to my feet and lean against the door. He stood up, facing me, his breath fast from the rage that had flown out of him.

'Happy now?' I asked far too hastily, the shrapnel of pain unable to stop my far too quick tongue.

'Far from happy, you smug bastard,' he said as he came for me again. He threw his right fist for my head and I managed to duck enough for it to just fly off my head and into the door. If it hurt him he didn't show it as his left fist flew into my stomach. Winded I hurtled forward head down into his stomach, and pushed him back into the sidewall. He hit it at speed with his back taking the full force of two bodies falling backwards. For a moment he was winded allowing me time to send a kick into his groin winding him still further. A street fighter would have moved in for more violence but I was no fighter. I simply stepped back, amazed at what had happened and hoping it would all just go away. All the fighting cards were in his favour and I didn't really want to trust to luck on this one. Part of me wanted to run but the fright of what had just happened seemed to glue my feet to the floor.

Callum looked up at me. I looked at him.

'What the fuck are you doing?' I asked. As I did I realised that blood was pouring quickly down the side of my face.

'You know what I'm doing you fucking wanker.'

'Such bad language' I let out, far too hastily. I had been flippant all my life and sadly the ability to keep my mouth shut was not about to find me now. On I went like a demented half-wit, lost in the belief that my fine words could tame the terror before me,

'This is not what Annabella would want?'

'How the fuck do you know you little shit,' he snarled. Clearly mentioning the name of Annabella was just about the worst thing I could have done. I had thought, and I use the word 'thought' in its loosest sense, that it was the best way out of my predicament but realised far too late I had said the one thing I should not have done. By mentioning Annabella I had to his mind confirmed that she, the object of his affection, and I were far more than just friends. I saw his head working overtime as no doubt pictures of Annabella and I naked in bed filled his brain. If only I could see those pictures too I thought. Still I had started something now and I realised at last that damage limitation was called for. Pay back could come later, but only if I had a later. Now was not the time to go on to mention that his mother was a lady of the night, rather now was the time for diplomacy!

'Look Callum she's with you, yea? You're the one she's chosen to be with all these years. Right, dude, right?'

Callum glared at me, hate filling his eyes. He pulled himself to his feet and walked towards me. When these threatening situations happened normally I had my friends around me and nothing ever happened that we could not control. Now I was on my own and things were far too out of control.

'You know quite a lot to say you are just new friends don't you?' he snarled.

'Well one of the first things she told me was that she was with you. With you, not me, yea?'

'So you're not the reason she told me earlier tonight that it's all over between us? What do you know about that eh? Wanker?'

I knew nothing about that. I looked at him and realised with dread that he had come tonight for one reason only and that was to harm me. Hopefully murder was not on the cards but looking at him as he snorted like a bull ready to charge I realised anything was possible. Of course I knew Annabella was not happy with Callum and of course I knew she had feelings for me, strong feelings I had hoped, but I did not know she was going to finish with Callum that night. She was probably saving it up as a surprise to crown what was to have been a glorious night. In fact as I faced the prospect of Callum charging into me I thought about Annabella and I in bed for the first time, her beautiful naked body in my arms. It was a calming thought. I looked up at Callum and for a brief moment our eyes locked. In his eyes I saw rage. In mine he may well have seen Annabella.

And then it was all too late, too much, too real, too sad. Callum charged me and let go of a dramatic right fist that caught my chin. My top front two teeth instantly shattered inside my tongue. I flew out a defensive punch that just caught Callum's nose in the vain hope of slowing him down. He didn't even seem to realise I had hit him. His second angry punch hit me full in the stomach for the second time and my insides felt as they were all about to come up at the same time. I turned to try and get to the door and shout for help. I managed to get my hand on the door as he pulled me back and threw me against the wall.

'You sad excuse for a man. If only Annabella could see you now, running away with blood dripping off your sad git of a face.' He was shouting these words, anger having clearly taken over any reason. I was now helpless. I had nothing left to give and I feared for my life. I fell forward from the wall that had caught me and tried desperately to again grab hold of him in an attempt to try my winding trick again. It was no use as my strength had all gone. He pushed me back and threw his right fist at me again, this time catching the side of my eye for a second time and opening the cut still further.

As I fell into the wall again I thought about Annabella's happy face and knew instantly how much this would hurt her. I hoped she would not come through the door to see us like this. A kick landed fully in my side and searing pain once again filled my body. Three or four further kicks followed, each one now just adding onto throbbing pain that was hitting me in waves of violence. As each blow piled into my sides, my arms, now totally battered and bruised, fell away from protecting me. Searing pain now mixed into a happy state of unconsciousness that was attempting to save me. I reasoned that I would now slip into being unconscious and who knows what else and I welcomed the feeling and waited for it to happen but all of a sudden, miraculously, his kicking stopped. I braced myself for another kick to follow but none did. He had finished what he came to do. He had a point to make and he had made it in the only way he knew how, by beating to a pulp the weedy band type who had dared to win the heart of his girl.

As he finished he said nothing. He spat at me. Twice. I then heard the door that we were about to go through open and close and then, in the distance, the outside fire door fling open into the back car park and into the night. The opening of the door set off the internal security alarm.

I lay holding myself as tightly as I could with what little strength I had left in my arms, fearing that to let go would allow my whole body to fall apart. I reasoned that I had to move, I had to get away before Annabella saw me like this. It wasn't a vanity attempt at hiding the mess that was my face and body. It was simply that I knew she would want to comfort me and if she saw me in such mess she would blame herself and, of course, it wasn't her fault at all. It was just life, some good, and some bad. This bit was certainly the bad bit. Amazing that it had followed so closely on from such a good bit!

I tried to pull myself to my feet, but it was impossible. Pain was now filling my whole body in a way I had never felt pain before. Prior to this, fillings at the dentists had been about as bad as any physical pain I had known had got. Behind me I heard a door open and as I looked up through my blood filled eyes I could just see that it was Vole, no doubt coming to check the security door.

'What the fuck…?' he said as he ran to my side and crouched down. He put his arm around my shoulder and helped me through the door that Callum had escaped through toward a seat by the now open fire door. Later it would strike me as funny that it was Callum who in effect had got help for me by opening an alarmed door that caused Vole to find me so soon.

'Help me!' Vole shouted down the corridors in an attempt to get people at his side, clearly upset at the state I was in.

'Who did this to you?' he asked as he dialled a number into his mobile phone. I looked at him and opened my mouth but could not find any words.

'HELP ME!!!' he screamed at the top of his voice. I heard voices fill the corridor and saw Steve break into a run as he saw me. I managed a small cracked smile as I realised it was the first time I had seen Steve run since secondary school. I tried to tell him this but again the words would not come. He reached me and held me as I fell into his body, the pain now taking over my whole being and causing my body to want to shut down.

'Ambulance! I need a fucking ambulance and quick!' I heard Vole shout. I felt Steve's tears fall on to my face as his hand stroked my blood stained hair. He whispered 'Everything will be alright' over and over again. I passed out.

18

Three and a half weeks later and the bruising had just about gone. One of the few benefits of being beaten up quite badly was the time off from work and the sympathy I got from even the most unexpected quarters such as Mr Wilde from work who sent a personal card with a record voucher. How surprisingly sweet!

Thankfully nothing was broken apart from my two front teeth, three ribs and my two little fingers on my right hand, which were not used for the guitar so I was miraculously still gig worthy. The bruising though was exceptionally severe and I did look the most hideous of sights. Stitches were applied liberally in various parts of my body as the nursing staff put me back together. They were quite simply brilliant. Of course any pride that I may previously have had as to how I would look after myself in a violent situation had totally evaporated and you can imagine how sorry I felt for myself. The dentist did a wonderful capping job in replacing my two front teeth, and the pain of the needles in numbing the area was even bearable compared to the kicking I had received a few days earlier.

The police interviewed me but I simply told them it was a fair fight with a punter who I did not know and I had come off worse. They had better things to do with their time than looking out for idiots who enjoyed fighting and so, to top it all off, they cautioned me for fighting and warned me against my future conduct. Charming.

The Band came to see me far too often, I spent the night of our glorious triumph in the Queens Medical Centre surrounded by many other accident cases, some of whom looked remarkably worse than me, although only marginally so. Steve had gone to the hospital with me whilst Keith and Tricks ensured everything got packed away correctly. By 2.00am in the morning Keith had joined us at the hospital along with Chloe and Annabella.

It was the first time Annabella had seen me since my beating. Thankfully the time delay had allowed the medical staff to at least clean me up a bit. I sat in a side cubicle in a wonderful NHS nightshirt with fifteen stitches in my head cut and bruising gradually building up around my face and body. At least only my face was on show. I had undergone X rays on my hand and ribs and a CAT scan to check my brain. The latter check would only check for abnormalities visible to the naked eye and not to how I was feeling inside, which was at that point numb, but would later turn to anger mixed with fear.

All the tests had come back and all were clear. This was perfect because to meet Annabella with worse news than the damage that was so plain to see would have been very hard. As she arrived I could see she had been crying, a lot.

'Anthony,' she cried as she walked into the cubicle with the others, 'what has he done to you?'

It was true that I looked a right sight. The cubicle was blessed with a mirror and I had caught several glimpses of a sad looking geezer who had obviously just returned from some war somewhere! She rubbed her hand along my wounded cheek and I mumbled through swollen lips,

'I'm OK, really I am…' and then, for obvious comic effect, '… you should see the other one. He was ugly before, but now…'

She didn't smile. None of them did. I was perhaps losing my comic touch in my hour of need. That and the obvious discomfort of me even trying to talk clearly was not helping my timing.

'I didn't know that was why he had come but I knew I didn't want the two of you to be alone.' As she spoke tears softly rolled down her cheeks. She looked even more beautiful when she cried. 'I knew I shouldn't have let him be with you on your own,' she was crying a lot now, ' It's my fault, all my fault.'

'It's OK, it's not your fault,' I said, speaking painfully through broken teeth that hid the now very enlarged flabby tongue that was suffering from the hole that my front teeth had caused. The nurses had very kindly fished out bits of teeth. Despite the painkillers it still hurt. I wanted to say more but I was floating on drugs and words were not easy to even put together in my mind, never mind speak them.

'Nobody could have known that he was going to attack Anthony,' said Keith who was by my other side, Steve having retreated to the bottom of the bed to be comforted by Chloe. It had been an ordeal for all of us and I knew it had upset Steve a lot seeing me so violently damaged.

'I let Anthony walk through those doors with Callum as much as you,' Keith said kindly to Annabella reaching over his arm to put around her shoulders, 'in fact that corridor had been so busy all night it was amazing that no one came upon them.'

'It was fate,' I mumbled, 'fate that he had his time…' I looked at Annabella through my blood stained eyes '…because he's now lost the most beautiful girl in the world.'

She gave me a smile and stroked my face far too vigorously for my bruising's liking.

Two days later Keith and Steve arrived for us to finalise our 'Get Callum Back (the bastard)' Campaign. After two hours of discussion we had cemented a wonderful list of constant made up pizza orders, book orders, taxi arrivals, escort arrivals, Inland Revenue visits, Health and Safety visits, Double Glazing telephone calls, Power supply telephone calls, Chinese Take-away, Fish and Chips Take-away, and of course the old favourite of asking every Window Cleaner in Nottingham to go to his club to clean his scabby club windows and bill him later.

Keith and Steve had also both taken to ringing Callum and shouting abuse down the phone as often as possible and whatever time they wanted. After a week of getting better, having my front teeth put in and finding my voice again, I joined in and did the same.

Three weeks later with my face showing few signs of the attack I went to see Callum at the gym. I didn't tell anyone I was going, knowing friends would want to talk me out of it. I had no choice. On my own in the dark middle of the night hours I was finding I was waking up and generally being terrified of being attacked again by the shadows that surrounded me. I realised that unless I faced down the initial aggressor, I would struggle to regain normality and whilst I knew that being alone in corridors would probably always hold a certain darkness, I needed to face up to what had been done to me. Callum could of course beat me in again and it was a huge risk, though a calculated one as I went in his peak teatime slot to ensure I wasn't alone. Here I was demonstrating the age old adage that 'he who is short of a bob or two upstairs will never find the loose change to make it up again!'

I walked into the gym and spotted him across the other side chatting with an attractive girl. What a surprise! I walked straight up to him and placed my arm around his shoulder.

'Hello you tart,' I said, as he turned to meet me, 'how are you?'

He looked at me, amazed at my audacity, anger flying across his face and yet I saw fear too. He was not used to being challenged. I turned to the girl he was talking to,

'I'm the guy he beat up a few weeks ago and sent to Casualty. I'd stay away from him if I were you.' She looked at me as though I were mad. I probably was. I turned back to Callum.

'Look I know you are bigger than me and stronger than me but there is one thing I think you need to learn.'

'And what could that possibly be from a pathetic little fucking twat like you?'

'That if you intend to fight for a lady you should do so with honour.'

'And what do you know about honour?' he snarled, hate filling his voice.

'So much more than you will ever know you bastard,' I replied.

I turned around and left the building, half expecting him to follow and sure enough I heard the door be pushed open behind me into the open street. I turned expecting confrontation but all I saw was the girl he had been talking to running down the street in the opposite direction. If I saw Callum again it would be too soon.

When I was a young boy I tried to listen to voices that said I could not touch the stars. I was a young lad being brought up in a mining town that was coming to the end of being a mining town. My place was to know that the world was hard and that my life would be hard too. If I had dreams, well remember they were just that – dreams! As regards living the dream, well this was akin to walking on water and this was simply not possible. The inevitability of life was like a book with no ending and I was swimming against the tide in trying to write in an alternative. When you get so tired of wanting to break out but still those same voices tell you that you cannot succeed, there are times when you are left with tears falling down your face, when you feel like your life is going to waste. Well, somewhere deep in me, lights still shone, lights wished to continue to guide me to being who I thought I could be. Little moments like standing up to a bully were my lights and these moments saw me find my place in the world. They fixed me up inside and whilst at times they meant I got hurt, well I would get hurt! That was me, a boy who got hurt, but a boy who found out that he would not stop going for his dreams and his place to smile in this life.

For the rest of that week I had the biggest smile on my face. The dam of hurt had been broken and now I was free to get on with building my life back up.

19

Saturday August the 11th, and we were on our way to London to take our place in rock stardom's hall of fame. Tom Brown, Keith's friend from London, had been so impressed with us at Rock City that he had got four more gigs lined up for us over the next month in The Big Smoke, all at exclusive venues. He had used a live tape recorded off the mixing desk at our Rock City gig to spread the Wide Eyed Wonder word. It was fantastic. We were getting all the London promotion we needed without having to do any work for it. As a result of Tom's excellent efforts he assured us that at least eight record labels would be present at our gig at South Kensington's The Orange Club that night, if not more. To the ever confident 'us' that meant only one thing, we would be signed.

The Orange Club would be the start of a record company fight to sign us and we would be spoilt as to who to go with. As we had gigged and practised leading up to this moment, we had ached over the virtues of different record companies.

The easy option, providing of course that they were interested, would be Creation Records. If Alan McGhee could sign up the magic that was Oasis then he would have to be interested in us wouldn't he? Steve argued that Creation would be looking for something different to diversify the label but to me it was a label that already held all the richness you would want. As well as Oasis, the stable included two bands that were torchbearers and Forefathers of the 90's music scene that was now developing. There was the tortured brilliance of Primal Scream with Bobby Gillespie showing how to make music move. Then there was the fabulous Teenage Fanclub. Here was a band without equal for me. They sang harmonies in a way that I could only dream about and admire. I figured that if the band made it then these would be the sort of people I wanted to sit down with and ask 'How do you do that?'

Polydor were a label to consider carefully. They already carried several of the new 'Indy' bands such as Cast and Shed Seven. We had played a gig in York where the Shed Seven boys often came to drink and in their earlier days had often played. Somehow this made us feel a little connected to them despite the fact we had not actually met them. The label also had the advantage of having The Wonder Stuff. I pointed out that Polydor would never sign another band with 'Wonder' in their title. Those boys though were a band to behold. I had been to see them with one of my good pals, Chris. We had known each other for years and it was he, being my friend away from the never never world of the band, that kept my feet firmly on the ground. When we hung out it was not to talk about my obsession about the band, though he was interested, but rather we talked football, family, jobs, hopes and how the girl across the bar was blessed with the most fantastic pair of virtues that we had ever seen! What we didn't talk through was the complexities of the right and wrong chord for a new song, or the song order for the next gig or whether we needed a new drummer. It kind of helped to have that normality away from the birds that filled my head every time I got lost in the band. Chris and I went to see The Wonder Stuff at the rather fine looking Leicester's De Montfort Hall and it was a gig where they came, they saw, and they conquered. We got there early and had a few drinks in a nearby pub. We joined the queue and made our way into the rather scruffy venue. Making our way towards the front we waited for Miles Hunt to lead his merry men onto the stage, which he duly did with a stunning performance of the Construction for the Modern Idiot album. It was fantastic. The evening was nicely finished when what seemed like a few hundred traveller-looking types somehow or other made their way in to the already crowded hall by a side door that had been pushed open by one of their associates. One of them repeatedly pushed into Chris, who consequently pushed him back with a force that compelled me to grab Chris and pull him away from the automatic violence that would have followed. 'Nottingham lads trampled to death at Gig' was not a headline I thought my mother would like. I was very lucky to watch these bands at their prime and live and raw. It left a lasting impression on me.

Oasis's greatest rivals, according to the press, were of course Blur and they were signed with Food and I really liked the idea of being on that label. Damon v Noel and Liam never seemed a fair fight to me but to Damon's credit he never seemed to flinch from facing up to the Gallagher boys. It must have upset Blur perhaps in a similar way to when the Beach Boys were devastated by The Beatles recording of the Sgt Pepper's Lonely Hearts Club Band Album in 1967. This eclipsed their Pet Sounds album and Brian Wilson was intimidated and deflated. Perfection just moved up several notches and the Beach Boys could only try again. Blur could have felt the same way. Parklife had been extraordinarily successful for them but the press only seemed to want to recognise Oasis. Noisy and angry brothers just grabbed the press by the balls more but Damon and the boys didn't seem to mind, in fact they almost seemed to revel in the differences between the two bands. For all Noel and Liam's goading, Blur just came out cooler, which pretty much reflected the styles in music of the two bands. For now Oasis were my main musical main influence, but sure enough as I got older it would be Blur who would interest me more. Yes I liked the idea of Wide Eyed Wonder signing with Food and I figured that the label would welcome a new rock Indy band that they could use exactly to face Oasis, and Blur in return could just get on with being Blur.

The classic labels were not to be ignored and with their spending power we could only hope they might give us a listen. Parlophone housed the incredible talents of both Supergrass and Radiohead. Island looked after the all-conquering U2 and Jarvis Cocker's Pulp. That other rather large Manchester band called The Stone Roses were on the Geffen label. The choices were wide and immense and with money flowing from the labels and UK music being in a good place, we felt our timing of introduction to the scene was pretty perfect. All we needed was a willing partner to believe in us.

We would spend hours weighing up the different bands we liked and the different approaches we should make to their labels to get us signed. The Levellers sat with China Records. We could do that. The Charlatans sat with Beggars Banquet. We could do that. Up and coming Sleeper with the luscious Louise Wener were on Indolent Records. We could definitely do that as often and as many times as possible.

Weller sat with Go! Discs and the thought of sharing a label with one of the true masters of our time was in fact unthinkable. It would be a dream come true. When one of your first records you listened to was 'In the City' and you heard the raw power of the perfection that was The Jam, well music would basically never be the same. 'In the City there's a thousand things I want to say to you,' snarls Weller through gritted teeth, 'but whenever I approach you make me look like a fool.' The Jam had been the best of bands. Angry and direct, focussed on themselves as they went about their business before imploding into what can only be described as a different direction. Most of my best friends from school all adored The Jam which, when your back catalogue consists hallowed vinyl that inspired a generation, meant that there was no wonder that the Gallagher's held them, and particularly Mr Weller, in high esteem.

Our list of hopeful record label homes went on and on. For example, Suede in all their unique glory were with Nude records and given my recent modelling background I felt this label may strangely suit us. I note I have not mentioned the results of the nude modelling. I have seen some of them. They ranged from rather complimentary to down right insulting. Annabella's work fell in the former camp, though her work had a rather scratchy style, which meant that interpretation was everything. In short I would not be hastening back to the model's chair!

Sheffield, our close city neighbour, was home to the excellent new Longpigs. To hear them sing 'Lost Myself' was to listen to raw emotions and rub them into your body like a lotion. They were signed to Mother Records and I considered that this might be a super selling point in finally getting my own mother to think the Band was not such a bad idea after all.

The amazing Bluetones, so young that they all looked 12 and yet with lyrics that had seen a thousand lives, were with Paradox Records and we couldn't help but think this was the sort of label that would take a chance with us.

It was with all this hope and blind faith in our potential future that we took the decision to hire a single Decker bus to take 45 of our fans and ourselves down to the big smoke for the big gig. I call it a bus when in fact other equally worthy definitions could happily have been used. 'Wind Machine,' 'Scrap Heap,' 'Death Trap.' All were equally good at describing the vehicle that took us down that old favourite road, the M1. This was the road that was the link between the grim North, land of flat caps, coal for money, whippets and lean to shacks, with our future in the affluent South and us bathing in, if not champagne, at least warm water that had not previously been used by the rest of the family. Of course I exaggerate, but as kids we had done without many home comforts that we now had and yet, and here's the rub, we were so very happy. However our happiness did not preclude us from looking at what we could have to add splendour to our lives and the great North/South divide that even saw the lights stop way down the M1 as a political statement that said drive any further north and we, the Government, will not be responsible to what happens to you!

I had the fortune of living in Mansfield and with that came the dubious privilege of being one of the first to catch the band bus. The coach was from a 'renowned' local firm who I had never heard of called Brown's coaches, so called I thought as I saw and heard the contraption arrive 15 minutes late, because of the enormous amount of rust that blended in seamlessly with the paintwork. I caught Keith's eye with a pleading look of 'surely this cannot be our bus' and he met my look with a smirk. I often got the impression throughout my life that I was actually part of a 'Keith's Film Productions' show. Somewhere along the line I had been given a leading role, without the obligatory audition, within a life long film put together by the great Keith Scott. He could become a big screen legend, the famous English Director and Producer rolled into one, the man who took film into the 21st century, and the man who made me look very silly indeed!

As the burly coach driver, and when I say burly read humungous, brought the 'bus' to a shuddering and wind inducing halt outside The Red, I actually looked around to see if I could see anyone filming this auspicious event. It was the sort of scene that would be played over and over again if we ever made it on those 'Before They Were Famous' shows which, looking at this bus, seemed highly unlikely. Still once the ten or so of us had got on and the heavily wheezing driver had helped us load our gear into the storage compartments underneath, we were ready to begin a new 'Wonder' adventure. Amazingly the bus did start on the first turn of the key, and we were on our way. An hour later and after two more stops, the bus was full and with several more cars in convoy, we were on the motorway and heading south.

I sat next to Steve towards the front. Annabella sat next to Chloe behind us. Since the Callum debacle Annabella and I had seen a lot of each other. She had not spoken to Callum at all since Rock City and he had stayed away from her, which pleased me greatly. We talked late into the night one evening and decided to play it cool for a while. Annabella said she didn't want me to be caught up as a rebound from her break up, and I told her I didn't want to be a rebound. Rather I declared grandiosely 'I want you to come to me when you know I'm the one.'

That night I had taken her home and we had held each other at the door for a long time, eventually with her pulling away from me and I saw she had been crying,

'What's wrong?' I said, gently wiping the side of her cheek with my fingers.

'I'm just really happy,' she looked at me, 'I think I'd forgotten what happy was.'

'Well I've just found out,' I smiled, broadly. I looked at her, taking in her soft face all at once, feeling my heart beating fast and my brain sending out every good feeling it could find.

'Do you want me to come in?' I asked, as sweetly and as matter of factly as I could manage.

'Yes,' she said. My heart along with other parts of my body jumped.

'But not yet…'

'Five minutes then?' I asked with as an inviting a grin as I could manage.

'…Soon, but perhaps not that soon. OK?'

'Yea. Cool.'

We kissed, a long lingering kiss that stayed with me all the way home.

And so here we were, on our bus to the most important gig we had played to date and with me was the girl who filled my dreams. On the scale of one to ten in the good vibe days, this was most definitely a ten!

Steve and I talked excitedly about the gig. It seemed to me that one important gig just led to another one and that just kept everything fresh and vital. Of course it had not been without hard work and we had paid our dues in gigs that you played and wondered why and times too when it would have been far easier to have been somewhere else than rehearsing the same songs over and over within a sweaty rehearsal studio. We had come through it all, even Tricks efforts to sideline us at the Rock City 'near passed out' disaster, had turned out OK. Since then he had tried harder and we all noticed and things had settled down. This was good because our fan base loved him and he was a great drummer most of the time. Even I tried much harder with my relationship with him and all was good. Steve couldn't help but point out to me that by me actually trying, things really were getting better. He was right. I was an arse.

Keith and Tricks however were still not right and they had said very little to each other since Rock City, apart from talking about the Band. Not that any of us talked about much else, particularly since Rock City! Our mailing list really had rocketed through the 2000 mark and was climbing quickly. It cost us a fortune to mail our monthly fanzine update, not to mention the time spent folding the letters, putting them into the envelopes and then sealing them all up.

By just after one o'clock the bus had remarkably got us down to the outskirts of London and as it made its way through the outer city streets Keith took hold of the coach microphone and gave us a very amusing tour guide. He was conductor of the trip and we were his orchestra! He waved his hand one-way and pointed out a landmark with a possibly made up fact and we laughed. He would then swap our gaze to the other direction and we would follow obediently and laugh again.

At two o'clock we were parked up in South Kensington and unloading our gear to the club. Everyone then split, with the Band agreeing to meet up at 5.00pm, an hour before the sound check. It was an exceptionally exciting time for us.

Walking around London that afternoon was different to any other time I had been down to the city. We didn't have long to sightsee but Steve, Chloe, Annabella and I made our way straight to Covent Garden and wandered around the back streets and shops. It all felt so unreal because in less than six hours I knew I would be playing to an audience that would include people that could change my life. Chloe reminded Steve and I that we should not assume A&R types would show. We had been promised 'visits' before but been let down.

Tonight though for the first time we had a man in the middle, a man with connections and therefore there was actually a real possibility that this could go somewhere.

We ate a hearty pub lunch and watched the world go by the window. We talked about the gig and what it meant to us as a band and then what it could mean to us as people. If we really did get signed then it could really change so much of who we were and what we could achieve.

'It's just a pipe dream,' I reasoned.

'But one that might be about to happen,' Annabella said, 'and it will change everything.'

'Not everything,' I said looking at her with my heart written all over my eyes. She smiled at me despite this.

'I can't wait,' declared Steve, 'no more menial work, just fun, fun fun!.'

'Oh, there will be work alright,' said Chloe.

'Yea, but nice work,' I replied.

'Like travelling together all the time?' asked Annabella mischievously.

'Well Tricks could perhaps have his own little coach,' I suggested with a naughty smile.

'For him and Roseanna to do what him and Roseanna do,' added Steve.

'Which is?' asked Annabella.

'Being extremely rude,' I said.

'What about constant sound checking?' asked Chloe.

'Dingy hotel rooms?' added Annabella.

'Late nights and early mornings,' laughed Chloe.

'Crazy fans,' said Annabella with an animated 'Look at me, I'm a crazy fan' face.

'Fans with bad breath and body odour problems…' said Chloe whilst looking at Steve and laughing.

We spent the next hour weighing up the pros and cons of

rock stardom, and eventually concluded that we would not really know until we made it, that is, if we made it.

We drank up and made our way to Covent Garden tube station, and then headed west back across the city to South Kensington and the Orange Club.

Keith had beaten us back and was discussing the advantages of being a bass player over being a teacher with several of our devoted sixth form fans.

Soon after, and remarkably on time and seemingly fully sober, Tricks arrived and we began to set up.

There were several bands playing and we had drawn the short straw of being on first, which meant that we would sound check last. As a result our gear was last on the stage in front of everyone else's leaving us little room to mesmerise the crowd with a mighty fine stage presence. Equally playing first meant it was unlikely that A&R would be there to hear us. Keith went to make a few calls and we patiently waited our turn.

Thirty minutes and three bands in and we were still waiting our turn. Tricks had disappeared at one point only for Keith to send Steve after him to 'stick to him like glue.' Keith was determined that the errors of our Rock City ways would not be repeated here. The two of them were gone for ten minutes with each minute seeing us both get more agitated. They returned with sheepish, and yet cheeky smiles. Whatever they had been doing I was just glad they were back.

A quarter of an hour later and we were summoned to the stage for our five-minute sound check. We quickly set up and then belted out 'Shooting Star', which went OK apart from Tricks fiddling around with his bass pedal and moaning about it not feeling right. Keith shot him a look that suggested the bass pedal might be the least of his worries. We left Tricks stretched out on the floor fiddling with his gear and made our way to the bar at the side of the room to chill. 7.30 arrived and with it Tom to tell us that John Stern from Food and Chloe Temple from Polydor had both arrived, and were very excited at seeing us live. Tom told us that he had personally given them copies of tapes from Rock City and backed these with his own personal view that we were one of the next big things. The adrenalin torch paper was now well and truly lit.

We were due on at 8.00 and so we made our way to the back stage area to have a team talk.

'OK,' I started with my pre gig address, feeling it taking on an urgency that we had not experienced before,

'This is as big as it gets. Most bands don't even get this chance so we are not going to mess it up.'

I noticed Keith looking at Tricks and in turn Tricks looking somewhat disinterested as he gazed at another band member who was smoking what looked like a home rolled cigarette. The guy was lying back on a battered old sofa with a wonderful enormous smile filling his face.

I stopped talking. All eyes returned to me, each pretending that they had never left me.

'We've got five songs and that's it so...' and as I talked I looked into each of the guys faces '... let's just really hit it hard.'

The last few moments just flew by as several of our fans came back stage to wish us well.

'Just enjoy it Anthony,' said Annabella giving me my final prep talk, 'you are brilliant. Just let them see that for themselves.'

With that she leaned over to me and whispered in my right ear,

'I could get used to this.'

'My smell?' I replied.

'Being with you, loads and loads,' she said.

With that she stepped back, blew me a kiss and disappeared into the audience.

In my head the Hallelujah chorus erupted, led by the Three Tenors and backed ably by the London Philharmonic. Gabriel and his mates flew overhead and the world and all his friends told me my world was right! Annabella wanted to be with me 'loads and loads!' Success was mine. I turned back to the Band who were mimicking a love struck lover. Still, fair play! I was Romeo and she was my Juliet. After all I had taken one hell of a beating, and that surely represented enough tragedy for any Shakespearean play.

8.00 had now arrived and we were at last ready to go on to the stage. The club was already nearly full which bode well. A quarter of these we knew and were here for Wide Eyed Wonder. We knew there was a vibe about us and we knew there were plenty in the crowd there for us and looking forward to hearing us for the very first time. The crowd was ours and now we would make the A&R people ours as well.

We stood behind the curtain listening to the guy announcing the evening and going through the band names for the night's entertainment in reverse order of appearance. Tricks stood at the front. I thought he looked very nervous and hoped he would hold it together for the songs. Keith stood behind him. The two of them were not talking, no back slapping encouragement was taking place, but I figured since when did being best friends make a good band. I was sure this was going to be good.

At the back Steve and I pulled faces at one another. Whenever pressure or serious moments arrived we faced them with the one attribute we possessed in abundance, childishness.

And then we heard it,

'Please welcome, all the way from Mansfield, Nottingham. They are the Band out of the city a lot of people are beginning to talk about. They are tipped for the very top. They are, of course, WIDE EYED WONDER!!!!'

One by one we stepped through the curtain to receive rapturous applause. The evening was surely made for us.

Tricks got sat down and the rest of us picked up our guitars. Tricks hit his drumsticks, one, two, three, four. That was it and we launched into Shooting Star.

Three and a half minutes later the song was over and the crowd were quite simply going wild. All our fans, including about thirty people from connections already down in London, had as soon as we had come on to the stage, pushed their way to the front of the stage. Throughout 'Shooting Star' they had jumped up and down like people possessed singing every word. It was a most impressive sight for a young man from Woodhouse to be able to enjoy from the birds' eye view from the stage.

Then, straight into 'Take You There,' which I suspected we had never played quicker but we were now so pumped up that there was no holding the energy back. Again, thunderous applause and cheers. I literally had never heard a noise like it.

As I looked over to Keith, who was always to my left, and he looked back at me, we smiled. Maybe our break truly was here at last. I turned to my right and to Steve to exchange the same smile but he was not there! I spun around to see his wonderful bottom poking out from under the drums as he tried to do something to Tricks drum kit. A dread began to fill my body. I looked to Tricks for re-assurance but there was none forthcoming. He simply looked to me and shouted above the noise that was just beginning to subside.

'My fuckin pedal's broken!'

'Well play on without it,' shouted back Keith angrily.

'I can't!' screamed back Tricks.

'You had better!' replied Keith, with authority mixed with a strange growl that gave the warning an even more threatening tone. 'Steve, come on, we need to keep on playing.'

Steve got back to his feet and, laughing nervously at the still friendly audience, picked up his guitar.

'Thanks a lot,' I said to the crowd, 'that was called Take You There, and this…' I could see Keith out of the corner of my eye making gestures to Tricks. I doubted that they were love signs,

'…well this is called I Wanna Be Me.'

The crowd roared and again Steve and Keith launched into the big song introduction. There was, though, something most obviously missing. No drums.

In the surreal moment that was the big band noise without its drummer I considered the choices that lay ahead of me. All I could think was this was hopeless! My heart was being pulled out of me as the colour drained from my face. We were like a ship without a rudder, a plane without wings, a heron without the 'h.' Keith and Steve were making a go of it. I turned to see Steve playing the normal opening whilst looking across at Keith with a look of horror on his face. I turned again to Keith who was again playing the right chords but who in turn was looking to the back of the stage to where I assumed Tricks was still desperately trying to fix his bass drum pedal.

It was hopeless. I considered stopping altogether but assumed that any moment now Tricks would spring back into action if for no other reason than the obvious one that we would all have to shout at him for hours, maybe even days, if he didn't. The introduction to the song came to its end and I steadied myself to launch into the opening line of 'And I looked out into my world and I said come look at me' when, amazingly, Keith simply stopped playing. He had endured enough and could clearly take no more. The crowd had gone quiet as I turned to see Tricks just sat on his stool. He was crying.

An empty pause filled the room. I looked across to Steve who seemed caught between running off the stage, to hiding behind his amplifier. I considered alternative career options. Lion taming perhaps, a shark cage operator, or maybe a circus cannon volunteer. Surely they all had to be safer than the grilling the audience would now surely give us.

'Wankers,' shouted a friendly local from the crowd, which I thought was somewhat unfair. Some one shouted back to him,

'Shut up you cockney bastard.'

It was a supportive gesture from one of our fans, but one that I couldn't help but think might lead us into trouble.

'Wide Eyed Babies!' our antagoniser shouted.

'Why don't you just fuck off?' shouted Steve in reply only to find a thrown pint of lager in a thankfully plastic glass hit his guitar. That was the final straw that broke Steve's camel humpy back.

Steve ripped off his guitar and without hesitation threw himself into the crowd. I couldn't believe it. I turned to Keith who had disappeared. I looked back into the crowd but could only see Steve ploughing his way through them like Moses through the parted Red Sea.

I turned back to see what Tricks was, or of course was not, doing. I was amazed to see Keith's arm being raised up and down in a pounding motion. As I listened carefully I could hear Tricks shouting,

'Do it man, HIT ME AS HARD AS YOU CAN!!! Ow! I am a cooked dude. Nice one, that really hurt. I deserve to be hit. That's a good one. HIT ME ON MY HEAD KEITH. Yea, Ow, Ow, Ow, that's the magic mushroom spot, that's killing me dude…Harder! Harder! Not that hard…'

I knew then I had seen and heard just about everything.

I turned to look for Steve and, spotting where he was, I

jumped into the crowd. After working my way through a lot of people I found Steve with several of our brave fans already at his side. He had squared up to the big daddy of a tormentor who had now gone a little sheepish at the prospect of a one to one discussion with a Wide Eyed Baby.

'I didn't mean anything mate, honest,' he whimpered in an attempt to get Steve to let go of his neck.

I noticed Steve was holding him very tightly indeed. Anger had taken over his body and I felt he was not in control and things could get very nasty.

'Let him go Steve,' I said, placing my hands on his shoulders, 'let him go. He's really not worth it.'

I kept my hands on Steve's shoulders, squeezing slightly in what I hoped was a soothing and calming manner. In turn I felt a hand on my shoulder and turned to see Annabella and Chloe at our side. They looked as worried and as upset as I felt. I hoped my face didn't betray as much emotion as their faces! With all this posturing behaviour following the band maybe wrestling might be an alternative area for us!

Slowly Steve released his grip and turned back to me.

'It's alright,' I said, looking straight at Steve's wounded expression.

'Yea, sure, he really is not worth it,' he replied unconvincingly, 'though it's really not alright is it?'

With that he turned back to the man and head butted him. Unfortunately Steve's nose is not made for head butting, being somewhat on the long and pointy side. As he turned back to me blood was trickling down out of his nose and falling gently on to his shirt. He was, though, smiling.

'Nice,' I said with admiration.

'Thank you,' he replied, the old sparkle returning. 'He is not worthy of listening to the Band Anthony, not worthy, you hear me!'

'Yea, I hear you.'

The crowd separated as we made our way to the back stage area. Silence was broken as one of our fans began to clap. Others quickly joined in and by the time we had reached back stage the crowd had erupted and were going wild again chanting 'Wide Eyed Wonder' over and over again.

Keith was waiting for us and the three of us took our bow, knowing that we had undoubtedly blown our biggest break.

We left the stage and were met by the sight of Tricks sat on the same sofa that he looked at so longingly only 10 minutes earlier. He was holding to his head a cold tin of lager that no doubt Roseanna had gotten for him to take down some of the swelling from the fists of my avenging brother. Roseanna was at his side holding another lager, or perhaps that was a cider can, to Tricks' left ear

I left Steve to look after them and in silence went to help Keith retrieve our guitars from the side of the stage. We said nothing. There was nothing to say. The venue promoter followed us around the stage helpfully leaving us in no doubt that we would never be invited again. In fact he even suggested our days in London were over. It was as though I was carrying a duffle bag and into it he was simply adding more and more heavy stones. It was all I could do to get off the stage without my legs giving way and me simply falling over.

Five minutes later we were all sat huddled together, the thought of going out into the auditorium a prospect none of us could yet stomach. We had let everyone down and it felt so utterly hopeless. Another band had begun to play, without bass pedal difficulty. Their sound bounced around us but we were not for listening. Each of us contemplated the long sad drive home. It had not been the night we had anticipated. Annabella and Chloe had joined us but still silence held itself over us, bar the occasional muttering from Tricks as he lamented 'I'm sorry dudes, I really am so very sorry. I've had a bad trip man, bad, bad, bad…'

He sat on the corner of the sofa, head in hands, tears still falling down his unshaven cheeks. He had simply been unable to cope and had, quite literally, broken down. How could we be angry with him? It had just been too much. Roseanna, at Tricks' side, cradled him in her lap. We looked at one another hoping to see something that would make it all alright, hoping to find one golden nugget to fire it all out again. This was surely something that we would laugh about in time to come, but that time was certainly not yet. Together we waited listening to Tricks' loud and long sniffles. What a delight, an anti-climax of the highest order!

'Absolutely fucking fantastic.'

We turned as one to the curtain through which a rather attractive and trendy young lady had walked with our LSE friend Tom. I wondered if ex friend should be a more suited phrase as surely we had let Tom down big time. Still, they looked remarkably cheery. Perhaps they were seeing one another or maybe one of them had just won on the pools?

'I have seen a few show stoppers in my time but that just about was the best!' She spoke in a manner that suggested she owned the Club.

We stood, bemused, a look of 'Who are you?' over all our faces.

'Chloe Temple is my name. I am from Polydor and you…' she looked Keith, Steve, and myself up and down undressing us and dressing us at the same time,

'… You, with a new bass pedal of course, will be our next big band, and I mean BIG band. You just put on a show that even Oasis would have been proud of. Wide Eyed Wonder…' she shouted producing a bottle of champagne from behind her back, '…here you come!'

'This is not the end. It is not even the beginning of the end. But it is, perhaps, the end of the beginning'

Sir Winston Churchill

ACKNOWLEDGEMENTS

This book would not have been possible without the band who were my family on stages around the country in the mad 90's. Steve has always been my wingman and Nigel has always been my hero. It is the way of things. We actually had around 16 drummers during the life of Wide Eyed Wonder but this book bows its head in great gratitude to Dave and Mark who brought us such great memories.

I would particularly like to thank Sarah Lambert and Nicola Matthews who have been so wonderful in reading the drafts and picking me up on things. You have been amazing. Also Nicola has been such a wondrous support as adviser and editor and I am totally indebted to you.

To David Donnan, a fine photographer, who kindly lent his talents to the book cover. You're a constant inspiration to me, David.

To you, my outstanding readers, who have been so encouraging about my writing. 'Being in a Band' most definitely would not be here without you keep asking me 'where's the next book!'

Finally my Karen and Flora. You make my days burn with sunshine. Love you.

Anthony
30th April 2019

ON ASHOVER HILL

Henry found his feet begin to break out into a run, because he had seen, quite clearly, the bones of a hand stretching out from the dug-up earth. 2046. A hand, skeleton in form, stands out in a pile of earth. Years of a hidden mystery are at last uncovered. 1943. In Naples, a squad of new British recruits are labouring under the hot Italian sun, and the story begins. Soldier William McTeer falls in love with a beautiful young Italian woman, Francesca, but the war tears them apart. Years later, a letter Francesca writes to William leads them to be reunited. They move to Edinburgh where their son Robert is born and the die is cast. The story then centres around Robert, his children, Taylor and Jasmine, Robert's best friend Angus and his family, and their entwined lives. Tragedy follows, but redemption too.

Behind it all lurks a secret too dark to even contemplate...

On Ashover Hill travels across Europe, spanning generations of the McTeer family and the love, hurt, pain and redemption that follows. It covers 103 years and a family in transition from a kiss to a birth, an act of inhumanity to a triumph act of love.

Primarily a story of true romance, it weaves together a tale of unending love and family relationships with an undercurrent of mystery, crime and betrayal.

THE BIRTHDAY GIFT

What would you do if you suddenly discovered that all you thought you knew turned out to be a lie?

How would you react if the foundations you had built your life upon turned out to not be foundations at all?

A moment in time caught between a grandfather and grandson, lost in utter joy at the end of a late summer's day. Click. Soon, devastation follows; the old man loses his fight to live, but leaves an extraordinary gift for his beloved grandson – a gift that will cause much heartache and cause decisions to be made that will put lives on the line. Noah Spearing is a young man teaching in St Ives, Cornwall, when his life is changed forever after the death of his beloved grandad. A gift left for him from the man he loved more than anyone else turns out to be a poisoned chalice that he must deal with in the best way that he can. All this comes at a time when the girl he wants is set to marry another man, and Noah must decide not only what to do with the gift from his grandfather, but also his love for Flora Trembath...

The Birthday Gift is a novel that sweeps through issues of love, of hope, of sorrow and of destiny. It spans across Europe, from Cornwall to London to France to Germany and then to Poland.

The book is a gripping combination of thriller and romance, revolving around the painting central to the book which featured heavily in the recent Hollywood blockbuster, The Monuments Men, written and directed by George Clooney.

THE BIRTHDAY GIFT

What would you do if you suddenly discovered that all you thought you knew turned out to be a lie?

How would you react if the foundations you had built your life upon turned out to not be foundations at all?

A moment in time caught between a grandfather and grandson, lost in utter joy at the end of a late summer's day. Click. Soon, devastation follows; the old man loses his fight to live, but leaves an extraordinary gift for his beloved grandson – a gift that will cause much heartache and cause decisions to be made that will put lives on the line. Noah Spearing is a young man teaching in St Ives, Cornwall, when his life is changed forever after the death of his beloved grandad. A gift left for him from the man he loved more than anyone else turns out to be a poisoned chalice that he must deal with in the best way that he can. All this comes at a time when the girl he wants is set to marry another man, and Noah must decide not only what to do with the gift from his grandfather, but also his love for Flora Trembath...

The Birthday Gift is a novel that sweeps through issues of love, of hope, of sorrow and of destiny. It spans across Europe, from Cornwall to London to France to Germany and then to Poland.

The book is a gripping combination of thriller and romance, revolving around the painting central to the book which featured heavily in the recent Hollywood blockbuster, The Monuments Men, written and directed by George Clooney.